Praise for Trice Hickman

"Hickman is spot on."
—*Library Journal* on *Deadly Satisfaction*

"Hickman's (*Playing the Hand You're Dealt*) narrative is engaging . . .
you'll enjoy the story's heart."
—*Publishers Weekly* on *Breaking All My Rules*

"Readers will enjoy the twists and turns in Hickman's tale, which
has a definite soap opera vibe . . . Hickman's name should be well
known by librarians. If not, this juicy tale is a great launching
point."
—*Library Journal* on *Secret Indiscretions*

"Fans of Mary Kay Andrews and Mary Monroe may enjoy this excellent, dramatic story featuring three smart women."
—*Booklist* on *The Other Side*

Also by Trice Hickman

Complicated Love series
The Other Side
Blindsided

Dangerous Love series
Secret Indiscretions
Deadly Satisfaction

Unexpected Love series
Unexpected Interruptions
Keeping Secrets & Telling Lies
Looking for Trouble
Troublemaker

Stand-alone titles
Playing the Hand You're Dealt
Breaking All My Rules

Blindsided

TRICE HICKMAN

www.kensingtonbooks.com

To the extent that the image or images on the cover of this book depict a person or persons, such person or persons are merely models, and are not intended to portray any character or characters featured in the book.

This book is a work of fiction. Names, characters, businesses, organizations, places, events, and incidents either are the product of the author's imagination or are used fictitiously. Any resemblance to actual persons, living or dead, events, or locales is entirely coincidental.

DAFINA BOOKS are published by

Kensington Publishing Corp.
119 West 40th Street
New York, NY 10018

All Kensington titles, imprints, and distributed lines are available at special quantity discounts for bulk purchases for sales promotion, premiums, fund-raising, and educational or institutional use.

Special book excerpts or customized printings can also be created to fit specific needs. For details, write or phone the office of the Kensington Sales Manager: Kensington Publishing Corp., 119 West 40th Street, New York, NY 10018. Attn. Sales Department. Phone: 1-800-221-2647.

The Dafina logo is a trademark of Kensington Publishing Corp.

ISBN: 978-1-4967-0935-6
First Trade Paperback Printing: November 2021

ISBN: 978-1-4967-0937-0 (e-book)
First Electronic Edition: November 2021

10 9 8 7 6 5 4 3 2 1

Printed in the United States of America

Acknowledgments

I give honor, thanks, and praise to God, for every single thing. Lord, you have blessed me to complete another book, my tenth, and I am so humbled and appreciative of Your amazing grace, tireless mercy, and abundant blessings. I know that through You, all things are possible. Thank You, Jesus!

From suffering with writer's block for nearly two decades, to writing ten books, I know that I'm blessed, and I have many people to thank for this amazing journey . . .

Thank you to my strong, kind-hearted, hard-working, God-fearing husband, Todd T. Hayes, Sr. You're not only my best friend, confidant, prayer partner, and cheerleader, you're my everything. I love you beyond measure, Baby! Thank you to my son, Airman Todd T. Hayes, Jr., for your love, genuine spirit, and dedicated service to our country. You're a wonderful father and I'm so proud of the man you've become. Thank you to my daughter, Eboni S. Hayes (my Sweetie!), whose drive and intelligence are matched by your beauty and talent. I'm so proud of the young woman you're growing into. Thank you to my sweet and adorable granddaughters, Gabriella and Raven. You two enrich my life with joy and laughter. Mama Trice loves you!

Thank you to my wonderful mother, Mrs. Henalmol Hickman, who is the sweetest, kindest woman I know. The valuable life lessons you taught me have shaped me into the woman I am today, allowing me to stand strong on the foundation you laid for me. I'm blessed to be your daughter and I love you to the moon and back. Thank you to my father, the late Rev. Irvin L. Hickman, for always loving me, giving me the BEST advice, and still watching over me from above. There's not a day that goes by that I don't think of you. Thank you to my late brother, Marcus Hickman. You were my first playmate and friend, and I still can't believe you're gone. I miss you so much, but like Daddy, I know that you are with me in spirit.

Thank you to my agent, Janell Walden Agyeman. My literary journey wouldn't be what it is today without your careful guidance, thoughtful advice, and expert knowledge. You are a light force, and I'm blessed to call you my friend. Thank you to my talented editors Wendy McCurdy and Elizabeth Trout, whose dedication helped bring this book to life. Thank you to my publishing family at Kensington, Dafina Books, for everything you do.

Thank you to my amazing group of forever girlfriends whom I've known for decades, and who always lift me up with your love; Sherraine McLean, Terri Chandler, Tammi Johnson, Jeneane Davis, Tiffany Dove, Tracy Wells, Tracy McNeil, Renee Alexander. Thank you to my talented and supportive literary sisters whom I love dearly and am blessed to have in my life; Kimberla Lawson Roby, Marissa Monteilh, Lutishia Lovely, and China Ball.

Thank you to all the bookstores (especially Indie stores), booksellers, book promoters, book bloggers, literary event organizers, and other industry professionals who have supported my work, sold my books, and helped connect me with readers. The work that you do is invaluable, and I appreciate all of you.

Thank you to my amazing readers and book clubs! Your support, encouragement, and dedication is absolutely phenomenal. I appreciate all that you do from purchasing my books, to spreading the word about my writing, to inviting me to your monthly meetings and other events. You ROCK, and I sincerely hope that you enjoy this book!

Thank you to Mrs. Michelle Obama, for your encouragement, sisterhood, great advice, and the many tips you've shared with me, even if those conversations were only in my head!

Many blessings to you all!
XOXO
Trice Hickman

Life has boundaries, but love does not . . .

Chapter 1

BERNADETTE

One year ago, Bernadette Gibson had moved from the political, power-hungry city of Washington, DC, to the sleepy, sip-sweet-tea-on-your-front-porch, slow-paced life of Bourbon, North Carolina, and ever since she'd celebrated her fiftieth birthday six months ago, her life had changed in sweeping and dramatic ways that she couldn't have predicted.

Back then, if anyone had told Bernadette that she would be in a committed, monogamous relationship with a compassionate man who loved her without reservation or conditions, she wouldn't have believed them. If they had told her that the man of her dreams, who had literally swept her off her feet, would be a debonair, dangerously handsome, night-club–owning ex-felon with a sly smile, sordid past, and a reformed trigger-finger, she would've flat out laughed in their face. But the most unbelievable and shocking proposition of all was the notion that at the seasoned age of fifty, she would be six weeks pregnant with her first child.

But Bernadette's late in life pregnancy wasn't just a shocking proposition, it was a very real and sobering reality, which for her, felt as though someone was playing a twisted joke, toying with her life and her sanity. And as Bernadette had learned over the years, things that happened in real life could tell a more outrageous tale than any work of carefully crafted fiction.

It had been two weeks since Dr. Vu, Bernadette's OBGYN—who her friend, Arizona, had recommended—had told her that the cause of her round the clock fatigue, increased appetite, and occasional nausea, wasn't menopause, as she'd originally thought, but rather, the early symptoms of pregnancy. Never in Bernadette's wildest imagination had she even considered the possibility that she might be pregnant. At her age, she'd thought that the baby boat had sailed long ago to distant shores, never to return.

Now, as Bernadette kicked off her three-inch stiletto sandals, and spread her freshly pedicured toes against the textured fibers of the Aubusson rug under her delicate feet, she closed her eyes and breathed out a sigh of physical and emotional relief. It had been a long and, at times, stressful day, and she was glad to be back in the comfort of her home. Most of her Saturday nights were spent at Coop's house, on the other side of town, where she felt happy and safe. But as much as she loved spending time there, especially in his king-size bed, she also relished being in her own home.

"It's been one heck of a day," Bernadette said, "and I'm ready to unwind."

Coop's lips formed a seductive smile. "Baby, you might be tired, but you still look just as fresh as a flower," he said in his deep, southern laced baritone. "Turn around and let me unzip you outta that pretty dress."

Bernadette loved the way Coop always made her feel special through his words and actions, and as she followed his gentle command she couldn't help but smile back at him. "Thank you," she whispered.

Her skin tingled when his fingertips gently grazed across the bare skin of her slender back, which had been aching for his touch. Bernadette wasn't surprised that Coop had just turned the act of tugging on a zipper into an exciting, sensual event, as he did most things involving their interactions. She wriggled side-to-side, allowing her elegant, knee-length cocktail dress to slide down her shoulders. "That wedding was beautiful, but I sure am glad to be out of this dress," she said, as she thought about her friend's nuptials.

Bernadette hadn't been sure if the wedding was actually going to take place because Arizona had been hesitant about marrying her fiancé, Chris. Several months ago, to Arizona's dismay and disappointment, she had discovered that Chris had a micropenis, which was no more than an inch and a half long, when fully erect. And, added to that, beyond his anatomical challenges, the two weren't sexually compatible in any way. Bernadette felt that their relationship was going to be an uphill struggle, and she hoped that her friend was prepared to deal with the troubles that were sure to come her way.

But in true, pie-in-the-sky, optimistic fashion, Arizona and Chris had tied the knot and then partied all night during their lavish, over-the-top, five-star wedding reception that had followed. It had been a day filled with happy tears, sentimental speeches, and nonstop dancing and celebration that had continued into the evening.

It was nearly midnight by the time Bernadette and Coop had finally left the St. Hamilton, the luxury hotel where Arizona's and Chris's reception had been held, and which happened to be only a short drive from Bernadette's exclusive neighborhood in the tony Palisades section of Bourbon. When she and Coop had walked through her front door ten minutes ago, she had felt an immediate sense of calm envelop her tired body. Other than the comfort of Coop's bed, Bernadette's home was her second favorite place to be. Not only had she grown to enjoy her home, she'd grown to love the town of Bourbon.

Living in the small, eastern North Carolina town was yet another thing that Bernadette would have never imagined for herself. She was a city girl, through and through, Washington, DC, born and bred. She had loved the excitement and adrenaline rush that came with living and working in the day-to-day bustle of the Nation's Capital. But last year when a lucrative job offer had brought her to Bourbon—whose claim to fame was its vinegar-based, pit-cooked barbeque and unbelievably sweet iced tea—she had packed up her fast paced but lonely life in the city, and traded it for the quiet, church mouse existence in a tiny southern town that she had now grown to cherish. Now, standing in the middle of her bedroom, with the man she loved, Bernadette knew that coming here was the best decision she had ever made.

"I knew you were tired after that last line dance," Coop said.

"I must've given it away when I started limping," Bernadette said with a laugh. She looked down at her designer dress that was puddled around her sore feet and swollen ankles. Normally, an expensive piece of clothing laying on the floor would have bothered her, not to mention the irritation of her aching extremities. But like many things in her life, she had learned not to sweat the small stuff. "Thank you, for unzipping me," Bernadette whispered to Coop.

He tossed her a sexy smile. "I should be thankin' you."

"You're something else," Bernadette said with a slight blush.

"My job is to make you happy every day that you open your eyes."

Bernadette tried to muffle the yawn that was on the verge of breaking free from her mouth, but she was too exhausted to contain it.

"That wasn't the reaction I'd expected, but I'll take it," Coop chuckled.

"I'm sorry honey, I thought I was tired before, but I'm really struggling now."

Coop reached for Bernadette and drew her into his broad chest. "It's okay, I was just teasin' you. I know it's been a long day."

"Yes, it has, from sunup until sundown. I'm exhausted, aren't you?"

Coop grinned and unbuttoned his crisp, white dress shirt. "Honestly, I feel great. Like I could run a marathon."

Coop's intensity always amazed Bernadette. In her position as vice president of operations at Bourbon General Hospital, she was used to being around Type-A corporate executives who operated at a high level, but being with Coop made her realize that he could run circles around everyone in the hospital's c-suite, including her. From the time they had started dating, right after her birthday five months ago, Coop had always tackled every endeavor with the intense energy of an engine running full speed ahead. He was a laser-focused man with the ability to multi-task better than anyone she knew. Between his successful and wildly popular jazz club, Southern Comfort, his highly foot-trafficked laundromats sprinkled throughout town, his multiple rental properties, and his financial investments in several black-owned businesses in Bourbon, Coop was the busiest man that Bernadette knew, and his drive was just one of the many reasons why she admired him.

"You have way more energy than I do," Bernadette said with another yawn. "The only running I want to do is straight over to that bed. I'm going to take a shower and . . ."

"I'll join you," Coop quickly interrupted, giving Bernadette a big smile.

A twinge of anxiety tugged at Bernadette's stomach because she knew that Coop wanted to make love. *That's how I got myself in this situation in the first place,* she said to herself as she looked down at her swollen ankles. Her constant fatigue and bouts of nausea were just a hint of what she knew was ahead for her. She rested her hand on her still flat tummy, knowing that in a few months it would reveal what she was hiding. She knew she needed to tell Coop that she was pregnant because this was the kind of life-changing news that needed to be shared sooner rather than later.

Bernadette thought the words "pregnant at fifty" were more fitting for the title of a reality TV show, or a headline grabbing news article, than her real life. She knew that she would be disappointed if Coop had been withholding any kind of information that directly involved her, so she had to come clean. Bernadette closed her eyes, let out a deep breath, and looked directly into Coop's eyes. "Coop, I . . ."

Bernadette's life altering words were perched on her tongue when Coop interrupted her once again. "Baby, I know you're tired, and that's exactly why I'm gonna join you in the shower."

Coop's words caused her mind to shift from divulging her secret, to the fact that doing something that normally brought her great pleasure, was now causing her temples to throb. Any other time she would have looked forward to what she knew would result in a steamy, sex-fueled romp with Coop as warm water rained on their skin, but not tonight. Bernadette's aching body and lack of energy gave her pause. "Honey, we both know that if you join me in the shower I'm going to be beyond tired once we finish."

"Woman, get your mind out the gutter." Coop shook his head and placed his hand on the small of Bernadette's back as he pulled her close to him. "Remember that subscription to *Men's Health* magazine that you got me?"

"Yes, I remember," Bernadette responded, slightly puzzled.

"There was an article in there that said water massage is good for tired muscles and stress. And since I know you've been stressed on your job, which is probably why you've been so tired lately, I was thinkin' a massage in the shower might help."

Bernadette's voice became soft and delicate. "You really are something, Coop."

He smiled. "So I've been told."

Twenty minutes later—after a short, but passionate and intense lovemaking session in Bernadette's large, marble tiled shower—she and Coop lay atop her bed, wrapped in each other's arms.

"I told you I could help you relax in the shower," Coop said with a satisfied grin.

"Yes, you did. And as usual, you were right. But so was I, because now I'm exhausted."

"But you have to admit, it was worth it."

Bernadette nodded. "Yes, it was." She repositioned herself so she could look into Coop's eyes. She felt as though she could melt when she thought about how Coop's gentle and initially innocent massage had turned into carnal-fueled lovemaking. He had lathered her loofah sponge with her favorite L'Occitane bath gel, covering her body with fragrant suds as he washed her soft brown skin. As he had promised, his slow, sweeping movements had indeed relaxed her, and they had also excited her.

Bernadette had collapsed her back against Coop's broad chest as he cupped her breasts in each hand and massaged them with care, tweaking her nipples between his fingers with just the right amount of pressure. Slowly he glided his strong hands down to her stomach before making his way to her delicate middle. He inserted his finger and caressed her, lingering in her hot spot until he knew that she was ready for him. He gently turned her so she was facing him, and he kissed her with quick heat as he positioned her against the shower wall.

Bernadette gasped with sweet pleasure when she felt Coop slowly enter her at just the right angle, with the perfect amount of force as he eased every inch of his hardened manhood inside of her. He took his time, delivering long, deep strokes that made her body tremble under his direction until she reached a powerful climax that had her calling out his name. She whimpered with pleasure into his chest as he quickly followed her lead, leaving them both with satisfied smiles on their faces.

"I was running on fumes before that shower, and now my gas tank is sitting on E."

Coop slipped Bernadette a sly smile. "I guess I should apologize, huh?"

"I wouldn't go that far," Bernadette said with a light laugh as she nestled further into his arms. "Coop, what am I going to do with you?"

"That's a good question . . . How about, marry me."

Bernadette looked into Coop's piercing, deep brown eyes, which were staring directly into hers. Even though she'd heard what he had just said, and knew exactly what his words meant, she asked for clarification. "What?"

"Bernie, I love you." Coop paused and then took a deep swallow, as if something were lodged in his throat. He looked at Bernadette with a soft vulnerability that she had never seen before. "From the moment I first laid eyes on you, struttin' through the lobby of the hotel the night of Arizona's birthday party, I knew you were special, and after our first date, I knew that I wanted to spend the rest of my life with you. I can honestly say that I've been happier the last five months than I've ever been in my entire life, and it's because of you. I want you to be my wife."

Bernadette was not only caught off guard by Coop's proposal, she was slightly startled by the fact that for the first time since she had met him, he seemed nervous. But even with his slight shift in confidence, his steady eyes were still fixed on hers as he gave her hand a tender squeeze while trying to regain his composure.

"Back in the day," Coop said as he continued, "old folks used to say, 'you'll know when you know.' I didn't understand what that meant back then, but now that I've done some livin', I see what they meant. We've only been datin' a short time, but I know what I feel, and I know this is right. Like I said, I want you to be my wife, Bernie, and I hope you want me to be your husband."

Bernadette stared at Coop, wanting to speak, but unable to say a word.

"I know this isn't the traditional, get down on one knee kind of proposal," Coop said, "but we're not the traditional type of couple. You and me come from two very different worlds. You got your degree from a prestigious university, while I got mine through correspondence courses in prison. You work around professionals every day in a fancy corner office, while I conduct business between laundromats and rental houses in low-income neighborhoods. You live here in the most affluent part of town, while I stay in what's considered the wrong side of the tracks. We move in very different circles. But what I love about us, is that we fit where it counts."

Bernadette's heart was beating so fast that she had to sit up in order to calm herself. The moment was more than she had expected, and her mouth was dry with the weight of it. She was overjoyed with happiness about Coop's proposal, overwhelmed with anxiety about her pregnancy, and filled with confusion about another secret that she'd been keeping—one which included Coop, and his involvement in an unsolved murder that could possibly destroy their future.

Coop planted a gentle kiss upon her bare shoulder. "I want you to be the first thing that I wake up to every morning, and the last thing that I see when I close my eyes at night."

There was a long pause between them, and although Bernadette knew she couldn't tell Coop about her suspicions that tied him to a cold case which had recently resurfaced, she knew she had to tell him what her OBGYN had told her during her visit a few weeks ago. She couldn't accept his proposal until he knew exactly what he was getting himself into, so she came out and said, "Coop, I'm pregnant."

Chapter 2

TESS

"It's been a long day," Tess said to Maceo as they walked through the metal and wood, industrial-designed door that led into his sparsely furnished condo. It was shortly after midnight, and they were both tired from a full day of non-stop action. They had celebrated and danced all night at Tess's friend Arizona's beautiful church wedding and extravagant dinner reception that had followed.

Much like her cousin, Bernadette, Tess had been unsure if Arizona would actually go through with marrying her fiancé, Chris, because the two had been having serious problems, which unfortunately centered around sexual dysfunction. Tess and Bernadette had sat on uneasy nerves, sending multiple texts between them while they wondered if Arizona was going to walk down the aisle.

It wasn't until the processional music had begun to play that they'd finally relaxed, knowing that Chris wasn't going to get stood up at the altar. Tess had breathed a complicated sigh of relief that had been laced with a heavy dose of lingering doubt. She had been relieved that Arizona had averted the drama of earning the label of "runaway bride," but she'd also felt doubt because her gut had told her that her friend was making a big mistake by signing up for a life that Tess knew Arizona would no doubt come to regret.

Tess stepped out of her champagne colored, three-inch Valentino heels and planted her long, narrow, bare feet against the cool-to-the-touch hardwood floors beneath her as she smiled at Maceo. "I had so much fun tonight," she said in a tired voice, "but I sure am glad to be off my feet because they're killing me."

"Or as Sandy would say, your dogs be howlin'," Maceo teased, referring to his long-time and less than tactful hostess and server at Sue's Brown Bag, the popular soul food restaurant he owned that was named after his dearly departed mother, and was a local favorite of residents throughout town. He looked down at Tess's stylish shoes that she had just taken off and sat near the door. "I don't know how women do it."

"Very carefully, and in my case, with great style," she said as she tossed Maceo a quick wink.

"Yes, I see, and I agree." Maceo stepped out of his equally stylish wingtips and placed them beside Tess's heels. "I know it must be hard, but it's worth the effort because baby, you look sexy."

Tess gave Maceo a seductive look as she walked toward his chef grade, galley kitchen. "You know I love you, right?"

"Yes, I'm glad you do."

"I need some water because all that wine that I drank at the reception has me feeling dehydrated." Tess opened his impressive stainless steel, Sub Zero refrigerator and studied its contents. She always felt in awe by how neat and organized Maceo kept his home, and in particular, his kitchen. He was a chef and restaurant owner by profession—which accounted for his meticulously arranged fridge and pantry—and he was a neat freak by nature, which accounted for all other areas of his well-organized life.

Tess was always amazed by how much they differed when it came to domesticity. Maceo cleaned his condo to perfection each week, while she relied on a housekeeping service for weekly cleaning of the luxury home that she owned in Chicago. He enjoyed going to the local farmer's market and browsing the aisles for fresh produce, while she preferred to use home delivery for the rare occasions that she bought groceries. He could cook anything from appetizing gourmet meals to a smack-yo-mama soul food feast, while her go-to dish was a mean turkey sandwich. "We're polar opposites in almost every way," she often said.

Tess held the refrigerator door open, trying to decide between regular bottled water or the sparkling Voss sitting on the top shelf. "What should I drink, the regular or the good stuff?" she causally asked Maceo, partly because she couldn't make up her mind, but mostly because she always wanted his opinion on all matters involving food and beverages.

"Regular, good ol' Dasani," he said in his deep, laid back voice. "Carbonation might be a little too much right now."

"You're right," Tess smiled as she glanced back at him. "You want a bottle?"

"No, I'm good," Maceo answered. He walked over to Tess and gently rested his hand on the small of her back. "It was a nice wedding, huh?"

"Yes, it was." Tess nodded in agreement. She kept her back to him and aimed her sights squarely on the contents inside his refrigerator. She knew that he had made the comment in order to spark a conversation, and she was hoping to avoid the question that she was certain was going to come next.

"Can I ask you something?" Maceo said in an inquisitive tone.

Uh-oh. Here it comes, Tess thought to herself. She knew what Maceo was going to ask her, and she knew it was a logical and reasonable question—when were they going to set a date and start planning their own wedding.

It had been over a month ago when Maceo had cooked Tess a late-night gourmet dinner, complete with candles, flowers, and her favorite Chardonnay, before he had dropped to one knee and presented her with a beautiful engagement ring. His proposal had been heartfelt and romantic, and Tess had been overjoyed, readily saying yes. The next day she had been giddy with excitement when she had called her mother, and then Bernadette, followed by just a handful of close friends.

When Tess had met Maceo just five short months ago, she had been on the heels of recovering from a traumatic break-up that had left her devastated. Maceo's kind and gentle ways had helped soothe the damage of Tess's broken heart. She loved the fact that he was a Southern gentleman with a laid-back swagger that was smooth and easy. His rich, honey-hued skin was smoother than most women's, and his sculpted physique added to Tess's visceral and instant attraction to him. And as her cousin, Bernadette, and her friend, Arizona, had both pointed out, they were a good match, because Maceo's calm, no-drama demeanor was the perfect balance to Tess's rambunctious and often melodramatic personality.

After Tess had shared the good news of her engagement with the chosen few, she'd almost immediately begun to feel a combination of guilt and nerves gnaw at the pit of her stomach, not because she hadn't been in love with Maceo, nor because she'd thought they were rushing in too soon. She'd felt apprehensive because of a secret that she'd been hiding, and was still holding onto, even today.

From the beginning of their whirlwind romance, Maceo had made it clear that he wanted to settle down, get married, and have children. During their second date, he'd let Tess know his desires while they dined on steak and lobster tails.

"I've seen and experienced a lot in my thirty-five years," Maceo had said, "and life has taught me that time isn't going to wait around for me or anyone else to get our act together. It's fluid, and it moves forward, regardless of the struggles going on in your own world. So you have to approach everything you do with purpose and intention. I want to have a real impact on this earth, and I want to leave a legacy behind once I'm gone."

"Through your business and the community work that you do?" Tess had asked.

Maceo smiled and shook his head. "Through a family. There's

no better way to leave your footprint on this earth than by having others to carry on once you're gone."

Tess loved the fact that Maceo was a solid, selfless, hard-working man of conviction who saw life beyond his own existence. He valued stability and discipline. He stood his ground on matters of integrity and honor. He was honest and straightforward. And best of all, he was the most genuine and sincere man that Tess had ever dated. She often had to remind herself that he was real, and that their relationship wasn't fanciful fiction like the books she wrote.

Tess knew that along with Maceo's philosophical thinking, his desire to be a father and raise a family was heavily driven by the fact that he'd grown up without his own father, or a sense of connection to a traditional family structure. And what shaped his view even more was the fact that five years ago a paternity test had proved that the daughter whom he'd help raise alongside his adulterous ex-wife, hadn't been his biological child. "It nearly broke me," Maceo had told Tess, "but it made me realize that, as cliché as it may sound, what doesn't kill you will truly make you stronger. After I healed from the pain and betrayal, I learned that I can handle anything that life throws at me."

Tess had thought about that conversation many times, and when she remembered the emotion that had peppered Maceo's words about wanting children of his own, it made it that much harder for her to tell him about her challenges.

A loving husband, at least two children, and perhaps even a family pet, had been Tess's dream life ever since her mid-twenties. But as she looked at her current situation, she knew that her chances of conceiving were about as likely as accurately predicting a seven-day weather forecast in North Carolina—the prospects of which were slim to none.

Tess had been told by her gynecologist, as well as two of the best fertility specialists in Chicago, that her fibroids and endometriosis, combined with her being forty years old, had culminated into the sad reality that she had a less than five percent chance of becoming pregnant, even with the help of medical intervention. Tess knew that she needed to tell Maceo about her condition, because he deserved to know that if he married her, he probably would not have the biological children that he longed for.

Tess knew that Maceo was growing tired of her excuses for why she didn't have time to sit down and set a date or plan their wedding. She'd cited her book events schedule, manuscript deadline, and anything else her mind could think up as reasons for not following through. She hadn't even posted her good news about being engaged on social media. Now, he was about to ask her about their pending nuptials once again.

"When are we going to start planning our wedding?" Maceo asked, "or at least set a date?

Tess took a deep breath and didn't utter a word as she continued to stare into Maceo's well stocked refrigerator.

"Is there something you want to tell me, but you just don't know how?" he asked.

A heat wave of panic swept over Tess's entire body. "Mace, you know I love you, right?"

Maceo shook his head in frustration. "Listen, if we're gonna have this conversation, I want you to at least look me in the eye when you break things off."

Tess quickly turned to face him. "Break things off? Mace, I'm committed to you and I have no intention of doing that."

"Then what do you mean by, 'You know I love you, right?' "

"Just what I said. I love you, and I hope that you know I do."

Maceo rubbed the beginnings of the goatee forming on his chin, and looked up at the ceiling for a brief moment before focusing his eyes back on Tess. She knew this meant that he was taking his time in choosing his next words so they would make a powerful statement. "I'm invested in what you think and how you feel," he began. "I know when you're happy. I know when you're excited. I know when you're pissed. And yes, I know when you need to drink regular water or carbonated. I said all that to make the point that right now, I know that something's very wrong." Maceo paused for a moment to give even more weight to what he was about to say next. "So, tell me the truth. What's the real reason that you don't want to set a wedding date?"

Tess wanted to open her mouth and tell him, *I can't have children.* But she couldn't bring herself to say those words, let alone accept them. Even though she knew it was a long shot, she still held on to the improbable hope that there was still a sliver of a chance that through some miracle, she might be able to conceive a child. But she knew deep down that the main thing holding her back from telling Maceo about her fertility struggle was fear. Fear of losing him. Fear of being alone. And fear of living an empty life full of unfulfilled dreams.

Tess felt that if Maceo knew the truth, he would no longer want to marry her. When she had turned forty several months ago, she had known that her prospects of finding an eligible mate, especially one who wanted a solid commitment, was only going to dwindle with each passing year. The prospect of being alone terrified her, and after the humiliating break-up that she had experienced with her ex-boyfriend, Antwan Bolling, Tess didn't think she could stand to be rejected by another man.

Tess looked into Maceo's eyes as she struggled to explain herself. "Mace, I love you and I want to marry you more than you know, but I . . ." she tried, but then stopped. Tess knew from the expression on Maceo's face that he wanted and needed to know about whatever was holding her back, but all she could do was close her mouth and look down at her bare feet.

"Like I said, I know you well, but Tess, I'm not a mind reader. You need to tell me what's going on. I deserve that much, don't you think?"

Tess nodded her head. "Yes, you do."

"Then talk to me. Look me in the eye, be straight up and tell me what's going on."

Tess moved her eyes back up to meet his. She remembered all the times that Antwan had looked into her eyes and told her bald-faced lies. She remembered all the times that she had pleaded with him to be honest with her and tell her the truth, no matter how angry it may have made her, or how much it might have hurt. And she remembered how she'd felt when he had either outright lied, or had said nothing at all. She knew that Maceo had done nothing to deserve the type of emotional roller coaster she was putting him through. *I know better, and I've got to be better,* Tess said to herself.

Tess lifted her eyes from the floor and stared into Maceo's soft, baby browns. She inhaled dread through her nose, allowed the emotion to fill her chest, and then slowly exhaled the truth. She reached for his hand and held it in hers. "Mace, there's a good possibility that I might not be able to have children."

Chapter 3

ARIZONA

"What an unbelievable day," Arizona said to Chris with a happy smile. "We did it, baby! We're finally husband and wife."

Chris smiled back at her. "Yes, we are, and I'm the luckiest man on the planet to have you by my side. I love you, Mrs. Pendleton."

It was nearly one o'clock in the morning, and after a long day of wedding pomp and circumstance, Arizona and Chris were finally settling into their romantic honeymoon suite at the St. Hamilton Hotel. "This room is beautiful beyond my imagination," Arizona said as she looked around in awe. Chris was the general manager of the upscale, boutique hotel, and several months ago he'd arranged for her to stay in the presidential suite to celebrate her thirtieth birthday. It had been a beautiful room, but as she stood in the middle of the posh living room, she realized that the honeymoon suite was a newlywed couple's dream come true.

Fragrant, fresh flower bouquets of hydrangeas, roses, and baby's breath, neatly encased in glass cylinder vases filled the room. Pillar, stick, and votive candles cast a soft, romantic glow from corner to corner, while strategically scattered rose petals on the floor along with a bottle of Arizona's favorite champagne added an extra layer of ambiance that elevated her visceral and emotional experience.

"I wanted to make sure that everything was perfect for you, baby," Chris said.

"You always think of everything. I love you."

"I love you too, baby."

Despite the seesaw of up and down feelings that Arizona had experienced right before their wedding, she was glad that she'd made the decision to marry Chris. She knew that he genuinely loved her, and that he was willing to go the extra mile to please her.

Arizona walked into the bedroom area of the expansive suite to where her overnight bag had been placed on the intricately carved, mahogany luggage stand, and reached inside to retrieve a hair tie from her accessories bag. "Are you as tired as I am?" she asked Chris. "I've been up for almost twenty straight hours and I'm officially beat."

"It's definitely been a long day," Chris replied.

"Yes, and even though it's been one of the best days of my life, I'm glad it's over because wedding fatigue is real."

After Arizona secured her freshly flat ironed, shoulder length hair into a neat bun, she kicked off her rhinestone embellished flats that she had changed into during the reception, and began taking off her crystal chandelier earrings and matching bangle. "Can you unzip me outta this dress?" she asked.

Chris nodded with a smile. "You don't have to ask me twice," he replied as he walked to where Arizona was standing. He clutched the tiny zipper with his large fingers and gently slid it down the length of Arizona's back. "Baby, you were absolutely beautiful today, and this dress hugged you in all the right places."

"Thank you, honey. You always know how to make me feel like a queen." Arizona blushed and took one last look at her wedding dress before she slipped off the heavy, crystal and rhinestone studded mermaid style gown. She'd been nervous in the hours leading up to the ceremony because she hadn't been sure if her dress would still fit due to her significant weight loss. Over the last several months, Arizona had shrunk several dress sizes, a result of the stress of worrying about whether or not she should go through with marrying Chris.

The couple had experienced some rocky moments, and all roads had led back to Chris's inability to please Arizona in the bedroom. She'd feared that his sexual limitations were a precursor to other troubles that could arise. But after weighing Chris's many virtues against his few negative qualities, which she thought were mostly superficial, she had decided that her life would be much better with him in it than without him.

"You looked so handsome in your tux," Arizona said to Chris. "I'm glad that you decided to go the custom-made route because it truly is a one of a kind and I love it."

Chris smiled, flashing his perfectly straight teeth. "I hoped you would. I knew you were going to look amazing, so I had to step up my game for our big day." Chris took a seat in the high back chair next to the plush sofa and removed his patent leather shoes. "When I saw you walk down the aisle, I thought, 'Wow, I'm the luckiest man on earth.'"

"Honey, you're gonna make me cry happy tears all over again." Arizona held the front of her wedding gown against her chest and trained her gaze on Chris with seductive intent. "I have an idea about how you can put a big smile on my face right now." She dropped her wedding gown to the floor, revealing her white lace bustier, garter belt, and matching thong. With an extra wiggle in her hips, she sashayed a few steps toward the king size bed that was covered with red and white rose petals, and slowly lowered herself onto the plush mattress. "Let's get our honeymoon started right."

Arizona spread her thick, shapely legs and struck a sexy pose. She was going to ask Chris to fill their champagne flutes with the Veuve Clicquot that was chilling in the ice bucket to toast their lovemaking as newlyweds, but she stopped short when she noticed an abrupt change in her husband's demeanor.

"Baby, to be honest, I'm wiped out," Chris said with a yawn. He raised his long, muscular arms above his head and stretched as if he had just completed a labor-intensive task. He removed his tuxedo jacket and began to unbutton his shirt. "Didn't you say you were tired? I thought you were ready to call it a night."

Arizona nodded her head. "Yeah, I'm beat, but I'm not too tired to do a lil' sumthin' sumthin'. It's our honeymoon night."

"Baby, I hear you, but . . ."

Arizona was trying to remain calm, but she could feel her internal temperature begin to rise, so she took a deep breath before she said her next words. "Chris, we haven't been intimate since way back in February, and now it's June. Plus, like I just said, this is our honeymoon night and I want it to be special."

Arizona bit her lower lip as she thought about the frustration and disappointment of their previous attempts at lovemaking. She and Chris had been practicing abstinence from the moment they had started dating more than two years ago, but in late January, the night before Arizona's thirtieth birthday, a moment of weakness had overtaken them. Their lust and desire for each other had led them to cross the physical line into sexual intimacy. But instead of the carnal ecstasy that Arizona had been so sure Chris would bring her, she had experienced the shock of her life—practically non-existent sex.

That night, Arizona had discovered that her gorgeous, six-foot-four-inch, Adonis-looking fiancé had a micropenis that was only an inch and a half long, when fully erect. And if that disappointment had not been enough, he hadn't been able to please her with his mouth or his hands, and even though they had attempted to make love a couple times after that first disastrous night, their lovemaking had gone from bad to unbearable. Arizona had been displeased and put-off that not only was Chris's tiny tool smaller than her pinky, his tongue's only skill was reserved for talking. And even though she'd been sexually unfulfilled, he'd reached orgasm each time, and had fallen into a satisfied sleep while Arizona had laid awake and frustrated from each dismal experience.

Arizona had been so fed up that she'd confronted Chris about her disappointment and deep concerns about the future of their relationship. She had even threatened to call off the wedding. Chris didn't want to lose her, and while he'd said there was nothing he could do about his size, he'd promised to work on improving other skills and techniques that would give her sexual pleasure. But instead of trying the "practice makes perfect" approach to see if he could improve their sex life, Chris had persuaded Arizona to return to their practice of abstinence until they got married. "Once we're husband and wife, we'll have a lifetime together to practice, explore, learn, and enjoy each other," he'd said.

Now, in the present, Arizona could see that Chris was clearly uncomfortable about wanting to make love, but she didn't care one bit because she knew from past experience with her new husband that she couldn't beat around the bush when it came to what she wanted in the bedroom. She had to let Chris know where she stood. "I think we need to start our married life off the right way, don't you?" she said with conviction.

Chris rose to his feet. "You know that I love making love to you, but I'm tired, baby." He wrapped his arms around Arizona. "We have an entire lifetime to make love, make babies, and make happy memories. Let's get some rest so we can both feel energized and ready . . . in the morning."

"But it's already morning! You told me the same thing months ago, that we would have a lifetime for sex once we got married. Well, we just did the damn thing and now you're trying to blow me off again."

"I'm not blowing you off," Chris said in near exasperation, "it's late, and we need to get some rest before we start our honeymoon trip because the sun will be up before we know it."

Arizona pursed her lips and shook her head. "We're gonna be so rushed when we get up that we probably won't have time to do much of anything. You know we have to go by my parents' house and say goodbye to Solomon before we head to the airport." Arizona knew that regardless of Chris's and her differing views, the one thing they both agreed on was that Arizona's five-year-old son—with whom Chris had stepped in and was helping to raise as his own—was a top priority, and they needed to make sure they saw him before they left town.

She knew that Chris could tell what she was thinking because the apprehension she felt was draped over her face. The subject of their sex life was a difficult one.

Chris sighed. "Like I said, we've got a lifetime ahead of us. If we make love in the morning, great. If we don't, that'll be fine, too."

"For who? Certainly not me."

Chris took a few steps to where Arizona was perched at the foot of the bed, and dropped to one knee. *Finally,* she thought. He kissed Arizona on her lips and squeezed her against his chest.

"Trust me when I tell you that our life together is going to be great. You trust me, right?"

Arizona nodded with relief and anticipation. "Yes, I trust you, Chris."

"Good, now we've got two bathrooms in this suite, so why don't we both take a shower, get some rest, and then make love when the sun rises."

And with that, Chris rose to his feet and walked toward the bathroom on the other side of the suite. Arizona was so stunned that she couldn't move, even if she wanted to. Her new husband had bamboozled her out of her one and only chance to have wedding night sex.

Twenty minutes later, Arizona lay in bed, wide awake, listening to Chris's heavy breathing that had just turned into a full-on snore. *I think I made a big mistake when I said, I do,* she thought to herself as she looked at Chris. Little did she know that a sexless wedding night was soon to be the least of her problems.

★ ★ ★

It had been one week since Arizona Mays had become Mrs. Pendelton, and in that time she had experienced a honeymoon fraught with pure frustration.

Arizona knew it had been wishful thinking to believe that her and Chris's love life would improve without the benefit of practice. But her love for him and her faith that her prayers would be answered had led her to suspend reality and cling to the hope of a miracle. She'd thought about what her two best girlfriends, Bernadette and Tess, had told her just two weeks before the wedding when they had met for dinner and drinks.

"I've been praying for you," Bernadette had said. "I know you feel frustrated and confused about what to do, and that's not the way anyone should feel in the weeks leading up to their wedding day. Are you sure you want to marry Chris?"

"Thank you for your prayers, 'cause I need them," Arizona had replied. "And you're right, I'm a frustrated ball of nerves. I keep going back and forth about what to do, and just when I think I've made the right decision, I second guess myself and I'm back at square one."

"That should tell you something," Tess had chimed in.

"You don't think I should marry him, do you?"

"Not if you're second guessing your decisions," Bernadette said in a gentle tone. "Is the sex your biggest concern?"

Arizona nodded. "Chris acts like all the sexual dysfunction never happened, and I'm scared that after we get married things will stay the same. I know sex isn't everything in a relationship, but it's a big deal to me, and our sex life, when we had it, was the pits."

Tess took a sip of her Chardonnay and shook her head. "Girl, I'm gonna give it to you straight. If you think that Chris has learned some new tricks, you're headed for a big disappointment. And even if he has learned a thing or two, there's only so much he can do with that little dick he's workin' with."

"You're so crude," Bernadette said. "Remember what I told you about thinking before you open your mouth?"

"She's asking for our advice and I'm giving my honest opinion," Tess shot back.

Arizona was too upset to eat her cobb salad, so she pushed her plate to the side. "So both of you think I should call off the wedding, right?"

"Listen Arizona," Tess replied, taking another sip of her drink. "I think that if you go into this marriage with the belief that sex with Chris will somehow magically improve, you're kidding yourself and you're going to end up more frustrated than you already are. Change requires effort, not just time."

Bernadette bit into her chicken salad sandwich and then dabbed her napkin at the corners of her mouth before she spoke. "Tess is right about that second part. You can have all the good intentions, faith, prayer, and hope that you want, but you have to put forth action to make change happen."

Arizona relied heavily on both her friends' opinions, especially Bernadette's, who was older, wiser, and more level-headed than both she and Tess. "You have a point," she said.

"The tricky part of your predicament," Bernadette continued, "is that because you agreed to go back to being celibate until you two get married, you haven't put in the physical work to make changes, so now you have to ask yourself, or more importantly, ask Chris, what has he done to make changes. Have you talked to him about it?"

"No, I haven't," Arizona answered. "I have so many back and forth emotions. I know Chris loves me and I love him, and that's hard to find in these crazy days."

"You have a point," Tess agreed.

Bernadette swirled two French fries in her ketchup-filled rame-kin and continued to eat as she talked. "Regardless of what the two of us, or anyone else tells you, no one can make this decision but you. If you're continuing to have reservations, don't force yourself into anything, and don't worry about what anyone will think, including Chris." Bernadette paused, took a sip of her water, and reached for the breadbasket that was sitting in the middle of the table.

"What's up with your appetite?" Tess said as she looked at Bernadette stuff food into her mouth. "I've never seen you eat so much. You better slow down before you end up as big as a house. You know they say that once you turn fifty, things start going downhill."

Arizona shot Tess a look. "Lawd have mercy, Tess. I know that I have trouble with my mouth, but Girl, you on a whole other level."

"Bernadette knows that I don't mean any harm. I'm just looking out for her."

Bernadette placed a piece of cheese toast on her plate. "Yes, and I know that you don't have good sense, Tess, and that's why I'm ignoring you," she said before directing her attention back to Arizona. "As I was saying, you're the one who will have to live with the consequences of your decisions, so make sure that marrying Chris is what you really want to do."

Arizona had also heard the opinions of the women in her family, who had all urged her to not let a good thing slip away.

"You better hold on tight to that man," Arizona's mother had told her. "He's a good one."

"Men like Chris only come around once in a blue moon," her aunties and cousins had all said.

"Girl, you better hurry up and marry that man before he changes his mind," her longtime girlfriends had offered.

Arizona had never been one to be easily influenced, but she had to admit that her mother, aunties, cousins, and friends had all made valid points for why she should marry Chris. He may have had literal shortcomings, but he was a kind, hardworking man, and she knew that pickings were slim, especially in Bourbon.

Now, in the present, as Arizona sat in the window seat next to Chris, preparing for their descent into Raleigh-Durham International

Airport, a thousand thoughts raced through her mind about what she should do once their flight landed. She knew that she needed to have a come-to-Jesus conversation with Chris, because she wasn't happy.

Not once during their seven-day honeymoon did they make love or even come close to it. When they had first entered their luxurious, five-star resort in Napa Valley, California, she'd had high hopes that she and Chris would rebound from their disappointing wedding night. But instead of redeeming himself between the sheets, Chris had come up with an excuse each time that Arizona had tried to initiate sex. Either he was too tired, or, he wanted to stay out all night so they wouldn't have to be alone in the confines of their room after dark.

Once again, Arizona thought back to how Chris had behaved after they had made love many months ago. Rather than facing the uncomfortable truth that he had a miniscule-size penis that had not been able to sexually satisfy her, Chris had completely avoided intimate contact with Arizona by pretending to be tired, and even faking as if he'd been asleep. She had wanted to confront him, but she'd known it would cause a huge blowup, and she didn't have the energy to deal with the emotional fallout. On their fourth day of Chris's ducking and dodging on their honeymoon, Arizona had finally given up. She had decided that she would concentrate on the beauty of the wine country instead of her troubling love life.

Arizona was pulled from her deep thoughts by the sound of Chris's voice.

"Baby, did you enjoy our honeymoon?" Chris asked with a wide smile. "Can you believe seven days went by so fast?"

Arizona looked at him with astonishment and shook her head. "I don't think I should answer that right now," she replied in a curt tone. She could see by the surprised expression on Chris's face that he hadn't expected her response. After all, she had played along during their entire honeymoon, tip-toeing around a snowball that had rolled into an avalanche of emotions.

"Baby, what's wrong?" Chris reached for Arizona's hand, but she withdrew hers and folded her arms.

"You know full well what's wrong."

"No, I don't." Chris said with concern. "Are you not feeling well? You look like you're coming down with something."

Arizona's eyes narrowed and her mood jumped from docile to hostile in less than the time it had taken her to blink. She wanted to tell Chris that she was pissed, and that she knew that he had intentionally avoided making love to her from the first night of their honeymoon, right up until they had gotten dressed this morning. And now, engaging her right before they landed was his passive-aggressive way of dealing with an inevitably touchy discussion that he knew would be coming once they got home. Arizona exhaled and stared at her husband. "You know that I can see through the game you're playin', right?"

Chris let out a deep breath filled with confusion. "I don't know what's come over you, but I don't like it."

"And I don't like feeling this way," Arizona shot back. "But how am I supposed to feel after a sexless honeymoon."

Not only had Arizona's mood changed with red-hot lightning speed, but the pitch of her voice had risen several notches, drawing curious stares from passengers in nearby seats. There had been a time in Arizona's wild and defiant past when she wouldn't have given a second thought about causing a loud and chaotic scene, right there on the plane. But she was a different woman now. She was a wife, mother, and entrepreneur, and she knew she needed to act accordingly. Thankfully, Chris realized the confrontation that was resting on her lips and refrained from engaging her any further.

Forty-five minutes later, Arizona and Chris were on their way to her parents' house to pick up Solomon. They had deplaned, retrieved their luggage, and put it into Chris's SUV, all without saying a single word to each other. As they approached her parents' house, Arizona's mood sank even lower when she saw more than a dozen cars parked along the street as she inhaled the aroma of charcoal-grilled food in the air. A colorful 'Welcome Home' sign hung on her mother and father's front door, and colorful balloons were taped to the mailbox pole.

Arizona took a deep breath and felt physically ill, knowing this was the beginning of a life that she did not want.

Chapter 4

BERNADETTE

Bernadette's eyes flickered, and her mouth formed a delighted smile as she felt the wet softness of Coop's lips on the back of her neck. The sun was just beginning to make its ascent into the sky, and as she felt Coop's hardness pressed against her thigh, Bernadette knew that he was rising as well.

"Good morning," Bernadette said, turning her body to face him. "What a wonderful way to wake up and start my day."

"I was just thinkin' the same thing." Coop's words were slow and easy, spilling out of his mouth with a heated intensity that Bernadette had come to love. She squinted her eyes, adjusting them to the light peeking into the room that allowed her to see Coop's face. No matter how many times she looked at him, Bernadette was still struck by his classically handsome features that were old Hollywood worthy. His smooth, baby soft, café-au-lait-colored skin defied that of a man in his early fifties, as did his fit body and sculpted muscles. She was glad that Coop was the type of man who recognized the importance of maintaining a physically fit and well-groomed appearance without being fussy about it. She often teased that his cover model looks could earn him more money than all his businesses combined.

There was a time when they had first started dating that Coop's attention-grabbing good looks had intimidated Bernadette, and had made her feel even more self-conscious about her own appearance. Because while she was blessed with a petite, well-toned body and smooth brown skin that was soft and supple from head to toe, Bernadette knew that her plain facial features, curveless figure, and basic updo hairstyle were all average at best. But what she had come to realize, and what Coop always reminded her of, was that she was beautiful in ways that mattered beyond the superficial.

"How'd you sleep, baby?" Coop asked, his sexy voice dripping with southern charm.

"Like a rock," she answered. "How about you?"

"I slept like a baby, and I feel energized. I'm gettin' kinda used to stayin' here at your place for a change."

Bernadette and Coop usually spent the bulk of their time together at his house across town, in the section of Bourbon known as The Bottoms. It was a tight-knit, predominately black section of town, and it had been that way for as long as anyone could remember. The Bottoms was a place where black leaders, teachers, doctors, businessmen, day laborers, and their families all thrived in unity, living in modest homes with well-maintained lawns. But during the 1960s, things began to change, and by the 1980s the drug epidemic had swept through the area, as it had most black communities across the country, and changed the landscape for generations to come. Coop's four-bedroom, ranch style brick home was situated at the end of a quiet, tree-lined street, and was considered one of the nicest in The Bottoms. But it was no match for Bernadette's *Architectural Digest*-worthy home that was tucked away in the most exclusive section of her Palisades neighborhood.

It surprised Bernadette to hear Coop say that he was getting used to staying at her house, because she knew that outside of coming to see her, he had very little interest in that side of town. He was one of the wealthiest men in Bourbon, black or white, but he didn't flaunt it. His impressive bank account afforded him the ability to live any-where he wanted, but he had chosen to stay in The Bottoms, where he had been born and raised, and he had adopted the mission of restoring his community back to the richness of where it used to be. But for now, Bernadette was glad that Coop was in her house, wak-ing up next to her in her king-size bed.

"I wish we could wake up like this every morning." Bernadette said.

"Me too." Coop squeezed Bernadette into his chest and kissed her forehead. "But we both know that ain't gonna happen. That's why we better steal these moments while we can, because once the baby's born, that's all she wrote."

Bernadette knew that Coop's straight-forward words had come from a place of sincerity and truth, and they only served to heighten her anxiety about what was going to be their new reality. Thinking about diaper changes and early morning feedings flatlined Berna-dette's good mood.

It had been nearly two weeks since she'd told Coop that she was pregnant—right before accepting his marriage proposal—and in that time they'd had lengthy discussions about how a baby would change their lives. They both knew that with Bernadette being fifty and Coop having turned fifty-two last month, they would face consider-able challenges as first-time parents raising an infant. And beyond that, by the time they reached their sixties, instead of coasting into retirement and traveling abroad, they would be attending parent/teacher conferences, helping with nightly homework assignments, and orchestrating drop offs and pickups from extra-curricular activities—all while adjusting to being senior citizens.

Bernadette looked into Coop's eyes and wondered if his words had dampened his spirits as well, but her question was answered when she felt his hand rub against her thigh. "Does anything deter you?" she asked.

Coop gave her a quizzical look as he pulled her even closer into his chest. "Whadda you mean?"

"I can't believe that talking about the baby, and how our lives are about to be turned upside down, doesn't kill your mood to have sex?"

"Absolutely not," Coop said with a smile. "First of all, you're sexy as hell, so that's a turn-on right there. And second, when I think about the life that we're about to bring into this world and all the good things that's gonna come from us gettin' married and buildin' a family, I feel nothin' but appreciation."

"You do?"

"Yeah. Don't you?"

Bernadette shrugged her shoulders. "I guess I didn't think about it that way," she said in an unsure voice. "There's so many unknowns . . ."

"Bernie, you're one of the most optimistic people I know. Baby, you just gotta trust that everything's gonna work out."

Bernadette pulled away from Coop's embrace so she could sort through her thoughts. She gathered the soft, 1600 thread count, sateen bed sheet around her chest and let out a deep breath. "I don't know if it's my hormones kicking in or my rattled nerves, but I'm all over the place with my emotions." She felt out of sorts, which was a foreign thing to her because she was used to dealing with life in a controlled manner. "Like I said, there's so many unknowns."

"Okay, what can I do to ease your worries?"

"You're already doing it. Just being present and knowing that you're here for me is comforting and reassuring."

"You know I got you, and I'm gonna always be here for you. No matter what."

"No matter what, right?"

Coop shook his head and looked deep into Bernadette's eyes. "Woman, you should know by now how much I love you, and that

I'll move heaven and earth to make you happy and give you anything that you need . . . you, and our child."

Coop didn't know it, but instead of his words calming Bernadette, they had unknowingly ignited a quiet fear that had been resting inside her for weeks. She'd discovered that Coop may have been involved in a murder thirty-five years ago, during his wild and reckless youth. It was a cold case that had recently gained traction, due to the victim's family's renewed push to get justice for their slain loved one.

Bernadette had found evidence hidden in Coop's home office that directly implicated him in the murder, and, if he was indeed the killer, he would most likely be convicted and spend the rest of his life inside prison walls.

Bernadette had always prided herself on possessing a high code of ethics, integrity, and sense of doing the right thing. Her mind told her that if Coop was guilty of the crime, he needed to face the penalty; after all, there was a grieving family that the victim had left behind and they wanted and needed justice. But the very human, hormonal, and emotional part of her couldn't fathom the thought of seeing the love of her life and the father of her unborn child locked behind the bars of a prison cell.

As Bernadette looked at Coop and once again thought about his baby growing inside her, she knew right then and there that she was going to do everything in her power to keep his secret buried beside the body of the dead man from the past.

"Baby, it's gonna be all right. Trust me, okay?"

Bernadette nodded and drew her attention back to the here and now. "I do, Coop. I'm still trying to process everything. I'd resigned myself to the belief that I'd never get married or have children. Now, I'm going to have both, and even though I know without a doubt that being your wife is going to be the best thing that's ever happened to me, and having our baby is going to be a blessing, I feel a little overwhelmed by the sheer weight of it all."

Coop reached for Bernadette's hand. "I know baby, and I understand what you're tryin' to say. It's a normal reaction considerin' our lifestyle and current circumstances. We're only accountable to ourselves, but havin' a baby means we're gonna be responsible for another human being. Plus, let's face it, even though we're both in good shape, we're gettin' up there in age."

Bernadette was glad he'd said that because it opened the door for her to say what was really on her mind. "To be completely honest, Coop, I'm terrified about the physical process of having a baby. I'm high risk."

"Yes, and that's something that I've thought a lot about, too, and that's why I'm gonna take extra good care of you."

Bernadette smiled. "Thank you, Coop. But my health is just one part of it. Because of my age our baby is also at risk. And even if I have a smooth pregnancy and our child is born healthy, our lives will change completely. We won't be able to go out whenever we want, plan a spur-of-the-moment trip, or leisurely lay in bed and watch the sun come up like we're doing right now. We're going to constantly be on the go because children require so much. My hours at work will have to change, your hours at the Southern Comfort, and how you do business in general will have to change as well. Everything will be different."

Bernadette studied Coop's face and could see that he was in deep thought about what she had just said. She knew that usually when people pondered complicated matters, one could tell what the other person was thinking by their body language or facial expressions. But Coop was always calm and controlled, from his carefully selected choice of words to his body language. He didn't give anything away. He had a well-earned reputation for being as cool as a fan. Bernadette knew she would have to wait until he spoke to know what was on his mind.

"Bernie," he began. "A lot will change, but I guarantee you it'll be easier than you think."

"What makes you say that?"

"Look at how we live our lives right now. You mentioned spur-of-the-moment trips, but we're not spur-of-the-moment kind of people. We plan everything we do, whether it's a weekend getaway to the beach or a date night at the movies. I can count on one hand with fingers to spare, how many times we've laid in bed and watched the sun come up. We're too busy for that, either hittin' the walkin' trail for a mornin' run, or you're headin' in to work while I head out to do my thing. Baby, we're already busy people."

"True, and that's kind of my point, too. With all that we do, how're we going to fit raising a child into our life?"

"The best way we can. We're smart, we're resourceful, and I know that we'll find a way."

Coop had just told her what he was thinking, and as Bernadette looked deeper into his eyes, she no longer questioned how he felt. She saw faith and hope all rolled into love, and it slightly eased her mood, but she still needed more assurance that things would work out. "I know you're right, but you've got to be a little scared, too," Bernadette urged.

"I'd be lyin' and half-crazy if I said that I wasn't. But I learned a long time ago that there's no reward that doesn't come without a certain amount of a risk."

Bernadette nodded. "It's the risk that has me worried."

"Bernie, you've been a risk taker all your life."

"No, Coop," Bernadette said with a sigh. "I've always played it safe. The only risks I've ever taken have been calculated ones."

Coop shook his head. "You took a risk when you left the projects to attend college at Georgetown. And I don't know many folks our age, man or woman, who would up and move from the city where they'd lived their entire life, to a small town where they didn't have family or know even one soul."

"You give me too much credit."

"And you don't give yourself enough."

"That's because what I did wasn't a big risk when you think about it. When I accepted that full scholarship to Georgetown, I went from Southeast DC to the Northwest side of town, which was less than twenty miles away. And when I moved here last summer, it was because Bourbon General offered to pay me more in one year than most people make in five, plus they covered all of my relocation expenses in addition to giving me a sweet signing bonus. So you see, my 'risks' were no brainers."

Bernadette knew that Coop was digesting what she had just said because rather than respond to her, he sat in silence, staring out the window at the sun that was now beaming high in the sky. She took a moment to admire him, and the way the brilliant light washed over his skin, making him glow even more than he normally did. As Bernadette continued to watch him, she was filled with appreciation for Coop. He always saw the best in her, even when she didn't acknowledge her own good qualities, like now. He was telling her that he recognized and appreciated her strength and courage, and that she, and they, would be just fine bringing a child into the world.

"Coop . . ."

"Yes?"

"I'm sorry."

"For what?"

Bernadette squeezed Coop's hand. "For letting my fears overtake my faith. I guess you're right, I don't give myself enough credit. I have a problem with that, and I know I need to work on it."

"I'm glad you realize it 'cause I can't be the only one in this relationship who thinks you're a superstar."

Bernadette laughed. "You're too much. I don't know what I did to deserve you, but I'm glad you're in my life."

"Baby, we're in this thing together. Just remember, like I said, whatever happens, I got you."

"And I got you, too, Coop," she said, taking a deep breath of relief. "I've read so many articles about the dangers and risks of being pregnant at my age, not to mention the fact that my mind feels numb when I think about the demands of having the day-to-day responsibility for another human being who will be completely dependent upon me, it got me doubting myself."

Coop leaned back against the soft, tufted headboard and focused his eyes on Bernadette's. "Do you want to have this baby?"

"Of course I do. I don't want you to think that because I have worries, that I don't want to have our baby. I know this isn't what either of us had planned, but I do believe it was planned for us by God, otherwise, I wouldn't be pregnant in the first place."

"I'm glad you said that, because I feel the same way."

Bernadette squeezed Coop's hand again. "We're aligned, and like you said to me on the night that you proposed to me. We fit where it counts."

"I love you, Bernie, and I can't wait to marry you." He planted soft kisses on her face, making her smile, then without warning he pulled away. "I'll be right back." Coop rose from the bed and walked to the bathroom.

Bernadette bent her knees and hugged her arms around them as she watched Coop leave the room. She thought about her eight-week prenatal appointment with her OBGYN that was scheduled for later that afternoon. She had taken the day off from work and Coop had pushed his meetings into the following week so that he could accompany her. She was glad that Coop had insisted upon going with her because she knew that having him by her side would calm her overactive nerves. She was pulled away from her thoughts when she saw Coop emerge from the bathroom with his hands behind his back. He walked over to her side of the bed and sat on the edge beside her.

"I didn't do this the right way when I proposed, but you still said yes anyway," Coop said as his mouth formed a smile. He presented Bernadette with a small, ivory colored box and opened it to reveal a breathtaking ring. "Bernie, this makes our engagement official. You're not just my lady, you're my fiancée, and I can't wait until you become my wife."

Bernadette's heart began to beat fast with excitement. Although she had accepted Coop's proposal nearly two weeks ago, she had completely forgotten about sealing the deal with a ring. Between her demanding job and constant fatigue, her mind had been too preoccupied to think about anything beyond what was right in front of her. Now, looking at the dazzling diamond that Coop had presented to her, she was overwhelmed with joy.

"Oh, Coop, it's absolutely beautiful," Bernadette said.

"You really like it?"

"Are you kidding me! Yes, how could I not? It's gorgeous and so unique. I love it."

Bernadette knew right away that not only had Coop put a substantial amount of money into her four-carat show-stopper of an engagement ring, he had invested a great deal of time and thought. Her keen eye could see that the ring was without a doubt custom-made, because of its unique setting, which was a combination of modern and vintage design.

Coop smiled with pride. "I'm glad you approve. It took a while for them to get the setting just right."

"How long have you been planning this?"

"I started workin' with the designer about three months ago."

Bernadette blinked her eyes in amazement as a thought came rushing into her mind. "Wait a minute. That was only two months after we started dating."

"Yep. Your ring was supposed to arrive the day before Arizona's wedding, and I'd planned to propose to you after we left the reception. But the jeweler called a couple days before and told me it would be another two weeks before the ring would be ready. Even though I didn't have it in hand, I still wanted to propose to you that night because it felt right."

Coop removed the ring from the box, reached for Bernadette's left hand, and gently slid the sparkling diamond onto her petite finger.

"It's perfect," Bernadette said as she admired the beautiful ring. "I even have a little room to spare, which will come in handy because judging from the way I look right now, my fingers are going to swell like crazy in the months to come."

"More for me to love."

Bernadette was so happy that she could barely contain herself. She hadn't told anyone that Coop had proposed to her, not even her mother. But with a large diamond sitting on her finger, she knew that she had to let those closest to her know. She decided that she would call her mother after her prenatal appointment, and then tell Tess and Arizona later tonight during their girls' night dinner.

"Have you been thinking about dates for the wedding?" Coop asked.

"Um, actually, no," she stammered. "I've been so busy and tired that I can barely remember my name some days."

"I understand, Baby. I know that you want time to plan, and I want to make sure that we have the wedding of your dreams."

Bernadette looked at her hand and once again admired her ring. She thought back to five years ago when she had been planning to marry her con artist of a fiancé, Walter Pearson. At forty-five, she had been so excited at the prospect of finally walking down the aisle that within days of Walter's proposal she had begun interviewing caterers and florists and had set the wheels into motion for a wedding that was befitting of royalty. But her entire relationship with Walter had been a sham. The diamond that he had given her had been meaningless, and had actually been stolen property, as she'd discovered a month after their breakup when the police had shown up at her door.

The invaluable lesson that Bernadette had learned from her failed relationship with Walter was lasting. She had come to see that material possessions and outward appearances meant nothing, and that it was the intent that rested inside one's heart and mind that really mattered. She knew that Coop's intentions, in everything he did, came from a place of authenticity. From the way he went about his business dealings, to his charitable giving and volunteerism that uplifted his community, to the fierce way he took care of the people he loved, Coop had proven to Bernadette that good men still existed in the world.

Bernadette realized that it didn't matter where or when she and Coop got married, just as long as they did it. But she didn't want to put off setting a date for too long, as her cousin Tess was doing with her fiancé. Bernadette knew that the sooner she became Mrs. Dennis, the more relaxed she would feel.

"I don't want a big, elaborate ceremony," she said. "But I do want to be your wife as soon as possible. How would you feel about doing something simple, like, getting married at the courthouse and then having a reception at Southern Comfort?"

Coop nodded his head, leaned in, and planted a kiss on Bernadette's lips. "Baby, this is another reason why I love you. I was thinkin' the same thing, but I thought you might want somethin' fancy and formal. But the Justice of the Peace and the club sound just fine with me. As a matter of fact, we can go down to the courthouse before your doctor's appointment and apply for our marriage license."

Bernadette raised both her thumbs to give Coop her seal of approval. Even with her worries about the unknown, she was happy, and she couldn't imagine being any more excited than she felt right now.

Several hours later, after applying for their marriage license and then driving across town to Bernadette's doctor's appointment, she and Coop sat it the exam room stunned and slightly dazed. Dr. Vu had finished Bernadette's exam, and he and his nurse had just left the room to give Bernadette time to re-dress.

Bernadette had felt as though she had been walking on a cloud when she and Coop had arrived for her first prenatal visit, but now she was numb from head to toe. She remembered the shock that she had felt when Dr. Vu had first told her that she was pregnant, and the anxiety that had followed. But as inconceivable as that revelation had been, it didn't hold a candle to the fact that she and Coop had just learned that she was pregnant with twins.

Chapter 5

TESS

Ever since Tess's confrontational blow out with Maceo two weeks ago, her mood had been melancholy, and she had stayed sequestered from the world, sitting behind her desk, staring at her computer. She was writing a new book and the words were coming slow because her mind couldn't focus on the characters she had created, or the plot that was struggling to unfold. To say that Tess was in a funk was putting it mildly, but this evening offered a bright spot that she was hoping would give her a pick-me-up. Tonight she was meeting Bernadette and Arizona for dinner.

Tess's girls' night out was coming at just the right time because she needed a good dose of sisterly love and support, and more important, she needed advice. Her relationship with Maceo had gone from exciting, tender, and loving, to dull and distant right before her eyes. After she'd told him that there was a high probability that she would not be able to have children, their communication became strained and uncomfortable. Tess had known that whenever she chose to tell him, the news would come as a complete surprise to Maceo. But what she had not expected was the heated way her revelation would unfold.

After Maceo had pressed Tess about why for weeks she had purposely avoided having a conversation about setting a wedding date, she'd told him the truth, in painstaking detail. She'd told him about her history of fibroids, endometriosis, and her premature ovarian failure, or in layman's terms, a lazy ovary. She had told him about the multiple surgeries and procedures she had undergone, all in her efforts to improve her chances of conceiving one day. She'd told him that each month she experienced severe pain that no amount of holistic remedies, healthy diet, herbal supplements, or pharmaceutical prescriptions had been able to alleviate. Then finally, she'd told him about the disappointing visit she'd had last month with her OBGYN, Dr. Gina, when she had taken a weekend trip to Chicago so that she could put her house on the market in preparation for her impending move to Bourbon.

Maceo had listened in silence for nearly a half hour as Tess had poured out everything she'd been holding inside, from the beginning of their relationship to the present. She'd even told him about the fact that she had been sick from an endometriosis flare up, and not a common cold—as she had led him to believe—when she'd had to cancel their first date. She had exhaled with relief after coming clean with the truth, glad that she'd finally unloaded the heavy weight of her secret. She had been prepared for Maceo to be shocked and even a little upset, but what she had not expected was the hurt and anger that had flowed out of him in a cool and steady stream.

"Tess, you know all about my past," Maceo had begun, "I poured my heart out to you the first night we met because I felt an instant connection with you that I'd never experienced with any other woman. It was powerful . . . like magic."

"I know, and I felt it too, Mace, and . . ."

Maceo cut her off. "Please, Tess, can you for once let me finish a sentence before you jump in," he said in an irritated tone.

Tess was startled that Maceo interrupted her in the middle of what she was about to say. It was true that she often interjected when he was talking, but she only did it in support of, or in agreement with any point he was trying to make. She had interrupted this time because she felt that she needed to let him know how much she loved him, too, and how sorry she was for keeping such an important secret from him. But right now she knew that Maceo was pissed, so she shut her mouth and listened. "I'm sorry, go ahead with what you were saying."

Maceo shook his head and continued. "I haven't kept any secrets from you, and I've always been straight up about everything that's going on in my life, and that's why I'm having a really hard time with this. When we talked while you were in Chicago last month, when I asked you how things were going, the only thing you talked about was the meetings you had with your realtor and that she already had a few people lined up who were interested in buying your house. Not once did you mention anything about going to your doctor or having fertility tests. You were being seen by a specialist and you didn't even tell me.

"When you had to cancel our first date because you were sick, you had me believing that you'd caught a cold. I remember I was on my way to pick you up, and instead of turning around and going back home, I drove to Bernadette's house where you were staying, and I made you homemade soup so you would feel better. You purposely misled me, Tess, and it makes me question how many other times you've misled me or outright lied about things."

"Maceo, I would never intentionally tell you an outright lie," Tess said with pleading eyes. "You've got to believe me."

"I don't have to do anything, and right now, I don't know what to believe. I thought I knew you, Tess, but it's obvious that I don't."

Now Tess was becoming nervous because instead of looking into her eyes with love or something close to it, as he always did, even when they had disagreements, Maceo's stare carried a vacancy that didn't register. Tess stood up and began to pace the floor. "I know you're doubting me right now, and you have every right to. But Mace, you have to believe me. I wanted to tell you, but it seemed like it was never a good time."

"There's always a good time for the truth."

"Maybe for you, but this was hard for me, Mace. And every time I thought it was the right time, something would always come up."

"That's bullshit and you know it."

Tess's eyes grew wide with surprise when she heard Maceo curse without hesitation. She was the foul-mouthed one in their relationship, and it was nothing for her to rattle off expletives with ease. But Maceo was like his Uncle Coop, they were the epitome of calm control. Maceo was always smooth in his approach and he rarely, if ever, allowed anything to rattle him. Tess knew she had really messed up now.

But instead of quieting herself so that their argument would not escalate out of hand, Tess became indignant. "It's not bullshit," she said right back at him. "It's the truth. This is a delicate subject, and it's hard to just tell someone, especially someone who wants to have a house full of kids that, 'Hey, by the way, I've been told by medical experts that it's very unlikely that I'll be able to have kids.'"

"First of all, I'm not just someone. I'm your fiancé. And second, it's not hard to tell the truth if you love someone, and you know that what you're holding inside is going to impact them, too. That's what responsible people do, Tess."

"You don't understand."

Maceo nodded his head. "Yes, unfortunately I do." He stood to his feet and folded his arms across his chest. "I've always known that you're an attention seeker, a drama queen, and at times, extremely self-absorbed. Then there's your mouth, that can cut people to the core with your choice of words. But I've dealt with those things because I love you, Tess, and because we all have flaws that we need to work on, including me."

"Wow," Tess interrupted with a sarcastic smirk. "I finally open up to you about the agony that I've been going through, and you use my pain as an opportunity to criticize me. That's really low."

Maceo took a deep breath and exhaled his frustration. "You still don't get it."

"Yeah, I get it all right. Now I hear loud and clear what you really think of me."

"No, Tess, there's one thing I left out, that up until this very moment I hadn't realized."

Tess stopped pacing the floor. She walked to where Maceo was standing, planted herself directly in front of him, and folded her arms across her chest, just as he had done. She stared him in the eye with a look that said she was ready for whatever he had to say. "Okay, Mace, tell me the great epiphany that you've just discovered about me."

Maceo returned her stare, and calmly said, "You're selfish."

"Selfish?" Tess balked.

"I didn't stutter."

"I may be a lot of things, but selfish isn't one of them. I'm one of the most generous people you'll ever meet."

"If you're talking about your generosity to charities, the way you give gifts, and things like that, then yes, you're generous. But that's not what I'm talking about."

"Then what are you trying to say?"

"You're selfish in your personal relationships, at least that's the way you are with me."

"Now you're talking crazy. I'm always looking out for you, trying to help you, and doing anything I can to please you. That's not the sign of a selfish person."

Maceo looked as though he was beginning to grow tired. "Let's be real with each other. The reason you didn't tell me about your infertility issues has very little to do with me and my feelings, but it has a whole lot to do with how my reaction to hearing that news might directly affect you." Maceo unfolded his arms, letting their weight hang to his sides.

"That's not true," Tess nearly shouted. "I was thinking about you this entire time, and how not having biological children would impact you. I kept my condition from you because I didn't want to say anything until I had exhausted every treatment option. As a matter of fact, I have an appointment in a few weeks with Bernadette's OBGYN, Dr. Vu. He's going to give me another opinion, and hopefully he'll have some encouraging news."

"So, Bernadette knows about this?"

Tess could see the disappointment and hurt in Maceo's eyes. "Well, yes. You know how close we are. She's my cousin."

"But I'm your fiancé."

Tess felt trapped by her own words. As a seasoned writer, she knew how to throw sentences together to weave a convincing story that could get her into or out of any situation. But this was one set of circumstances that had rendered her tongue helpless to defend her.

Maceo walked toward the slim, marble-top table in the foyer, retrieved his keys from the silver bowl where he always kept them, and opened the door without saying a word.

"Where're you going?" Tess asked.

"Out."

In the two weeks that followed, their conversations had been strained, and the normally effortless vibe between them had become decidedly different. Maceo had thrown his time and energy into Sue's Brown Bag, where he now spent most of his time during the day as well as at night. Tess had thrown herself into working on the manuscript for her next book, secluding herself inside Maceo's guest bedroom which now served as her writing cave. They had even put house hunting on hold, and not once had Maceo brought up any mention of setting a wedding date as he'd normally done.

Now, as Tess sat in the posh entryway of the Magnolia Room, she was looking forward to relieving some stress and catching up with Bernadette and Arizona, neither of whom she had seen since Arizona's wedding. Just as she was about to send them a group text to let them know she was there, she heard the familiar sound of Arizona's hearty laughter followed by Bernadette's controlled shushing, no doubt trying to quiet Arizona inside the tony, Michelin-rated establishment.

"Tess!" Bernadette called out with excitement. Even though her voice remained at a respectable decibel, her tone and wide smile screamed with emotion and let Tess know that her cousin was happy to see her.

"Hey Girl!" Arizona chimed in beside Bernadette, practically running toward Tess with outstretched arms. "It's so good to see you! It feels like it's been forever."

Tess had missed the two women, and seeing how much they had missed her in return made her feel wanted, which as of late, was a distant emotion. After they exchanged hugs and a short debate about where they wanted to be seated—Tess preferring the breezy heat of the picturesque, outdoor patio, and Bernadette and Arizona electing for the comfort of the air-conditioned dining room—a server led them to an area near a large window in a quiet section inside the restaurant.

"See, you get to enjoy the beauty of outdoors without sweating in this oppressive heat," Bernadette said to Tess as she perused her menu.

"It's not the same," Tess responded as she peered outside. "Looking through a window at the sun and feeling its heat on your skin are two very different things."

Arizona shook her head. "Girl, you must be outta your mind. It's two hundred and ninety-five degrees outside, and I'm not tryin' to melt this makeup straight off my face."

"It's not that hot," Tess said with a laugh.

Arizona chuckled as she took a small sip of her sweet iced tea. "I've lived in Bourbon all my life and I'm still not used to the heat or the humidity. Chile, it's more than a notion."

"I will say this," Bernadette said with a thoughtful smile, "I don't know whether it's this blazing summer heat or your newlywedded bliss, but Arizona, you're positively glowing."

"You can say that again." Tess nodded. "Tell us all about your honeymoon because you know we can't wait to hear the juicy details."

Arizona uncomfortably shifted her weight in her seat and looked down at her salad. "That glow you're seeing is because of my make-up and nothing else," she responded in a dry tone. "Let's talk about something else for a minute while I calm myself down."

Tess exchanged a worried look with Bernadette. She wasn't surprised that Arizona was already having problems with Chris, and she knew it must be worse than she'd imagined if her friend had to take a few minutes to compose herself before she spoke about her honeymoon. Tess was glad that Bernadette was ever the consummate diplomat and always knew how to handle delicate situations, so she followed her cousin's lead to relieve Arizona's pressure.

Bernadette smiled. "We should have ice cream for dessert to cool us down," she said in Tess's direction. Bernadette removed a tissue from the small packet in her large handbag and dabbed the tiny beads of sweat populating her forehead. "When I moved here last summer, I was too busy settling in to pay attention to how hot it was. But now that I'm actually living here and not just going through the motions, I don't know how I'm going to survive this heat."

Tess noticed that not only was Bernadette sweating as though she had just run two laps around the restaurant, she looked as though she had put on a few pounds in the two weeks since she had last seen her. Bernadette had always maintained her weight along with a physically fit appearance, thanks to her healthy eating habits and daily workouts. But Tess knew she shouldn't be surprised that Bernadette was putting on the pounds because she had settled into a routine with Coop that included putting on "happy" weight. Between preparing meals for Coop, eating takeout from Sue's Brown Bag, and indulging in the meals served up at Southern Comfort, Tess surmised that no matter how much Bernadette had been working out, her steady consumption of down-home, southern style comfort food was beginning to catch up with her cousin. She remembered how Bernadette had practically inhaled her food when the three of them had met for lunch a few weeks before Arizona's wedding, and now Bernadette's appetite was growing.

Tess thought it was a strange twist of irony that Bernadette was gaining weight as Arizona seemed to be dropping pounds virtually overnight. In the months leading up to her wedding, Arizona had lost a whopping fifty pounds, and in the two weeks since she had said her *I Do*'s, Tess could see that she had slimmed down even more, as was evidenced by her figure hugging, bodycon dress that accentuated her curvy figure. As Tess studied Bernadette, who usually wore strapless sundresses and slim fitting capris during the summer months, but was now sporting a formless, floral print maxi dress that swallowed her body, she knew that she needed to say something to help her cousin.

When the server brought their food to the table, Tess's thoughts were reconfirmed that Bernadette needed an intervention before her weight got out of hand. Tess couldn't believe Bernadette's plate, which consisted of a quarter pound Magnolia Angus beef cheese-burger, steak fries, and a side order of mac and cheese. Conversely, she and Arizona had opted for garden salads.

"How is your book coming along?" Bernadette asked Tess, no doubt wanting to introduce a new subject that would help Arizona get her mind in a better place. "I haven't texted or called you in the last two weeks because I know you're back in your writing cave, working on your next masterpiece."

"That's exciting," Arizona said, seeming to come back around. "You're my girl and everything, but I still think it's wild that I'm friends with the famous Testimony "Tess" Sinclair, *New York Times* bestselling author."

"I'm hardly famous," Tess said with a shrug of her shoulders.

"Yes, you are," Bernadette jumped in. "I'll never forget, years ago, when I turned on my TV as I was getting dressed for work and I saw you being interviewed by Robin Roberts on *Good Morning America*, and then later that evening you were on *Entertainment Tonight*. I said, my cousin has officially arrived."

Arizona nodded as she pierced a tomato with her fork. "That's what I'm talkin' about."

"I still don't think I'm famous," Tess said, "and I'm certainly not on anyone's radar, especially lately."

Arizona leaned in close to Tess. "How do you figure that? Your last book was a huge hit, you finished a new book a few months ago, and now you're already working on another one. You're on everyone's radar because all of your readers, including me, can't wait to get our hands on your next novel."

"She's right," Bernadette agreed.

Tess felt mentally exhausted. Normally during the writing process she preferred to be tucked away in her writing cave without the outside distractions of the outside world. But ever since she had been dating Maceo, she looked forward to stealing quiet moments with him each day, and lying next to him at night after her long writing sessions. She thought about how empty her bed had felt the last two weeks and the fact that she would most likely be alone again tonight.

Tess looked at Bernadette and then toward Arizona. She let out a deep breath and shook her head. "Can I be honest with you guys?"

Bernadette and Arizona sat in silence with questioning stares that bordered on alarm. "What's wrong, Tess?" Bernadette asked in a gentle tone.

"I think Mace is going to break up with me and call off our engagement. Hell, he might even ask me to give back this ring," she said as she looked down at her diamond. "This love shit is for the birds."

"What did you do?" Arizona asked.

"Damn," Tess shot back with frustration. "Why're you coming after me like that? How do you know that it's not something that Mace did to me?"

Arizona patted the sides of her mouth with her napkin before she spoke. "I've known Maceo all my life, and he's one of the most chill, easy goin' brothas I know. He's just like his Uncle Coop," she said, glancing at Bernadette. "And those men don't do nothin' to nobody unless somebody's done somethin' to them. I love you like a sista, but you keep mess stirred up, so I just figured you did somethin'."

Bernadette spoke up again. "What happened, Tess?"

Now it was Tess's turn to shift uncomfortably in her seat. "I told him about my infertility issues."

She leaned her body in close to the table and lowered her voice because she didn't want nearby patrons to hear the details of her personal business. "I poured my heart out to Mace about all the physical and emotional problems that I've been going through, not to mention the fact that I'm still doing book events and I'm under a deadline for my next novel, but it was as if he didn't care. He actually had the nerve to tell me that I'm selfish. Can you believe that?"

Arizona sipped her tea and Bernadette took a bite of her cheeseburger. Tess expected them to come to her defense, especially after hearing that she had finally told Maceo about her fertility challenges. But they were as quiet as if they were sitting inside a library.

"So, you two have nothing to say?" Tess asked.

Arizona cleared her throat. "I'm still workin' on my tact issues, so I'm just gonna let Bernadette take this one."

"What's that supposed to mean?" Tess snapped.

Bernadette raised her hand as if to say, wait. "Tess, you know that we love you, so what I'm getting ready to say is coming from a place of genuine care and concern."

"Oh, hell. This is getting ready to be some bullshit," Tess said in an annoyed voice.

"No, it's getting ready to be some truth-telling," Bernadette responded in an even tone.

"You asked for it," Arizona threw in.

Bernadette gave Tess a serious look. "What prompted you to finally open up and tell Maceo that you might not be able to have children?"

Tess took a deep breath to calm herself and told Bernadette and Arizona about the nearly hour-long argument between her and Maceo that had started the night after they had returned home from Arizona's and Chris's wedding. She told them that Maceo accused her of being a drama queen and always wanting to be the center of attention. She watched carefully as Bernadette and Arizona nodded their heads, as if they were in agreement. She knew deep down that a small part of what Maceo had said about her being a drama queen could possibly be true, but she also felt as though he had been unsympathetic following her painful revelation. She felt that if anyone had created the drama it had been him.

From Tess's perspective, she was simply unlucky when it came to crazy situations happening around her. She didn't know why she routinely found herself involved in sticky situations, but what she did know was that whenever she found herself in peril, she wasn't one to lay down to a challenge. So yes, that could possibly make her a drama queen. But she reasoned that she was a drama queen born of circumstance rather than nature.

"Okay, I get that you poured your heart out to him," Bernadette said, "and I'm glad that you finally told him what you should have had a conversation about several months ago. But that still doesn't answer my question, Tess. What made you finally tell him?"

Tess shrugged her shoulders. "I decided it was the right time."

"Are you sure it wasn't because he called you out about not setting a wedding date?"

Tess's eyes grew large with surprise as she stared at Bernadette. "How did you know?"

Arizona pursed her lips and tilted her head. "Tess, if you didn't have that big rock on your finger, no one would have a clue that you're engaged. Most women start planning their wedding before they even get a ring, or at least start tellin' folks. But you haven't mentioned a date or even posted it to your Instagram, Twitter, or Facebook, accounts 'cause I've checked, and beyond telling me over the phone the day after Maceo proposed, you haven't mentioned it again. And hey, with my situation being what it was, I wasn't gonna ask you about it. But I have to admit I've been curious."

Tess nodded. "You're right. I haven't been acting like someone who recently got engaged because I couldn't set a wedding date before telling Mace that I might not be able to have children. I was hoping it wouldn't come to that, especially if Dr. Vu gives me good news this week."

Bernadette stopped eating and furrowed her brow. "You're going to see Dr. Vu?"

Tess nodded. "Yes, I have an appointment with him, Monday morning."

"You'll love him, won't she, Bernadette?" Arizona chimed in. "I've been going to Dr. Vu for years. He delivered Solomon, and half of my friends' kids, and the fact that he specializes in infertility issues is a plus for you."

"I hope so," Tess responded. "After you recommended him to Bernadette, and then she gave him a glowing review after she saw him, I figured I should make an appointment."

"I'm gonna say a prayer that he can give you some good news," Arizona said.

Tess could see that Bernadette looked concerned. "Cuz, what's wrong."

"Oh, nothing," Bernadette answered, seeming preoccupied.

Tess studied Bernadette's face and she could clearly see that her cousin had something on her mind. Then it came to her in a flash. She realized that Bernadette was most likely feeling the effects of menopause, which would account for her ferocious appetite and surprising weight gain. "Oh, I know exactly what's going on with you," Tess said with a knowing look. She reached out and placed her hand on top of Bernadette's. "You might need to make another appointment with Dr. Vu, and quick."

Bernadette nervously folded her napkin and set it on the table beside her plate. "Um, I'm not sure if I'm following you."

"You're at that age," Tess said in a consoling voice. "Bernadette, you're going through the change of life."

Arizona shook her head. "That sounds like somethin' my mama and my aunties would say. Stop being so dramatic and just say menopause."

Tess rolled her eyes. "The change . . . menopause . . . it's all the same," she said, looking to Bernadette. "Even though it's a natural thing, you need to watch it. A huge burger, fries, and mac and cheese. That's a disaster just waiting to happen." Tess bit off a small piece of toasted bread as she looked at Bernadette's plate. "And like I said a few weeks ago, you're putting on weight. You better make your appointment quick."

Bernadette gave Tess an annoyed frown. "We haven't seen each other for two weeks, and in the midst of me trying to help you with your never-ending problems that you bring upon yourself, the first thing out of your mouth to me, about my life, is criticism and sarcasm."

"You don't have to get so damn huffy and defensive," Tess responded. "I was just making an observation, which by the way, is for your health and well-being."

Arizona jumped in. "Tess, cool it. Let Bernadette eat what she wants, and so what if she's gettin' as big as a house. She's earned the right to do whatever she wants at her age."

Bernadette shook her head. "I know that Tess doesn't have much couth, but Arizona, I thought you had gotten a little better when it comes to thinking before you say things that can hurt a person's feelings. But I guess negativity breeds negativity," she said, glancing at Tess.

"Bernadette, you know that Arizona and I aren't trying to hurt your feelings," Tess said.

"I'm sorry, Bernadette," Arizona said. "You look good no matter what size you are, and I know that Coop feels the same way, so as long as y'all are happy, that's all that matters."

Tess nodded and put her head in her hand. "Bernadette, instead of me worrying about your weight gain and eating habits, which can easily be corrected, I need to worry about the fact that Mace is going to break up with me."

Arizona smirked. "You know good and doggone well that Maceo's not gonna break up with you."

"No, I don't know that," Tess responded. "He's really hurt that I didn't mention my infertility issues before he proposed. He thinks that I should have told him when we first started dating. But it's such a personal, sensitive thing. It's hard to tell a man who wants children that you might not be able to have any."

Arizona put her elbow on the table and leaned forward as she spoke. "I can relate to Maceo on that one. I love good sex, and it was one of the things that I told Chris when we decided to practice abstinence right after we had started dating. I wish he'd told me about his issues from the jump. But he didn't. He dated me for over two years and managed to get me to fall in love with him, knowing full well that he couldn't please me in bed. But because I loved him, I went ahead and married him, and now I think I made one of the biggest mistakes of my life."

Tess and Bernadette were rendered silent by Arizona's honest admission. Tess knew that she had issues in her relationship with Maceo, but as she would soon discover, their challenges were miniscule compared to the avalanche of problems that had cropped up in Arizona's life since she and Chris had returned home from their disastrous honeymoon last week.

Chapter 6

ARIZONA

"I should've listened to my head, and not my heart," Arizona said with frustration as she poured her heart out to Bernadette and Tess.

What was supposed to have been a fun and relaxing girlfriends' get-together at the Magnolia Room had turned into an intense, armchair therapy session back at Bernadette's house. Arizona had been looking forward to today all week because she had known it would be an opportunity for her to let loose with her two best girlfriends, but what she hadn't anticipated was that letting loose would bring on a firestorm of emotions. At one point, Arizona became so frustrated that her rising voice had drawn the stares of several dinner patrons who had begun filling up the tables around them. When Tess told one woman to mind her own damn business, Bernadette signaled to their server that they were ready for their check. After that, Arizona and Tess had followed Bernadette on the five-minute drive to her house.

Arizona hadn't realized how stressed and angry she had become until she had started talking about how her brand-new marriage had taken a nosedive in the days since she and Chris had returned from their honeymoon a week ago.

"Tell us what's going on," Bernadette asked with concern.

"And don't spare any details," Tess threw in.

Arizona nodded. "All right, but I'm gonna warn y'all, you're gonna need wine and maybe even hard liquor if you listen to what's been goin' on with me."

"Oh, my," Bernadette responded.

Tess walked over to Bernadette's bar cart and picked up a bottle. "I'm already ahead of you."

Arizona began by telling her friends that from the moment that she and Chris returned home from their honeymoon, they'd been doing something that neither of them had ever practiced in their relationship—engaging in the art of pretending.

After getting into a short but heated argument as their plane had landed, Arizona and Chris had driven from the airport to Arizona's parents' house in complete silence. They had planned to pick up Solomon, go home, and unpack their week's worth of clothes as they decompressed from their blowout. And after spending a little time with Solomon, Arizona had made up her mind that she was going to need some alone time in a separate bedroom from Chris so she could sort out her feelings.

But when they had driven up to her parents' front yard and had seen that her family had planned a welcome back party for them, Arizona and Chris decided that they didn't need to let anyone see them at odds, especially not on the heels of their honeymoon. So they plastered fake smiles on their faces, playing the role of happy newlyweds. They had laughed and talked as though they'd enjoyed a wonderful honeymoon filled with heated passion and sweet romance. When one of Arizona's cousins had teased that the two probably had not seen much of California's wine country during their trip because they'd probably been holed up in their room, both Arizona and Chris had simply tossed out an uncomfortable smile and sipped their drinks, rather than respond.

Once they had arrived at their house, Arizona had done exactly what she had initially planned to do. She had unpacked her suitcases, talked with Solomon for a couple hours, showing him honeymoon pictures as she scrolled through her phone, and then once he was sound asleep, she had asked Chris to sleep in the guest bedroom for the night. "I need time to clear my head," she had told him. She had been both surprised and relieved when he'd offered no resistance.

"I understand," Chris had said. "It might be best for us to take a night to cool down."

Arizona had been glad that while they had been away on their honeymoon, a few family members and friends had moved most of her and Solomon's clothes, as well as a few small pieces of furniture, from her house into Chris's. They had even hung her clothes in the large walk-in closet where Chris had cleared out a substantial amount of space to accommodate her things. But after she finished her shower and settled into the empty king-size bed that she and Chris were supposed to be sharing, Arizona knew that there was no getting around the fact that everything about their first night home as a married couple was very, very wrong.

Even though Arizona had known she was idealistic, at best, when it came to the nitty gritty of her relationship with Chris, she wasn't completely oblivious. On their first night home, she had known that she and Chris should have made love and then snuggled in each other's arms until they drifted off to sleep, and even if their first night hadn't been filled with satisfying lovemaking, they should have at least been sleeping in the same bed. But instead, they had started off their marriage with her sleeping on one side of the house, and Chris sleeping on the other.

That night had set the stage for how they had slept ever since their return from their sexless honeymoon. Each day they would awake, Arizona would cook breakfast, get Solomon ready for school, pack his and Chris's lunches, kiss Chris goodbye before he headed off to work, and then she would drop Solomon off at summer camp. Each evening, Arizona, Chris, and Solomon ate dinner as a family, watched a movie together, and once Solomon was fast asleep, Arizona would retreat to the master bedroom while Chris scurried off to the guest room.

But last night, Arizona had had enough of their dysfunctional routine. After she had completed her last client consultation for the day, she called Chris on her way home and told him that they needed to talk.

"Baby, this is a busy time for me," Chris had told her.

"But it's the end of the day."

"Yes, it is, but the hotel is at full capacity, and after being gone all last week, a few things have fallen through the cracks that I need to address."

"Does that mean you'll be working late again?"

"Unfortunately, yes."

"How late?"

"I don't know, maybe around six or seven."

Chris had been coming home later and later each night, and now Arizona was beginning to lose patience. She wanted to be understanding because she knew what it was like to have to play catch up with work. As it stood, she was swamped as well.

Between scheduling new clients, purchasing equipment to film makeup tutorials for her new YouTube channel, and making adjustments to her ever-changing business plan—not to mention daily cooking and housework—Arizona felt overwhelmed. But no matter how busy she was, she knew that she needed to make time for her marriage, which she knew was hemorrhaging. She needed to find a way to stop the bleeding before their relationship ended up in critical condition, barely clinging to life. "Okay, fine," she had said, "stay at work as long as you need to so you can get caught up. But after Solomon goes to bed tonight you and I need to have a serious talk about what's going on in our marriage."

"I agree," Chris immediately said in an understanding voice. "I've been wanting to talk with you, too, but with all the stress at work along with the fact that I know you're unhappy, I thought I'd just wait until you were ready to sit down and discuss things."

Instead of feeling relieved, Arizona felt annoyed. From the moment she and Chris had started having problems several months ago, she'd been the one who initiated the hard conversations that they needed to have. Now, she wanted him to step up to take the lead on working to resolve their issues, especially because she felt that he was the one causing their problems. But instead of showing her frustration, Arizona nodded in agreement and told him that she looked forward to their conversation.

Later that night after Solomon was fast asleep, the result of an active day at summer camp, Arizona asked Chris to join her in their bedroom. She'd prepared a platter of cheese and grapes, along with a glass of wine for her and Hennessey for him, hoping to soften the mood for the frank discussion she planned to have.

"I want to start by saying, I love you, Arizona," Chris said. "I know that you're disappointed in me, just like you were a few months ago when we first made love."

Arizona took a sip of wine and cleared her throat. "I'm not disappointed in you."

"You're not?"

"No, I'm pissed and frustrated, and my next step is going to be anger if we don't resolve some things. It makes no sense that we've been married for almost two weeks and we haven't made love one single time. That's not right."

"I know, and I'm sorry."

"Don't be sorry," Arizona said with a heavy sigh, "be proactive. Be assertive. Be present and talk to me."

Chris took a sip of his drink and nodded. "Arizona, do you love me?"

"What kind of question is that? I married you, didn't I?"

"Yes, but plenty of people get married who don't love each other."

"True, but you know me. I don't do anything that I don't want to do. But I'm not gonna lie, it was touch and go up until a few days before the wedding, because I was afraid that what we're going through right now would happen. I prayed on it and I said to myself, 'Arizona, Chris is a good man, he loves you and Solomon, and we love him right back, so what is there to think about? Marry him and become his wife.'"

Chris turned his drink up to his lips and gulped down the remaining liquor in his glass. "You just turned me on," he said as his eyes roamed over Arizona's body. He set his empty glass on the bedside table to his right and then reached for her.

Arizona didn't think what she had just said was anything more than common sense, but she was glad that her simple words had moved Chris into action, and that it had turned him on. She eagerly melted into his arms, ready to make love. She was under no illusion that it would be mind-blowing sex, but she did hope that it would at least be tolerable, and that Chris would put effort into pleasing her that could serve as hope for better days to come. She smiled seductively. "I've been waiting for you to say that."

"Good," he said with a seductive wink. "Now let me show you."

He clasped the spaghetti strap of Arizona's brightly colored, geometric print sundress between his large fingers, and slid it off her shoulder, while at the same time she reached for his t-shirt, eased it up his finely chiseled six pack, and ran her hand over his stomach. One of the things that had initially attracted Arizona to Chris was his extraordinary physique. Chris was what her southern aunties called "built." He was a six-foot, four-inch Adonis who looked as though he had jumped off the pages of a men's fitness magazine.

Arizona's eyes took in all of his milk-chocolate perfection, and her desire was now at a level that made her hunger for a night filled with pleasure. She said a quick, silent prayer that their lovemaking would be measurably better than in the past.

Arizona enjoyed the feel of Chris's strong hands against her baby soft skin, which was a good sign because the last time they had attempted to make love, his touch had felt rough, like sandpaper nudging against her flesh. When his lips made contact with hers, they felt soft, and full, making her heart race with anticipation. But as he continued, both the speed and force of his kisses jumped from zero to one hundred in the blink of an eye, and before Arizona knew it,

Chris's lips torpedoed her entire face. She felt as though he was literally pecking her, like a chicken, and her mind was drawn back to how he'd kissed her months ago.

"Please," Arizona whispered in the gentlest voice that she could muster. "Let me guide you." She knew she needed to slow him down, otherwise their lovemaking session had the potential to end before it got started.

Slowly, Arizona kissed the top of Chris's mouth and then pressed her full lips against his. She briefly opened her eyes to look at him and she saw that his were shut tight. His lids were creased with intense concentration and it made her nervous because she had seen that same look when he had underperformed in the past. She didn't know if he was trying too hard or if he just didn't know what he was doing, but it began to irritate her. Arizona didn't want to become even more frustrated, or worse, get upset, so she decided to move on from kissing to touching. She reached for Chris's right hand and placed in on her left hip.

"Baby, you're so sexy. I love you, Arizona," Chris said as he caressed her through the delicate cotton fabric of her sundress.

Arizona was glad that for once, his touch actually felt sensual. This gave her hope and she encouraged him by telling him that she loved the way he was caressing her. She knew that Chris was responding positively to her coaching because with gentle precision, he lifted her sundress as she wiggled out of it. Within a matter of seconds he had unhooked her bra, and then slid her panties down her long, thick legs. Chris took a moment to study Arizona's body, and it made her smile.

There had been a time not too long ago when Arizona would have been too self-conscious to have her nude body on full display without the protection of a sheet to cover the bulges and extra weight that she had acquired, especially after giving birth to Solomon five years ago. But today was a different story. Five months ago when Chris had seen her naked for the first time, she had been a size 20. But the sundress that he had just tossed to the floor was a size 12, and she had plenty of room in it to spare. Arizona was glad that even though she had dropped several dress sizes, she hadn't lost her curvy hips and sensuous thighs that served to accentuate her small waist even more, giving her a true hourglass figure.

"Wow, baby," Chris said with a wide smile. "Your body's always been sexy to me, but seeing you now, I know without a doubt that I have the most beautiful wife on the planet."

Arizona blushed. "Thank you, baby."

"I knew you'd lost a lot of weight, but until seeing you like this, I didn't realize how much. You look damn good," Chris said, as if he was seeing her for the first time in years.

If we'd been making love like normal newlyweds you would've known, Arizona thought but didn't say. She knew that she needed to switch gears before she became frustrated all over again.

"I love you, Arizona," Chris said. He quickly removed his shirt and shorts, and then pulled Arizona close to him as they lay on top of their bed.

"Oh, Chris," Arizona cooed. "This is what I've been wanting and needing."

They lay in bed holding each other close, despite the sweat beading up on their skin. Arizona was grateful for the ceiling fan above that served to cool their heated bodies. Even though the central air conditioner kept the temperature cool throughout the house, they needed extra reinforcement to fight the steamy, Bourbon heat that engulfed every molecule of air.

Arizona felt happy. She was finally in her husband's arms, about to make love, and for the first time since their disappointing honeymoon night, she felt as if she and Chris might have a fighting chance at resurrecting their love life. She looked into his eyes. "This will be our first time making love as husband and wife. I've been looking forward to this moment."

Chris kissed her forehead and nodded in agreement. "Then I better bring it."

Arizona wanted to tell him, *You sure better!* but she remained silent instead because she didn't want to say or do anything that might jinx the moment. She placed Chris's hand back on the lower part of her hip so she could feel his touch against her skin. But right away, Arizona noticed that things felt decidedly different. When he had caressed her while she'd been wearing her sundress, his touch had aroused her and had made her desire grow. But now he had gone back to the stiff, wax on, wax off, *Karate Kid* style movements that she remembered from when they'd had something that vaguely resembled sex, months ago.

Arizona tried to guide Chris's hands in a direction that would give her pleasure, but it was nearly impossible because not only was the motion he used disruptive; he had a heavy-handed approach that felt as though he was trying to rub a pet, instead of caressing her delicate skin.

Once again, Arizona didn't want to get upset or frustrated because she knew if she did, things would go from bad to worse in a hurry, and it would leave her nowhere. So she took a deep breath to calm her nerves. But from out of nowhere, Arizona's fears sprang to life when Chris started grinding against her thigh as if he were a wild animal who was out of control. His rough movements caused friction that irritated her skin like a rug burn.

"Ouch!" Arizona said in discomfort. "Chris, slow down."

"Baby . . . you feel so good!" he panted, still grinding against her at jackhammer speed.

Arizona was aghast when she saw sweat covering Chris's entire face, as though someone had thrown a pitcher of water over his head. She sucked in a deep breath of dread because she knew what was literally coming next. Chris's breathing became heavy and labored, his eyes clinched like two balled up fists, and his grip on Arizona's body was akin to a suffocating bear hug. *Lord, please don't let what I think is about to happen, actually happen*, she said repeatedly, over and over inside her head.

But before Arizona had a chance to pull away in her hopes to prolong the inevitable, Chris let out a loud, *"Uggghhhh,"* sound, signaling his release. His grinding slowed to a snail's crawl and his body's full weight collapsed on top of Arizona.

Damnit! Arizona shouted to herself. She felt so defeated that she couldn't move, and Chris must have been following her lead because he didn't move either. They lay still, taking shallow breaths in the dark for what seemed like hours, but was only a few minutes. Finally, Arizona shifted her body so that Chris was forced to do the same. She pulled the sheet over her naked curves and laid there in complete silence.

"I'm sorry baby," Chris said slowly. "It's been so long, and you felt so good."

Arizona felt as if she were experiencing deja vu because those were the same words that Chris had said months ago when he'd done the exact same thing. She was pissed that not only did he have an orgasm without even entering her, he was still wearing his boxer briefs, which were now damp against her skin from his secretion. The thought of it all made Arizona want to scream.

"Baby, did you hear me? Chris asked in a weary voice. "I didn't mean to come so fast, but I couldn't help it. You're incredible."

Arizona couldn't bring herself to respond because she knew that whatever she said would obliterate Chris's already fragile ego, ripping what was left into shreds. So, she lay there, as still as a statue, not saying a word. She watched the blades on the ceiling fan spin round and round. She wanted to shout, but she couldn't. She wanted to run out of the room, but she was too numb to move. Arizona's emotions were jumbled and her mind began to race with thoughts of what to do next.

"I'll try harder next time," Chris said in a sheepish voice. He planted a wet kiss on her cheek and within a few minutes he was fast asleep.

Now, back in the present, as Arizona sat in Bernadette's living room looking at the stunned expressions on both of her friends' faces, she could see that Bernadette and Tess felt sorry for her, almost as much as she felt sorry for herself.

"Oh, Arizona," Bernadette said with concern. "I was praying that things had gone well on your honeymoon and that you and Chris were settling into a happy newlywed phase. That's why I waited to reach out to you after you got back in town last Sunday."

Tess shook her head. "This sounds like the same shit he pulled before you two got married."

Arizona nodded. "It's exactly the same, and the bad part about this whole situation is that I should've known better."

Arizona looked at Tess, who was reclined on Bernadette's chaise, directly across from her. She knew from the expression on her friend's face that she was thinking, *"Arizona, how dumb can you be?"* Then she turned her eyes to Bernadette, who was sitting at arm's distance from her on the large leather sectional sofa, and she could see that Bernadette's facial expression was more sympathetic. Arizona braced herself for a sarcastic, "I told you so," from Tess, and a motherly lecture on decision making from Bernadette.

"So he came in a matter of seconds?" Tess asked after she took a sip of wine from her glass.

"Yes," Arizona answered in exasperation. "And it happened so quick, I didn't see it coming."

"Pun intended!" Tess said with a burst of laughter.

Arizona looked puzzled. "Huh?"

"Lord have mercy," Bernadette said with a muffled laugh and a shake of her head.

"Arizona, that's truly fucked up," Tess said as she regained her composure. "I'm not going to sugarcoat things . . . I really feel sorry for you because I don't think your situation is going to change."

"But it's got to," Arizona said with desperation, "'cause if it doesn't, I won't be able to stay in this marriage. It's only been two weeks and I already know that I can't put up with this long term." Arizona looked down at her hands and mumbled, "I thought things would change once we said our I Do's."

Bernadette raised her brow and asked, "What made you think that?"

"Okay, let me rephrase it," Arizona responded. "I had hoped that things would change. I prayed on it, and I thought I had made the right decision, but now I'm not so sure."

Bernadette nodded. "The change that you want will only happen if both of you are willing to work at improving your relationship," she said as she rubbed the lower part of her back and relaxed her shoulders against the sofa cushion. "It sounds to me like Chris's problems are just as much emotional and mental as they are physical."

"Yep!" Tess interjected. "I've been thinking that something was wrong with him from the jump."

Bernadette nodded and continued. "I'm glad that you pray, because that will definitely help. But you're also going to need couples counseling because I think Chris's problems run deeper than you know."

"What do you mean?" Arizona asked in a worried voice. "Do you think he's suffering from some kind of deep-rooted trauma?"

Tess took a sip of the wine she'd poured before she chimed in again. "Didn't you say that he transferred colleges during undergrad because some girl on campus told everybody about his little dick?"

Bernadette shook her head. "You're an author, Tess. Surely you can put words together better than that."

Tess shrugged her shoulders, ignored Bernadette, and turned her attention back to Arizona. "But that happened, right?"

"Yes," Arizona answered. "And Chris told me that he felt humiliated after the incident."

"I'm sure he did," Tess said. "And if that didn't traumatize him, I don't know what would. Plus, just think about it, he barely has a penis. That alone has got to be a source of constant anxiety for any man. Chris's problems run deep, and like Bernadette said, you two are going to have to seek couples counseling, plus he's going to need individual therapy."

"I had thought about that while we were on our honeymoon, but chances are slim that Chris will agree to go."

Bernadette spoke up. "Agree? Arizona, unfortunately, you don't have the luxury of asking him because your marriage is already on life support. You need to tell Chris that you two are going to have to get some professional help. The way he rushes through sex and doesn't seem to even put forth any effort to control himself or please you, signals that he has some latent control issues."

Arizona thought about what Bernadette had just said, and it was something her friend had brought up a few months ago. Arizona knew that Chris's actions in the bedroom were selfish, but she also knew that he was thoughtful, giving, and full of compassion for others—things that selfish people were not capable of. It was as if he was two different people, which worried Arizona. "I know both of you are right," she said, "and I appreciate your honest opinions and advice, 'cause I'm at my wits end, and I'm so frustrated over this that I feel sick. I can't eat and I can't sleep."

Tess sat up in her seat. "I can tell that you're not eating because you look like you've lost even more weight since the wedding."

"I have," Arizona acknowledged. "I haven't been this size since junior high school, and even back then I was heavier than I am now. I've been wanting to slim down for years, but this definitely isn't the way I'd wanted to do it."

"It may not be, but you still look good," Tess said. She glanced at Bernadette, and Arizona could tell that Tess wanted to say something yet again about her cousin's weight, but something made her stop. Arizona was glad that Tess had exercised control and had held back from saying something that could have turned into a fourth of July explosion.

Arizona had noticed right before the wedding, and especially today, that Bernadette looked as though she had picked up a few extra pounds. She also noticed that Bernadette's always smooth skin looked even more subtle than usual. She didn't know if Bernadette had been using a new facial serum, or if she had recently gotten a treatment at the upscale spa that she frequented, either way, she was glowing.

As Arizona studied her friend from head to toe, she noticed that

Bernadette's ankles were swollen, and that she kept rubbing her back, as if she were in discomfort. Until now, she hadn't realized that the symptoms of menopause were similar to pregnancy. She remembered that when she was pregnant with Solomon, she had eaten everything in sight, was constantly tired, and her feet and ankles were always swollen. Her hair had grown lush and full, and her skin had glowed, like Bernadette's was now.

Arizona thought they had escaped a blow up about Bernadette's weight, but Tess couldn't control herself. She opened her mouth and Arizona knew that things were going to get ugly, quick.

"Now that we're on the subject of weight," Tess said as she turned her attention to Bernadette. "The same way I've been honest with Arizona, I have to be honest with you."

"No, you don't," Arizona spoke up.

"Honest with me about what?" Bernadette asked.

Tess cleared her throat. "You've always worked out and been healthy, I'll give you that. So I don't know whether it's menopause or all that fried chicken and ribs you're probably eating at Sue's and Southern Comfort, but you're picking up a lot of weight and I don't want you to keep going until you're out of control."

Listening to Tess, Arizona realized how offensive and hurtful it was to tell someone exactly what was on your mind without filtering it through a combination of kindness and common sense. Arizona knew she was guilty of doing what Tess had just done, many times, but over the last few months she had been working on how to bridle her tongue, and she knew that her situation with Chris was a prime example of how far she had come. But hearing the way Tess had just spoken to Bernadette made Arizona cringe. And as someone who until recently had always carried extra weight, she took offense to Tess's insensitive words.

"What's wrong with you?" Arizona said, looking into Tess's eyes. "What you just said was way, way outta bounds and just plain uncalled for."

Tess set her empty wine glass down and raised her brow. "Arizona, you've got to be kidding me. You're the last person to be correcting anyone about what they say."

Bernadette jumped in. "Tess, I'm not sure what's going on with you, but you need to get yourself together. If you're angry about your relationship problems, don't take it out on me by criticizing my weight." Bernadette sat upright and spread out the fabric on her dress. "And so what, if I've put on a few pounds. I'm healthy and I'm happy. Why can't you comment on that instead of looking for something negative to say."

Arizona looked back and forth between the two cousins and didn't know what to say next. She usually tried to stay out of the middle of Bernadette's and Tess's relationship, because she knew that many times when the two went back and forth, it was more of a cousin/sibling type of egging than outright arguing, but today, she sensed something different. Tess's words seemed to carry the hurt and sting of a person who was lashing out.

"Your anger, rudeness, and self-absorption is going to cause you to lose more than a fiancé," Bernadette continued. "I love you, Tess, but I refuse to put up with your one-sided, mean-spirited, ego-driven ways."

The room fell silent. Arizona had known from the moment they had been seated in the Magnolia Room a few hours ago, that it would only be a matter of time before either she, or Bernadette, told Tess off, because she had been snippy from the jump. Arizona had thought she would be the one to do the honors because Bernadette was much too diplomatic to go off on anyone. But she also knew that you could only push a person so far before they began to push back.

Tess took a deep breath and nodded her head. "I'm sorry, Bernadette, and I apologize to you, too, Arizona. I'm in a really horrible mood and I shouldn't be taking it out on the only two women who are patient enough to put up with my shit."

"I'm gonna forgive you because that's the first smart thing that you've said all evening," Arizona said with a laugh to lighten the mood.

Tess put her head in her hands. "My period just started this morning," she confessed, "and I was hoping that it wouldn't because that would've meant that I was pregnant. Every month that it comes I want to cry because not only does it dash my hopes of having a baby, I end up with terrible cramps, heavy bleeding, and pain like you wouldn't believe. But I would suffer through all of it a thousand times if it meant that I could have a baby. I think about all the women out there who don't even try to get pregnant or want kids at all, and voila, they end up with a baby. But here I am, desperately wanting children and unable to have them."

Arizona could hear the longing and pain in Tess's voice and her heart went out to her friend because she knew that she had once been one of those women that Tess was talking about. Solomon had been born of irresponsibility and bad decisions, but he'd ended up being the best blessing that had ever happened to her, and she couldn't for one second imagine life without her sweet little boy in it. She considered motherhood to be her greatest accomplishment to date.

Arizona was expecting Bernadette to say something comforting that would lift Tess's spirits, but she remained silent. She could see that Bernadette was in deep concentration about something, which would account for the fact that she hadn't opened her mouth or accepted Tess's apology.

"Cousin," Tess said. "If a heathen like Arizona can accept my apology, surely you can."

"You can't do right to save your life," Arizona said with a shake of her head.

"Of course I accept your apology," Bernadette responded. "But Tess, you really need to watch how you talk to people. Just because you're upset or things don't go the way you want them to, it doesn't give you the right to make everyone else around you miserable."

"You're right, and again, I'm sorry."

Arizona was glad that the uncomfortable tension that had engulfed the room had left just as quickly as it had come. Over the next two hours the women laughed, consoled, and leaned on each other, which was mostly Arizona and Tess receiving sage advice and guidance from Bernadette. Arizona was happy for Bernadette, and she decided to use her friend's life as inspiration for her own because if at the seasoned age of fifty years old, Bernadette could turn her love life from lackluster to fabulous, Arizona knew she stood a chance at happiness as well.

Chapter 7

BERNADETTE

Bernadette's mind was flooded with a mixture of thoughts and up and down emotions as she stood in her massive doorway and waved goodbye to Arizona and Tess.

"What am I going to do?" Bernadette whispered to herself as she walked to her kitchen. She opened the freezer of her Sub Zero and removed the half-eaten carton of rocky road ice cream that she and Coop had shared yesterday afternoon once they had returned from her first prenatal visit with Dr. Vu. They had sat at her large, marbled top kitchen island and eaten half the carton—with Bernadette doing most of the eating—as they had discussed the fact that they were going to have twins.

"God sure does have a sense of humor," Bernadette had said. "I've been petrified at the thought of having one child, so I guess He said, 'Here you go, now try juggling two.'"

Coop burst into laughter.

"You think this is funny?" Bernadette asked.

Coop swallowed a spoonful of rocky road and gave Bernadette a wink. "We've gotta find humor where we can."

"I guess you're right, but I'm too frazzled to find anything funny about the fact that two middle age people who don't have a clue about raising kids are going to be first-time parents to twins!"

Coop stopped laughing and thought about what Bernadette had said. "I know that our lives are about to change, and I'd be lyin' through my teeth if I said that I haven't had a couple 'what the hell' moments. But this is the hand that we've been dealt, and I like our odds."

Bernadette nodded. "It still feels like a crazy dream, and when Dr. Vu told us that we're having twins, I literally thought he was joking. But when I saw that he had the same look on his face that he did when he first told me that I was pregnant, I knew he was serious, and this was real."

"I sure wasn't expecting him to tell us that we're havin' twins," Coop said. "I was bracing myself for all the information that I thought he was gonna give us about high-risk pregnancies, and all the do's and don'ts, but twins . . . that blew my mind."

"I wonder if we're going to have girls, boys, or one of each. I can't wait to find out."

"I hope one of each, that way we can get two for one."

Now it was Bernadette's turn to laugh. "You make it sound like we're getting a deal on the price of eggs."

Coop reached out and put his hand on Bernadette's stomach. "Just think, right now you have two little raspberries inside you," he said, referring to the comparison that Dr. Vu had given them to illustrate the current size of the embryos, "and by late January, maybe even on your birthday, we'll have two little human beings that we made."

"It's amazing. I already feel like I'm eating for a family of five," Bernadette said as she scraped the bottom of her bowl, filling her spoon with the last bit of ice cream. "Lord knows how big I'll be once the babies are born."

Coop smiled and slid her his half-eaten bowl. "We gettin' ready to make a family," he said in his deep, rich voice.

"As terrified as I am, I'm also excited. I mean, I always wanted to have two kids, a husband, and a dog."

"I'm with you on everything except the dog . . . but if you twist my arm . . ."

"We'll travel that road when we get to it."

Now, as Bernadette reached inside her upper cabinet for a bowl and then her lower cabinet for a spoon, a myriad of thoughts raced through her mind. "I really don't need this ice cream, but I sure do want it."

Ten minutes later, Bernadette licked the last remnants of rocky road from her spoon, and felt sad, not because she had just polished off the remainder of the delicious treat, but because she didn't have another carton on standby. "I need to go to Harris Teeter before it gets too late," she said as she put her bowl and spoon inside her stainless-steel dishwasher. She walked back to her bedroom to get her handbag and keys when she heard the garage door open. She had not been expecting Coop to come back to her house until the wee hours of the morning because other than Saturday night, Friday was Southern Comfort's busiest time.

Bernadette admired the fact that Coop was such a dedicated businessman. He had opened Southern Comfort nearly ten years ago, and in that time, the establishment had gained a reputation as the premier jazz club throughout North Carolina. Every weekend the club was packed with regulars who lived in Bourbon and the surrounding towns, as well as visitors who hailed from other parts of the Tarheel state. Unlike most night clubs in the area where people went to strictly dance, party, and get their drink on, Southern Comfort catered to an audience that wanted an experience. Not only did the club specialize in live performances and a mixture of classic and modern jazz, it served amazing food, top shelf cocktails, and a sophisticatedly good time. Southern Comfort kept Coop busy, in addition to his rental properties, laundromats, and car wash locations. And even though he worked tirelessly, he always found time for Bernadette, and that made her feel loved.

"I wonder why he's back here so early?" Bernadette said to herself as she clutched her handbag. "I hope nothing's wrong at the club."

Bernadette walked to the kitchen and saw Coop smiling as he entered through the mudroom.

"Hey Baby," Coop said as he greeted Bernadette. He looked down at her handbag and keys. "You goin' somewhere?"

"Yes, I was on my way to Harris Teeter," Bernadette answered as she placed her handbag on the counter, "but now I'm not sure. Is everything all right at the club?"

"Everything's fine."

"Whew, I'm glad . . . but if everything is fine at the club, why're you home? It's only ten o'clock, and things are just starting to get busy down there."

Coop leaned forward and gave Bernadette a kiss on her forehead and then took a seat at the kitchen island. "I wanted to come home to check on you. Your cousin called me."

"Tess called you?"

"Yep. She told me that she said some things to you that she shouldn't have, and that even though you seemed okay when she and Arizona left this evening, she could tell that you weren't your normal self."

Bernadette pulled out a barstool beside Coop and sat down. "If she was so concerned about me, why didn't she call and check on me herself instead of calling and interrupting you while you're trying to run your business."

"She said that she called you, but you didn't pick up, so she left a voice message."

Bernadette looked inside her handbag, retrieved her phone, and sure enough she had a missed call and a new message from Tess.

"She must've called while I was in here because I didn't hear my phone ring," Bernadette said. "Did she tell you exactly what she said to me?"

"No, she didn't go into detail, but I know Tess, and her mouth can be pretty rough. I figured you would tell me once I got here."

"She basically told me that I need to stop eating because I'm getting fat." Bernadette thought about the fact that she had been on her way to the grocery store to get more ice cream before Coop had come home, and it gave Tess's words more sting.

Coop rubbed his clean-shaven chin and nodded his head. "In a few months she'll understand why." He looked at Bernadette's bare engagement ring finger. "I hope you start tellin' folks that we're gettin' married before then."

"I wanted to talk it over with you to see when you think we should announce it, now that I have a beautiful ring," she said as she thought about her engagement ring that she had tucked away in her nightstand drawer. "I was thinking we can start calling our family and friends tomorrow."

"Sounds good to me."

"I'll call my mom first, then I'll let Tess and Arizona know."

"They'll all be excited and happy for us," Coop said with reassurance.

"My mom will be skeptical, so get prepared for it. Arizona will be overjoyed. And as for Tess," Bernadette said with a sigh, "I honestly don't know whether she'll be happy or mad."

"I know Tess is raw, and she can be a certain kinda way, but she loves you, Bernie, and I believe she's gonna be happy for us."

"I'm not so sure about that."

"Why not?"

"Have you talked with Maceo?" Bernadette asked. She watched as Coop's expression changed, and she immediately knew that he was aware of the fact that Tess and Maceo were having problems.

"Yeah, I talked with him," Coop answered.

"What did he tell you?"

"He said that Tess told him that she can't have kids, and that she's known for a long time, but she purposely kept it from him." Coop bent forward, placed his elbows on the island, and let out a deep breath. "Bernie, you know I try to stay outta folks business, 'cause I damn sure don't want 'em in mine. But your cousin was wrong for that. She knew from the beginning that Maceo wants kids, and she knew what his ex-wife did to him. But she still didn't level with the man. That's why he feels hurt, and right now, he's angry."

Bernadette nodded. "She wanted to tell him, but she didn't know how."

"You just open your mouth and say it."

"True, but in Tess's defense, she didn't tell him that she *can't* have children. She said it's a strong possibility that she *might not* be able to conceive."

"Whether she can or can't, if she knew that she had any kind of issues, she should've told Maceo. And she damn sure shouldn't have accepted his proposal knowing that."

"I can relate to how Tess felt because I didn't know how to tell you I was pregnant." Bernadette thought about the fact that for six weeks she had kept her pregnancy a secret from Coop, not to mention the fact that she had not breathed a word about her discovery that directly linked him to an unsolved murder case thirty-five years ago. "People withhold information for all kinds of reasons."

Coop's eyes softened. "Baby, our situation is completely different from Maceo's and Tess's. For one thing, I think you were in shock, and still are, about being pregnant. And before you accepted my proposal, you told me the truth. Tess has been walkin' around wearing the ring that Maceo gave her, and she hasn't even announced it to anybody besides you and Arizona. How do you think that made Maceo feel?"

"I imagine not too good."

"That's an understatement. And he told me that every time he tried to talk to her about settin' a date, she would change the subject.

That kind of behavior is intentional, and it's wrong. If he'd gone about things the way she has, she would be mad as hell."

Bernadette knew that Coop was right, and she couldn't defend Tess's actions. But she still hoped that her cousin could salvage her relationship. "She thinks that Maceo is going to break up with her," Bernadette said to Coop, more as a question than a statement.

"It's lookin' that way," Coop said. He rose from his barstool and walked over to the freezer. "Listen, instead of talkin' about Maceo and Tess and their problems, let's talk about me and you over a bowl of ice cream."

Bernadette gave him a sheepish grin. "Um, we don't have any more ice cream."

"You and your girls ate the rest?"

"No, it's more like, I ate the rest."

Coop walked over to Bernadette, took her by her hand, and helped her off the barstool. "Then we need to make a late-night ice cream run."

Later that night after finishing their ice cream, Coop and Bernadette lay in bed watching their favorite movie, *The Godfather*. It was a hot summer night, but with Bernadette's thermostat set to sixty degrees, they felt cool and refreshed.

"Coop," Bernadette said. "I love the fact that you're concerned about me and that you want to make sure that I'm okay, but I don't want you dropping things that you need to do just to come check on me like you did tonight. As the months go on, there will be times when things will happen, and I want you to know that I'm going to be all right."

"Woman, you sound crazy," Coop said. He turned on his side to face Bernadette and reached for her hand. "That club, or nothing else is more important than you, period. I don't want to hear you say anything like that again, and I want you to promise me that from this moment forward, if you need anything, and I mean anything, you'll call me no matter where I am or what time it is. Okay?"

Bernadette nodded. "Okay."

"Good." Coop looked down at Bernadette's hand and secured it inside his own. "I know we're gonna start tellin' people that we're engaged tomorrow, but have you thought about a date that you want to tie the knot?"

Bernadette smiled. "I'd love to do it as soon as possible. I was even thinking about eloping."

"Really?"

"Yes, but if I did, my mother would never forgive me."

Bernadette knew that, as it stood, her mother would have extreme skepticism about her getting married in the first place, and she would be incredulous at the thought of Bernadette eloping, which she saw as a glorified shotgun wedding. Bernadette also knew deep down that one of the main reasons why she wanted to elope was because she didn't want to run the risk of her mother coming to any kind of ceremony or celebration and ruining it with her negative energy.

When Bernadette had booked her mother a first class, roundtrip airline ticket to Bourbon a few months ago, she had been extremely nervous because she knew that Rosa Francine Gibson was a true piece of work. But she had wanted her mother to finally see where she now lived, and more important, she had wanted Rosa to meet Coop. But almost immediately, Bernadette had known that her mother's visit was going to be a nerve splitting disaster.

Rosa had complained from the moment that Bernadette and Coop had picked her up from the Raleigh Durham International Airport, right up until they had dropped her off at the departures skycap stand two days later, cutting her originally planned week-long visit short by five days. Bernadette had been embarrassed when on the two-hour drive back to Bourbon, Rosa had said, "So, Coop, do you have a criminal record?"

From asking Coop to stop multiple times so she could take bathroom breaks, to complaining about how bad the pollen was in the south each time she got out of and back into Coop's SUV, to asking him to change from the satellite jazz station that they had been listening to, in favor of an oldies station that in her words played, "regular music," Rosa had made Bernadette begin to regret inviting her for a visit.

When they had turned onto the street where Bernadette lived, and then finally reached her beautiful home, Rosa had been impressed and had beamed with pride that her daughter had risen from the hard scrabble neighborhood where they had once lived many years ago, in southeast DC, to the exclusive enclave where she resided today. Bernadette had been glad that her mother seemed to be pleased, and she had thought that things were beginning to look up.

That evening, Coop and Bernadette took Rosa to dine at Sue's Brown Bag, and Tess had joined them. Rosa had been happy to see her niece, and had been even more thrilled when Tess told her that she was going to send Rosa an advance copy of her next book once they were ready. The three had devoured plates of delicious food and all had been going well until Maceo had come out from the kitchen to meet Rosa, bringing a slice of his famous brown butter pound cake for her to try. When Tess introduced him as her boyfriend, Rosa looked as if she had just been told that she'd been eating dog food all night. She shook her head and said, "I can't believe that my daughter's dating an ex-con, and my niece is shacked up with a short order cook. What's this world coming to?"

Tess had been outraged and embarrassed, Coop had sat in silence, and Maceo had been so taken aback that he had quietly retreated back to the kitchen without saying a word. But Bernadette had experienced the worst feeling of all. She had felt regret for having invited her mother for a visit in the first place. Rather than cause a scene in the restaurant, Bernadette waited until Coop had dropped them off back home to tell her mother exactly what she thought about her behavior.

"I've always known that you're bitter," Bernadette said to her mother, "but I didn't realize that you're also cruel and cold-hearted."

Rosa raised her perfectly arched brow. "Have you forgotten who you're talking to?" she asked Bernadette as she gave her daughter an incredulous stare.

"No, I haven't, and that's the only reason why I haven't cursed you out, because if you were anyone other than my mother, I would've done it."

"Hmph, I just call it like I see it. I'm looking out for you and Tess. Y'all got so much education, but you're dumb in life. I just want better for you than . . . never mind."

Bernadette shook her head. "Do you know how you even sound right now?"

"Like a woman who has seen things and knows which way is up."

"No, Mom. You sound like an unhappy old woman who can't see past the mistakes that you've made in your own life. You're so blinded by your negativity that you can't see that I'm the happiest I've ever been, and so is Tess."

"Oh, so now y'all are happy because you think you're in love. Just wait till Snoop and Julio . . ."

"Their names are Coop and Maceo," Bernadette shot back.

"You know who I'm talking about," Rosa said, not missing a beat. "Just wait till those two show you and Tess their real colors and end up breaking your hearts. You won't be thinking I'm a bitter old woman then."

Bernadette let a long moment of silence hang in the air as she and her mother stared at each other without blinking. "Not every man is like my father was," Bernadette said.

Rosa looked as though she had been mortally wounded. She tucked a stray strand of her long, silver hair behind her ear, and continued to stare Bernadette in the eye as she spoke. "Every time I think about all the men who have gotten over on you ever since you were old enough to date, I beat myself up for not teaching you how to stand up for yourself. And then, after Walter nearly destroyed your life, I vowed that as long as I lived, I would never stand by and let you make the same mistake twice. I'm telling you right now, Bernadette, that nightclub hoodlum is no good. He's gonna end up back in the slammer where he belongs, and he's gonna break your heart just like all the rest."

The only reason why Rosa was not on a plane back to DC the next morning was because all the flights had been full. But the following day, Bernadette had risen at the crack of dawn in order to drive her mother to the airport so she could catch the first thing smoking out of dodge. It had taken Bernadette a solid month before she could bring herself to have a decent conversation with her mother, and it had only been a few weeks ago that they had finally gotten back on good speaking terms. She had never told Coop about her mother's incendiary comments later that night, which had hurt Bernadette and had caused her to have a setback with her self-esteem.

Back in the present, Bernadette thought about her pending nuptials and how Rosa might react. "Honestly," she said to Coop with a heavy sigh, "when it comes to my mother, it wouldn't matter whether we elope, go to the Justice of the Peace, or get married in a grand cathedral with all the bells and whistles, she's going to find fault and she's going to do or say something that will ruin everything."

Coop nodded. "Yeah, from what I've seen she probably will. But the bottom line is that she's your mama, and just like Tess, she's got a mouth on her, but she loves you. You're her only child and she just wants you to be happy."

"But Coop, she's so bitter that she can't see that for the first time in my life, I'm blissfully happy. I don't want her negative vibe around me. I've come too far to backtrack, and trust me, if my mother comes anywhere near me anytime soon, I think I might have a breakdown."

Coop looked at Bernadette with concern. "I'm not lettin' anything jeopardize your health and well bein', not even your mama. I'll let you call all the shots about how, when, and where we get married."

Bernadette was glad that Coop was so understanding. That night, after Coop had fallen asleep, Bernadette laid in bed watching TV, unable to get her mother's words out of her mind. Rosa had said that Coop was going to end up back in prison, and that he was going to break her heart in the process. All Bernadette could think about was the murder from thirty-five years ago that she was almost sure that Coop had committed. The cold case hit closer to home than Bernadette wanted to acknowledge, because the man who had been shot in cold blood was Morris Fleming, Maceo's biological father.

"I better get some sleep," Bernadette said with a yawn. She flipped the channel to the local station so it would be cued up for the morning news when she awoke in a few hours. She was about to press the off button when she saw Morris Fleming's face appear on the screen. Bernadette looked over at Coop, who was lightly snoring, and turned the volume down low. She eased out of bed and stood in front of the sixty-inch screen so she could hear what the newscaster was saying.

Not since last summer, shortly after she had moved to Bourbon, had she seen any news reports about the Morris Fleming cold case. But now, the newscaster had just said that because of new and credible evidence that had recently been uncovered, the Bourbon Police were once again reopening the case.

Bernadette felt as though she was walking in slow motion as she entered her large corner office. She closed the door behind her, sat down on the upholstered love seat near the large window, and watched the rain fall in a heavy downpour as she tried to figure out what her next move should be. "I wish I had never discovered that hidden compartment in Coop's office," she whispered aloud.

Bernadette thought back to the day, a little over a month ago, when she had discovered evidence that linked Coop to Morris Fleming's murder. She had been cleaning and purging papers in Coop's home office when she'd stumbled upon a hidden compartment in a makeshift space at the base of one of his file cabinets. Curiosity had driven her to investigate, and when she did, she found an old, rusted metal box. Her gut had told her that whatever was inside would not be good, so rather than open it and find trouble that she'd not been looking for, she decided to place it on top of Coop's desk and let him deal with it. But when she had picked it up, the box's tiny lock swung open, and its damaging contents spilled to the floor.

Bernadette's heart raced when she saw a gun wrapped inside a dusty, gray colored cloth along with newspaper clippings and a police report detailing Morris Fleming's murder. But what had made her heart go from racing at record speed to a near standstill was a note in Coop's handwriting that included Maceo's name, date of birth, and a short message underneath that read, "I can't bring him back, but I can raise his son." When Bernadette had looked at the photo of Morris Fleming, it had been like looking at a picture of Maceo, and at that moment, everything began to make sense.

Bernadette had remembered that Tess had told her that Maceo never knew his father, and for good reason. His mother had told him that his father had been a successful sales executive who lived up north and traveled to southern towns as part of his business territory. Sue had met him on one of his trips when he'd passed through Bourbon, and they began a secret affair. Eventually, Sue became pregnant, but her lover had been married with children at the time, and he didn't want to risk losing his already established family. In a fit of rage, he had beaten Sue badly, hoping she would miscarry, but she and her baby survived, and she never heard from him again. She had even told Maceo that years later, when she had tried to reach out to him so that Maceo could meet him, she'd learned that the name he had given her, as well as the company that he said he'd worked for, were both fake.

After Bernadette's discovery in Coop's office, she had pieced together the puzzle of the tale that Sue and Coop had come up with to explain the identity of Maceo's father. Bernadette had learned through Google searches that Morris had been from Washington, DC, and he had just completed his residency at Johns Hopkins at the time of his murder. He had no doubt met Sue during a business trip, as her and Coop's long-standing story had suggested, but that was where reality ended. It hadn't been hard to cover up the truth back in those days, because Coop's reputation for ruthless danger, and the fact that he had dirty cops on his payroll, had led people and the authorities to mind their own business and not ask any questions.

But times had changed, and now Morris's family were demanding long overdue answers that would give them closure about what had happened to their loved one.

Bernadette's legs felt wobbly under the weight of her worries, but they managed to carry her back to her bed where Coop was sound asleep without a care in the world. Bernadette turned off the TV, and said a silent prayer that her mother's words would not come to pass.

Chapter 8

TESS

Tess had been a bundle of tightly woven nerves when she walked through the door an hour ago after returning from her girl's night out with Bernadette and Arizona. She had needed to decompress and sort through her feelings, so she lit the lavender and chamomile scented candle that Maceo had given her as a gift, and then sat in silence, taking in the soft glow and healing scent. Before moving in with Maceo a few months ago, Tess had briefly stayed with Bernadette, and thanks to her cousin, who kept a fragrant candle in every room of her house, Tess had become hooked and now kept one in every room as well.

Usually, after practicing her healing ritual, Tess felt uplifted with a clear train of thought, but not tonight. Her cramps were steadily getting worse and her anguish over her relationships, all around, had her feeling melancholy. "I need some medicine for these damn cramps, and a hot shower to ease my body and relieve my stress," Tess said aloud.

She swallowed two pain pills to keep her cramps at bay, and then walked to the bathroom to take a long, hot shower. She stood directly under the rainfall style showerhead and allowed the hot water to caress her body and relax her sore muscles. And instead of rushing to wash her hair as she normally did, she took her time working the shampoo through her thick curls as she gave herself a therapeutic head massage. But after fifteen minutes of pampering, Tess only felt slightly better, which again, was unusual because a hot shower normally did the trick.

"I've got to get my groove back," Tess mumbled to herself. "And I've got to find a way to shake off this shitty mood I'm in." She flipped on the Bose sound system that Maceo had installed throughout the house and scrolled through several playlists until she found what she was looking for. "This is more like it," she said as she hummed along to the soulful rhythm of the sounds flooding the room. She rubbed her Philosykos-scented Diptyque lotion on her freshly shaven legs. But by the time she had finished moisturizing her skin, her funky mood had returned. "I can't seem to shake this horrible feeling I have," Tess said with frustration.

Ever since she'd opened her eyes this morning and looked at the empty space beside her in the bed she shared with Maceo, Tess had felt a heavy weight of sadness. And what had made her feel even worse was when she had put her feet on the floor and stood up, she'd realized that she had just started her period. It had been yet another blow to her already fragile state of mind. She had been a few days late, which rarely happened, and she had hoped that by some miracle she was pregnant. She had even purchased a pregnancy test last night, just to increase the chance that her positive thinking had willed her desires into existence. She had fully intended to take the test first thing this morning, but after her unfortunate discovery there had been no need.

Now, after a disappointing start to her morning and a contentious end to her evening, Tess wanted and needed relief. She slathered a handful of leave-in conditioner onto her thick curls and used her Denman brush to form a messy ponytail high on her head. "It ain't pretty but it'll have to do."

Tess wished that Maceo was home with her because even when

she was in her most depressed moods, he always made her feel better. She walked to the bedroom and searched through her dresser drawer trying to decide what to wear to bed. She didn't want to run the risk of ruining one of her silk negligees because of her period, so she slipped her oversized Winston-Salem State University nightshirt over her head. "I guess it doesn't matter how I look in the company of one."

Tess rubbed her aching stomach as she thought about her visit with Bernadette and Arizona. Even though their dinner plans had not been the rousing good time that she had hoped it would be, she was grateful that she'd been able to get out of the house and spend time with them. But she felt bad when she thought about the fact that they had to cut their get together short and leave the Magnolia Room early because she had raised her voice and cursed at a fellow patron.

Tess shook her head as she thought about how inappropriate and potentially dangerous it had been to yell at a perfect stranger inside a restaurant, regardless of the establishment's exclusivity and sophisticated clientele. She would not have dared attempted that kind of outburst if she'd still been living in Chicago. For one, she was well-known and recognized throughout the city as Chi-town's number one, bestselling author, and she would have found herself trending on social media with the hashtag, #tesssinclairgoesoff, before she could blink her eyes. She also knew that had she pulled the same stunt in the Windy City she would have surely received the same cursing that she had dished out, and she would have likely been on the receiving end of a few blows to top it off. Thinking about the trouble that she had narrowly escaped at dinner made Tess glad that she was in small-town Bourbon, where Southern hospitality was extended even to foul mouthed city slickers like her.

"I've got to do better," Tess said to herself as she thought about the crass things that she had said to Arizona about her dysfunctional sex life with Chris, and the hurtful words she had said to Bernadette about aging and gaining weight. She had been stressed, depressed, and frustrated about her deteriorating relationship with Maceo, and she had selfishly taken her bad mood out on the only two women whom she knew had her back in times of trouble, and in particular, her cousin, Bernadette.

Tess walked from the bedroom back into the bathroom, and reached for her skin serum on her side of the long, quartz countertop. She looked into the mirror as she smoothed the creamy white liquid onto her skin, lightly massaging it over her forehead, cheeks, and chin. She wasn't vain, but she also had no problem owning the fact that she was a strikingly beautiful, forty-year-old woman who did not look a day over thirty. She was blessed with her father's height, her mother's svelte, shapely figure, and both her parents' natural good looks. Her thick, curly dark brown hair perfectly framed her slim face, and her taunt, wrinkle-free, honey colored skin glowed as if she had been born that way.

As Tess peered closer at the image in front of her, she was suddenly struck with a startling realization. She walked out of the bathroom and into the large, walk-in closet where she examined herself in the full-length mirror from head to toe.

"I'm beautiful, I'm smart, I'm successful, and I have close to eight figures sitting in my bank account," she said out loud to absolutely no one. "So why am I alone on a Friday night, standing in the middle of a closet, talking to my damn self?"

Tess walked back to the bedroom, sat on Maceo's side of the queen size bed they shared, and snatched her phone from the nightstand. It was close to eleven o'clock, and she knew that Maceo was just beginning to close the restaurant for the night, so she dialed his number, hoping he would answer her call. "C'mon, Mace, pick up," she said after the fourth ring. When she heard his voicemail come on she hung up rather than leave a pleading message for him to come home. Up until their big fight, Maceo had gladly handed over the duty of closing the restaurant each night to his senior employees, which allowed him to come home early so that he could spend time with Tess. But for the last two weeks he'd been going into Sue's early each morning and he stayed later and later every night. His behavior and attitude toward her made Tess uneasy.

She had wanted to call Bernadette again, but she had offended her cousin so badly that, much like Maceo had just done, Bernadette had refused to pick up the phone when she had called a few hours ago. Tess knew that her cousin must have still been mad because even if Bernadette had been unable to answer her phone, she would have definitely called back by now.

As Tess mulled over the insensitive and outright rude comments that she had blurted out tonight, and thought about how she had hurt Bernadette's feelings, another startling realization came to her, and if she hadn't been sitting down, her discovery would have knocked her off her feet. "Oh no! I'm just like Aunt Rosa!" Tess nearly screamed with a gasp.

Tess thought back to a few months ago when Bernadette's mother had come to town for a visit. Tess had been excited to see her Aunt Rosa, because beyond quick phone calls for holidays and birthdays, and brief visits when she happened to be back in DC to spend time with her parents, Tess had not been around her aunt for any significant length of time since she had been in high school. She knew that Bernadette had routinely complained about how negative, caustic, and downright rude her mother could be, but Tess had never given it much thought because her Aunt Rosa had always been pleasant when she had spoken with her.

Little did Tess know that she would get a front row seat to witness her Aunt Rosa's antics, up close and personal, when Bernadette and Coop had invited her to join them for dinner to celebrate Rosa's first night in town. The evening had started off well, and Tess had felt a sense of pride when she saw that her aunt was highly impressed with the décor in Sue's Brown Bag, as well as the quality of the delicious food that had been served. So when Maceo had come out from the kitchen wearing his apron and carrying a plate of his ever-so-popular and oh-so-delicious, made from scratch, brown butter pound cake, as a special welcome for Rosa, Tess was eager to let her Aunt know that she was dating the man behind the wonderful food. But Tess never got the chance to say that not only did Maceo prepare the food that she had raved about, but he owned the restaurant as well. To Tess's astonishment, Rosa insulted Maceo with demeaning words, and then managed to spew an underhanded putdown in Coop's direction.

"Damn," Tess hissed as she felt a stab of pain in the lower part of her stomach. Her stress level was through the roof, which made her cramps kick in until she was nearly doubled over in pain. Just then she heard the door unlock and the clanking sound of Maceo's keys as he tossed them into the small dish sitting on the console table in the entryway. He usually called out her name to let her know that he was home, but lately he'd simply entered without a word. Even though he was apparently still pissed with her, Tess was glad that he had come home earlier than he had been doing over the last two weeks, and it gave her hope that he would be in the mood to talk so they could get their relationship back on track.

"Hey Mace," Tess said in a low voice as Maceo walked into the bedroom.

"Hi." Was his one-word response.

It was clear to her that he had no intention of engaging her. Up to this point, Tess had not put forth much of an effort to engage him either, because she had hoped that Maceo would come around on his own. But after some hard, self-evaluation, Tess knew that if she wanted to continue her relationship with Maceo, she had to step up and fix the mess that she had created. *Here I go . . .* "How was work?" she asked in an eager voice.

"It was okay."

"Was the restaurant crowded tonight?"

"Yes."

"That's great. I'm sure everyone loved the new menus."

"Uh huh."

Tess watched as Maceo removed his clothes while giving short answers without looking in her direction. She knew this was a bad sign. "Mace, we need to talk, and I mean really, really talk."

"It's been a long day, and I need to take a shower."

"Damnit, Mace, it's bad enough that you've been avoiding me and acting like I don't exist, but now that we're in the same room you can at least acknowledge me by looking in my direction when you speak."

Maceo turned and gave Tess an icy stare. "Like I said, I need to take a shower." And with that, he walked into the bathroom and shut the door behind him.

Tess sat on the bed unable to move after the shocking way that Maceo had just spoken to her. It was as if someone had turned off a switch inside him, and had abducted the man who had stolen her heart. The Maceo whom she knew was the calmest, most tender and gentle person who she had ever known. He was thoughtful, kind, and compassionate to a fault, and he always thought of her needs, as well as the need of others, above his own. But the man who had brushed her off a few minutes ago was cold and unfeeling, and it made her more afraid than ever because it brought to memory something that her ex, Antwan, had once told her.

After one of her and Antwan's knock-down drag-out arguments, Antwan had told her that despite the harsh words he had said to her, he still loved her.

"I know I still love you because of the argument we just had," he'd told Tess.

"That sounds absolutely asinine." Tess had balked.

Antwan shook his head. "No, it's not. When you're able to get a rise out of someone, like you just did with me, it means that person still cares. But if they can take whatever you dish out to them without blinking an eye, and then walk away from you, it means that the person, especially if we're talking about a man, has checked out and it's over."

Tess knew that what Antwan had said was true because when she had discovered that he had cheated on her for the umpteenth time, and in retaliation she had broken into his house, ransacked the place, destroyed his property, and then stolen his alcohol, he had never said another word to her. He didn't press charges as she had thought he would, nor did he beg her forgiveness. He'd gone silent because it was over. He had checked out. And now, as Tess thought about the way Maceo had just acted, her heart sank, and she burst into violent tears.

Tess's head was buried against Maceo's pillow when she felt his hand on her shoulder. He sat down on the bed beside her and held her in his arms.

"Baby, please don't cry," Maceo said, lowering his smooth, deep voice to a whisper.

"I'm so sorry, Mace," Tess managed to say through body jerking sobs. She continued to cry as Maceo rubbed her back and placed her head on his bare shoulder. "I don't want to lose you," she continued. "I love you and I'll do anything that you want me to. I want to make things right between us. Just please, don't check out on me."

Maceo rocked Tess back and forth in his arms until her tears soaked his skin and she stopped crying. He placed his finger under her eyes and wiped away the last of her tears. "I'm sorry, too, Tess. I didn't mean to make you cry."

Tess raised her head from Maceo's shoulder and looked into his eyes. The man she had fallen in love with was back, and he was looking at her with compassion and care. "I thought I'd lost you. I thought you were going to break up with me and call off our engagement."

"I've been in my feelings, but I still love you, Tess."

"You do?"

"Of course I do. Why would you even question that?"

Tess sniffled. "Because of the way you've been acting toward me. Someone once told me that when you're able to walk away from someone, with no emotion, that it's over because that person has checked out. You've been treating me like I'm invisible ever since our fight, so I thought . . ."

"That I was through with us?" Maceo said, completing Tess's sentence.

"Yes." She nodded and then wiped her nose on the back of her hand.

"Hold on, I'll get you some tissue."

Tess watched Maceo's naked body as he rose from the bed and walked into the bathroom. She thought about the fact that he'd heard her sobs and had immediately come to her side to make sure she was okay. His words told her that he still loved her, but it was his actions that let her know that what he had said was true. And when he walked back into the room wearing a towel gathered at his waist, as he carried tissues and a bottle of water that he'd gotten from the kitchen, she knew that it was further proof.

"Here, you go," Maceo said in a gentle voice as he handed Tess several tissues.

Tess blew her nose and wiped her remaining tears. "Thanks Mace."

"You're welcome."

"I'm so sorry about everything that's happened. I know I was wrong, and I was selfish. I kept my fertility issues from you because I thought you would break up with me if you knew there was a possibility that I can't have children."

"You could've just told me, like you're doing now."

"I know, but somehow I couldn't bring myself to do it. It never felt like it was a good time to deliver bad news." Tess cast her eyes on Maceo's as she continued to speak. "It's also another reason why I've been hesitant about setting a wedding date or announcing that we're engaged."

Maceo shook his head. "All this time I thought it was because you had doubts about marrying me. I remember what your Aunt said about you dating a cook, and I thought, man, maybe there was a little truth to what she'd said."

Tess raised her brow. "Are you serious? You know I'm not like that. Why didn't you say something to me."

"I did. Many times. Why do you think I kept asking you over and over if you were sure about us?"

"I just thought you wanted to hear me say yes, and that I love you." Now that Tess thought about what Maceo had just said, it explained why he'd acted as though he had needed reassurance about their relationship. It also made her realize that he had done the very thing that she had done. He'd kept her in the dark. "Mace, you know that you're wrong for that, right?"

Maceo nodded. "I didn't realize it until now, but yes, I was wrong. I should've explained why I asked if you were sure." Maceo let out a deep breath. "I want children, but I also want you."

"I promise that from here on out I'll be completely honest and straight up with you."

Maceo smiled. "I'm glad to hear that. We need to keep the lines of communication open, Tess, no matter how difficult a situation may seem. I'm going to hold you accountable to that, and I want you to do the same with me."

"It's a deal, and in the spirit of transparency, would you like to go with me this Monday when I have my appointment with Dr. Vu? He's Bernadette's OBGYN, and he also specializes in infertility issues and high-risk pregnancies. From what I've heard about him, he's a great doctor."

Maceo nodded. "Sure. It'll help me understand what's going on with you, and what some of our options are." He leaned in and kissed her slowly.

Tess felt as though she was floating on a cloud until a sharp pain nearly took her breath away. The medicine that she had taken shortly after she'd come home had only given her a temporary illusion of relief. She winced and gritted her teeth from the sharp stabs in her stomach.

"Are you okay?" Maceo asked.

"Cramps," was all Tess could say. She had to take a moment to gather herself before she spoke again. "I suffer like this every month, and when it's bad, like it is now, I do my best to just bear it without letting you know. But now that I'm being all see-through . . ." She had tried to make a joke about their newfound relationship with transparency, but her pain stopped her.

Maceo handed Tess the bottle of water that he'd set on the nightstand. "Here, drink this."

Tess drank small sips, grateful that Maceo was there to help her. But she could feel another round of pain coming on the heels of what had just taken her breath away. She knew from experience that what was about to come was going to be even worse than what she had just endured, and although Maceo had said he wanted them to be open about everything, she wasn't quite ready for him to see her in such bad condition. "Why don't you go and take that shower that I interrupted with all my crying." She gave Maceo a half smile and muffled her pain.

An hour later, Tess felt much better thanks to the heating pad across her stomach. She and Maceo had fully made up, and now they lay in bed eating popcorn from the same bowl as they discussed wedding dates. Tess told him that she would like to get married during the Christmas holiday season, which she thought was the perfect way to celebrate love, and because it was already June, they would have to start planning soon because December would be there before they knew it.

As Tess drifted off to sleep, she was thankful that she and Maceo were back on track. She knew that she had almost blown a good thing, and she made up her mind that she wasn't going to let that happen again.

"Hello," Tess said in a groggy, half-asleep, half-awake voice. She wasn't sure what time it was, but she knew it was much earlier than she normally rose to start her day. She was a night owl who was notorious for keeping late hours, especially if she was working on a new manuscript. So morning phone calls that greeted the sun were not her cup of tea. She knew there was only two people who were bold enough to call her at such a hellishly early hour—her mother and Bernadette.

"Good morning sleepy head. Rise and shine," Bernadette's perky voice practically sang through the other end of the phone.

Ever since Bernadette had started dating Coop, she had transformed from a glass-is-half-empty type of person into a champagne-flute-is-overflowing type of optimist. The sudden change had taken Tess some time to get used to, but now she was beginning to come around, and after last night's realization that her own negative thinking and bad behavior were eerily similar to her Aunt Rosa's, Tess knew that she needed to adjust her outlook on life as well.

"Good morning, Bernadette," Tess said, trying to sound more awake as she rubbed her puffy eyes. "I'm trying to rise, but I don't think I'll start shining for a few hours." She smelled a delicious aroma coming from the kitchen and she thanked the Lord above that she and Maceo were back on track.

"Were you up late, writing into the wee hours of this morning?" Bernadette asked.

"No, I wasn't writing, but I did stay up pretty late talking with Maceo about a date for our wedding."

"Oh, wow! You two made up?" Bernadette asked with excitement.

Tess's smile beamed through the phone. "Yes, we did, and I'm so happy. But I'll fill you in on all the details later because before I say another word, I want to apologize again for the way I behaved yesterday."

"You already apologized, so you don't have to do it again."

"Oh yes, I do. Bernadette, I thought about all the terrible things that I said to you, and the pissy attitude I had yesterday. I took out my frustrations about my own unhappiness on you, as well as Arizona. Neither of you deserved that."

"I accept your apology again. Sometimes circumstances can get the better of the best of us, and that's what happened to you. I'm just happy that you and Maceo have made up, and that you're talking about setting a date."

"I still can't believe that I'm actually going to get married. And now that Mace and I are back on track, I'm going to announce it and post a picture on social media."

"That's great, but get ready for a barrage of messages because regardless of how you try to deny being a celebrity, you're well known, and people are going to be curious."

Tess thought about what Bernadette had just said, and she knew there was some truth to it. A part of her wanted to keep her private life hidden from the bloggers, readers, and entertainment magazines that would be writing stories and speculating about her relationship with Maceo. But she also wanted to celebrate her happiness and stand as an example of the fact that love can come along when you least expect it. It was something she had written about in her novels, and now it was happening to her. "You're right," Tess replied. "But I think it's time that I stepped into happiness instead of always wading in the shallow pool of despair."

Bernadette chuckled. "It's times like this that I know you're a writer."

"Damn straight."

"By the way, did you and Maceo set an actual date?"

"No, not yet. But we agreed that it's going to be during the holidays."

"That's a beautiful time of year," Bernadette said as she perked up even more.

"Yes, it is. I love it because everything will already be so festive and it's a great time to get people together for a wedding."

"And, speaking of weddings," Bernadette said, and then paused. "Coop proposed."

Tess sat straight up in bed. "What?!!" she screamed. "Girl, why the hell didn't you tell me that when I first answered the phone."

Maceo came rushing into the bedroom. "Baby, are you all right?" he asked with worry.

"I'm fine," Tess answered. "I'm on the phone with Bernadette. Coop proposed to her!"

Maceo nodded and smiled. "Tell her I said congratulations. I better go back to the kitchen before our omelets burn." And with that he was gone.

"Mace said congrats," Tess said.

"Awww, tell my nephew that I said thanks."

"Your nephew?! . . . Oh my goodness, you're so disgustingly in love," Tess said with a playful roll of her eyes.

"I sure am."

"And that's why I'm so happy for you cuz, and I'm not at all surprised that Coop proposed. That man loves you up, down, and sideways."

"And I love him just as much."

"Can you believe that we're both engaged and crazy in love, with good men at that?"

Tess thought for a moment about the fact that just six months ago when she, Bernadette, and Arizona had all celebrated milestone birthdays on the same day, turning forty, fifty, and thirty, respectively. How very different their lives had been back then than they were today. She could honestly say that Bernadette's life, as well as her own, had drastically improved, but Arizona was still in the middle of a sticky situation.

Tess wanted to be hopeful and think positive about the fate of Arizona's marriage, but she had a sinking feeling that it was doomed. But for now, Tess refocused her thoughts on the happiness at hand.

"I know that Coop just proposed," Tess said to Bernadette, "but have you guys started talking about dates of when you'd like to have the wedding?"

"Actually, yes, and it's going to be sooner rather than later."

"How soon?"

"Like, within the next week or two."

Tess's eyes got big with surprise. "You're kidding me."

"No, I'm not. We're thinking about doing something low-key,

like going to the Justice of the Peace and then having a reception at Southern Comfort."

"Justice of the Peace! Damn cuz, it's not like you're knocked up and you have to piece together a shotgun wedding."

The line fell silent, and Tess realized that she had just made an insensitive joke that had rendered Bernadette quiet. She'd agonized over the hurtful comments that she had made yesterday, and here she was, less than twenty-four hours later doing the very same thing. But this time Tess knew that her words carried more sting because she had just made light of something as special and sacred as marriage. She knew she had to correct herself.

"Bernadette, I'm sorry about what I just said."

Bernadette spoke in a low voice. "You sound like my mom."

Tess's breathing almost stopped when she heard her cousin say those words. Just last night she had realized that her negative attitude mirrored her Aunt Rosa's, and now, Bernadette had confirmed it to be true.

"I called her right before I called you," Bernadette continued. "And I should've known she wasn't going to be encouraging, or even happy for me."

"Aunt Rosa's happy for you, she just doesn't know how to show it . . . Bernadette, I'm sorry, and I'm apologizing for both of us."

"It's okay. Listen, I've got to go," Bernadette said in a rush. "I'll give you a call sometime tomorrow."

Tess lowered her head. "Okay, and listen, don't let anything steal your joy. Not me, not your mom, not anybody."

Tess hung up the phone and felt awful. She wished she could rewind the clock and start over from yesterday. She knew that she couldn't just say she was going to do better, she had to put action behind her words and actively do it. Until that very moment, she hadn't appreciated just how remarkable Bernadette was. Tess knew her cousin was calm, diplomatic, and said all the right things, and now that she was trying to practice that same kind of discipline, she realized that it wasn't easy.

Tess was drawn from her thoughts by the buzzing sound on her phone that signaled another call was coming in. When she looked at the name on her screen she nearly dropped her phone. It was Antwan Bolling.

"What the hell?" Tess mouthed to herself as she looked at her ex's name. She did not pick up, and his call rolled into her voice mailbox. She stood and paced the room, then she listened to the message that he had left. It was only seven seconds long, and he had simply said, "Hey Tess, It's Antwan. I hope you're doing well. Give me a call so we can catch up."

"Catch up about what?" Tess whispered to herself. She didn't know why Antwan had called her after all this time, but one thing she did know was that whatever the reason, it couldn't be good.

Chapter 9

ARIZONA

Arizona squinted and placed her hand above her eyes to form a shield against the early morning sun that was just beginning to peek over the tall trees at the edge of her well-manicured front yard. "Okay Solomon, have a good time," she said to her son with a loving smile before casting a disapproving eye toward Chris. She was still upset with him from what had happened last night. She wanted to erase him from her sight, but she knew that she needed to at least say a few parting words before he left. "I'll see you when you get back tomorrow," she forced herself to deliver in a flat tone.

Arizona stood in her front door and watched as her husband and her son began to walk toward the white church van that was parked in the front of their house. Today was St. Mark AME Zion's Annual Sanctified Warriors Retreat, and both Chris and Solomon had been looking forward to the experience for the last couple months. The event was designed to bring the men in the church—both young and old—together through bonding and mentoring activities that centered around their Christian faith. Chris had been excited about spending father/son quality time with Solomon, and Solomon had been excited about the fact that the event included an overnight stay at a hotel where he could eat pizza, go bowling, and play with his friends from Sunday School.

Initially, Arizona had told Chris that while she believed the Sanctified Warriors Retreat would be a great opportunity for him and Solomon, she didn't think the timing was right because it was set to take place the week after they returned from their honeymoon, and things would be too hectic with them just settling back in. But now she was glad that Chris had insisted that he and Solomon participate, because she needed to be by herself so she could sort out her complicated mixture of emotions.

Arizona knew that Chris could tell by her distant body language and the irritated tone in her voice that she wasn't happy, not even a little bit. She had smiled at Solomon and wished him an enjoyable time, but she'd given Chris a tepid glance and basically said she would see him later. She was actually proud of herself for the fact that she'd been able to remain civil, and she was glad that Chris had not tried to pretend as though nothing was wrong when he knew that it was. Just as she had thought she had avoided making a scene, Chris turned around and walked toward her.

"Don't I get a little sugar before we leave?" Chris said playfully.

Arizona immediately knew that Chris's sudden need to be lovey-dovey was for the benefit of his fellow church brothers' curious eyes that were on him. Arizona was beginning to see that keeping up appearances was very important to Chris, and in this case, he didn't want the upstanding men of the church to think there was anything but happiness between him and his new wife. But just as Chris had known his fellow church brothers were looking, Arizona felt he should have known that his wife was not about to play along with his game as they'd done at her parents' house last week.

"Sugar?" Arizona said, then put her hand on her hip. "Do you mean you want a kiss?"

"Baby, c'mon," Chris nervously said, trying not to look over his shoulder as he continued to walk toward Arizona.

"If you come any closer, you're gonna get embarrassed," Arizona said in an "I'm not playin'!" tone. "I'm not for playin' games, Chris, so if you know what's good for you, you'll turn around and get in that van."

"Arizona!" Chris hissed in a low voice, through clinched teeth, as he continued to walk toward her. "Don't be like this."

"Take another step and I promise you, I will show the hell out right where I'm standing."

Chris stopped and froze in his tracks as if someone had flipped his off switch. Arizona could tell by the look on his face that Chris knew she was serious, so he turned around and forced a smile across his face, "Okay baby, we'll see you later."

As Arizona watched the van roll away, she thought about last night, and the growing desperation she was beginning to feel about her marriage.

She had shared her frustrations about her honeymoon and her disappointment about her and Chris's disastrous attempt at love-making with Bernadette and Tess. She knew that of all the people in her life, including her mother and lifelong girlfriends, that Bernadette and Tess would keep whatever she told them confidential, and they would give her honest, heartfelt advice that would help her make the right decisions. She knew they'd been right about the fact that she and Chris needed to seek counseling, but after the horrific act that transpired between them last night, Arizona felt that her marriage was a hopeless cause.

When Arizona had gotten home last night, she'd hoped that Chris would be asleep, especially because she knew he had an early morning and a busy day ahead of him with the Sanctified Warriors Retreat. But to her surprise, he was in their bedroom, wide awake, and he'd placed a candle on each nightstand to set a romantic mood. Soft music was streaming from the music app on his phone, and a bottle of wine was chilling in an ice bucket atop their mahogany dresser.

Arizona knew that she should've been thrilled that her husband had put thought into initiating a romantic evening, but instead of feeling excited, her first emotion was anxiety followed by apprehension. She was extremely skeptical after Chris's uninspired performance the night before, and she didn't want to engage in any physical intimacy that would once again leave her frustrated and downright angry.

"I'm glad you're home, baby," Chris had said. "I've been waiting for you to get here so we can have a good time tonight."

Arizona gave him an unenthused half smile. "I already had a good time . . . with my girlfriends."

Chris swung his legs to the side of the bed and stood. He was wearing a pair of gray colored boxer briefs, looking like he'd just stepped off the set of a photo shoot for an underwear ad. Arizona had to admit that her husband was a fine specimen of a man; tall, dark, and oh so handsome, with the type of smooth looks and sex appeal that could make a woman want to throw caution to the wind and submit to his will. Arizona remembered how everywhere they went on their honeymoon, women had done doubletakes when Chris had walked by. His chiseled, muscular body, along with his megawatt smile, made him practically irresistible. And now, looking at her husband in all his milk chocolate covered glory, a part of Arizona felt the attraction of the same magnetism that had drawn her to him when they had first met a little more than two years ago.

"I'm glad you had a good time with Bernadette and Tess," Chris said, "and now I want us to have an even better time."

He flashed Arizona a smile that made her heart beat fast, but the thrill was gone in a flash when she looked at the area that she had been trying to avoid. Her eyes zeroed in on Chris's flat groin and she let out an audible sigh.

"What's wrong?" Chris asked with concern. "Are you okay?"

No, I'm not okay, and I have no interest in having mystery sex with you, Arizona wanted to say, but decided to refrain. If her time spent with Bernadette and Tess had taught her anything, it was that she should think before she spoke. So rather than destroy Chris's feelings, Arizona contained the truthful but brutal words perched on the tip of her tongue. "I'm just a little tired," she said. "I'm going to take a shower."

"Okay, baby," Chris said. "Do you want me to join you? I can wash your back," he said with a sexy wink.

"Um, no, that's okay," she responded as she made her way to the bathroom. "I'm good. I'll be out in a minute."

Arizona made a beeline to their en suite and shut the door. She prayed that Chris wouldn't come in behind her, and she literally stopped breathing when she heard the door open and saw his head peek inside.

"I'm going to pour you a glass of wine so you can relax once you finish your shower," Chris said.

Arizona nodded and tried to act excited, but "Thanks," was all she could say.

Once Chris was gone, Arizona was able to regain her breath. She reached for the showerhead handle, turned it to hot, and then placed her shower cap on her head. "Damnit," she said under her breath as she peeled off her sundress and left it on the floor. "What am I gonna do?" she said to herself. Arizona stepped into the shower and let the warm water wash over her body, but it didn't give her any relief or relaxation because she was too nervous about what might happen next.

After nearly thirty minutes, and the longest shower she'd ever taken, Arizona emerged from the water with worry still etched on her face. She dried her body with one of the plush towels that she and Chris had received as a wedding gift, and slathered her skin with her Bath & Body Works lotion. She tied her silk robe at her waist and hoped that Chris would be asleep when she walked back into the bedroom.

"If you had been in there a minute longer I was going come in to make sure you hadn't drowned," Chris joked, wide awake in the bed.

Arizona was so disappointed that she could have screamed, but she didn't acknowledge his comment or say a word. Instead of engaging Chris, she walked to her nightstand and gulped down half the wine in her glass in just a few sips.

"Slow down, we've got all night," Chris said with a sly smile.

That's what I'm afraid of, Arizona thought to herself. She put her nearly empty glass down and walked to her dresser in search of a nightgown. She skimmed past the sexy, lacey lingerie that she'd received at her bridal shower last month. She didn't want to put on anything that would further encourage Chris, but then she thought for a moment. *Maybe I should give it a try.*

Arizona knew that if she had negative thoughts, she'd reap negative results. She loved Chris, and she wanted their marriage to work, not just for her sake, but for Solomon's as well. So she decided to change her attitude. She reached for her see-through, cream-colored, lace teddy, minus its matching thong, and willed herself to put a positive smile on her face. She dropped her robe to the floor, giving Chris a birds-eye view of her voluptuous hips, and slipped the barely there material over her head. Slowly, Arizona turned toward the bed, stood in place, and struck a sexy pose.

"Baby, you look amazing," Chris said. He rose from the bed and walked to her. He pulled her in close to his body and held her in a romantic hug.

Arizona was pleasantly surprised by how good it felt to be in Chris's arms. His sculpted body was warm and soothing, and his skin smelled of the woodsy scented shower gel that he'd used earlier that night. She wrapped her arms around his neck and shoulders and rested her head in the middle of his broad chest. When he began to hum the sultry Luther Vandross ballad serenading them in the background, Arizona allowed herself to give in to the rhythmic, soulful sound as they swayed their bodies back and forth in a slow and sultry dance. This had to be one of the most romantic feelings that Arizona had ever experienced. All the love and desire that she had felt for Chris over the last two years came rushing back to her all at once, making her throb between her legs, ready to make love to him.

"I want you," Arizona whispered into Chris's ear.

He kissed her gently on her forehead, and then softly on her full lips as his hands caressed the small of her back through the thin material of her silk negligee. He took Arizona's hand into his and slowly led her to their bed. "I want to try something new," he said in a seductive voice.

Arizona was so excited that she could hardly contain herself, and she was thankful that she had changed her attitude because she was now getting the positive results that she'd prayed for. "Okay," she whispered softly back to him. "What do you have in mind?"

"Let's both receive pleasure at once." And with that, Chris removed Arizona's teddy and gently laid her body across the bed.

Arizona was growing more excited by the minute . . . until Chris reached for the lamp on his nightstand, turned on the light, and removed his boxer briefs. Arizona had seen glimpses of her husband's thimble of a penis on the few occasions that they had made haphazard love, but she hadn't examined it thoroughly until now. Her emotions veered between shock and fascination, but mostly shock, followed by acute anxiety sprinkled with a heaping dose of *Oh heeeellllll no!*

Buried between Chris's thick, curly pubic hair and two small ball sacs of wrinkly skin was a penis so small that Arizona had to look hard to identify it. His one-and-a-half-inch penis was erect, poking out of his midsection like a small growth of flesh. Arizona remembered the photos that she'd seen when she had Googled 'micropenis' after she'd discovered that Chris had one, and she was experiencing the same cringe-worthy feeling that she had back then.

Arizona knew she should be trying to concentrate on how she was going to salvage this train wreck of a moment, but all her mind could think about was the fact that she would never be able to look at a gherkin pickle in the same way again. Just as she was trying to formulate a plan in her mind, Chris climbed on top of her and positioned his head between her legs. Arizona had to stop herself from screaming when he lowered his hairy little genitals over her face. But as much as she tried to stay silent, she let out an audible gasp when his two wrinkly ball sacs of flesh grazed her mouth.

In that moment, Arizona realized what Chris had meant when he'd said that he wanted to try something new, and that it would be something that would allow them to both receive pleasure at once. He had been referring to a sixty-nine. It was a sexual position that Arizona had performed many times in the past, and had enjoyed. But she'd experienced it with partners who were anatomically equipped. Arizona closed her eyes tight when she saw Chris's micropenis dangle like a misshapen skintag in front of her face. She didn't think things could get any worse, but what Chris did next made her know that she'd been very wrong in her assumption.

From out of nowhere, Arizona felt a cold, hard metal object being thrust inside her with a force that made her scream out in pain. She kicked her legs in a reflex motion and sent Chris's naked body tumbling off the bed and down to the floor.

"What the hell are you doing!" Arizona yelled at Chris. She looked at the footlong, nearly four-inch thick, pink-colored metal vibrator that Chris had dropped and was now lying near her feet. As she sat up to take a closer look, a fresh hot burst of pain shot through her vagina reminding her of the force that Chris had used to impale her with the sex toy. "You're fucking crazy! What the hell's wrong with you?!!" she gritted in pain as she reached for the bed sheet to cover herself.

"What's wrong with me?" Chris screamed back in bewilderment. "What's wrong with you? I was just trying to pleasure you, and . . ."

"By sticking a damn piece of metal inside me without warning? You rammed that thing inside me so hard, I feel like you did some damage." When Arizona rose from the bed she felt another sharp stab of pain. She put her hand between her legs and saw blood on her fingers. "Oh, no!"

Chris's eyes got big with horror when he saw the bright red

blood, and he realized the severity of what he had just done. "Baby, I'm so . . . I'm so sorry," he said, barely able to get out the words as he quickly rose to his feet and came toward her.

"Get away from me," Arizona hissed. She was thankful that Solomon's room was on the other side of the house, and that he was such a heavy sleeper that he could lie perfectly still through an earthquake on top of a tornado.

Slowly, Arizona inched her naked body off the bed and limped past Chris on her way to the bathroom, but she became enraged when she realized he was right on her heels. "Didn't you hear me? I said get away from me," she hissed again.

"Baby, I want to help you."

"Then do like I asked and get away from me." And with that, Arizona closed the bathroom door behind her.

But instead of doing as Arizona had repeatedly asked of him, Chris opened the door and tried to plead his case. "Arizona, please listen to me, baby. You know I would never, ever try to hurt you on purpose. I thought you'd like it."

Arizona gave Chris a death stare as she reached for her fluffy towel that was hanging on the hook near the shower. She secured it around her body and slowly walked to the linen closet and retrieved a washcloth. She limped over to the faucet in silence, completely ignoring Chris, and wet the cloth with cold water. Slowly and gently, she pressed the cool dampness against her aching flesh. She winced with pain as she tried to soothe herself, then she turned her growing anger on Chris.

"What in the hell made you think that I would like or even want that huge thing rammed inside me from out of nowhere?" Arizona said as her chest heaved up and down. "How would you like it if someone stuck a pole up your ass and expected you to take it, and like it? Huh? And when did you even get that thing?"

"I ordered it from Amazon the day after we got back home from our honeymoon."

"I can't even deal with you right now."

"Baby, please forgive me. I didn't mean to hurt you." Chris looked down at the floor as if he was embarrassed. "I know I can't give you what you want when I'm inside you, so I thought I would give you something you could feel. I wanted to please you."

"Bullshit!" Arizona spat out. "If you'd been interested in pleasing me, you would've eased into it. You stuck that thing inside me without any thought of how it might make me feel. What's wrong with you?"

"I've never used one before," Chris pleaded. "I did it like I saw the guys in the videos use it, and I thought you would like it because the women they used them on did."

Arizona bucked her eyes wide. "You thought you could please me by watching some made up craziness that you saw on a porn site? And by the way, since when did you start watching porn? Is that what you're doin' at night in the guest room? Is that why you want to stay in there now?"

"No!" Chris yelled.

"Don't you raise your voice at me," Arizona said as she pointed her finger at him.

Chris shook his head. "I only watched a few videos so I could see how it's done. I knew you were frustrated, and I wanted to please you," Chris said in a sad voice. "So that's why I thought this would be a good idea. I didn't know what else to do."

"How about talk to me, Chris . . . that's what you could've done," Arizona said as she wrung out her washcloth in the sink. "I'm not sure what's going on in your mind. You just went from avoiding intimacy, to going hog-wild like a crazed sex fiend. I'm gonna tell you right here and now, I don't get down like that and I'm not here for it. Period!"

There was a long pause of silence between them. Then finally, Chris spoke. "Are you hurt bad?"

"You mean did you hurt me bad?" Arizona corrected. "Because you did this to me."

Chris hung his head. "I know I did, and like I said, I'm sorry. But please, just answer my question, Arizona. Are you hurt bad? Do you think you need to go to the emergency room?"

"No, Chris. I don't need to go to the ER. I'll be fine once I heal. But I think you need to sleep in the guest room tonight."

Now, as Arizona sat at her breakfast table, alone, drinking a cup of dark roast coffee, she had to shake her head about the fact that Chris had the nerve to ask her for a kiss right before he and Solomon had left the house for their retreat. She hoped that in between bonding with Solomon over the next twenty-four hours, that Chris would think about what he'd done and consider going to therapy as Bernadette and Tess had suggested yesterday. If she didn't know before, she fully understood now, that Chris's problems were greater than she had realized.

Arizona was in deep thought when the sound of her phone stole her attention. She wasn't in the mood to talk to anyone, especially not this early in the morning, but when she saw that it was Bernadette she picked up. "Is everything okay?" she asked. She knew that Bernadette wasn't in the habit of calling people early in the morning or late at night, so she wondered if something was wrong.

"Yes, everything is fine," Bernadette answered. "How're you doing this morning?"

"You don't sound like everything is fine, plus it's early and you don't normally call folks, interruptin' their Saturday morning. Are you sure you're all right?"

"Yes, Arizona . . ." Bernadette paused and let out a heavy sigh. "I have some good news to share."

Arizona wrinkled her forehead in confusion. "If you're about to tell me good news, I would hate to hear what's bad."

Bernadette chuckled a bit. "Actually, it's very good news. Coop proposed to me."

Arizona set her cup down with so much force that she splashed coffee on the table. "Girl, that's not good news, that's fantastic news! I'm so happy for you!" Arizona was ecstatic for her friend, but as overjoyed as she was, she couldn't understand why Bernadette wasn't jumping for joy, and it didn't make an ounce of sense as to why Bernadette was sounding down in the dumps. "Bernadette, I can tell by the sound of your voice that something is wrong, so please tell me what's going on?"

"I'm happy about my engagement, but my mother and Tess . . . well, let's just say they both know how to rain on a parade."

"Girl, what in the world did they say?"

"Where do I begin?"

"From the beginning."

"It's a lot."

"I'm not sure what your mama could have possibly said, but as much as I love Tess, and you know I do, she has some issues, so you can't listen to half the mess that she says."

Bernadette let out another sigh of frustration. "You know what, I don't want to spoil my good news or this bright and sunny morning with negativity," Bernadette said with an injection of pep in her voice. "Girl, I'm engaged!"

"Wooohoooo!!" Arizona cheered. "I knew that it was only a matter of time before that man put a ring on it. I'm so happy for you two."

"Thanks Arizona. I can hardly believe it, and if it wasn't my actual life, I'd be skeptical that an untrusting and emotionally damaged fifty-year-old woman could leave a big city, relocate to a small town, and then find the man of her dreams. I never would've thought that a man would love me the way Coop does. Girl, I'm just thankful."

"You're surprised, but I'm not." Arizona said. "I remember when we had dinner on our birthday, and I told you that once you let go of all that negative energy and anger that you had against your crazy ex, you would free yourself and love would come. You got out of your own way, unblocked your blessings, and found love. You should write a book about it."

"Has anyone ever told you that you're wise beyond your years and that you give great advice?"

"All the time," Arizona said as they both laughed. "Have you and Coop talked about setting a date?"

"As a matter of fact, we have. We don't want a lot of fanfare, we just want to start our life together as soon as possible. We were thinking about going to the Justice of the Peace and then having a reception at Southern Comfort."

Arizona clapped her hands. "Now that's all right! I love it! If I had to do it all over again, I'd do the same thing," Arizona paused and then sighed. "Let me stop lyin'. If I had to do it all over again, I wouldn't do it at all. And after last night, Girl, I need to really pray hard on what to do next."

Bernadette's voice turned from lighthearted to concerned. "Oh no, what happened last night?"

Arizona wanted to tell Bernadette the crazy details of her traumatic encounter with Chris, but she didn't want to dampen her friend's happy news. And just as Bernadette had decided to put negative talk to the side and embrace joy, Arizona knew that she needed to follow suit.

The two friends laughed and talked a while longer before ending their call on an upbeat note. Arizona was happy for Bernadette, but she was also sad about her own situation. Just as Bernadette had said that she couldn't believe that she was happy, madly in love, and engaged to a good man, Arizona couldn't believe that she was miserable in a marriage to a man with a teeny weenie penis and a graveyard full of deeply buried emotional issues.

"I've got to regroup and refocus before I end up feeling depressed," Arizona said aloud. She rose from the kitchen table, still feeling a slight twinge of pain from last night, and walked over to the sink to wash out her coffee mug. "I definitely need to put some plans into action," she said as she headed down the hallway to her home office that also doubled as her makeup studio. She sat in her desk chair, reached for her notebook and pen, and began to develop a plan. She spent an hour on Google, researching the topic of sexual dysfunction, another hour looking up mental health providers in her area, and yet another hour educating herself about the laws surrounding annulment and divorce in the State of North Carolina.

Before Arizona knew it, it was noon, and she was hungry because she had not eaten since yesterday. "At the rate I'm going I'll be skin and bones by the end of the summer. I need to eat." She decided to do something that she rarely did, and had only done once before, on her birthday. She decided to pamper herself to an "All About Me Day." She was going to treat herself to an early dinner, followed by a trip to the movies, and then end her day with a relaxing soak in her jetted bathtub.

After Arizona was dressed, she looked at herself in the full-length mirror inside her bedroom, and she was happy with what she saw. She'd always felt confident about her looks, regardless of her expanding size over the years. She had natural curves in all the right places, and her pretty face along with her above average height, only served to enhance her physical appeal. Arizona smoothed down the sides of her shoulder length, freshly flat ironed hair, and tucked a few strands behind her ears to highlight her medium size gold hoops. She had decided on a summer casual look, and slipped on a pair of white capri pants paired with a chambray, off-the-shoulder blouse. She dabbed a bit of iridescent gloss in the middle of her pink lips to give her mouth the perfect shimmer effect, and she complemented her sultry eyes with a warm brown and soft peach eyeshadow.

Arizona decided to drive out to the Palisades section of town, where Bernadette lived. She rarely ventured to that side of town unless she was visiting her friend, but she felt that after the rough night she'd had, she deserved the royal treatment. She was thankful for the small reprieve, and with no husband to annoy her, or child who demanded her time and attention, she was free to concentrate on herself, and she planned to enjoy every minute of her All About Me time.

But just a little over an hour later, Arizona's grand plan was cut short by the staggering heat. She had decided to go shopping before eating an early dinner, which had not been a good idea. The thermometer in her SUV read ninety-nine degrees, but the sweltering humidity made it feel twenty degrees hotter and had left her exhausted.

Rather than dining at one of the ultra-formal restaurants in the area, Arizona decided to order her meal to go and take it home so she could eat and relax in peace. She had heard about a popular restaurant called Fried Green Tomatoes that was supposed to be the upscale version of Sue's Brown Bag, back on her side of town. Arizona doubted the food was better than Sue's, but she wanted to give it a try. She had perused the menu on her phone and called in her order, and now she was about to pick it up.

When Arizona walked into the chic restaurant, she was impressed by its on-trend décor. Where the Magnolia Room was a refined, old money restaurant where exclusivity was valued, Fried Green Tomatoes was its edgy and modernly hip counterpart, where chic sophistication ruled. Although each establishment differed in style and atmosphere, they both were high-end, high-dollar properties with top shelf accoutrements. Arizona strutted up to the hostess stand and was told that she could pick her order up at the bar on the other side of the room.

Arizona glided across the restaurant and was glad she had decided to call in her order and pick it up because she could see that the Saturday night dinner crowd was going to pack the place. As she walked toward the bar she made a mental note that whether she was in the down-home Bottoms or the ritzy Palisades, her curvy figure and sultry good looks were able to turn the heads of men, black and white, young and old. She was only a few feet away from the large bar when a man caught her attention at the same time that she caught his, and when their eyes met, Arizona nearly lost her balance.

At first glance, she thought she must have been mistaken, so she blinked twice to make sure that her eyes were in proper focus. *That can't be Jaquan,* she said to herself in disbelief.

Jaquan Williams had been one of Arizona's many boyfriends during her wild and crazy heyday. He was tall, dark, and handsome, and on top of his physical appeal, Jaquan had brains to match. He had been born and raised in Raleigh, the state capital, and had lived in one of the toughest public housing projects in the city. To keep him alive and out of trouble, his mother had sent him to stay with relatives in Bourbon during his junior year of high school, and that was when he and Arizona had met.

Jaquan had been considered a city boy, and all the girls at Bourbon High had flocked to him, including Arizona. Despite the fact that Jaquan had made good grades when he'd decided to show up for school, had earned a high SAT score, and been accepted into three colleges that his mother had sent applications to on his behalf, Jaquan had decided to drop out of school so he could major in dealing drugs in the streets. Over the next few years, Jaquan lived between Bourbon and Raleigh, and had established himself as a player in the drug trafficking business. After Arizona had graduated from high school, the two began a tumultuous, on again-off again relationship that had ended when Jaquan had been sentenced to fourteen years in prison on federal drug trafficking charges.

"Arizona, is that you?" Jaquan said as he walked toward Arizona.

"Jaquan?"

"Yeah, it's me."

Arizona was taken aback. She remembered how dangerously sexy Jaquan had been when he had gone away to prison, and from what she could see, his appeal had only increased over the years. The goatee that he'd once sported was now replaced by a clean-shaven face that revealed smooth, soft-to-the-touch-looking skin that had not aged. His once closely faded haircut was now a slick bald head, and his brown eyes now carried an even deeper allure than Arizona remembered. But she could also tell from the scar near the cleft in his chin that prison life had not been a walk in the park. And although he was still ruggedly handsome, as was evidenced by the swagger in his walk when he had approached her, Arizona could instantly see that

Jaquan possessed a calmer, more serious demeanor than he had in his younger days.

The two embraced, and Arizona could feel a magnetic energy between them, so she quickly let go. "Wow," she said, slightly shaken. "What're you doing here, and when did you get out the pen?"

Jaquan shook his head and chuckled. "I see you haven't changed, at least not in that respect . . . still keepin' it one hundred," he said, referring to the fact that Arizona was always one hundred percent honest in her opinions and thoughts.

"You know me." She smiled. "But seriously, when did you get out, and what're you doin' in here?"

"I've been out about two weeks now, and I just started working here last week."

Until that moment, Arizona had not realized that Jaquan's black button-down shirt and black pants was the staple uniform of the servers buzzing around the restaurant, carrying food and drinks to customers' tables. "You're a server here?"

He smiled. "Not quite. I'm washing dishes and busing tables for now. But they're going to move me up to the dining room in another week or two, then I'll be a server."

"Oh." Arizona knew this was a far cry from the Jaquan that she had known back in the day. He had driven a late model Mercedes Benz, had worn expensive clothes from designer brands, drank top shelf liquor at the best bars, and had looked forward to ordering food, not serving it. But prison—as she had witnessed from many examples—changed people in unexpected ways.

"Are you dining in?" Jaquan asked.

"Look at you, already got the server lingo down pat," she teased. "No, I'm picking up my order to take home."

"Whatever you ordered, I think you'll enjoy it. The food here is pretty good."

"As good as Sue's?"

Jaquan shook his head. "Nobody can hang with Maceo, but it's decent."

They both shared a laugh. Jaquan's was slow and easy, but Arizona's was slightly uncomfortable, which was unusual for her. As they stood in silence, Arizona could see that Jaquan was taking inventory of her looks. The last time he had seen her was nearly six years ago, right before his conviction, and she had been much heavier. That thought made Arizona realize why she had been so surprised to see him, and it wasn't because he was working at a high-end restaurant in the upscale part of town, it was because he was out of prison so early. So she posed the question that she had meant to ask when he had first walked up to her. "I thought you got fourteen years," she said. "Why're you out?"

Jaquan chuckled again. "Your subtly is amazing, Arizona." He looked around and smiled. "Do you have plans after you pick up your order?"

"Why do you ask?"

"I was just about to go on my break, so if you have time, I can answer your question and fill you in."

Arizona spent the next thirty minutes eating her southern fried chicken wrap and fried green tomatoes, which were delicious, while she talked with Jaquan. Under any other circumstances, she would not have allowed herself to be seen sitting in a parked car with a man other than her husband. But she figured that no one she knew would see her on this side of town, especially not sitting in the parking lot of Walgreens, where Jaquan had parked away from the restaurant.

During their short time together, Arizona learned that Jaquan had been released early because his lawyer had produced evidence in his favor, that had reduced his sentence to time served. While he had been in prison, Jaquan earned a GED and had obtained his Bachelor's degree in Business. He'd used his education and life experiences to start a mentoring program for younger inmates, and had also worked with the Wake County Public Schools to help educate and mentor young men of color about the perils of choosing the wrong path. Once he was released he spent one week in Raleigh, visiting with his mother, before returning to Bourbon, where he was staying with his

Uncle Clem. He knew that in order to make a fresh start he could not remain in Raleigh, where most of the crime that he'd committed had taken place. And even though he had been dealing drugs in Bourbon, its slower pace and close-knit community was what he needed.

"You've been in Bourbon for a whole week," Arizona said as she put her half-eaten wrap back inside the to-go container. "Usually word travels fast around here, but I had no idea you were back in town."

"I don't have the same type of profile that I used to." Jaquan rubbed his smooth chin and looked at Arizona with a quiet pause. "You look good, A," he said, calling her by the nickname that he had once given her. "I can tell that life's been good to you."

"Thanks," Arizona blushed. "I can't complain."

"So tell me what's been going on with you?"

Arizona knew this part was coming, and she'd already rehearsed the short version of her life that she had come up with twenty minutes ago. "I went back to school and got my Bachelor's degree in business, and six months ago I quit my job at Bourbon General to do makeup full time, which is my true passion. But my biggest accomplishment of all is Solomon, my son."

"Wow, that's great, A," Jaquan said with a smile. "So . . . how old is your son?"

"He's five."

Jaquan nodded, and Arizona could tell that the wheels in his head were already turning. She didn't want to get into logistics and possibilities, so she quickly changed the subject. "Oh, and I almost forgot, I'm married."

Jaquan raised his brow. "Whoa, what? You're married?"

Arizona nodded. "Actually I got married two weeks ago."

"Congratulations, I guess," Jaquan responded as he looked down at her bare finger. "You're not wearing any hardware."

Arizona knew that Jaquan was shocked, and so was she because she had actually forgotten to put her ring on her finger before she left the house. She'd worn her engagement ring for an entire year, and she'd worn her complete wedding set since she'd gotten married two weeks ago. But here she was, out without it today. Nervously she said, "I accidentally left it home."

"Why didn't you tell me that you were married from the jump?"

"Because I was listening to you talk about what's been going on in your life."

"No, I mean . . . when I asked you what you've been up to, you told me about being married last. You're a newlywed, and I would think that's something that you would share right away."

Arizona didn't have a good answer to give him, and she wasn't about to say what was on her mind, so she remained silent.

Jaquan turned his key in the ignition and moved the gear shift into drive. "I'm sitting in my car, in a parking lot, with a married woman. I better take you back to your car so you can go home to your husband."

They rode in silence during the short drive back to Fried Green Tomatoes. Once he parked, Jaquan finally spoke. "Listen, A . . . I mean, Arizona. I meant no disrespect and if I had known that you were married I would've never asked you to spend my break with me."

"I'm the one who needs to apologize," Arizona said. "You can probably tell that I'm having trouble in my two-week-old marriage. My husband and son are at our church's father/son retreat, and since they're gone until tomorrow I decided to treat myself to a good meal tonight and clear my head."

Jaquan nodded. "It was good seeing you again, Arizona. You take care of yourself."

There was so much more that Arizona wanted to say, but again, she couldn't find the words. She told Jaquan that it had been good seeing him, too, and then she walked back to her SUV and drove away.

Later that night as Arizona lay in bed, all she could think about was Jaquan. She thought about how good he looked. How he had made her laugh and tingle inside. How wild she had been when they had dated. How intense their lovemaking had been. And how he had been respectful tonight, not wanting to cause problems in her new marriage. But the thing that she had thought about most, was the fact that there was no doubt in her mind that Jaquan was Solomon's biological father. And as Arizona tossed that reality around in her head, something told her that Jaquan knew the truth, too.

Chapter 10

BERNADETTE

"I should've known the minute that I called my mother to share our good news that she was going to spew negativity," Bernadette told Coop. "You would think that she'd be happy for me. I've finally found love, real love, and all she could do was bring up my failed relationships from the past. If I didn't know any better, I would think that she wants me to be unhappy for the rest of my life."

Coop had just placed a cup of hot chamomile tea in front of Bernadette to soothe her nerves and her stomach. They were at his house, in his family room, relaxing together until it was time for Coop to head out to Southern Comfort. There were many nights that Bernadette went to the club with him, but there were some where she didn't, and this was one of those nights. She had initially wanted to enjoy a fun evening at Southern Comfort to celebrate all the good things happening in their lives. But between her upset stomach, constant fatigue, and her now dampened mood, all Bernadette wanted to do was rest. Her nerves had been frazzled ever since she had spoken with her mother and then her cousin earlier that morning, because they had both been negative. Then just thirty minutes ago, her mother had called her again.

"Bernadette," Rosa had said. "I forgot to ask you something when we spoke this morning."

"What did you forget to ask me, Mom?"

"Are you going to get a prenup?"

"I beg your pardon?"

"You're smart, so I know that you know what a prenup is, don't you?"

Bernadette blew out a deep breath of frustration. "Of course I know what it is. I just can't believe that of all the questions that you'd want to ask me, 'am I getting a prenup,' is one of them. How about asking me when we plan to set a date for our wedding, or just saying congratulations, which you still haven't done."

Rosa glossed over what Bernadette had just said. "You need to protect yourself. You're successful, Bernadette. You've got a big house, a nice car, and I know your bank account and retirement fund are loaded. Joop knows that, too."

"Mom, you know full well that his name is Coop, not Joop, and I don't appreciate you purposely mispronouncing it."

"It don't matter whether his name is Humpty Dumpty, the bottom line is that you better get a prenup to protect yourself. Listen to me because I know what I'm talking about."

Their conversation lasted only five minutes longer before Bernadette told her mother that she had to go. Rosa had upset her so much that she had to take deep breaths while she slowly counted to one hundred.

"We were finally getting back on speaking terms after that fiasco of a visit when she came here a few months ago and managed to thoroughly piss off everybody," Bernadette said to Coop, before taking a small sip of tea. "Now, she's on the verge of me not wanting her to be involved in any part of my life."

Coop rubbed Bernadette's hand in his attempt to calm her. "Baby, don't let what your mother said upset you."

"But Coop, you would think that she'd want to be there for me, and encourage me instead of tear me down every chance she gets. It's hurtful."

"I know, baby. But it's hard for Ms. Rosa to be happy for you because she's not happy, herself. I learned a long time ago that there comes a point in certain relationships where you have to accept things as they are, and not how you want them to be."

"So, you do think I should just give up?"

"No, that's not giving up, it's called coping. Sometimes you have to make adjustments in how you deal with people, even people who you love, so you can live your life without a bunch of mess."

Bernadette thought about what Coop had just said, and she knew that he was right. She had lived with her mother's negativity all her life, and she knew it was the reason why many of her own relationships had failed miserably. But her life was different now. She was happy, and she had joy, and she wanted her mother to be excited about the fact that her only child had beaten the odds. She was successful and she was about to marry the love of her life and start a family.

Bernadette sighed. "If she acted like this about us getting married, I can only imagine what she's going to say or do when I tell her that I'm pregnant."

Coop shook his head. "Bernie, don't even think about that right now."

"But how can I not? God willing, before we blink I'll be going into my second trimester and I'll have to start telling people. I'm already starting to show, Coop."

"We'll cross that bridge when we get there. Right now you just need to focus on the here and now. Stayin' healthy and keepin' yourself stress free is what's most important. Now drink some more tea."

Bernadette took another sip of the soothing liquid. Even though it was a hot, muggy night, she had been craving chamomile tea, which always calmed her.

"Is that better?" Coop asked.

"Yes, and thank you, Coop."

"I have to look after you, and our children."

Bernadette smiled. "When I think about the little ones inside me, I already want the very best for them, and I'm going to make sure they know that they're loved, and that I've got their backs, no matter what. Because I'm their mother."

"I know you will, baby. And as their father, I'm gonna do the same. We're gonna make a hellava team, and I'm gonna work hard to make sure our family thrives. We're in this together."

Bernadette gave Coop a warm smile. "I don't know what I'd do without you."

"You'll never have to wonder as long as I'm alive."

"Hearing you say that makes me think that maybe that's the very reason why my mother is so bitter. My dad divorced her when I was five years old. He'd been having an affair and he just up and left us high and dry, and my mother never got over the abandonment and feelings of rejection. She didn't have anyone in her corner to encourage her, support her, have her back or show her love, so she put up a wall and wouldn't let anyone back into her heart. Not even me. I've tried to please that woman all my life. But now, it's just way too much, and it's exhausting."

"I know, and I understand," Coop said in a gentle voice. "I never knew my father, and my mother OD'd when Sue and I were little kids. We bounced from relative to relative, basically raising ourselves." He swung his arm around Bernadette's shoulder and pulled her closer into his body. "I'm glad that our children are gonna have it better than I did . . . than we both did."

"Me too."

★　★　★

It was almost nine o'clock when Coop walked out the door on his way to Southern Comfort. After a quick shower and a small bowl of Rocky Road ice cream, Bernadette settled into bed. She picked up the TV remote and searched for a good movie to watch that would take her mind off of a thought that had been gnawing at her ever since she and Coop had talked about her phone call with her mother. Bernadette felt in her gut that not only would her mother have negative things to say once she found out about Bernadette's pregnancy, but she believed that Tess would as well.

The thought that her own mother, and her first cousin—who was more like a sister to her—would not be happy about her new-found joy hurt Bernadette to her core. She knew that she would be over the moon with excitement if her mother was blessed to find happiness with a man who loved her, and she was already thrilled when she had found out this morning that Tess and Maceo had made up and were working on setting a wedding date. Although Bernadette felt that her mother might be a bit of a lost cause, because as Coop had pointed out earlier, Rosa would most likely continue to be the same unhappy person that she'd always been, she felt that Tess might be a different story.

Bernadette reasoned that Tess was younger, more adaptable to change, and had a more willing and open heart than her mother. But Tess was also an attention-seeking drama queen who could be vindictive and petty if she felt slighted or hurt, and that, Bernadette felt, was a storm that was brewing. But even with those strikes against her, Bernadette knew that Tess stood a fighting chance at happiness because she was in love with a man who brought out the best in her.

Bernadette was drawn from her deep thoughts when she looked at her phone and saw that Arizona was calling her.

"Hey Arizona, how's your evening going? Are you enjoying your 'me' time?"

"Bernadette, I've got some real problems goin' on."

Bernadette sat straight up in bed at the sound of Arizona's voice. She had heard Arizona sound sad, stressed, anxious, happy, angry, and every emotion in between, but this was the first time that she'd heard her friend sound desperate. Bernadette pressed the power button on the TV so she could give Arizona her full attention. "What's wrong?"

"Are you at home or are you over at Coop's?"

"I'm at Coop's tonight. Why . . . what's going on?"

"Damn, I was hoping you were home because I'm not too far from your house, and I really need to talk right now."

Alarm bells were ringing inside Bernadette's head. She knew that Arizona rarely ventured out to the Palisades unless she was coming to her house for a visit. Having been born and bred in Bourbon, Arizona still stuck to the old school town rules, the Palisades was for the white folks and The Bottoms was for the black folks. Now, not only was she in a section of town where she felt uncomfortable and unfamiliar, she was there, alone, at night. "Come on over here," Bernadette told her. "Coop just left for the club a little while ago, so we'll have plenty of privacy to talk."

Fifteen minutes later, Bernadette was greeting Arizona at the door. She was surprised that Arizona had been able to get to Coop's house so quickly, given that she was a good thirty minutes away when she had called.

"You're already in your pajamas," Arizona said as she walked inside. "I'm sorry to be coming over here so late, but I didn't know who else to turn to."

Bernadette tied her silk bathrobe at her waist as she ushered Arizona inside. "As soon as I heard your voice, I knew something was wrong, so I'm glad you're here."

"I was so rattled that I almost hit two cars. I was tearin' up the road tryin' to get here."

Bernadette's eyes grew large with even more concern at Arizona's statement. Bernadette knew that as happy-go-lucky as Arizona was in most areas of her life, she was overly cautious when it came to getting behind the wheel of her car. "I drive below the speed limit," Arizona often said, "because I don't want to do anything crazy to make Solomon an orphan." The fact that she had been so desperate to get to Coop's house that she had sped let Bernadette know that Arizona's troubles ran deep.

"Come and sit in here and calm your nerves while I get us something to drink," Bernadette said as she led Arizona into Coop's large family room.

Bernadette scurried into the kitchen and poured a large glass of sweet iced tea for Arizona, which was her favorite drink, and another cup of Chamomile tea for herself. As she carried the beverages to the family room where Arizona was sitting, Bernadette said a quick prayer because she had a bad feeling that whatever her friend's problems were, it was something that would not be easily fixed.

"Let me take a look at that rock!" Arizona said with excitement.

Bernadette extended her hand and blushed. "Coop had it custom-made."

"I can tell. The setting is beautiful."

"Thank you. I love it, and the fact that he took the time to help the jeweler design it makes it even more special."

"You can say that again, and you ain't gonna find a diamond that big at Kay's or Zales. How much did he pay for it?"

Bernadette blinked twice, but remained silent.

"This is the first time that I've been inside Coop's house," Arizona said as she took a sip of tea and looked around. "It's very nice, just like I thought it would be."

Bernadette nodded. She knew without a doubt that Arizona was troubled because she had fully expected her to follow up on her inappropriate question about the cost of her engagement ring with an even more inappropriate comment about Coop's house, but instead she kept her words short and sweet. "Tell me what's going on?" Bernadette inquired.

"There's so much happening in my life right now that I don't know what to do. I've got some serious decisions to make."

"About you and Chris?"

"Yes, and also about Solomon's biological father."

"What?"

"Yeah, he's back in town and I saw him tonight."

Bernadette didn't know how to put a delicate spin on the question that she was about to ask, so she just came right out and said it. "I thought you didn't know who Solomon's biological father was. Didn't you say it was between one of two people?"

"Actually, three," Arizona said without a hint of shame. "But tonight left no doubt in my mind who it is."

Bernadette listened as Arizona told her the details about how she had run into Jaquan Williams earlier tonight at Fried Green Tomatoes. She noticed that each time Arizona said Jaquan's name, her voice changed and carried a different lilt. Bernadette remembered that when she had first met Coop, Tess had told her that her voice had carried a different tone when she had mentioned Coop's name, and although Bernadette had tried to deny it at the time, she'd known that Tess had been right. Sitting and listening to Arizona talk about Jaquan, Bernadette had no doubt that Arizona was already on the road to committing adultery, just two weeks into her marriage.

"Girl, it was so crazy," Arizona said. "Until a few hours ago, I hadn't seen Jaquan since he went to prison almost six years ago, but as soon as I laid eyes on him in the restaurant, it was like looking at Solomon as a walking, breathing grown man. And the wild thing is that Solomon actually looks like a combination of Chris and Jaquan, but his actions, movements, the way he smiles, and even the way he cuts his eyes when he looks at you, is like Jaquan to a tee."

"And you're absolutely sure that the timeline makes it possible for Jaquan to be Solomon's father? Bernadette asked.

"I was rollin' back then, I ain't even gonna lie. But yes, I'm sure."

"Okay, I'm just asking because if Jaquan's been in prison for six years and Solomon is five, the full gestation period would have had to have been slightly longer than ten months." Bernadette realized that she had recited pregnancy terms that she'd heard from Dr. Vu, and she had said too much, so she reached for her tea and took a sip.

Arizona looked at Bernadette as if she'd just asked her to perform long division math. "Dang, Bernadette, you're gettin' real scientific on me. All I know is that I had sex with Jaquan about a week before his sentencing in Raleigh, maybe not even that long, and Solomon is five now, so that would account for the time between when I got pregnant and when I had him. And guess what?"

"I'm afraid to ask."

"I think Jaquan knows it, too, because when he asked me how old Solomon was and when I told him, he had a strange look on his face. I could tell he was doing the math in his head."

Bernadette took another sip of tea. "And you're confident that he's Solomon's father?"

Arizona pressed her back deep into the couch and nodded her head. "Honestly, a part of me has always known that Jaquan was Solomon's father. We had an on-again, off-again relationship for years. We would go strong for a few months and then break it off, but we always drifted back to each other. A few months before he went away, we had been seeing each other undercover because we'd both been dating other people at the time."

Bernadette nodded. "And you're still sure that Jaquan's the one."

"Yes, because I had stopped having sex with the guy I was seeing."

"Okay, that takes care of guy number two, but how about guy number three?"

"I'd only slept with him once during the time I was with Jaquan. I know what you're thinking, and trust me, I know it sounds sketchy, but I believe in my heart that Jaquan is Solomon's father."

Bernadette rubbed her temples. "So, obviously, after he went to prison you stopped all contact?"

"I had to put him out of my mind because he was locked up, and I didn't think he would live long enough to get out of prison."

"Why not?"

"Because he was on the verge of being big time when he went in, and word on the street was that he had rivals inside those prison walls waiting to take him out. One of my uncles said he didn't think Jaquan would last six months. I felt awful about it, but I knew there was nothing that I could do on the outside. Then about a month and a half later I realized that I was pregnant."

Bernadette shook her head. "I can't imagine how hard that must have been. You had to go through your pregnancy with so much on your mind."

Arizona took a sip of her iced tea and then blew out a heavy breath. "Bernadette, you don't know the half of it. There was no one I could talk to or confide in. I love my mama, but she gives horrible advice, and if I'da told any of my aunties, my business would've been all over town, and my girlfriends at the time were having their own baby daddy drama. I just did what I had to do."

"Arizona, I'm sorry that you didn't have the support that you needed back then, but I'm here for you now."

"Thanks Bernadette. I knew I could count on you."

"Absolutely." Bernadette sat forward and stretched her aching back. "You were right, you have some serious decisions in front of you. Do you think Jaquan is going to be in Bourbon for a while?"

"I don't know. Right now he's staying with his Uncle Clem, which is actually only a couple miles from here."

"I know how we can easily find out," Bernadette said. "All I have to do is ask Coop after he gets in. You know that man knows everything that goes on from one end of the state to the other."

"Girl, that's the truth!" Arizona nodded. "Jaquan said that he's been keeping a low profile on purpose, and it's like he doesn't even exist because he's been back for a week and I haven't heard a peep about him from anyone. But if anybody knows the 411, it's Coop."

"Yes, and just so you know, Coop is going to ask me why I'm fishing for information on a young man that . . ."

Arizona interrupted before Bernadette could finish her sentence. "Go ahead and tell him everything. Even though Coop knows everybody and he's always up on what's going on, he's discreet, and he stays outta folks' business."

"He sure does," Bernadette agreed. "Coop will want to know details only so he can find out what you want to know, so consider it done."

"If Jaquan plans to stay in Bourbon for a while, things are gonna get complicated real quick because I'm having so many issues with Chris," Arizona said with frustration. "He pissed me off so bad last night that I don't want to even see his face for a few days."

"Oh goodness, what did he do now?"

"I can't even form the words to explain it all, so I'm gonna put a pause in that one and save it for later."

Bernadette knew that if Arizona, of all people, was at a loss for words to describe a situation, whatever Chris had done, it must have been horrific. He'd already been on shaky ground for how he had behaved during their honeymoon, and now, judging from the tight-ness in Arizona's voice when she mentioned his name, their marriage was already on the edge of collapse.

"Okay," Bernadette said. "Just tell me later, but I do want to suggest something. I know you said that you're sure that Jaquan is Solomon's father, but before you say or do anything, you need to confirm it, and I'm not talking about what you feel in your gut, I'm talking about what you can prove on paper, and the only way to do that is through a paternity test."

Arizona looked worried. "I was afraid you were gonna say that."

"So you've been thinking it as well?"

Arizona nodded. "Yeah, I mean . . . I know that it's the right thing to do."

"It most certainly is, because what you're talking about has the potential to change a lot of lives, not the least, Solomon's. Chris is the only father he knows, so you need to be one hundred and ten percent sure before you do anything," Bernadette said. "You're going to need to get Jaquan to submit to a DNA sample."

Arizona fiddled with her hands and nodded her head in agreement. "Right."

"I know this is a lot, and you're stressed about it all, but trust me, it's going to work out, Arizona. Just remember that everything, and I mean everything, that happens to us happens for a reason. There are no accidents."

"You're a very wise woman, Bernadette, and you know a lot about life. I want to believe that you're right about this, but I just don't know how things are gonna turn out well. I've got an ex-con baby daddy who just popped up from out of nowhere, a new husband that I don't even want to be in the same room with, and my precious, innocent son is caught in between."

Bernadette reached over and took Arizona's hand into hers. "Listen, if you can go through a pregnancy by yourself, knowing that your unborn child may never see their father, and then raise that kid to be as awesome as Solomon is, you can conquer anything, Arizona."

Arizona took a deep, cleansing breath. "Wow, you're right. I was a crazy, wild, and irresponsible twenty-something back then, but once I looked into Solomon's eyes everything changed. I can't describe the feeling, Bernadette, but as a mother, it's like . . . before your child is born you go through life without a care, but after they get here, everything matters. Every single thing becomes real."

Bernadette was only in her first trimester, but she understood what Arizona meant because she had begun feeling that way almost from the moment that she had learned she was pregnant. She nodded, acknowledging Arizona's words. "That's got to be a special feeling."

"It is." Arizona squeezed Bernadette's hand. "I'm not sure how far along you are right now, but when you have your baby, you'll know what I mean."

Bernadette raised her brow and looked into Arizona's eyes with shock. The two friends let a moment of silence hang between them. Finally, Bernadette spoke in a soft whisper. "How did you know?"

"I just had a feeling . . . Wow, you really are pregnant!" Arizona said with a wide smile. "I knew it was more than just menopause."

"I honestly thought that's what it was at first, and that's why I had made an appointment with Dr. Vu, so he could give me some pills or something, but then he told me that I was pregnant."

Arizona chuckled. "When I saw you yesterday, you were sweatin' like crazy, then you were eating like it was your last meal, and tonight, as hot as it is outside, you're sipping tea, and I know that's to calm your stomach because it's what I did when I was carrying Solomon. Plus, you got that pregnancy glow."

Bernadette perked up. "You think I have a glow?"

"Yes, and it's the kind of shine that no amount of highlights or bronzer can give you. How far along are you?"

"I'm only eight weeks."

Arizona clapped her hands and pumped her fist in a cheering motion. "I'm so happy for you, Bernadette! Girl, I thought I was hyped when you called this morning and told me that Coop had proposed, but this right here, it takes the cake! This is the best news that I've heard in a long time."

Just as Bernadette's heart had been heavy at the thought that her mother and Tess were not genuinely happy for her, her heart swelled with gratitude that Arizona was. Bernadette was thankful that a chance meeting on her fiftieth birthday had brought her dear friend into her life. But then a startling realization came to her, causing her to reflect on what she had just said to Arizona, and the magnitude of it nearly took her breath away.

It had not been chance that had brought Arizona to the same restaurant where Bernadette had been dining alone the night of her birthday. It had not been a coincidence that Arizona and Bernadette had been born on the same day. And Bernadette absolutely knew that it was not by chance that Arizona was there tonight, speaking affirming words over the birth of her babies in the months to come. Arizona had said "when you have your baby, you'll know what I mean." Those words were surprising, but validating to Bernadette's ears.

Being a fifty-year-old, first time mother, she knew the risks were extremely high, and there had not been a day that had gone by since she'd found out that she was pregnant, that she had not thought about the possibility of a miscarriage. But now, Arizona's words gave her newfound peace of mind. For the first time in eight weeks, Bernadette was not worried. She leaned over and gave Arizona a hug. "Thank you," she said. "I can't tell you how much you mean to me, and how much your words just gave me the courage I need to let go of my worry. I've been a ball of nerves ever since I found out that I'm pregnant. I was too nervous to tell Coop."

"I can only imagine."

"He proposed to me the night of your wedding, and that's when I told him because I couldn't agree to be his wife without telling him what was on the horizon."

"Wait. He proposed to you the night of my wedding?" Arizona said. "Why're you just now telling me this wonderful news?"

Bernadette smiled. "For one thing, you were on your honeymoon, and then when you came back I knew that you were busy trying to get settled into your new home with Chris. I had planned to tell you and Tess yesterday but . . ." Bernadette stopped herself. She had almost told Arizona that she had been in such shock from learning that she was pregnant with twins, that she had completely forgotten to mention her engagement. It was one thing for Arizona to know that she was pregnant, but Bernadette didn't want her to know just yet that she was having twins.

"I know . . ." Arizona interrupted. "Once Tess started acting funky it probably ruined your mood. I get it."

Although Arizona was only partially right, Bernadette nodded in agreement.

"I'm gonna tell you right now, Tess is a negative force. I love her to death, but she's got issues."

"Yes she does, but I'm hopeful because now that she and Maceo have made up she can concentrate on thinking and living in a more positive way."

Arizona gasped. "What?! I didn't know that they made up. Yesterday she was cryin' the blues about how they were barely speaking, to the point that she thought he was gonna call off their engagement."

"When I talked with her this morning she said that they worked everything out, and they're even looking at getting married during the holidays."

"If she doesn't mess it up between now and then."

"We'll just have to pray that she doesn't. Maceo is a good guy, and I'm not just saying that because he's Coop's nephew. He's decent and kind, and I can tell that he genuinely loves Tess. But, that said, he's a lot like Coop in the fact that there's only so much he's willing to take. I just pray that Tess stays calm with him."

Arizona laughed. "Calm and Testimony Sinclair don't go hand in hand. I remember when she told me about how she cut up her ex's clothes, and that's when I knew homegirl was straight crazy."

The two friends shared a long, hearty laugh until Bernadette started to yawn. It was now close to midnight, and they were both getting tired, especially Bernadette.

"I'm gonna head on home because it's getting late and I know you're tired," Arizona said. "Get some sleep and I'll call you tomorrow."

After Arizona left, Bernadette washed the glass and cup that she and Arizona had used and then went to the bedroom to wait for Coop. Bernadette was tired, but she was also happy. Although Arizona had come over tonight in need of help, it was her friend who'd helped her instead, and had lifted her spirits. She knew that Tess, in her own way, was happy for her as well, but her cousin's deep-seated issues prevented her from fully sharing in Bernadette's joy. She hoped again, that once she was at a point in her pregnancy to let everyone know, that Tess would receive the news even half as enthusiastically as Arizona had. Bernadette was pulled from her thoughts when she heard Coop walk through the back door.

"Baby, I'm home," Coop called out in his deep voice as he walked back to the bedroom.

An automatic smile came to Bernadette's face. "How did it go at the club tonight?"

"Same ol' same ol'," Coop said. He walked to Bernadette's side of the bed and gave her a kiss on her cheek. "The place was packed, as usual. They'll be winding down in another hour or so."

Coop removed his tan linen jacket and walked toward the walk-in closet as he undressed. Fifteen minutes later, after taking a quick shower, Bernadette felt him slide under the bed sheets next to her. She was glad that Coop had not taken long in the bathroom tonight because she was tired, but she wanted to stay up long enough to ask him about Jaquan.

"How ya' feelin', Baby?" Coop asked.

"I'm good, just a little tired, but I can't complain."

"Good."

"Coop, do you know a young man named Jaquan Williams?"

Coop let out a low sigh. "Bernie, I know that you and Arizona are close, but Baby, stay outta whatever she and Jaquan got goin' on."

"I didn't say a word about Arizona," she said with surprise. "How did you know I was asking for her?"

Coop became quiet, and Bernadette could see by the look in his eyes that he was concentrating on what to say. He took Bernadette's hand into his. "Baby, just stay out of it. Arizona's a married woman and given the circumstances, things can get ugly before you know it."

Bernadette knew that her gut had been right when she'd had a feeling that Coop knew all about Jaquan, but it came as a surprise to her that he knew about Arizona's involvement with Jaquan, because according to Arizona, she and Jaquan had been dating in secret. But as Bernadette would soon come to discover, secrets could not stay hidden forever, and it was only a matter of time before they came bubbling to the surface.

Chapter 11

TESS

It was a hot, muggy, and overcast Monday morning, the kind that Tess dreaded, and especially today because she saw the gloomy weather as a telltale sign of things to come. She glanced over at Maceo, who was scrolling through his phone.

"You okay?" Maceo asked.

"Yes, I'm fine," Tess replied. "Just ready to get this exam started."

They were sitting in the exam room at Moonstone Women's Wellness Center, waiting for Dr. Vu to enter and begin Tess's appointment. She had initially thought that inviting Maceo to accompany her had been a good idea, but now she wasn't so sure. Not since her mother had taken her to her first pelvic exam right before she had begun her freshman year at Winston-Salem State University, had anyone accompanied her on a gynecological appointment. Tess had asked Maceo to come with her last Friday night, in the spirit of transparency, and, because she had been so happy that they had made up. She had wanted her openness to signal that they were in it together.

But a lot had changed between then and now, and the situation that was quickly developing with her ex had her worked up. Tess had known when Antwan had called and left her a short, nondescript voice message two days ago, that whatever the reason for his call, it wasn't going to result in anything good. The responsible and rational thinking part of Tess had told her that she should immediately text Antwan and let him know that she was engaged and that she did not want to communicate with him. But the petty part of her that still bordered on messy, had wondered what was going on with him and his new wife. And although she'd wanted to engage him, she had held off.

The next evening after a full day of writing, Tess had decided to wind down her day by posting the happy news of her engagement. She knew that her legion of loyal readers would be happy for her, and that thought had given her a jolt. She snapped a picture of the engagement ring on her left hand and posted, "He Put a Ring On It." #offthemarket #sweetlove #ifoundtheone. Then after posting the happy news to all her social media accounts, she had checked her email in order to get caught up on her messages for the week ahead. Her body had instantly stiffened when she saw a message from Antwan sitting in her inbox that he had sent at three o'clock that morning.

What in the hell does his trifling ass want? Tess had thought to herself. The fact that Antwan had been wide awake, sending emails at that time of morning didn't give her alarm. He was a Pulitzer Prize winning journalist for the Chicago Bureau of The Washington Post, and it was like second nature for him to be up working, researching, and writing all times of the day and night. Plus, she knew that he was a serial cheater, and most of his galivanting was done under the cover of night or the wee hours of the morning. But Tess also knew that the fact that he had contacted her not once, but twice, first through phone and then through email, had filled her with curious anxiety.

"Let me see what this asshole wants," she had said when she opened his message. Her eyes widened with worry from the opening line down to the last word.

To: tessthebest@testimonysinclair.com
From: abrotherwhowrites@antwanbolling.com
Re: Reconnecting

Hi Tess,

It has been a while. How are you? I reached out by phone yesterday and left you a voice message, but I'm not sure if you received it so I'm following up with this email. I'm working on an investigative piece that is bringing me to Bourbon, NC. Sonya told me that you are living there, and I thought it would be good to reconnect with you. I arrive in town Monday afternoon, and will be staying for one week.

Hope to see you soon,
Antwan

She read the message over and over, and each time she shook her head with skepticism. She found it hard to believe that out of all the places in the country and the world where Antwan had traveled on assignment for his groundbreaking investigative stories, that Bourbon would be on the list. Typically, his stories involved high crimes, complicated conspiracies, global revolutions, and world-changing events. Tess could not imagine what type of credible, newsworthy story could possibly draw him to the small eastern North Carolina town whose claim to fame was sweet iced tea and vinegar–based barbeque.

Tess had not spoken to Antwan in a year and a half, and that conversation had ended with her threatening his life. She had been devastated that he'd cheated on her. Antwan had strung her along for two years, and within six months of their breakup he had married someone else. Tess had felt that he had thrust a dagger through her heart, and to add insult to injury, she felt that he had twisted it even deeper by marrying his new love on Tess's birthday. She remembered reading about Antwan's grand Ritz Carlton wedding.

His new wife was Marie Jett, a gorgeous ex-model turned celebrity makeup artist and fashion influencer with a huge Instagram following. In Tess's estimation, the woman was probably naïve about Antwan's philandering, otherwise she wouldn't have married him after only dating for such a short amount of time.

Tess had been furious, hurt, and an emotional wreck after her discovery about Antwan's marriage. But even though she had been devastated, curiosity had led her to Antwan's social media pages, as well as to that of his new wife's, because she had wanted to see proof for herself. She had looked on in shock as she perused loving posts that featured beautiful pictures of the happy newlyweds. The entire situation had sent Tess spiraling into a mini meltdown and the stress had caused her fibroids and endometriosis to flare even more.

But what Tess had not known then, was that the heartbreak that she'd experienced had been the breakthrough that she had needed. If she hadn't been so depressed from Antwan's betrayal, Bernadette probably wouldn't have asked her to come to Bourbon for a visit, and in turn, Tess wouldn't have met Maceo. As she read Antwan's message again, she realized that she actually needed to thank him for her newfound happiness instead of cursing him for reappearing in her life. Then a thought came to her. *That bastard knows I'm living in Bourbon, but he doesn't know that I'm engaged.*

Antwan had said that Sonya, their busybody mutual acquaintance, had told him that she was living in Bourbon, and Sonya knew that information because her cousin happened to be the realtor of a couple who were interested in buying Tess's luxury home in Chicago's gold coast.

Now, as Tess gathered the blue tissue paper thin gown around her body, she wished she could hit a restart button and go back to Saturday morning. She was sure that if she had posted the picture of her engagement ring that morning instead of waiting until late evening the next day, Antwan would have never reached out to her, even if he really were in Bourbon for the purpose of an investigative assignment.

"You look like your mind is a thousand miles away," Maceo said, drawing Tess's mind back to the present.

"Just thinking . . . and hoping," she responded.

Maceo put his phone away and rose from the uncomfortable chair where he was sitting. He walked to Tess and kissed her forehead. "No matter what the doctor tells us today, we know that life is gonna keep on moving. We're going to get married and we're going to build a life together, Tess."

"But what if he says that he agrees with all the other specialists . . . that it's unlikely that I'll be able to have children."

"What if he says you can? What if we're blessed to have two or even three kids? What if we have a happy life and grow old to see the birth of our grandchildren? Baby, there's all kinds of what ifs in life. You need to concentrate on the possibility that good things will happen instead of fading into your fears."

Tess smiled and was thankful that she had a good man like Maceo who loved and encouraged her. She knew that he was right, and that she needed to change her way of thinking. "I guess I've been stuck in a negative place for so long that I'm still figuring out how to join the world of hope."

"You write about it in your books, now you have to be about it in your life."

"Damn, you just hit me with some powerful shit."

Maceo shook his head. "That's my Tess, always profound."

They shared a laugh that was interrupted when they heard the door open and saw Dr. Vu and his assistant walk into the room. Tess took hold of Maceo's hand, inhaled a deep breath, and willed her mind to fight against the feeling that was punching in her gut.

"Hello Ms. Sinclair," Dr. Vu said with a wide smile. "It's a pleasure to meet you."

"It's nice to mee you, too," Tess said as she returned his smile. "This is my fiancé, Maceo Dennis," she said with pride.

After they exchanged more pleasantries, Dr. Vu began his exam. He told Tess that her period was perfectly timed because while it may not have been ideal for her, it actually aided in the tests that were necessary to determine her chances of fertility, which needed to be done between the second and fourth day of her menstrual cycle. After Dr. Vu drew her blood and pressed his hands on the top of her stomach, it was time for the part of the exam that she always dreaded. When Dr. Vu reached for the stirrups, Tess watched as Maceo's eyes squinted with intensity. She could see by the look on his face that he must be having flashbacks to when he had gone to prenatal visits with his ex-wife.

Dr. Vu looked at Tess, "I'm going to try to make this as quick and comfortable for you as possible."

Tess nodded and took a deep breath to prepare herself for the mini torture that was about to begin. She looked up into Maceo's eyes, who was standing right by her side, and gripped his hand in anticipation of the pain that was about to come. Even though Tess had been through the procedure more times than she cared to count, each ordeal brought about physical and emotional stress. She winced and clenched her teeth when Dr. Vu inserted the hard, cold speculum into her vagina. She had thought that she'd made a bad decision by asking Maceo to come, but now she was thankful that he was there. He rubbed her arm with one hand and held her hand with the other, and it served to comfort and soothe her. Before she knew it, Dr. Vu had finished the exam.

After she got dressed, Dr. Vu told her and Maceo that they would have her Follicle Stimulating Hormone test results ready within twenty-four hours. But then he hit them with news that neither of them wanted to hear.

"I reviewed all of your records from the three previous doctors you've seen," Dr. Vu began, "and I can tell you from the pelvic exam, your fibroids have grown larger, and have multiplied, and because they have worsened, my guess is that your endometriosis has as well. I use the word guess because as you know, unlike fibroids, measuring the growth and spread of endometriosis is a little trickier. But judging from the increased level of pain you've been experiencing, I believe that's the cause."

"This isn't what I wanted to hear," Tess said, and she knew what was coming next.

Dr. Vu nodded and confirmed with his eyes what she knew he was going to say. He told her that even though her test results would come in within the next twenty-four hours, based upon her medical history, along with the exam that he had just performed, it was his opinion that her previous diagnoses had been correct. She only had between a one and five percent chance of becoming pregnant, and even if she were able to conceive, she would most likely miscarry due to the severity of her fibroids and endometriosis. But the blow that really deflated Tess was when Dr. Vu strongly recommended that she have a total hysterectomy, which would eliminate even the tiniest sliver of hope of having biological children.

Tess and Maceo walked out of Dr. Vu's office in silence. She wanted to cry, but her spirit was so broken that she didn't have tears to spare. She thought about the hopeful, optimistic words that Maceo had spoken right before Dr. Vu had entered the room and crushed their dreams. She thought about all the women in the world who had children, and how lucky they were to have been blessed to experience the joy of motherhood, and before she knew it, her mood turned from sadness to anger, and she could see that Maceo had noticed her shift.

Maceo turned the ignition in his Jeep and looked at Tess. "Is there anything that I can do?"

Tess shook her head.

"I'm sorry baby, but I want you to know that this doesn't mean we can't have a family."

Tess tried her best to hold back her tears, but she couldn't, and as much as she wanted to control her angry words, they came spilling out. "But we can't have our own kids."

"Says who? If we adopt children, they'll be our kids."

"Stop with all that fluffy bullshit, Mace. You know exactly what I mean. You said yourself that you want your own kids so you can leave a footprint on this earth."

Maceo put the car in drive and pulled away from the office as he spoke. "I can still leave my mark on this world whether we have kids biologically or not. Hell, there's people who have kids with their DNA running through their veins who are nothing like them, who disappoint them, who disrespect them, and don't amount to shit."

"Maybe so, but at least you know that it's of your own doing. Adoption is a crapshoot."

"I can't believe you just said that. What's wrong with you?"

"I'm a realist."

"No, you're negative, and Tess, as much as I love you, your attitude has got to change."

"Why? Because I don't agree with your pie in the sky philosophy?"

"Because your attitude ruins any chance for happiness."

"I think about all the women walking around in this world who've been blessed to have kids but don't even want them. They're irresponsible, terrible mothers who couldn't care less about raising a child, yet they can get pregnant and pop out babies at will. And here I am, desperately wanting to have children with the man I love, but I can't." Tess began to cry. "It's not fair. It's just not fair."

Maceo reached for Tess's hand and held it. They rode in silence all the way back home as rain poured in heavy sheets against the windshield.

Later that night, Tess lay in bed snuggled next to Maceo. He had decided to stay home from the restaurant so he could comfort Tess. He'd made her a bountiful chef's salad for lunch, and had cooked a delicious vegetable soup for dinner. But she had barely nibbled on the food that he'd made with love and care.

After Maceo had drifted off to sleep, Tess went into her writing cave because she needed to find a distraction from her thoughts. She logged on to her computer and checked her email, hoping to find a message from her literary agent about the updated production schedule for her novel. She scrolled through the messages and saw that Antwan had emailed her again.

Why is this fool contacting me again? She thought to herself. "He must be looking to cause some trouble because by now he's got to have seen my post and know that I'm engaged," she said aloud, but when she saw the subject line of his email that read, "Confidential," she became more confused than ever. But the one thing she did know was that the only way she would find out what Antwan was really up to was to open his message and read it. *Here we go.*

To: tessthebest@testimonysinclair.com
From: abrotherwhowrites@antwanbolling.com
Re: Confidential

Hi Tess,

I arrived in town a few hours ago. I've made an interesting discovery about the cold case murder that I'm investigating, and I believe you can help me. Please reach out to me tomorrow afternoon if you are able. I'm staying at the St. Hamilton Hotel.

Hope to hear from you.
Antwan

Tess was more puzzled than ever. "Why in the world does he think I can help him with a cold case murder?" Tess mumbled in a whisper as she scratched her head. "I've only been living in Bourbon for six months, and I barely know anyone in this town." After reading the message again, the only thing that was clear to Tess was that Antwan had no doubt seen her post because his message was serious, to the point, and all business.

Tess had to admit that she was more than a little curious. She knew that while Antwan may have been a despicable, lying, cheating boyfriend, he was a hell of a journalist with a stellar reputation for dogged professionalism and a passion for honest reporting. Tess knew that if Antwan had gone so far as to contact her regarding his story, he must have some solid, airtight evidence that had led him to believe she could help him in some way. She looked at the clock and saw that it was almost midnight. She knew that if she reached out to Antwan right now, either by email or phone, he would respond right away because he was most likely still up, as was the case with most fellow writers whom she knew.

She was about to press return on the email and send Antwan a message, but a little voice inside her head said, *Girl, don't reach out to that man unless you have a plan of how you're going to deal with him.*

Tess's eyes scrutinized Antwan's email again, and it struck her that he had ended his message by conveniently sliding in the name of the hotel where he was staying. She thought it was an interesting co-incidence that Arizona's husband happened to be the general manager of the St. Hamilton. *Why did he tell me where he's staying? Does he want me to meet him at the hotel?* Tess wondered. *Yep, I need to figure out a plan for what to do.*

Tess knew that in order to develop a good strategy she needed great advice. "Bernadette!" she whispered out loud. She knew that if anyone could help steer her in the right direction it was her cousin. She needed to talk with Bernadette anyway because she had promised to call her and let her know how her appointment with Dr. Vu had worked out. Although she had disappointing news to share with her cousin, she knew that Bernadette would give her the comforting, listening ear that she needed in order to deal with the disappointment and realization that she wasn't able to have children.

Tess rose from her computer, went back to the bedroom, and reclaimed her space next to Maceo. She knew she would have restless sleep, if any at all, and she knew she was going to have to do something that she absolutely detested. She was going to rise early in the morning so she could talk to Bernadette before her cousin started her busy day.

Tess was so tired that her head hurt. It was seven o'clock in the morning, which felt almost sacrilegious to her. She was thankful that unlike her, Maceo was an early riser who started each day with a burst of energy that, lucky for her, produced a fresh pot of home brewed coffee each morning, and on weekends a delicious breakfast.

Tess rose from bed and stumbled into the kitchen. "Thank you, Mace. And thank you, Lord, for giving me a man who knows his way around the kitchen, 'cause God knows I sure don't," she said as she inhaled the rich aroma of the French Roast coffee that Maceo had brewed. "This $20 Mr. Coffee maker does the trick every time," Tess mused. Maceo's coffee maker was the only appliance in his chef grade kitchen that didn't cost the equivalent of a month's mortgage payment. Some men's vices included cars, video games, athletic shoes, and sporting goods, but Maceo was a true epicurean, and he'd been known to spend his last dollar on a good set of paring knives.

After filling her large coffee mug to the brim, Tess walked back to her writing cave, sat down at her desk, and proceeded to call Bernadette.

"Uh, oh, you're up early. Is everything okay?" Bernadette asked in a concerned voice.

"I'm fine," Tess answered, still trying to keep her eyes open. She took another sip of her coffee. "Are you on your way to work?"

"Yes, I'm about five minutes away from the office. It's raining like a monsoon out here."

Tess swirled her desk chair to face the window and peered outside. "It's been raining like this since yesterday. It was depressing then and it's depressing now."

"Oh, Tess, your appointment didn't go well, did it?"

Tess shook her head on her end of the phone. "No cuz, it didn't. Dr. Vu is still waiting on my lab results, but after examining me he told me that he agrees with the other doctors that I've seen who've basically said I can't have kids. Plus, he told me the same thing that Dr. Gina recommended last month, that I should have a hysterectomy."

There was a stretch of silence on the line before Bernadette finally spoke. "I wish I had the words to say that would make you feel better, because I know how much you want to have children, but as you know, there are many paths to motherhood."

"My egg quality is so low that I can't even go the surrogate route. Mace keeps mentioning adoption, so I guess that's what we'll be looking at."

"Tess, you say it like adoption is a bad thing. I think it's wonderful. Do you know how many children need a good, loving home?"

Tess blew out a breath of fatigue. "Of course I do, but it doesn't change the fact that I want to have kids of my own. I want to give birth and look into the eyes of a mini me."

"A mini you?!" Bernadette said with a chuckle. "Do you think you and Maceo could handle a little Testy Terror running around the house? Be careful what you ask for."

Tess shared a laugh with her cousin about the nickname, Testy Terror, that her mother used to call her when she was a toddler. "I was a bad ass kid, wasn't I?"

"You were a handful for sure."

"I'll never know if my child will be a Testy Terror, or if they'll be a well-behaved angel like Mace probably was. And that's the thing about adoption. All the things that are inherent to you disappear in place of someone else's DNA, habits, quirks, personality, and looks."

"That's true, but you also have to look at the bottom-line fact that when it's all said and done, adoption leads you to motherhood, and that's your path, Tess. Whether your child emerges from your womb or someone else's, they will still be your child, and you will be their mother."

"You need to either open up a therapy practice or write books because what you just said sounded so damn convincing that I actually feel better."

Bernadette laughed. "There's nothing to feel bad about as long as you have hope and options."

"Hmmm, hope and options," Tess repeated softly. She was glad that she had Bernadette as not only her close relative and friend, but as a confidant. She told Bernadette things that she didn't even feel comfortable sharing with her own mother. Tess knew that she needed to call her mother at some point to break the news, which she felt both her parents would receive as a hard blow.

"Tess, as long as you keep things in perspective and develop a plan you'll be fine," Bernadette said. "I hate to cut this conversation short, but I'm at work now."

"Damn, when you mentioned having a plan I almost forgot the main reason why I called."

"I thought you called to tell me about your appointment with Dr. Vu."

Tess took another sip of her robust coffee. She hoped she would have enough time to get her cousin's advice because she could hear Bernadette shuffling around in her car, preparing to gather her things so she could head into her office. "That was part of it, but the main reason I called you at this ungodly hour is because of Antwan."

"Your ex?" Bernadette asked with surprise.

"The one and only. He called me Saturday, emailed me Sunday, and then emailed me again yesterday. And Girl, he's in town."

"What in the world is Antwan doing here in Bourbon?"

Tess heard Bernadette's car door shut behind her, followed by the chirping sound of her locking system, and the clicking of Bernadette's heels as she walked across the concrete parking deck that led to her office in the c-suite at Bourbon General. Tess knew that she needed to make it quick. "He's in town on assignment investigating a cold case murder. Can you believe that?" Tess said in a hurry. She waited for Bernadette's reaction, but she got no response. *She must have gone into the elevator and the call dropped,* Tess thought to herself. "Bernadette, are you still there?"

"Um, yes. I'm here . . ."

"Oh good. I thought the call dropped."

"What cold case is he investigating?"

"I don't know. His message said something about a murder that he's investigating. And get this, he said that he thinks I can help him with it."

"Help him how? Tess, what's going on?"

Tess could hear the concern and near panic in Bernadette's voice. She knew that anything involving wrongdoing made Bernadette nervous, which was why she still found it hard to believe that her cousin was in love with, and was going to marry, an ex-felon. "Antwan said something about an interesting discovery that I could help him with." Tess heard Bernadette's heels clicking fast, as if she was doing a slow jog, followed by the *beep beep* sound of her door unlocking.

"Did you just go back to your car?"

"Yes, I forgot something," Bernadette said as she sat in her car and closed the door. "So, tell me again, what exactly did Antwan say?"

"I know that you're in a rush, but if you have a minute or two I can open his email and tell you because I'm sitting at my desk."

"Yes, I'll wait."

Tess logged onto her computer and searched her inbox for Antwan's message. She read it out loud, word for word, to Bernadette. "I don't know how he thinks I can help him," Tess said. "The fact that it's a cold case means it happened a while ago, and I've only been in town for six months."

"I wonder what he meant when he said that he's made an interesting discovery?" Bernadette asked.

"That's the same thing I was wondering, and whatever that discovery is, it sounds like Antwan believes that I either know something about it or I'm linked to it."

"Do you know anything about any unsolved murders in Bourbon?"

"Cuz, you know who you're talking to, right?" Tess said with a laugh. "I write about that stuff in books, but I don't know anything about murder in real life. Besides, like I said, I've only been here for six months, and half of that time I've been in my writing cave. Antwan would be better off asking you than me, especially because of your connection to Coop."

Bernadette coughed as if she was choking on something.

"Bernadette, are you okay?"

"Um, yeah, I'm fine," Bernadette said as she fought to regain her breath. "What does my connection with Coop have to do with anything?"

"I didn't mean that the way it sounded. What I meant to say is that Coop knows everybody in Bourbon, and if anyone knows anything about a cold case in this town, Coop would."

"I guess . . ."

Tess's eyes got big. "You guess? Girl, I wouldn't be surprised if Coop knows Barack and Michelle." Normally, a joke like that would have made Bernadette laugh, but instead she sat silent on the line. Tess knew that her cousin was probably itching to get off the line so that she could go into her office and begin her demanding day of running things at the hospital, so she blurted out what she needed to ask. "Antwan wants me to contact him this afternoon, and Bernadette, I think he wants me to meet with him at his hotel, because he slid into his message that he's staying at The St. Hamilton, of all places. Do you think I should go?"

"Oh Lord, that's Chris's hotel."

"Exactly. Can you believe how crazy that is?"

"Have you told Maceo about any of this?"

"No, you're the only person I've talked to. I wanted to get your advice about what I should do. I need a plan."

"Don't meet Antwan anywhere in public, face-to-face, especially not the hotel. It's not a good look to be seen in a hotel with your ex. Call him and see what he has to say, but whatever you do, please don't go and see him."

Tess nodded and let out a deep breath. "Do you think I should mention this to Mace?"

"No, not right now. Just talk to Antwan first and find out what case he's investigating, what the development is, and how he thinks you may be able to help him. But don't say a word to Maceo, or anyone else until you get enough information to know what's going on. Okay?"

"Okay, you're right."

"And remember, don't meet with him."

"Damn, Bernadette. You already said that, and I get it."

"Okay, I just know how you are."

"And how's that?" Tess asked slightly annoyed.

"Listen cuz, I've got to go. Call me as soon as you finish talking with Antwan."

"I will."

After Tess hung up the phone she felt a small sense of relief. She knew that Bernadette was right about not meeting with Antwan in person, and her advice was on point about not saying anything to Maceo about Antwan contacting her until she had full details about her ex's motives. Suddenly, Tess thought of something. She knew that Antwan was the consummate professional, but she also knew that he was notorious when it came to women. *What if he's trying to mix pleasure with business, and he's just feeding me a line to sweet talk me into a quick hookup while he's in town on assignment? There's no way in hell that I can possibly help him with an unsolved murder in Bourbon.*

Tess did something that she'd not done since she had started dating Maceo—she went to Antwan's Facebook page. She noticed that he no longer had a photo of him and his new wife as his profile picture, and instead, it was the same photo of him standing in front of the Chicago Bureau of the Washington Post building that she remembered from when she and he had dated. *Interesting,* Tess thought to herself. She scrolled through his timeline and drew in a sharp breath when she saw that all the photos of Antwan and his wife were gone. She quickly opened another browser window to check out his Instagram page, and sure enough, all of the newlyweds' pictures had vanished from that page as well.

"That tricky dick bastard is definitely up to something," she huffed. Now he had made her mad. Tess rose from her desk and paced back and forth in the small space of her writing cave as she fumed. "He knows I'm engaged, so now he's trying to lure me in about needing my help with his investigation."

Tess thought about the fact that Antwan was up to his old tricks again, only this time she didn't know what kind of game he was playing. But one thing she did know for sure was that she was going to teach him a lesson. She knew that Bernadette had advised her not to meet with Antwan in person, but Tess also knew that there were some things that required a face-to-face meeting, and the cursing out that she intended to put on Antwan could only be done by staring straight into his lying, conniving eyes. Tess picked up her phone, and texted Antwan.

Tess: Meet me at The Magnolia Room restaurant at noon

Antwan: I will see you then

Tess shook her head when she saw that Antwan had responded to her message almost as quickly as she had sent it. "I've got a plan for him, all right," Tess mumbled.

Chapter 12

ARIZONA

Tuesday was in a tie with Monday as Arizona's least favorite day of the week, but on this particular Tuesday morning she was beyond overjoyed, and not even the dark clouds hanging in the sky or the heavy rain that had been falling since yesterday could dampen her good mood because Chris was at work. Arizona was glad that her husband would be gone all day and she hoped that just like yesterday, he would work late into the evening.

When Chris and Solomon had arrived back in town Sunday afternoon, she had been happy to see her son, and she'd tried to change her mindset about her husband. Arizona had felt guilty for having the thoughts about Jaquan that had been running through her mind since seeing him the night before. She knew how quickly thoughts could turn into actions, and although she had researched the grounds for annulling a marriage, she wasn't certain that she wanted to remove Chris from her life.

Arizona knew that despite how angry she was with her husband, Chris was a good, decent, and hardworking man. When she had wanted to quit her unfulfilling job in the payroll department at Bourbon General so she could pursue her career passion as a full-time makeup artist, it was Chris who had encouraged her to go for it. He had paid off all her credit cards, taken care of her mortgage and monthly bills, and was still providing for her and Solomon ever since she'd turned in her resignation six months ago. He spent quality time with Solomon and was teaching him the foundational building blocks required to raise a boy into a man. Arizona reasoned that his good points outweighed his bad, and she was going to do her part to work on improving their rapidly declining relationship.

Arizona had listened intently as Solomon told her about all the fun activities that he had enjoyed with his father, from playing a father/son game of dodgeball, to working on puzzles, to bowling, and then worshipping that morning at their sister church, Mt. Olive AME Zion, before returning home. Although Arizona had attempted to engage Chris about how he had enjoyed the Sanctified Warriors event, he'd barely said two words to her since his return, and instead, he had busied himself with the work of unpacking his clothes and then organizing his suit and tie for work the next day.

When dinner time rolled around, Arizona ordered a pizza, and they ate in front of the TV while they watched a Disney movie. She had tried to engage with Chris once again, but he had seemed more interested in talking with Solomon about the cartoon characters than giving her any attention. By the time Arizona helped Solomon with his bath, read him a bedtime story, and then turned out his light, Chris had already retreated to the guest bedroom for the night.

Part of Arizona had been thankful that she didn't have to sleep next to Chris, but another part of her was angry, hurt, and deeply disappointed that after being gone for a day and a half, and then basically ignoring her upon his return, that her husband of just two weeks didn't make the effort to talk about their problems, especially given that he was largely responsible for the thick tension that was standing between them.

That night, when Arizona had settled into her bed, she'd felt a type of loneliness that she had never experienced. Because she was tall, voluptuous, and beautiful, she'd never had a problem attracting men to occupy her time. Even after she had sworn off dating right after Solomon had been born, she'd had her son to fill the void in lieu of a romantic relationship. Then, when Chris had come along, her life had felt complete. But now that she had her husband, her son, a nice home, and a thriving new business, she felt vulnerable and unwanted.

That night as Arizona settled into her empty bed, she allowed her mind to drift from her frustrating troubles with Chris, to the excitement she felt at the very thought of Jaquan. She had wondered if Bernadette had been able to talk to Coop and get the details about Jaquan's presence in The Bottoms, so she dialed Bernadette's number.

"Hi Arizona," Bernadette said with a happy tone in her voice.

"What did Coop say about Jaquan?"

"I'm doing well, and yourself?"

"Oh, I'm sorry Bernadette. I'm so frustrated that I can't think straight." She quickly told Bernadette about how Chris had ignored her all afternoon and was now sleeping down the hall in their guest bedroom.

Bernadette exhaled a deep breath of air. "It sounds like he's pulling away from you on purpose so he can avoid having an honest conversation about your relationship. But honestly, Arizona, he did the same thing months ago when you first learned about his . . . um . . . his situation."

"Yeah, when I found out that he has a tiny dick. He tried to act like nothing was wrong, like everything was just fine."

"Oh boy."

"You can say that again. And now he's at it again, tryin' to avoid the trouble that's starin' us in the face."

"At the rate that you and Chris are going, if you two don't talk or seek some kind of couples counseling, things are going to go from bad to worse before you know it."

"You're right." Arizona turned over and looked at the empty side of the bed where Chris had only slept twice. She was beginning to feel even more frustrated, so she changed the subject to the reason why she had called Bernadette in the first place. "So tell me, what did Coop say about Jaquan?"

"He told me not to get involved in your business."

Arizona smirked. "That sounds just like somethin' a man would say."

"Exactly. But what Coop and most men don't understand is that women have a sisterhood, and we must protect each other. I'm not getting in your business, I'm looking out for your best interest."

"Thank you, Bernadette, and that's exactly how I feel."

"We have to stick together. Now let me tell you what I found out from Coop."

Arizona listened as Bernadette gave her the 411 about Jaquan's reappearance in town. Just as Jaquan had said, he'd been released early, and his sentence had been reduced to time served because his lawyer had presented the court with evidence of witness tampering and conspiracy to commit a cover up by two of the arresting officers who had been revealed to be dirty cops. When Jaquan had gone to prison, he'd had a sizable amount of money in the bank, expensive jewelry, and several luxury vehicles. But his attorney's fees as well as other debts had wiped all his gains away. When he was released two weeks ago he reemerged into a world that had vastly changed over the six years that he had been gone. The only material possessions he had left was a few of his clothes that his mother had still kept.

"Coop said that Jaquan decided to come back to Bourbon because he wanted to distance himself from the people and the life that he used to live in Raleigh," Bernadette said. "He's pretty much starting over from scratch, and the only thing he has are the clothes on his back and an older model Jeep that his Uncle Clem helped him buy when he came to town last week."

"That explains why he's washing dishes and busing tables at Fried Green Tomatoes."

"Yes, and he got that job through the owner's son."

Arizona squinted her eyes in confusion. "That's a high-end place on the white side of town, and excuse me for sayin' it but, how does Jaquan know folks like that?"

"Coop said that the owner's son, Jerry Hammer, served time with Jaquan. Jerry's the typical spoiled and deeply troubled rich kid who likes to walk on the wild side."

"Figures."

"Jaquan had looked out for Jerry while they were in prison, and he even saved Jerry's life during a fight that was so bad that Jaquan ended up having to be sent to the prison health center."

Arizona sat up in bed. "That explains the scar that I saw on his chin last night."

"Maybe so."

A part of Arizona felt sad when she thought about what life must have been like for Jaquan while he had been incarcerated. She'd heard stories about prison life because many of her cousins, uncles, and classmates had lived to tell the tale. But knowing that the father of her child was among that number made Arizona look at things from a different perspective. "So Jerry and Jaquan are buddies?" she asked.

"Apparently, because when Jerry was released, he told Jaquan that he would help him with a job whenever he got out. From what I understand, Jerry's had a few setbacks and he's still trying to get his life together. His father has him washing dishes and busing tables right alongside Jaquan."

Arizona was shocked. "His own father won't give him a hookup? He must be tryin' that tough love method."

"Sometimes you have to."

"I hope Jaquan doesn't go back to that life. He seemed different than I remember, in a good way."

"Actually, Coop spoke well of Jaquan. He saw him at Sue's last week when his Uncle Clem took him there for dinner on his first night in town. Coop said, and I quote, 'The young man seems to have his head on straight, and I think he's gonna be just fine.'"

"That's big coming from Coop. 'Cause I'm sure he remembers how Jaquan used to be when he was living in Bourbon."

All Arizona could do was shake her head at the thought of how time could drastically change things in unforeseen ways. She had once been a wild, reckless, and irresponsible party girl who didn't think beyond her own wants and needs. But now she was a married woman with a child and a thriving new business. Jaquan had once been a popular bad boy who lived the high life and spent hundreds of dollars on a single meal on any given day, and now he was an ex-felon whose goal was to move up from washing dishes to serving people food in the same kind of restaurant that he used to rule.

"Did you tell Coop about Jaquan being Solomon's father?" Arizona asked.

"No, I didn't, because that has yet to be verified."

"You're so technical, but I guess you're right."

"Arizona, you have to be one hundred percent certain about this before you say anything to anyone."

"I know, and that's why you're the only person that I've breathed a word to."

Bernadette let out a long sigh. "Good, and keep it that way until you've had time to really think things through. And whatever you do, don't contact Jaquan until you've had a chance to have a heart to heart with Chris. He deserves to know because you don't want this to blow up in your face."

After Arizona had ended her call with Bernadette, she had thought about Jaquan all night as her husband slept in another room on the other side of the house. She had thought about how her body had tingled when Jaquan hugged her in the restaurant, which had led her to reminisce about how he used to give her sensual pleasure when they had been together back in the day. Jaquan was hands down the best lover that Arizona had ever had. Not only was he well endowed, he knew exactly how to use the nicely packaged tool he'd been blessed with. Arizona smiled to herself because she remembered that Jaquan had taken the time to learn her body and anticipate her needs.

Arizona had known that lying in bed, reminiscing and fantasizing about another man, was a roadmap designed for trouble. "I'm in a sticky situation all the way around," she whispered to herself. She thought about Solomon, who would be confused and emotionally distraught to learn that Chris wasn't his father. She had known that there would come a day when Solomon would learn that Chis was not his biological father, but not now, and not under the current circumstances. She knew that Solomon would be doubly devastated because if things continued as she thought they would, not only would Solomon lose a father, he would lose the family unit that he loved.

Now as Arizona settled back into her house from dropping Solomon off at day camp, she walked into her home office and turned on her ring light and repositioned her camera so she could film her first makeup tutorial to post on her brand-new YouTube channel. This was something that she had been meaning to do for several months but had not gotten around to until now. Arizona's business was doing well, and she was accumulating new clients every day through word-of-mouth referrals. But she knew that once she started producing videos, her business would rise to a whole new level, which would generate new streams of income.

After a few hours of starts and stops, Arizona had successfully filmed her first makeup tutorial. It had been a lot harder than she'd imagined it would be, and she knew that the next hurdle would be the editing phase, but she was excited that she was off to a great start. As she looked in the mirror, she had to admit that she looked gorgeous. She had given herself a made up but natural look, and because she had a pretty face and great skin to begin with, her expert makeup application had taken her good looks through the roof.

"I'm lookin' good with nowhere to go on a rainy, dreary day," Arizona said to herself. Then her mind drifted back to Jaquan. She'd been thinking about him on and off since last Saturday, and had been fighting the urge to call him. "I wonder if his number is the same?" she said to herself. She knew that the only way to find out was to reach out to him and see for herself. She scrolled through her contacts in her phone and located his number. She was about to call, but then she stopped herself. She thought about how irritated she felt at times when people dialed her phone looking for someone else, so she decided to send a text message instead.

She felt as though she had five thumbs as she nervously typed a short message.

Arizona: Is this Jaquan's number?

Arizona didn't realize that she'd been holding her breath until she pressed send, and then finally exhaled. Never in her life had she ever been nervous about anything that involved contact with the opposite sex, regardless of who the man was. But at this moment, she felt as though she could barely control the butterflies in her stomach and the jittery anticipation she felt, wondering if she would hear back from him.

When an hour had passed with no word from Jaquan, Arizona felt slightly dejected and realized that her message had been a waste of time. It was approaching lunch time, so she decided to prepare a quick salad before she started working on the color scheme for an upcoming wedding that she had been hired to style this weekend. She was on her way to the kitchen when her phone chirped, signaling an incoming text message. "This is probably someone telling me that I texted the wrong number," Arizona said aloud and then looked down at her screen. She swiped to open the message and was stopped in her tracks by what she read.

Jaquan: Yes Arizona. It's me. How are you today?

Arizona felt giddy inside and was literally beaming like a schoolgirl who had just been kissed for the first time. She sat at her kitchen table and stared at Jaquan's message. She knew that even though she and Chris were having troubles, she shouldn't be communicating with her ex-lover under any circumstances. But as soon as that thought came into her mind, she pushed it out along with a return message to Jaquan.

Arizona: I'm good and I hope you are. I just thought I would reach out and say hi.

Jaquan: Glad you're well. And yes, I'm good. What are you up to?

Arizona: Nothing much. Just taking a break from a project I'm working on.

Arizona giggled as she waited for Jaquan's next text to come through, but she was caught off guard when instead of a text, her phone rang. He was calling her. Arizona's heart started beating fast. She couldn't avoid his call by pretending to be on another line while they had been messaging because she had just told him that she wasn't doing anything and was taking a break from work. By the third ring she knew that she needed to pick up the phone and deal with what she had just started.

"Hi," Arizona said, sounding out of breath.

"Hey," Jaquan responded in a smooth, sexy voice. "I hope you don't mind that I called. Texting has never really been my thing. Sometimes meanings can get lost in translation."

Arizona nodded as if Jaquan could see that she was agreeing with him through the phone, and then she realized that she needed to give him a verbal response. "Yes, that's true."

"Are you okay with me calling you like this. I know you're a married woman."

One of the things that Arizona had always liked about Jaquan was that he was forthright, even when he was doing dirt. He was the type of man who didn't beat around the bush because as he used to say, "Time is money, and I don't like to waste either." Arizona cleared her throat and said, "Honestly, it's complicated."

"I already figured that out."

"You always were perceptive."

"Arizona, it's kind of obvious. You're a newly married woman who doesn't wear her wedding ring."

"You got me there."

"And you reached out to me in the middle of the day. That means I was on your mind . . . not your husband."

Arizona had to shake her head because she was guilty as charged. She had opened a window of opportunity for Jaquan to slip right on in.

"I can't deny that my marriage is already on shaky ground," she admitted, and then paused because she didn't know what else to say. She was waiting for Jaquan to speak up and piggyback off of what she had just told him. But he remained silent. She knew that by sending Jaquan that text, she had set the wheels of adultery in motion, and now he was waiting for her to explain herself. Arizona was beginning to sweat when finally, he broke the silence.

"Why did you text me, Arizona?" Jaquan asked.

"Like you said, you were on my mind . . ."

"I was just thinking about you."

"What were you thinking?"

Arizona had already begun to sweat and now her heart was racing again. She did not want to tell Jaquan that ever since last Saturday night she had been thinking about how he used to make her cry out with pleasure when they made love, or that she felt a tingling sensation course through her body at the thought of him, or that just this morning she had fantasized about what it would feel like to wake up in his arms. She had a good idea that he most likely knew those things, but she wasn't foolish enough to say them aloud, so she told him a half truth. "I was thinking about my past, and you came to mind."

"Actually, you've been on my mind, too, Arizona. Can you meet me for lunch?"

"Oh, umm . . ."

"Wait . . . you don't have to answer that, and I apologize for even asking," Jaquan quickly said in a softened, gentle tone. "I know that because of your circumstance, any contact with me might put you in a situation that you don't need to be in."

"I appreciate you saying that." Arizona took a deep breath and jumped feet first. "What do you have a taste for?"

A half hour later, Arizona was parking her car at the Magnolia Room. This was the third time in just a few days that she had been in the Palisades, and the second time she'd been at the Magnolia Room. When Jaquan had suggested that they meet there, several thoughts had raced through Arizona's mind. Her first thought had been that The Magnolia Room was a good choice because no one that she knew would be dining at a place where a basic lunch entrée was the price of three meals, and the second thought that occurred to her had been, how was Jaquan going to afford to eat there on a dishwasher's salary. But before her mind could begin to create fanciful stories, Jaquan had told her that his friend's father not only owned Fried Green Tomatoes, he also owned The Magnolia Room, and Jaquan had the hookup to eat at both restaurants for little to nothing.

Arizona opened her umbrella and dashed through the rain, careful not to ruin her perfectly coiffed hair or her expertly applied makeup. Once she was safely inside, she closed her umbrella and began smiling when she saw that Jaquan was already at the hostess stand, waiting for her. She loved the way he was dressed, which was a combination of preppy meets swag. His natural stance looked as if he was striking a pose, with one hand tucked into the front pocket of his slim-fit tan khakis. His white button-down shirt was untucked, complementing his light blue, checkered pattern blazer. Arizona thought the three-peak fold of his solid, light blue pocket handkerchief set off his entire vibe. She knew by the look in Jaquan's eyes, that he was equally impressed when he saw her. She watched as he tried his best to use discretion while he roamed her body from head to toe. She was glad that she had quickly changed into her cream-colored silk blouse that draped the voluptuous curve of her breasts, then slipped on a red pencil skirt that hugged her round hips, tying it all together with a pair of leopard print pointed-toe stilettos that accentuated her long shapely legs.

They greeted each other with hugs that maintained a respectful distance between their bodies. Arizona felt a rush of excitement when she smelled his cologne that lingered from their chaste embrace. When the server asked them their preference of seating, Arizona was glad that Jaquan had told her that they wanted a private area near the back.

Arizona felt as though she was gliding on air as they followed the server to a part of the restaurant that she had not dined in on her previous visits. It was a section that was reserved for discreet power lunches and those engaging in private rendezvous. Arizona smiled and nodded her thanks as Jaquan pulled her chair out for her, and helped her get situated in her seat. She was still all smiles as the server handed her a menu, but in a flash, her bright and cheery smile turned into an expression of sheer surprise when she looked past Jaquan's shoulder and saw a woman who bore a striking resemblance to Tess sitting at a table with a fine-looking specimen of a man who was not Maceo.

Even though the woman's back was facing her, Arizona had no doubt in her mind that it was Tess. The woman's slender shoulders moved back and forth as she spoke and her full head of beautiful brown curls bounced from side to side, apparently giving the poor man whom she was dining with a piece of her mind. Arizona could see from the angle where she was sitting that Tess had even begun to point her finger at her lunch companion. Arizona wondered what was going on, and she hoped that Tess would calm down because if she didn't, she would be forced to leave the restaurant in a repeat of what had happened when she and Bernadette had dined with Tess last weekend.

Arizona watched as Tess grew more and more agitated by the minute, and it made her wonder what her friend was up to, and why was she so upset with the handsome man. She wanted to walk over to their table and ask Tess exactly what was going on, but at the same time she also wanted to disappear from sight because she did not want loud-mouthed Tess to see her with Jaquan.

"Are you okay?" Jaquan asked as he casually glanced over his shoulder to see what had caught Arizona's attention. "Do you know them?"

"Yes," Arizona whispered, not taking her eyes off of Tess. "That woman over there in the floral print shirt is my girlfriend, Tess. I love her to pieces, but she's got a really big mouth, she's loud, and she loves causing a scene. I don't want her to know that I'm here."

"Say no more. I'll ask our server to move us to a different section." Jaquan was about to motion for the server who was headed in their direction, but he stopped when he heard Arizona let out a gasp.

"Oh no," Arizona said with concern when she saw Bernadette and Coop walking toward Tess's table.

Chapter 13

BERNADETTE

Ever since Bernadette had opened her eyes this morning, she'd known that just like the hard rain falling outside, her day would be filled with dark clouds. She'd also known from the moment of her discovery in Coop's office that Morris Fleming's murder would one day lead back to the man she loved. But what she hadn't anticipated was that that day would come so quickly, or that Tess would unknowingly play a part in the truth coming to light.

"Of all the people to get caught up in this, why Tess?" Bernadette mumbled as she thought about the conversation that she'd had with her cousin on her drive to work. When Tess had told her that Antwan was in town investigating a cold case murder, Bernadette had known right away that it had to be Morris Fleming, and when Tess had said that Antwan had made an interesting discovery, and he thought she might be able to help him, the shock of hearing those words had made Bernadette literally feel weak.

Thankfully, Bernadette could tell that Tess was clueless. But she also knew that Antwan was a seasoned journalist with the resources of a powerful news organization behind him, so she was prepared for the fact that things were going to get messy real fast. And what made Bernadette most afraid was that Antwan was about to use an unknowing Tess to lead him directly to Coop.

"Why didn't I just tell Coop about the gun and the papers when I found them?" Bernadette pondered out loud. But she knew exactly why she had kept her mouth shut, and it was because she'd been afraid of the answer that Coop might have given her. It was one thing to think that Coop may have murdered someone, but it was another thing entirely to know that he'd actually done it. And although she had felt sad for Morris's family, especially his grieving parents, their need for closure didn't supersede her love for Coop, or her desire to protect the man she loved.

Bernadette picked up her desk phone and asked her secretary to hold all her calls until after lunch. Even though she had a mountain of work in front of her, she put it aside because she had more important things on her mind than hospital business. Just as Coop always looked out for her, she knew she had to do the same for him, so she logged onto her computer and got busy doing some investigating of her own into Antwan Bolling.

After two hours of Google searches, Bernadette was more worried than ever about what she found. She knew that when Tess had dated Antwan, she'd said that he was good at what he did, but she had made it seem as though he was a merely a seasoned reporter with a cushy job and an A list group of friends in high places. In actuality, that was only half the story. Not only was Antwan one of the most respected investigative journalists in the news business, he specialized in complicated, hard-hitting stories that usually resulted in convictions of the parties in his line of sight, whether they were corporations, countries, or individuals.

Bernadette also learned that last year, Antwan had worked with leaders in the Black Lives Matter movement to highlight the untold stories involving the wrongful deaths of black men and women throughout the country. But the thing that made Bernadette panic was Antwan's new project, which centered on the unsolved murders of black men in the south that spanned decades without any type of arrest, conviction, or justice.

Bernadette sat back in her leather, high-back office chair and exhaled in frustration. Then out of nowhere a thought came to her. While she had been researching Antwan's professional resume, she had neglected to look into his personal life. She quickly typed, *Is Antwan Bolling Married*, into the Google search bar and began scrolling. She was surprised that buried under the seventh page of his search results was the first mention of his marriage. She clicked on a link that took her to the Instagram page of celebrity entertainment columnist Shartell Brown, who had posted about Antwan's marriage to Marie Jett. "She's beautiful," Bernadette said. "I see why Tess was jealous." But when Bernadette tried to find information about their relationship she came up empty-handed, which she found to be very strange.

Bernadette searched both Antwan's and Marie's social media pages and discovered that they both had deleted their pictures of each other from their pages. It was as if they'd never known each other, let alone been married. "That's very odd," Bernadette said aloud. "There's got to be a backstory that those two are hiding." She was sure she could get to the bottom of it if she had more time, but it was quickly approaching lunchtime and she hadn't done an ounce of the work that Bourbon General was paying her a hefty mid six-figure salary to do.

Bernadette sat back in her chair, rubbed her tired eyes and yawned. Thinking about the cold case was enough to exhaust her, and added to that, she faced constant stress from her demanding job. She knew the adverse effect that stress could have on the body, and now that she was pregnant she had to be extra careful. "Lord give me strength," Bernadette said. She was drawn from her thoughts by her ringing cell phone, and Coop's name flashing across her screen. She swiped to the right to answer his call and she smiled when she heard him greet her before she even had a chance to say hello.

"How's the most beautiful woman in the world doin," Coop said.

"You know how to make an old pregnant lady feel good."

"Pregnant, yes, but old?"

"I'm a half century old."

"And fine as wine."

Bernadette couldn't help but smile again. No matter how low she felt, Coop always lifted her spirits. She looked out the window at the rain that was still falling and wished she could wash all her troubles away with each drop. "How's your day going so far?" Bernadette asked.

"Busy as always, but I can't complain because it's all good. I was just thinkin' about you and I wanted to call and let you know how much I love you."

"Oh, Coop. I love you, too."

"I told you, lovin' you is my job. I thought I had a pretty good life before we met, but you showed me what real livin' and genuine love is all about. And now that we're gettin' married and gonna have a family, I thank God for blessing me with more than I deserve."

"You're deserving of so, so much, Coop."

"I guess that makes us even. And as a matter of fact, one of the reasons I was callin' is because I want to take you to lunch today."

"I would love to, but I can't. I've been tied up all morning working on a complicated project," Bernadette said, feeding Coop a half-truth.

"Baby, I hear stress in your voice, and that's the last thing you need right now. Work, projects, and complications will always be there, but it's how we handle them that counts. I admire your drive, I really do, but I value your health even more. So I'm not askin', I'm tellin' you that I'm takin' you to lunch today."

"Okay, Coop." Bernadette nodded and smiled. "You talked me into it because as always, you're exactly right. Where do you want to go?"

"I'm gonna surprise you, and as a matter of fact, I'm almost at your office right now."

"Coop!" Bernadette said with a laugh. "You had this planned all along, and you knew I was going to give in."

"Yep. I'll be there in five minutes."

"Now this is a surprise," Bernadette said to Coop as he steered his black Escalade up to the valet stand at The Magnolia Room.

"I know you like this place, and since you had to cut your dinner short last weekend because of your cousin, I figured we could have a nice, relaxing meal together and break the stress of your day."

Bernadette leaned over and planted a soft kiss on Coop's cheek. "I think I could get used to this."

Coop took Bernadette's hand into his as they walked inside the restaurant. "I haven't been here in a long time," he said, "but from what I can remember, the food is excellent."

"It sure is," Bernadette said with a nod. "And even the bad weather can't keep folks away because this place is packed. I wonder how long we'll have to wait to be seated."

"We won't have to wait."

They approached the hostess stand and was greeted by a pleasant young woman. "Lunch for two?" the hostess asked.

"Yes," Coop said with a nod.

"We have a thirty-minute wait," she responded, and began programming a timed call buzzer.

Coop gave the hostess a smile. "That's not necessary. My name is Coop Dennis, and we'd like to be seated in the private lounge."

The hostess looked a bit startled. "Oh . . . yes sir. Just one moment." The hostess spoke into her headset, mentioned Coop's name, and then listened to the directions being given from her manager on the other end.

"Private lounge?" Bernadette asked as she raised her brow.

A distinguished looking older gentleman who was just as pleasant as the hostess, came up from the back. "Sir, Ma'am," he said as he retrieved two menus, "please follow me."

"Is there nothing that you don't have top access to in this town?" Bernadette teased.

Coop simply winked and smiled.

Bernadette had eaten at The Magnolia Room a few times since she had first dined there six months ago on her birthday, but in all those visits she had never seen the area where the hostess was leading them, which seemed as if it was an extra addition to the already sizeable restaurant. But she could see that this wasn't just an ordinary addition, and to her surprise, the space was actually a bit more elegantly appointed than the regular dining room. She knew that this is what access of the privileged few was like.

"This is a private, quiet area," Coop said. "I think you'll like it."

Bernadette nodded. "I'm sure I will." The stress that she had felt earlier was now a distant memory. Her headache was gone, her shoulders were relaxed, and she felt like a new woman. Not only were there extra plush high back chairs at each table, there was fine drapery adorning the floor to ceiling windows, and flickering candles throughout the secluded space that gave the area an intimate feel.

Bernadette's stomach growled as she thought about the delicious crab cake that she was going to order and the butter pecan pie that she was going to eat for dessert. Just as her mood was brightening, she and Coop turned the corner into the seating area, and she felt as though she'd been hit in the middle of her head with a hammer. She blinked her eyes twice to make sure that she wasn't seeing things, and even though she didn't want to believe it, there was no denying that Tess and Antwan were seated at a table to her far right, tucked away in a corner. And if that surprise wasn't enough, Arizona and a handsome young man who Bernadette could only assume had to be Jaquan were dining only a few tables away.

Bernadette could see both of her friends, but because of the angled position where she and Coop had just been seated, neither Tess nor Arizona could see her. Bernadette's legs felt wobbly as she took her seat. She prayed that Coop hadn't spotted Tess or Arizona, but she knew that as observant as he was about everything, he had not only seen them, he'd already sized up the men they were with and had formulated what might be going on.

Bernadette nearly jumped when their server came to the table, filled their glasses with water, and told them about the lunch specials. He scurried away to bring them a fresh, hot basket of assorted breads and an Arnold Palmer for Coop. Bernadette was so nervous that she could barely remember what she had wanted to eat.

"Do you know what you're gonna order?" Coop asked.

"I'm not sure." Bernadette busied herself by looking at the menu that seemed blurry through her thick fog of worry.

"I know you saw that your girls are over there, didn't you?" Coop said, slow and easy. "I have a good idea about why Arizona's here with Jaquan, but Tess . . ."

Bernadette knew that Coop had said all he was going to say for the moment. She watched Tess, who seemed to be giving Antwan a piece of her mind, judging from her body language. Her head was bobbing back and forth, and she had even pointed her finger at him as though she was chastising a child. Bernadette knew that Tess thrived on chaos and that she enjoyed creating a scene. But now her antics were becoming too much to deal with because the stakes were higher, and people's lives were on the line. Bernadette loved her cousin, but now her foolishness was beginning to bleed into a situation that had the potential to explode.

"Do you know that man who Tess is with?" Coop asked.

"Yes, that's Antwan."

"The guy she used to date?" Coop said, more as a statement than a question.

"Yes, he's her ex."

"Do you know why she's here with him?"

Bernadette knew that she had one of two choices. She could either lie, and say that she had no idea why Tess was with Antwan, or why he was even in town for that matter, or, she could divulge the truth and tell Coop that Antwan had come to Bourbon to investigate the cold case murder of Morris Fleming. Bernadette had already kept the secret from Coop about her discovery in his office, but she didn't want to continue hiding things from him, even if it mean trouble.

Just then their server appeared, carrying a basket of hot-from-the-oven bread and Coop's half sweet tea, half lemonade drink. "Are you ready to order?" the young man asked.

Coop spoke up. "I think we need a little more time."

The server nodded and handed Coop a wine list that he had forgotten to give them when he had seated them at the table. Bernadette watched Coop as he listened to the server who was giving him pairing suggestions to complement the list of lunch entrees. She noticed the intensity in Coop's eyes and the way he seemed to give his full attention to the young man, even though she knew without a doubt that he had his mind fixed on her, Tess, Arizona, and both their lunch dates at the same time.

Bernadette's nerves had been rattled, but strangely, by the time the server walked away, a calm had blanketed her spirit. Right then and there, Bernadette's entire attitude toward everything that was happening took a dramatic shift. *Coop is going to be my husband,* she thought as she looked into the eyes of the man she loved. *I'm going to have his babies. We're going to build a happy life together, and I'm not going to let anything or anyone come in between that. Not Tess, not a murder from long ago . . . not anything,* Bernadette whispered inside her head.

"So, do you know why Tess's ex is here, and why they're havin' lunch together in this private area?" Coop asked again, picking right up where he had left off.

Without hesitation, Bernadette knew what needed to be done. She folded her napkin that had been sitting on her lap, placed it on the table, and rose to her feet with purpose. "Let's go to her table and find out."

Chapter 14

TESS

What had started out as a civil lunch meeting with Antwan had escalated into a heated confrontation in less time than it had taken Tess to call him a lying sonofabitch.

When Antwan had agreed to meet her at The Magnolia Room for lunch, she'd known that she had to be smart about how she was going to deal with her ex-boyfriend. She had been curious about why he thought she would be able to help him with a murder investigation, especially given that it was a cold case, in a town with which she was largely unfamiliar. But aside from that, she had actually become more curious about why he and his wife had both deleted their pictures from their social media accounts.

After she had texted Antwan about meeting her for lunch, Tess had gone back to her computer and made a beeline to his wife's Instagram page. Tess realized something right away that she hadn't noticed the first time that she'd looked at the brown beauty's profile picture. Right under her stunning photo, Marie's name had changed from Marie Jett Bolling, back to Marie Jett. "This is crazy," Tess said. She wished that she had remained on speaking terms with a least a few of her and Antwan's mutual friends because if she had, she would've called them and gotten to the bottom of the mystery.

But there was one thing that Tess knew for sure, and that was that Antwan was not the monogamous type, and even though he had been able to corral his wandering eye and appetite for women long enough to get married, he had probably broken his vows shortly after saying 'I Do' which would explain the reason why the once happy couple were apparently split.

Even though Tess had no interest in rekindling any type of relationship with Antwan, she still wanted to look good when she saw him, and she planned to give him an eyeful of just what he was missing. She had put extra time and attention into applying her warm honey foundation, and she had even painted her mouth with a soft berry, matte cream lipstick that gave her a sexy pout. She used her eyeliner pen to draw the perfect cat-eye, and then accented her already long lashes with a mink strip that gave her a sultry vibe. She raked mousse through her thick mane of curls, bent her head forward, and shook from side to side until her hair bounced with volume. She completed her look with a vibrant, floral print shirt that highlighted her perky breasts without showing too much cleavage, and then slipped on a tight, knit miniskirt that showcased her long, well-toned legs.

When Tess had looked at herself in the mirror, she had given herself a fist pump along with two thumbs up because that was how good she looked. She was already a pretty woman, but now she looked just as good as any model in a magazine. "Eat your heart out, Marie Jett," Tess had said to herself. She fished through the closet until she found the accessory that she had known would seal the deal on her gorgeous look. "Perfect," she had said with a smile as she slipped on a pair of super sexy, strappy three-inch heeled sandals. "I'm gonna blow Antwan's mind and dash his hopes, all at the same time."

Tess had known from experience during the two years that she and Antwan had dated that he always arrived early for everything, so she had made sure that she pulled up to the valet stand ten minutes before their scheduled lunch date. But when she had walked inside,

Antwan had already been sitting in a chair in the lobby. It had been a year and a half since the last time that Tess had seen Antwan in person, and she hadn't been prepared for how his presence was going to affect her. She'd known from the photos that she had seen on social media that he had maintained his fit physique, handsome face, and piercing hazel-colored eyes, but when he stood to greet her, she unexpectantly felt the same rush of attraction and excitement that had drawn her to him the first time they had met.

Tess had been confused by the strange mixture of emotions that had flooded her body. Agitation and anger were emotions that she had prepared herself to feel, so she'd been caught completely off guard when she had the urge to hug Antwan and hold him close to her body. She had mentally scolded herself. *Come on, get it together and deal with this asshole like the lyin', cheating bastard that he is.*

As Tess had approached Antwan, she could tell that he was checking her out from head to toe, and more than that, she could tell that he liked what he saw. This wasn't the way she had wanted things to unfold, and her mind fell on Maceo. He had made her a fresh pot of Colombian roast coffee before he had left the house this morning, and he had told her to be prepared for some good food tonight. *I know that Maceo is honest and good to his core, so why in the hell am I having this reaction to Antwan?* Tess had asked herself.

When Antwan reached to hug her, Tess had summoned the strength and good sense to extend her hand instead. She gave him a firm shake, but when she had felt the warmth of his palm, no matter how hard she'd tried to fight and deny it, her body tingled from his touch.

Antwan gave her a sly smile. "It's good to see you, Tess. It's been a long time," he said, letting his hand linger against Tess's for much longer than was appropriate or safe.

Tess withdrew her hand. "Is there a wait?" she asked the hostess as she ignored Antwan's comment.

The hostess looked at them with caution plastered across her face. "No ma'am. The gentleman requested seating in our private lounge upon your arrival, and now that you're here I can seat you to-gether."

After following the assistant hostess, Tess and Antwan were seated in a private area that was tucked away from the rest of the restaurant. Tess made a mental note that she was going to request to be seated here from this point forward because of its cozy intimacy that carried an air of exclusivity. She liked that unlike the main din-ing room that had begun to fill with a robust lunch crowd, the pri-vate lounge was just that—private, and more importantly, it was discreet. The few smattering of customers who were seated in the area did not even look in her and Antwan's direction when they had walked by.

Tess tried to busy herself by looking at the lunch menu that she had already memorized last Friday.

"You made a great choice selecting this place," Antwan said. "I can tell the food is going to be excellent."

"Yes, the food is very good," Tess responded without accepting his compliment. "By the way, how did you know to ask to be seated here?"

"When I arrived, I asked to speak to the general manager, and I told him that I was here for an important meeting that required a cer-tain level of privacy. You know how these types of exclusive places work," Antwan said as he leaned in close, "they always have areas like this."

"No, I didn't know that because when I go to restaurants my main purpose is to eat, not conduct private meetings."

Antwan nodded. "Okay . . . let's start over. It's good to see you, Tess. How've you been?"

Just then their server came to take their drink order. Tess had wanted to order a glass of wine or something stronger to settle her nerves, but she decided on water instead. She watched Antwan as he flashed his sexy smile and ordered a bottle of Chardonnay for their table, along with an order of calamari for starters. It was Tess's fa-

vorite wine and appetizer, and she knew he had made the gesture as
a peace offering.

Now, as they sat across from each other, Tess's mind raced between getting right to the point of their meeting so she could find
out what in the world kind of connection she could possibly have to
a cold case murder in Bourbon, and finding out why he and his wife
had deleted each other's pictures from their social media accounts.

"I meant what I said. It's good to see you, Tess."

She smirked. "Uh, huh."

"I wouldn't say it if I didn't mean it."

"From what I remember, you say a whole lot of things that you
don't mean."

Antwan nodded. "I deserve that, and you're right. From what
you remember, I did. I made a lot of mistakes, Tess, and before we
go any further in this conversation I want to apologize and ask for
your forgiveness."

Tess leaned back in her chair and studied Antwan's eyes. She
knew that he had the ability to lie with a straight face, so she wasn't
impressed by the steadiness in his eyes. "What exactly are you apologizing for?" she asked.

"The way I treated you."

"Antwan, you're a very intelligent man, and I know that your
cognitive skills are sharp, so I'm going to ask you again . . . what *exactly* are you apologizing for?"

"For lying to you. For cheating on you. For taking you for
granted. And for all the hurt that I caused you. I did things that I'm
ashamed of, Tess, and I don't blame you for still carrying some level
of resentment toward me, and honestly, I didn't think you would actually agree to meet with me, but I'm grateful that you did."

"How do you know that I didn't agree to this little meeting just
so I could lure you out here and set you up?"

Antwan squinted his eyes. "What do you mean?"

"All I gotta say is, watch your back when you leave," she said and then paused. "The south is gun country, and you never know who's lurking in the weeds, ready for a kill."

Just then the server set their wine and appetizer on the table. "Are you ready to order your entrees?" the server asked.

Antwan tried to compose himself. "We need a little more time."

Tess stared Antwan square in the eyes as their server walked away, and she could see that he was actually a bit frightened, which made her feel an eerie combination of satisfaction and confusion. She had never known Antwan to be the type who flinched at anything, let alone a veiled threat that she might make. He was used to being in the crosshairs of danger, given the nature of his work, and added to that, when they had dated there were many times when she had cursed him out and threatened him with bodily harm. He had always brushed off her antics, never fully taking her seriously. But this was different, and Tess could see that Antwan had tensed up, so she waited for their server to retreat before she spoke again.

"Relax, I was joking," Tess said.

"I'm a black man, and whether I'm in the south or any other part of this country, what you just said is a very real possibility. Trayvon Martin, Michael Brown, Walter Scott, George Floyd, Breonna Taylor, Ahmaud Arbery, and the list goes on and on, filled with black men, women, and even children, who never saw their deaths coming. Shit is real, Tess. I'm here investigating the murder of a young, unarmed black man who was shot in cold blood right here in this town, thirty-five years ago, and that same type of madness is still happening today. What you said wasn't funny . . . at all."

Tess realized the danger and insensitivity of her ill-intentioned joke, and she could see that she had gotten under Antwan's skin. "I know all too well about the injustice in this country, and what both men and women of color are up against, so for that, I'm sorry for what I said."

"Thank you."

"But trust and believe, there've been times that I wanted to kill you myself, with my bare hands."

Antwan took a sip of his wine. "I believe you because the way you destroyed my house, not to mention cutting up all my clothes, I was lucky to walk away with my life."

Tess remembered how she had snuck into Antwan's house after catching him cheating on her for the last time that she was going to put up with. She had cut his clothes and towels in half, snipping one leg off of every pair of pants, one sleeve off of every shirt, and all his towels and wash clothes straight down the middle, before moving on to trash each neatly decorated room in his well-kept home. And for her coup de grace, she had taken as much of his expensive wine as she could fit into a canvas bag before she had shut the door behind her. "You deserved every bit of it," Tess said. She could feel her emotions beginning to bubble up, so she took a deep breath and tried to calm herself.

"Yes, you're right. Like I said, I did you wrong and I know that now. I wish I could go back and change things, because trust me, if I could, I most definitely would."

Tess knew this was her opening, so she asked the question that had been eating at her. "What's up with your marriage?"

Antwan shook his head from side to side and said, "I'm not married."

Tess rolled her eyes. "You know what, I should've known you were still full of shit. Just be honest for once in your sorry, low down, muthafuckin' life."

"Tess . . ."

"Unlike you, I'm not gonna sit here and play silly ass mind games."

"Tess, listen to me. I'm telling you the truth, and I'm not playing games with you. I'm not married."

Tess could see that she had Antwan on the ropes because of the nervous look on his face, and the fact that he was looking around, as if to shield their conversation from prying ears. But she didn't care who heard what she had to say, so she poured a glass of wine and took a large gulp to give her the boldness to speak what she was about to say next. "I'm not ashamed to admit that I've looked at your social media pages, as well as hers, and I know that your wife is an ex-model turned makeup artist, and you married the bitch on my birthday. That's right, I saw all those lovey-dovey honeymoon pictures that you two took. So if you're on the outs with her, or you just want a quick lay while you're in town, just say so, but don't sit here and lie, because there's no need to anymore."

"Tess, I'm not lying. I'm not married because I got the marriage annulled."

For the first time since she and Antwan had been seated at the table, Tess fell silent, partly because of what Antwan had just said, but also because she saw Bernadette and Coop walking her way.

If there was a photo next to the phrase, piss your pants, Tess's face would be prominently displayed. She hadn't expected to see Bernadette and Coop at The Magnolia Room during the middle of the day, given their hectic schedules. The sight of the two made so many competing thoughts race through Tess's mind that she couldn't speak.

On one hand, Antwan had just told her that his marriage was over, and miraculously, for the first time since Tess had known him, she was one hundred percent certain that he was telling the truth. But on the other hand, Bernadette's disapproving eyes were threatening to cut her like a knife for doing the very thing that her wise cousin had warned her against, which was being foolish enough to get caught in a compromising situation, in public, with her ex-boyfriend. But Tess's most troubling predicament that rendered her frozen in place was the fact that Coop's eyes were firmly planted on Antwan, and she was sure that whatever their exchange was going to be, Coop would be calling Maceo quicker than she could say, relationship over.

I bet Coop asked Bernadette, "Who's that man with Tess?" Tess thought to herself. And she knew that Bernadette, not wanting to tell a lie, had probably told Coop that Antwan was her ex. *Damn!* she thought. Tess knew that because of the way she had been acting, that it looked as if she and Antwan were having a lovers' quarrel. *I should've just kept my cool, or better yet, I should've listened to Bernadette and never met with this asshole to begin with.* For the first time in her life, Tess didn't want to make a scene and she wished she could quietly walk away without fanfare. But she knew without a doubt that it was too late for that.

"Hello Tess," Bernadette said. She cut her eyes toward Antwan but did not speak. "We thought we would come over and say hi."

Tess stood to her feet. "Hey Bernadette," she said with a nervous smile. She reached for her cousin and gave Bernadette a quick hug before doing the same with Coop. They shared a silent, awkward moment between the three of them. Tess wasn't sure what she should say next, and to her discomfort, and without warning, Antwan rose to his feet and inserted himself into the middle of an already sticky situation.

"Bernadette, it's good to see you," Antwan said with a smile, darting his eyes between Bernadette to Coop. "Tess and I were catching up over lunch. Would you and your guest like to join us?"

Tess shot Antwan a nasty look. "You do the damn most, you know that?"

"I'm simply being cordial, and there's nothing wrong with that," Antwan shot back.

"Didn't you just hear Bernadette say that they only came over to say hi," Tess hissed through clenched teeth. "She didn't say one word about joining us."

Coop spoke up. "I'm Cooper Dennis, Bernadette's fiancé." Coop stepped forward and extended his hand to Antwan.

Tess watched as the two men shook hands, and she knew that even though Coop's poker face gave no indication of what he was thinking, he was sizing up Antwan, and she could tell by the look on her ex's face that he was slightly unnerved. Tess glanced down at Coop's baseball mitt-size hands that were in a forceful grip with Antwan's, and her own palms began to sweat from the sheer tension.

"Nice to meet you, Mr. Dennis," Antwan said.

"Most folks around here call me Coop."

Antwan nodded. "Coop and Bernadette, the offer still stands. Would you like to join us?"

"Did you not hear what I just said?" Tess said in a slightly raised voice.

Bernadette cut in and looked Antwan directly in the eye. "What brings you to town?"

"I'm working on a story involving a cold case murder," Antwan answered. He folded his arms across his chest, cleared his throat, and looked at Coop. "You're the owner of Southern Comfort, right?"

Tess's eyes grew big with surprise. "How did you know that?"

Antwan smiled at Tess. "I'm an investigative reporter, it's my job to know all the major players in town when I'm working a story. Coop is a pillar of the community," he said, and then directed his attention back to Coop. "Coop, I'm sure you can be a big help to me with the story."

Tess put her hand on her hip and stared daggers at Antwan. "Wait a minute, that's the same bullshit that you told me, and it's the only reason why I agreed to meet with you," she said, throwing in that bit of information to let Coop know that her involvement with Antwan was strictly business and nothing more.

"How do you think I can help you?" Coop asked in his deep, smooth voice.

"Are you familiar with Morris Fleming?"

"I am," Bernadette interrupted. "I saw a clip about his unsolved murder on the local news last weekend."

Coop looked at Bernadette and then toward Antwan. "Yes, I'm familiar with Morris Fleming. That must've been, what . . . thirty plus years ago."

"Thirty-six, to be exact," Antwan said.

Coop nodded. "He was killed in an area of The Bottoms that we call Frog Pond," he said as he glanced at Bernadette before directing his attention back to Antwan. "He was from up north, but he found his way down here and ended up dead."

Antwan nodded. "That's right. It was a very personal crime because Mr. Fleming was shot straight through the heart. One clean shot," he said with a shake of his head. "I would love to sit down and talk with you about it, if you have time."

Coop reached into his charcoal gray blazer, pulled out a small gold case and handed Antwan his business card. "How long you gonna be in town?"

"As long as it takes to find out what I need know. Could be a week," he said, then turned his attention to Tess, "could be a month."

"Why the hell are you looking at me? I don't want you here right now in the present," Tess said with hostility.

Coop raised his brow and slid a smile across his lips. "Call me and we'll set somethin' up. You two enjoy your lunch."

Coop motioned for Bernadette so they could return to their table, but she stood in place with her eyes locked on something beyond Tess's shoulder. When Tess followed the direction that Bernadette was staring, she was shocked to see Arizona sitting at a table with a handsome man. *Who is he and why is Arizona here with him?* Tess wondered.

Tess and Bernadette exchanged a worried glance between them. Tess could tell that Arizona had seen them too, but she was trying hard to pretend as though she had not. *Oh, Lord, this can't be good,* Tess thought. She knew that Arizona only came on this side of town to visit Bernadette, and that her wallet couldn't afford her the luxury of having a casual lunch at the most expensive restaurant in town. And the fact that not only was Arizona here, but that she was dining in the private lounge made Tess wonder even more. She watched as Arizona nervously moved her salad leaves around on her plate, and kept her eyes focused on the man she was dining with.

I have to say, Arizona knows how to pick them when it comes to looks because he's fine and sexy as hell, Tess thought.

Tess wasn't the least bit surprised that Arizona was already on the hunt for someone who could scratch her itch, and she couldn't wait to call her friend later tonight to get the details. But then a thought occurred to her. Just as Coop was likely thinking that she was up to something with Antwan, Arizona probably did as well. The fact that she had been spotted by Bernadette and Coop, and now Arizona as well, made Tess's head throb, and once again, she wished she had listened to her cousin and had never met Antwan for lunch. When she thought about the fact that Antwan had lured her there under the false pretense of telling her that she could help him with the cold case, Tess wondered what Antwan was really up to. *I need to get rid of Bernadette and Coop so I can deal with Antwan's lyin' ass.*

"I'll call you later, Bernadette," Tess said. She hugged Bernadette and Coop goodbye, and then returned to her seat.

Tess watched Antwan as his eyes followed Bernadette and Coop all the way back to their table. She was so pissed that she could barely control her anger, but she knew that she had to. She took another long sip of her wine, and then looked into Antwan's eyes. "Okay, asshole. Tell me the truth about why you asked me to lunch?"

Chapter 15

ARIZONA

If Arizona could have sunk into a hole and buried herself inside, she would have. She tried her best to avoid the glaring eyes of Bernadette and Tess by concentrating on her food as well as on Jaquan.

"They see me," Arizona said through the side of her mouth, trying to act inconspicuous.

Jaquan kept his eyes on hers. "Do you think they're gonna come over and say hi?"

"No, I don't think so. As a matter of fact, it looks like Bernadette and Coop are about to leave."

"Coop, now he's the truth. He's a good man."

"Yes, he is. Coop's always been a good guy, always helping folks."

"Yes, and I'm one of them. I owe him."

"What did you say?" Arizona asked, half-listening to Jaquan and half-watching Tess continue to bicker with Antwan.

"I owe him," Jaquan repeated. "Coop is a big part of the reason why I'm the man that I've grown into today." He stopped and then shook his head. "I should probably keep my mouth shut."

Arizona was now fully engaged in what Jaquan was saying. "No you shouldn't. Tell me what you're talking about."

"Coop's private, and he might not want me telling his business."

"He probably won't mind, especially if it's something good. Besides, you're not telling his business to a stranger who's gonna spread it across town. You know me, and so does Coop. Plus my girlfriend who's here with him is his fiancée."

"Fiancée?"

"I know, right? Coop turned in his player card the minute he laid eyes on Bernadette."

"She must be a real one."

Arizona nodded. "Yes, she is. Bernadette is a great person, and she's been a mentor to me. She gives me sound advice and she's one of the few people that I can trust without question."

"That's ironic. I think the same thing about Coop."

"So then tell me. Why do you owe him?"

"Back in the day after I moved here from Raleigh, I got to know the lay of the land and I started moving product in The Bottoms. One night, Coop approached me and told me to stop. I knew his reputation, and I wasn't going to cross him. So, since I couldn't do my thing here, I started living between here and Raleigh."

"I'm confused for a couple reasons," Arizona said with a puzzled look. "I know how wild and crazy you were back then, and even though Coop rules The Bottoms, I'm surprised that you left that easy."

"Coop told me that either I take my hustle somewhere else, or I would be taken out of The Bottoms in a box."

Arizona put her fork down and leaned in close to Jaquan. "Coop threatened to kill you?"

"People threaten when they want to communicate their intentions for you to do, or not do something. Coop isn't the type of man who threatens. He takes action," Jaquan said with a serious voice. "Like I said, I knew from his reputation, and from what my Uncle Clem had told me, that Coop was only going to tell me once, and if I kept dealing in The Bottoms, my mom was going to be planning my funeral."

"Now I'm more confused than ever," Arizona said. "Why do you owe him for that? The way I see, if you hadn't gone back to Raleigh, you would've stayed away from that life, and you probably wouldn't have spent the last six years of your life in prison."

"Whether I went to Raleigh or any other city, I would've ended up in prison because I wasn't ready to give up the streets and the fast life. But here's the part of my story where Coop really comes in, and why I owe him."

Arizona blocked out all other sounds except Jaquan's voice, as he told her a story that gave her greater insight into who Coop was. Jaquan had still been dealing drugs in prison, when three years ago he had gotten into a bad fight. Jaquan had vouched for one of his friends who was serving time as well. He was a rich white boy whom Jaquan had known when he had briefly attended Bourbon High School. Jaquan's friend had been high on meth when he had mistakenly crossed the wrong clique of inmates. Jaquan took up for his friend and ended up on the receiving end of fists, feet, and a makeshift knife that nearly took his life.

Coop had heard how badly Jaquan had been beaten, and he had come to see him after he'd been released from the prison infirmary. During Coop's visit, he had told Jaquan things that had changed his life and set him on the path to being a truthful, hardworking man, and he vowed to never again bring harm to his community.

Arizona knew from what Bernadette had told her last weekend that Jaquan's rich friend had to be Jerry Hammer, but what she didn't know was how could Coop have possibly known about Jaquan's fight, so she asked. "How did Coop know about what had happened to you in prison?"

Jaquan moved the plate of half-eaten grilled salmon that he wasn't going to finish to the side, and continued his story. "Not many people know this, but Coop travels to prisons in the state, mentoring inmates. That's how he found out what had happened to me, and he remembered me from the night he confronted me in The Bottoms. Coop sent me money for textbooks to help me complete my degree, as well as books about black empowerment and entrepreneurship. I told him that when I got out, I wouldn't disappoint him, and I wouldn't be looking for a handout. I'm going to make it on my own."

Arizona shook her head. "So you'd rather wash dishes at Fried Green Tomatoes than work at Southern Comfort, or one of Coop's other businesses?"

Jaquan smiled and nodded. "I understand how that might seem crazy, but I know what I've got to do. Plus, Coop's already done a lot for me. I wouldn't be driving that Jeep out there if it wasn't for him. He knew that I needed transportation to and from work, so he made sure that I had a ride waiting for me at my Uncle Clem's, when I got to town two weeks ago."

Arizona had known that Coop was kind-hearted and generous, and that he did a lot for the community. Over the years, her relatives and friends who had been incarcerated had told her that he contributed to non-profits that helped reduce the recidivism rate and helped ex-offenders with their reentry to society. But she had no idea about the extent of his personal involvement.

"I know I don't have to say this," Jaquan said, "but this conversation is between you and me, and no one else, not even your girl, Bernadette."

"Of course," Arizona said as she nodded her head. But as she looked into Jaquan's eyes, something about the way he stared at her would not allow her to tell him a lie. "I have to be honest," she said. "I'm probably gonna tell Bernadette, 'cause like you said, she's my girl."

"That's one of the things that I've always liked about you, A," Jaquan said, calling Arizona by the pet name that he had used when they had dated. "You keep it one hundred."

Arizona felt a warm and tingling feeling inside. She knew that things between her and Jaquan were starting to heat up, so she tried to train her focus on Tess and her lunch date, who looked as though they were getting ready to leave. Their argument must have smoothed over because Tess's body language had calmed down. Arizona sipped

her sweet iced tea and watched as Tess and her lunch date got up
from their table and walked out.

"What're you thinking about?" Jaquan asked.

"Just watching Tess and her lunch date. They're leaving."

"I guess you can relax now."

Arizona batted her eyelashes and smiled. "I won't lie, I'm a little
nervous because . . ."

"Your husband."

If Arizona had been fooling herself before, she wasn't now, because she knew that she was definitely approaching dangerous territory with Jaquan. It was one thing to have lunch with him, and even
flirt a little, but it was another thing entirely to venture into the
strained state of her and Chris's dysfunctional marriage. Even though
she knew that Jaquan was already aware that things between her and
Chris weren't right, given the very fact that she was sitting in the
restaurant with him in the first place, a part of her was reluctant to
open up and let him in.

When their server came to clear away their plates, Arizona knew
that she should leave and walk away from certain danger, but Jaquan
ordered apple pie a la mode for dessert, and asked their server to
bring two spoons.

"You still haven't answered my question," Jaquan said.

Arizona shifted in her seat. Jaquan's piercing eyes and full, soft-
looking lips were drawing her closer and closer to him. She wanted
to look away, and just when she thought she needed to throw in the
towel, their server came back with their dessert.

Jaquan practically licked his lips. "This looks good."

"I certainly don't need any of this, but you're right, it does look
good." Arizona dipped her spoon into the sweet treat and when she
put it into her mouth, she closed her eyes and hummed to herself,
"It's delicious." She opened her eyes and saw Jaquan staring intently,
with an expression that was between a smile and a question.

"Seeing you smile and enjoy yourself brings back old times,"
Jaquan said.

"We had some good ones."

"Yes, we did."

Arizona and Jaquan reminisced down memory lane, and to her relief and surprise, he did not try to press her further about her marriage, and he kept their conversation light, bordering just on the edge of flirtation. When the check came, Arizona didn't want to leave but she knew that she needed to because she had a video that needed to be edited, a child to pick up from summer camp, and dinner to cook.

By the time they walked outside the sun had replaced the rain, and had brought a hot mugginess that made Arizona's fresh, silk press hairdo begin to puff up under the stifling humidity. As she and Jaquan walked in step beside each other, Arizona wished that she had parked even farther away than she had because she didn't want her time with Jaquan to come to an end.

"I really enjoyed talking with you, A," Jaquan said. "You don't mind if I call you that, do you?"

"No, I don't mind."

"Good, because I don't want to make you any more uncomfortable than you already are."

"What makes you think I'm uncomfortable."

"You've got to be. You're a newly married woman who's out with her ex, and, we still have feelings for each other. That's enough to make anyone uncomfortable."

Arizona could have tried to deny what Jaquan had said, but she knew that it would be a lost cause. He'd said that he liked that she had always been honest, and she could say the same about him. So instead of beating around the bush, she confronted it head on. "A part of me feels uncomfortable because you're right. I'm a married woman, and being here with you definitely presents a problem. But I also have to admit that there's another part of me that feels free because it's easy to be with you."

"Can I ask you a question?"

"Sure."

"Why did you marry your husband?"

Arizona figured that Jaquan would be curious about why after just two weeks of marriage, she would already be walking toward the tipping point of adultery. And just like everything else, she decided to tell him the truth. "He's good to me, and my son. He's a very responsible, hardworking, and giving man. He encouraged and supported me with starting my business, and even though he's not Solomon's biological father, he stepped in and treats him no different than if his DNA was running through Solomon's veins."

Jaquan was listening intently and had nodded his approval. "Your husband sounds like a good man, and those are admirable reasons to marry someone."

"But? . . ." Arizona said. "I know you're thinking something."

"I am."

"Well, say it. You know I have thick skin and you won't hurt my feelings."

They had reached Arizona's SUV, and she clicked her key fob to unlock her vehicle. She moved to the side as Jaquan, being a gentleman, opened her door for her. Instead of stepping inside, Arizona and Jaquan stood in the middle of her open driver's side door, as he thought about his answer.

"Admirable means deserving of respect, and according to what you said about your husband, he's earned that, and it's why I made that statement. But of all those great qualities that you named, you didn't say the one that's going to keep your marriage solid, and that's love. You didn't say that you married him because you love him."

Arizona sighed. "Jaquan, that's a given. I wouldn't have married him if I didn't love him."

"I'll rephrase it. Are you in love with him?"

Arizona was suddenly unsure of what to say. There had been a time when she'd been madly in love with Chris. But from the moment they'd promised to love each other until death did they part, the only emotions she'd felt toward him were anger, frustration, and resentment. And if she were being completely honest with herself, she knew that in the months leading up to their wedding, she'd had signs that this would happen. So she answered as truthfully as she knew how. "I don't know."

"I get it . . . love can be complicated. But A, this doesn't make sense to me."

"You're right. It's complicated," she said, trying to avoid the truth.

"Maybe I'm missing something," Jaquan said. "If your husband's done all the things that you said he's done, and you're still not sure if you're in love with him. He's not giving you something that you need."

The heat outside was nothing compared to the roasting that Arizona felt between her legs when Jaquan said the words, "something that you need." She knew that he had always known exactly what she needed and how she wanted it. Arizona had to look away to avoid asking him to meet her later tonight.

"I thought about you while I was away," Jaquan said.

"You did?" Arizona's voice lowered to a whisper.

"Yes, and I wondered how you were doing, and if you had changed. Were you that same ride or die chick who was down for whatever, or did you flip and become someone different."

"Now that you see me, what do you think?"

"You're still fine as hell and that ain't never gonna change," he said with a wink, "and you're still blunt with your words. But you're also a lot different in some ways. Good ways," he said with a smile. "You're focused, stable, level-headed, and calm. That's a big change from the way you used to be, and I like it."

"Thank you," Arizona smiled back at him. "You've changed a lot, too, and I don't mean the fact that you're a dishwasher." Arizona put her hand to her mouth. "I guess that's my bluntness that you were talking about."

"Yes, A, that's what I was talking about."

"Anyway," Arizona continued. "You're humble and very grounded, and I can tell that you're on the straight and narrow for real. You know, it's got me to thinking, what did Coop say to you that made you change?"

Jaquan smiled. "That's something that'll always stay between Coop and me, but what I can tell you is that what he said to me was said to him by an old man on his deathbed, who he'd served time with, and Coop passed it on to me," Jaquan paused for a second and looked directly into Arizona's eyes. "One day I hope to pass those words along to my son."

Arizona's heart began to beat fast. "Yes, I hope you do."

"When can I meet Solomon?" Jaquan asked.

Chapter 16

BERNADETTE

After Bernadette and Coop had left The Magnolia Room, it had been clear that there was a lot that they needed to discuss. So rather than go back to work and sit behind a desk where she knew her mind would not be able to focus, Bernadette called her secretary and told her that she wouldn't be back in the office the rest of the day. Coop dropped her off to pick up her car and they both headed over to her house.

An hour later, Bernadette was lounging in her comfy Kenta-print caftan as she and Coop sat close to each other on her large sectional and prepared themselves for a serious conversation. Bernadette wasn't quite sure if she should start with Tess and Antwan, Arizona and Jaquan, or the cold case murder and the fact that she knew that Coop had the gun that had been used to kill Morris Fleming in his possession.

"I know you've got a lot on your mind," Coop said, "so I'll start."

Bernadette nodded in agreement. "Okay."

"I'm gonna have a conversation with Maceo tonight, and I'mma let him know that we saw Tess and her ex havin' lunch."

Bernadette tilted her head in confusion. "Wait a minute. The other night when I was asking about Jaquan for Arizona, you told me to mind my own business, but now you're inserting yourself into Tess and Maceo's relationship."

"Baby, that's totally different."

"How?"

"Because Arizona and Chris are married, and married folks' business is a lot more complicated than single folks. Tess and Maceo don't even have a confirmed wedding date, and they're just now gettin' back on speakin' terms."

"I understand what you're saying. But at least give Tess the opportunity to talk to Maceo first, that is, if she already hasn't."

Coop ran his hand over his closely cropped, curly, black-and-silver hair and let out a sigh. "Just like Tess is more of a sister to you than a cousin, Maceo is more like a son to me than a nephew. After I got outta prison I helped my sister raise him, God rest her soul. I promised Sue that I'd look out for him, and that's what I'm gonna do. So whether Tess tells him now, tonight, or tomorrow, I'm gonna ask him to come by my house tonight so he and I can talk."

Bernadette rubbed Coop's shoulder because she could see that his body was tense. She'd come to learn that the only thing that could move Coop to anger or frustration, was if he thought that his loved ones might be in emotional or physical danger. Bernadette remembered when Coop had told her how hurt Maceo had been by his cheating ex-wife, and that his nephew had been crushed even further when he'd found out that he wasn't his daughter's biological father, and that the little girl whom he'd helped to raise had been the result of one of his ex-wife's numerous affairs.

Bernadette knew that Coop wanted to protect Maceo from further hurt, and if that meant stepping in the middle of his and Tess's relationship, that was what he was going to do. "Coop, I know that you're not a big Tess fan, and she gets on my nerves at times, too, but I believe that she loves Maceo."

"Bernie, you know this don't have nothin' to do with whether or not I like Tess, this is about me lookin' out for Maceo, and makin' sure that as a man, he knows what's up."

"I'll be honest with you, Tess called me this morning and told me that Antwan had contacted her because he was in town working on a story, and he wanted to meet with her."

"Hmmm," Coop said, mulling over Bernadette's words.

"I told her point blank that she should only talk to him by phone, and that she shouldn't meet with him face-to-face. But you know how stubborn Tess is. That's why I was so shocked when we saw her today."

"She's stubborn, but maybe she's also not over Antwan." Coop leaned against the soft cushions and draped his arm across the back of the couch. "I want to ask you about somethin'."

"Okay." Bernadette held her breath, nervous about what Coop might ask.

"When Antwan said that he wanted to talk with me about the cold case, Tess said that was the reason why she was meetin' with him, because he told her that she could help him with it. Tess ain't been in town but a hot minute, and she barely knows anyone. Do you know why Antwan would think she could help him?"

Bernadette bit her bottom lip and exhaled. "Yes, I think I do."

"Okay, please tell me."

"Even though Tess only posted pictures of her engagement ring and no photos of her and Maceo, Antwan, being the investigative reporter that he is, was obviously able to find out who her fiancé is."

Coop stared into Bernadette's eyes. "You know that Maceo is Morris's son, don't you?"

Bernadette felt her heart beating a mile a minute. "Oh, Coop. I'm so sorry. I should've told you before now." Bernadette put her head in her hands and burst into tears.

Coop pulled Bernadette into his arms and rocked her back and forth in a soothing motion. "Sshhh, it's all right, Baby. Breathe."

Bernadette did as he said and took deep breaths to regain her composure. "Last month when I was helping you clean out your office, I stumbled across the small gray box in the hidden compartment at the bottom of your cabinet."

Bernadette went on to tell Coop, in specific detail, about the contents she had discovered, as if Coop didn't already have knowledge of what that box contained. She wanted to suspend reality and naïvely believe that Coop would be shocked and would declare that someone must have planted the evidence to frame him because he didn't know what she was talking about. But when she looked into his steady eyes, they were fixed on hers with a definite sense of knowing. Bernadette wiped the last of her tears on the back of her hand and pulled away from Coop. "This whole time, you knew that I'd found that box, didn't you?"

Coop sat forward from his relaxed position and nodded his head. "Yes, I knew."

"How?"

"Even though I haven't touched that box since I moved into my house over twenty years ago, I remember exactly how I left it, and I could tell that it had been disturbed. I don't let many folks come into my house to begin with, and Bernie, you're the only woman I've ever even allowed to spend the night, let alone go into my office, so I knew right away that it had to be you."

Bernadette's mind had been wrestling with stressful scenarios ever since the day of her fateful discovery, and now she felt exhausted. "Coop, I just want to put everything out there, right here and now, because I can't take any more stress."

"I agree, and that's the last thing I want, especially now that you're pregnant. You just don't know how much I hate like hell that this is happenin'."

"Coop, I need to ask you a question, and I don't care what the answer is, I just want the truth, and . . ."

Coop placed his finger on Bernadette's lips to silence her. "Baby,

I don't want you mixed up in any of this. I love you with everything I have in me, so I'm askin' you now, please don't ask me who killed Morris Fleming."

Bernadette looked into Coop's intense brown eyes and she knew that if he answered her questions, she would have direct knowledge of his confession, which would be more indicting than the purely circumstantial, albeit powerful, evidence that she had found in the small gray box.

"Do you trust me?" Coop asked.

"Yes," Bernadette answered, barely above a whisper.

Coop brought Bernadette's hand to his mouth and kissed it with the tenderness that only true love could produce. "I knew that one day, things from my past would come back to haunt me, and I was prepared for it. But what I wasn't prepared for was you. Bernie, I love you more than I thought it was possible to love anybody, and I'm not gonna let anything or anyone come in between our happiness."

Bernadette's heart swelled with emotion. She had known that Coop was her soulmate ever since the night of their first date, and now he had just confirmed it by saying the very words that she had said to herself earlier today.

A few hours later, Bernadette kissed Coop goodbye and watched him drive off. He was on his way to run a few errands, and then he planned to meet Maceo at his house for a heart to heart. Without going into details, Coop had texted Maceo and asked him to come over to his place because he wanted to talk with him. When Maceo had responded with a simple, OK, instead of asking what his uncle wanted to discuss, Bernadette wondered if Tess had already told Maceo that she and Coop had seen her with Antwan. She hoped that Tess had come clean with Maceo because he loved her, and he deserved the truth.

But Bernadette also knew that she couldn't continue to worry about Tess and her relationship troubles because she had concerns of her own. She was going to do as Coop had said, and try not to worry about the Morris Fleming murder case. She knew that Coop was smart, that he knew how to handle Antwan and anything else that came his way. He had successfully eluded trouble for thirty-six years, and he had no intention of getting caught now.

Bernadette had to admit that a part of her felt sorry for Morris Fleming's parents. She remembered the anguish on his mother's face during the news segment about her son's unsolved murder, and the gut-wrenching way she had said her baby boy had died alone, in an alley, with no one to hold his hand when he took his last breath. She and his father wanted justice, and they had said they would not rest until they got it. Now that Bernadette was about to be a mother, she felt a maternal pull that made her understand why Mrs. Fleming couldn't let the case rest. She felt that way about her own unborn children, and she was prepared to do whatever was necessary in order to protect what was hers.

After a long, hot shower, Bernadette went straight to her freezer for a bowl of Rocky Road ice cream. She walked back into her bedroom, and relaxed while she enjoyed her dessert. She was about to turn on her TV when her phone rang. "Oh, no," she said when she looked at the name that popped up on her screen. It was Tess, and she knew without even saying hello that it was going to be drama. Bernadette couldn't decide whether she wanted to answer her phone now and ruin her night, or wait until tomorrow and ruin her day. If it was one thing that life had taught her, it was that dreading something was always worse than actually doing it. So she picked up. "Hey Tess, what's going on now?"

Chapter 17

TESS

"I need a Valium," Tess said aloud as she sat down at her desk. She was a bundle of nerves, and she had been that way ever since her ill-fated lunch meeting with Antwan.

Tess wished she had listened to Bernadette, and had never asked Antwan to meet her for lunch at The Magnolia Room. She had known the minute that she saw Bernadette and Coop approach her table, that it was the nail in the coffin of her relationship with Maceo. Just as she would have told Bernadette if she had seen Coop having a private lunch date with another woman, especially if that woman was one of his exes, she knew that Coop was going to tell Maceo, and she needed to get to him first.

Once Bernadette and Coop had walked away, Tess had calmed herself and tried to put a quick end to her time with Antwan, but before she left, she wanted him to be honest with her about his real motivation for seeing her.

"Don't act like I'm speaking a foreign language that you don't understand," Tess had said. "I asked you to tell me the real reason why you wanted to see me. You and I both know that I don't have a clue about the case that you're investigating, or how it involves me,

Coop, or the man on the moon, and frankly I don't care. All I want to know is why am I here?"

Antwan took a casual sip of his drink. "You're the one who asked me to meet you for lunch," he said with a smile. "You could have easily picked up the phone and called me instead, but you didn't, and here we are. So maybe you need to ask yourself why are you here."

Tess hadn't been prepared for Antwan's response, and as much as she had hated to admit it, he'd been right. Even though Antwan had reached out to her first, and had asked to meet with her, the ball had been in her court, and she'd made the decision to play rather than sit on the sidelines.

"Don't try to turn this around on me," Tess volleyed back at him. "As a matter of fact, I'm getting ready to leave."

"Before you go, I want you to know that I wasn't lying when I said that I thought you could help me with the investigation. But honestly, now that I have a more significant lead, I don't want to get you involved at all." Antwan paused and leaned in closer to the table so he could make his point. "This could get messy, and I want to keep you safe, Tess."

"Why do you always have to lie and bullshit your way out of things when it comes to me? Just be honest."

"I'm telling you the truth. Listen, I know you don't trust me because of all the lies that I told you in the past. You don't know how much I wish I could change things, but since that's not possible, all I can do now is try my best to protect you."

"Protect me from what? . . . from who?"

"I can't give you those answers right now because if I do, it'll jeopardize the investigation and like I said, now that I have a more significant lead I want to leave you out of it."

Tess looked into Antwan's eyes, and just as she could see that he had been telling her the truth about annulling his marriage, he was telling the truth about the case, and the fact that he wanted to keep her safe. "Okay, I believe you, but I still need to leave."

"Thank you for believing me, but just because things got off to a bad start, that doesn't mean you have to go. We haven't even ordered our entrees. At least let me buy you lunch."

"My fiancé can cook me anything I would've ordered off the menu."

Antwan looked at Tess with an expression that was void of his normally confident posture. "Does he make you happy?"

The genuine concern in his voice shocked Tess. She knew that Antwan could be cocky and a bit aloof, but she also knew that he could be sensitive and caring, which had been one of the reasons why she had fallen in love with him. But Tess didn't want to fall victim again to Antwan's slick ways. So instead of giving him a window into her relationship with Maceo, which was still on shaky ground, she threw a question back at him. "Why did you get an annulment?"

Antwan exhaled a deep breath and placed his hands on the table. "You have to promise that you won't use what I tell you in one of your novels."

After Antwan had told Tess a story that sounded so bizarre and downright crazy that she couldn't have written it if she had tried, she left The Magnolia Room knowing that she needed to talk to Maceo as soon as she could, and she hoped that Coop had not gotten to him first. She dialed Maceo's number and when he had answered and told her that he was on his way to Sue's because he was short-staffed and wouldn't be home until late tonight, Tess knew that she needed to tell him right away, before he spoke to Coop.

Tess told Maceo from beginning to end how Antwan had contacted her, how she had met with him only to discuss the investigation, and how Bernadette and Coop had seen her. When she finished, Maceo was silent.

"Are you going to say anything?" Tess asked.

"I'm not sure what to think, let alone what to say right now."

"I can tell that you're upset by the tone of your voice."

Maceo blew out a frustrated breath of air into the phone. "Of course I'm upset. You met with your ex, and the only reason that you're telling me is because Coop and Bernadette saw you."

"That's not true."

"Then why didn't you tell me this morning when you asked him to meet you for lunch?"

Tess couldn't think of a quick answer, so instead of making up something that Maceo could punch holes through, she told him the truth. "Mace, I love you and I would never do anything to purposely hurt you."

"Whether it was purposeful or not, the result is the same, and it's always the same with you, Tess. I've tried my best to love you, and I've tried to give you the benefit of the doubt in every situation. Even when you kept your infertility issues from me, I tried to be understanding, and now, you kept a secret meeting with your ex from me. What other landmines am I gonna step on in this relationship? Do you have more secrets?"

"No. I promise," Tess said in a pleading voice.

"I've got to go. Don't wait up for me." And with that, Maceo hung up the phone.

Now, as Tess sat in front of her computer sipping from a glass of wine, unable to write, she prayed that she could salvage what was left of her and Maceo's relationship. "I'm a gigantic mess," Tess said to the empty room. She looked around Maceo's guest room that she had turned into her writing cave, and was struck with the uneasy feeling that she would soon have to look for a place of her own. Although she had an interested buyer for her house in Chicago, her gut told her that she needed to call her realtor and let her know that it needed to be taken off the market.

Tess felt low, but she knew the one thing that always lifted her spirits was her soul-searching talks with Bernadette and Arizona. She reached for her phone and dialed Bernadette's number.

"Hey Tess, what's going on now?" Bernadette answered on the fourth ring.

"I didn't think you were going to pick up."

"I was debating it, so please don't make me regret my decision."

"Cuz, I know you're pissed with me, but before you say anything else, hold on for a minute because I'm going to connect Arizona on the call."

Before Bernadette could say another word, Tess put her on hold and dialed Arizona's number.

"Hey, Bernadette," Arizona said in her loud, chipper voice. "Tess got us on this call so she can explain herself."

"No," Tess corrected, "I'm doing a group call because it's been a hell of a tough day and I want to talk with my girls."

"I had to blink twice when I saw you and Antwan," Arizona said, "and Bernadette, when you and Coop rolled up, I said, 'Oh, hell!'"

Tess spoke up. "Before we get into all of that, I want to know who was that fine ass man you were with?"

Arizona told Tess about how she had reconnected with Jaquan last Saturday night, and that Bernadette already knew.

"I feel left out," Tess said, with slightly hurt feelings.

"You didn't call me to tell me that you and Maceo had made up, so that makes two of us," Arizona responded.

Bernadette jumped in. "Ladies, this is not fifth grade."

"All right, I get it," Tess said. "So, Arizona, what are you going to do? You know that sexy man isn't going to leave you alone, and you can't start sneaking around because trust me, all that's done in the dark will jump right out into the daylight and get you."

"I know this sounds awful, but I wish I never married Chris, and I mean that."

"Oh Lord," Bernadette breathed into the phone. "I knew this was coming. But before you do anything, you need to have a serious talk with Chris."

"He's working late tonight, but I plan to talk with him once he gets home. It might get ugly around here, so I asked my mom and dad if they could keep Solomon for the next couple days. They think

Chris and I are still trying to get everything settled into the house and that it'll be easier if Solomon isn't there. But the truth is I might be moving right back into my little old house in the Bottoms. I'm glad I listened to you, Bernadette."

"What did you tell her, cuz?" Tess asked.

Bernadette spoke up. "Honestly," she said in a motherly tone, "I gave her the same advice I gave you."

"Which is?"

"That she should hold on to her house as a rental property so she could have another stream of income, but also as a back-up in case she ever needed a place to stay," Bernadette paused, "Arizona listened, but as usual, you didn't."

Tess wanted to tell Bernadette to go to hell with her high and mighty advice, but she knew that Bernadette's jab at her was absolutely right. As she thought about the situation that she was in right now, once again, she wished she had listened to her cousin. Tess had known that Maceo's two-bedroom condo had always been a temporary arrangement, and they had decided to start looking for a larger place in time for their wedding. But all of those plans might soon come to an end. Arizona's voice drew Tess from her thoughts and back into their conversation.

"Look at God," Arizona said. "I was mad because I didn't have a renter lined up after I got back from our honeymoon, but now I see it was for the best."

"Wow, Arizona," Tess chimed in. "You sound amazingly calm about all this. I mean, I knew you were in for the challenge of your life because of the situation with Chris, but I didn't think you would throw in the towel this quick."

Arizona huffed. "After the stunt that Chris pulled last Friday night, he's lucky that I didn't go all the way off."

"Oh, boy," Bernadette said. "Tess, do you have wine in front of you?"

"You know I do."

"Well, take a sip, or two or three. You might need a whole bottle after you hear what happened," Bernadette said in a joking but se-rious voice.

Arizona let out a loud sigh. "Girl, we were foolin' around, and I was hoping that I might get a little satisfaction that night. Well, Chris wanted to do a sixty-nine."

"Oh, no!!" Tess yelled out and then took a big gulp of her wine. She cringed at the thought that the sexual position that Arizona was speaking of required her friend to be face-to-face with Chris's teeny weenie peenie. "I'm weak," she said as she reached for the bottle of Chardonnay and poured more wine.

"Well, get ready for this," Arizona said with exasperation. "From out of nowhere, Chris pulled out a gigantic vibrator and basically jammed it inside me."

"What?!" Tess screamed.

"Yes, girl. It was a foot long and about as thick as your fist. I wouldn't want something that big from a real, living and breathing man, let alone a hard, metal object."

"Lord have mercy," Bernadette said.

"It hurt so bad that I kicked him with all my strength, and he fell off the bed. He's been sleepin' in the guest bedroom ever since."

"What in the hell?" Tess said, still in shock.

Arizona let out a long sigh. "That's what I said. And get this . . . I didn't realize until yesterday that he has a bruise on the side of his face, I guess it's from where he fell."

Bernadette sucked her teeth on her end of the line. "I've been thinking about what he did, and Arizona, it was so sneaky. He asked you to do a sixty-nine, but he didn't mention anything about intro-ducing a sex toy into the act, and he had to have planned it because he didn't get that vibrator from thin air."

"I was completely stunned, not to mention sore for an entire day. But yeah, I agree with everything you said."

Tess shook her head. "Something's definitely wrong with Chris. His little dick aside, some of the things that you've said he does sound bizarre."

"I know I've told you this before," Bernadette said. "But I believe Chris has some larger, no pun intended, and deeper issues that go way beyond his penis size and lack of sexual skills. The way he purposely avoids talking with you about the issues that you two have, as if they don't exit, and the selfish, passive aggressive way he acts whenever you do have sex, is extremely troubling. He needs therapy right away, Arizona. And if you intend to stay with him you're going to need it, too."

Tess took another sip of her wine and was beginning to feel its effects, which helped loosen her tongue. "You should've stayed celibate and waited until after you were married to have sex with Chris."

"And be even more frustrated than I am now?" Arizona said.

Tess let out a chuckle. "You might be frustrated, but you'd also have a strong legal case for annulling your marriage."

Tess went on to tell Bernadette and Arizona that Antwan had quietly and without fanfare gotten his marriage annulled three months ago because Marie had turned out to be a complete fraud, ultimate manipulator, and a dangerous psychopath. She had played the role of the dutiful girlfriend and successful entrepreneur who was going to be the perfect wife. But after she and Antwan had returned from their honeymoon, the real Marie had emerged.

To Antwan's shock, the charismatic beauty was a deviant social climber who had played him from the moment they'd met. He had come home one evening to find a used condom on the floor that Marie had forgotten to discard. She began to disappear for hours on end, and she only answered Antwan's phone calls when she needed something from him. A week after they had been married, Antwan found out that Marie had been sleeping with three different men the entire time they had dated. But it wasn't until after he had put Marie out of the house that he found out the true depths of her deception.

Once he had been away from her for a week, a cloud seemed to lift from his mind, as if he'd been drugged and was suddenly free. Antwan instinctively knew that something wasn't quite right, and as an investigative reporter, he knew that he needed to think critically about what was really going on that had made his life and his marriage crumble around him. He started by doing something that he'd uncharacteristically neglected in the beginning, which was to start with the source right under his nose.

Antwan discovered that ever since their first date, Marie had been giving him doses of a Colombian produced street drug, often referred to as the Devil's Breath, which had impaired his judgement to make rational decisions, and had basically rendered him helpless under her spell. It was the reason why he'd experienced an overnight conversion from a serial bachelor into a committed husband.

"He filed his annulment under the grounds that he was mentally incapacitated due to being under the influence of drugs when they got married," Tess said. "The only reason she's not in jail and there wasn't a huge story about it is because Antwan is private as hell, and he didn't want that shit to get out."

Bernadette and Arizona were quiet on the phone.

"Hello?" Tess said.

"I'm here," Bernadette and Arizona said in unison.

"Growin' up in a small town like this, you hear some crazy mess," Arizona said. "But that right there? I can hardly believe it. I Googled the chick and she's gorgeous, but you'd never think she was a lunatic. Girl, this is better than a book."

Bernadette let out another long sigh. "It reminds me of my ex, Walter."

"Oh, my goodness," Tess said. "You're right."

"He was a fraud and a con artist," Bernadette said, "and if I hadn't overheard him on the phone talking to a loan shark that he owed money to, I would've probably ended up marrying him and dead, all inside six months."

"And I thought I had problems with Chris," Arizona said.

Tess laughed. "You do, just not the kind that will kill you."

"It's true that what doesn't kill you makes you stronger," Bernadette added. "I guess Antwan is a changed man from that experience."

Tess poured more wine into her glass. "Yes, he is, Arizona. That's why I was telling you that if you hadn't slept with Chris before you two got married, you could've gotten an annulment based on the fact that you were deceived into thinking he had a dick when he doesn't."

"You're not funny," Arizona said.

Bernadette lightly chuckled. "But there's some truth to Tess's statement."

"Well, there's something that I have to tell you that's very serious, which is what I'm gonna tell Chris tonight," Arizona said with the weight of worry in her voice. "Jaquan is Solomon's father."

"What?!" Tess yelled into the phone.

Bernadette spoke up. "Arizona, you don't know that for sure and that's why you need a DNA test before you declare him Solomon's father."

"I know in my heart that he is. Plus, Jaquan does too, he even said so today."

"Okay, wait a minute," Tess said. "I thought there was about five or six guys that you thought could've been Solomon's father, how did you narrow it down to just Jaquan?"

"Tess!" Bernadette scolded.

"You know that you can be a real bitch, right?" Arizona shot back. "And to answer your question, no, it was three, not five or six."

"Oh, I was way, way off."

"Cousin, you need to put that bottle away," Bernadette said.

"Yes she does," Arizona agreed. "Anyway, I've always known that Jaquan was Solomon's father, but because he was in prison, and I didn't think I'd ever see him again, I had put him out of my mind as much as I could. I was a single mother who had to get down to the business of raising a little black boy on my own. That's why when Chris came along, I was so thankful. I thought things were perfect, but I just didn't know, and now my baby is caught in the middle of a mess that I created." Arizona's last words rang with emotion, and Tess could hear the tears and hurt in her voice.

"I'm so sorry, Arizona," Tess said. "I know I talk a lot of shit, but I truly want the best for you."

"I'm torn up inside because whether or not Chris and I stay together, I'm going to have to tell Solomon that Jaquan is his father."

Bernadette interjected. "I'm not trying to be insensitive, and I know that I'm repeating myself, but Arizona, you've got to have a paternity test before you can make that claim."

"I agree with Bernadette," Tess said, nodding on her end of the phone. "What you feel and what a test can prove might be two different things."

Arizona let out a deep breath. "Before I took Solomon over to my parents' house, I used a sterile cheek swab on the inside of his mouth that came in the DNA Paternity Kit that I bought at CVS this afternoon, and when I see Jaquan tomorrow I'm gonna do the same thing to him, as well as myself. We should have the results back in a couple days. I'm gonna tell Chris tonight so he'll be prepared."

The line was silent once again, this time from Arizona's confession. Tess's heart went out to Solomon because he was innocent in the midst of the troubles brought on by the adults around him. Tess knew it would be hurtful for Arizona to end her marriage before it could really begin, but for Solomon, it was going to be devastating to lose the only father he had ever known. When she thought about her problems with Maceo, which was no walk in the park, she knew that it in no way could compare to what was in store for Arizona.

Arizona sighed. "Now that Tess and I have laid out our problems, you have the floor, Bernadette."

"Yeah," Tess said, beginning to slur her words as she felt the full effect of her wine. "Antwan was saying that he thinks Coop can help him with the murder case that he's investigating. What's going on with that?"

"What murder?" Arizona asked. "Who was killed and what does Coop have to do with it?"

Bernadette let out a heavy breath of what sounded like worry. "It's a cold case, and the murder happened before you were born, Arizona. But because Coop grew up here and he knows so many people, Antwan wants to talk to him to get some information."

"Oh wow," Arizona said with curiosity. "I should ask my mom if she knows anything about it. What's the name of the victim?"

"I have a call coming in," Bernadette quickly said. "I've got to go but we'll chat later."

Tess knew from her cousin's rushed and abrupt departure that there could only be one reason why Bernadette had bolted quicker than a sprinter, and that was because Coop had to be calling her on the other line. "Well, Arizona, it's just you and me," Tess said.

"No, it's gonna be just you," Arizona responded in a clandestine whisper. "I see Chris's headlights pulling up in the driveway, so I've got to go. I'll talk to you later."

"Okay."

"Oh, Tess, one more thing. Can you do me a favor?"

"Sure, what do you need?"

"Put that bottle down and go to bed before you get yourself into trouble. I can tell you're drunk."

"Bye Arizona."

Tess looked at the clock on the wall, and it was only ten p.m. Even though it felt much later, the night was still young. She knew that the dinner crowd at Sue's was winding down to a crawl, so she called Maceo and hoped that he would pick up. Her heart beat fast with nervous anticipation when he picked up on the first ring, which she thought was a good sign.

"Hello," Maceo answered in a dry tone.

"Hey Mace, I'm glad you picked up. I know you're probably busy shutting things down, but I just wanted to hear your voice."

"I'm not at Sue's."

"Oh," Tess said with surprise. "Where are you?"

"Have you been drinking?"

Tess looked around the room, as if Maceo could see her. "Um, a little . . . where are you?"

"I'm at Coop's."

"His house or Southern Comfort?"

"Does it matter?"

Tess rose from her desk, picked up her nearly empty wine glass and completely empty bottle of wine, and slightly stumbled to the kitchen. "Uh, yes, it matters. I want to know where the hell you are."

"You didn't give a damn about telling me where you were earlier today, so why should I let you know where the hell I'm at right now?"

Tess was used to cursing at people, but she didn't like it when the language she used was tossed back at her, and just like that, her temper jumped from zero to one thousand. "Oh, so now you're gonna play some bullshit, tit-for-tat mind game with me? Is that your strategy?"

"This isn't a game, Tess, and I'm not a character in one of your books that you can write off if you decide to."

Tess could hear Coop's voice mumbling something in the background. She didn't know if he was talking with Bernadette, or if he was in Maceo's ear, trying to coach him on what to say, but it made her uneasy. Deep down, Tess felt that Coop didn't particularly like her, and that he only tolerated her because she was Bernadette's cousin. As she thought about the uncharacteristically hostile way that Maceo was talking to her, she wouldn't have been surprised if Coop were behind his comments. "Write you off? What the hell are you talking about? Do you know what you're even saying, or is this coming from someone else?"

"I'm a man, and whatever I say to you is coming straight from my heart. But what I'm finding out about you is that you don't know how to deal with a real man, and you definitely don't know how to speak from your heart. You don't have a clue about real love."

"Where the fuck do you get off telling me about real love? Who do you think you are?"

"You're drunk, so I'm going to end this call before things get out of hand."

"Hello? . . . hello?" Tess said into the phone. "I know he didn't just hang up on me!"

Tess's head was spinning. She looked at the wine that was left in her glass and was about to bring it to her lips, but then she stopped herself. "My life is fucked up," she said. She poured the remaining contents of her glass down the kitchen sink, lumbered over to the refrigerator, and took out a bottle of water. "Mace was right. I'm drunk and I don't know shit about love. I'm in here talking to an audience of one, and even I don't want to hear what I have to say."

Tess walked back to the bedroom, sat on the bed, and looked at Maceo's empty side. She knew that whatever time he came in, whether it was later tonight or the wee hours of the morning, he would be sleeping on the couch and not beside her in bed. Tess put her hand over her heart because it was in that moment that she knew that her journey with Maceo had come to an end, and worse, she knew she had no one to blame but herself.

Chapter 18

ARIZONA

Arizona sat on the couch, waiting for Chris to walk through the door. She was glad that she had been able to talk to Bernadette and Tess because it had calmed her nerves and prepared her for the conversation she needed to have with her husband once he walked through the door.

After Arizona's lunch with Jaquan, her head had been filled with emotion and her heart had been filled with regret. She wished that she had faced her fears a long time ago because if she had, she knew that she wouldn't be in the situation that she found herself in today—existing in an unfulfilling marriage that was disintegrating before her eyes.

After talking with Jaquan earlier that afternoon, Arizona had returned home and thought long and hard about their conversation. While she had not disclosed to him that she and Chris were experiencing issues of sexual dysfunction, she had admitted that the communication between them was nearly non-existent, and when they did talk their conversation was strained. She had told Jaquan that she knew they needed counseling, but she didn't think Chris would agree to go.

"You know that communication is the key in any type of relationship," Jaquan had said.

"Yes, you're right." Arizona acknowledged. "What's so strange about the way things are between us right now is that we used to talk about everything when we dated, for what was a little more than two years. We didn't start having problems until a few months before we got married, and once we said I Do, everything took a nosedive. We went from what I thought was a happy couple, to two unhappy people who barely speak to each other."

Jaquan wrinkled his forehead in thought. "Is there something that you're not telling me, A?"

"Why do you ask?"

"Because your husband isn't shutting down for no reason. When things abruptly change there's always something behind the shift. Do you think he's cheating on you?"

"Haaaahhh, haaaahhh, haaaahhh," Arizona couldn't contain her laughter. She could see that Jaquan was looking at her as though she was in the middle of having a full-on nervous breakdown. She wanted to tell him that she was more worried about her sleek silk press hairdo reverting back into frizzy curls than she was about Chris cheating on her. Arizona wanted to tell Jaquan that Chris could barely have sex with her, let alone go out and find another woman who would be willing to deal with his practically nonexistent penis. But she knew she couldn't reveal that information, so she pulled herself together. "I didn't mean to laugh, but no, I don't think he's cheating."

Jaquan shook his head and then looked away, as though he was trying to solve an equation. "I can tell you feel very confident he's not, and if you're that confident you're probably right because a woman's intuition is usually on point. But if your husband's not cheating, that means something else is holding him back from connecting with you."

"Did you take psychology classes while you were getting your degree, 'cause you sound like you know a li'l summin' summin'."

Jaquan smiled. "No, I didn't. But what I do know well is human behavior. Especially when it comes to how men act in relationships."

"And how do y'all act?"

"It depends on the man and his maturity level. But if a dude is a real man, and he's dealing with a real woman or any real situation for that matter, he'll rise to the occasion that the woman or the situation sets for him."

"Hmmm."

"Look at how crazy and reckless I was back in the day. I knew I wasn't doing right. I was endangering my own community just to make quick money so I could show everybody that I was 'somebody', that I was 'the man.' I had money, women, cars, and clout. I thought I was running things, but I was really running from myself. When I got locked up and all those things were stripped away, I had to deal with who I really was."

"And who was that?"

"A scared boy pretending to be a man." Jaquan turned his body and moved in close so he and Arizona were face-to-face, standing only a few inches apart, their chests nearly touching. "I had to own my shit, and I had to admit that I wasn't in prison because of the fact that somebody dropped a dime on me and I got caught, or because my pops wasn't around and didn't give a damn about me or my moms, or because I grew up in the projects learning how to hustle from the time I was elementary school, or because of any emotional or societal issues. I was in prison because I, alone, made the choices that put me there. I took the easy way out instead of putting in the hard work that's required to be a real man, for myself and for the community. I didn't realize that God had already made me great, but I know that now."

Arizona's breathing became shallow, and she was overwhelmed

by the passion, raw honesty, and depth of Jaquan's words. She wanted to tilt her head forward and kiss the lips that she remembered were soft and succulent. But at the same time, there was a part of her conscience that reminded her that no matter the state of her marriage, she had a husband, and standing in the parking lot of a restaurant, wanting to kiss another man, was wrong on more levels than she could climb.

"I care about you, A, and I always have," Jaquan said in a soft whisper. "But don't worry, I'm not going to put you in a compromising situation because I respect you, and I also respect myself. So, I'm not going to step out there into something that's not right."

"You really have changed, Jaquan. And I like it."

He smiled. "Thank you."

"You know, sometimes I wonder why certain things happen, and what life would be like if . . ." Arizona stopped herself because the next words out of her mouth were going to be that she wondered what would have happened between the two of them if he hadn't gone to prison. "I guess I shouldn't question anything, because it's all God's plan."

"A fourteenth-century philosopher named Hafiz said, 'This place where you are right now, God circled on a map for you.' So you see, even if we don't understand the things around us, and why they happen, we're exactly where we're supposed to be, doing exactly what we're supposed to be doing."

"I know that right now, at this very moment, I'm glad that I'm standing here talking with you. It was something that I didn't even think was a possibility just a week ago. There's so many things . . ."

Jaquan looked deep into Arizona's eyes and then took a small step back. "I want you to be happy, but you're the only one who can determine what that looks like."

"Things are complicated, more than you know."

"I believe you, and trust me, I don't want to add to your troubles," Jaquan said and then paused for a moment. "But there's something that I want to ask you."

"You want to meet Solomon, don't you?"

Jaquan nodded. "I do, but I want to go about it in a responsible way. I've made a lot of mistakes, and I don't want to mess this up."

"I need to tell my husband about all of this, and we also need to have a paternity test done."

"I understand, and I agree. I think we both want a definitive peace of mind."

Arizona told Jaquan that she was going to stop by CVS on her way home and pick up a DNA Paternity Kit, and they would have the results back within two days. Jaquan reached into his pocket, took out his wallet, and handed Arizona two crisp, one-hundred-dollar bills to cover the cost. Before they parted ways, they hugged and when Jaquan kissed Arizona on her cheek, she knew that the philosopher who Jaquan had quoted was right, she was where she was supposed to be.

Once she had returned home, she'd swabbed Solomon's cheek and then fixed him a snack before posting a few pictures to Instagram, Facebook, and Twitter. Then she hurriedly uploaded the makeup tutorial she had filmed earlier that day. After she dropped Solomon off at her parents' house she came home and had a cathartic phone chat with Bernadette and Tess, which had helped her relax.

Now, as she watched Chris walk through the door, she tried not to question the fact that she didn't feel right in her current situation. She didn't feel right living in Chris's house, and she definitely didn't feel right being his wife.

Arizona could see the surprise on Chris's face when he saw her sitting on the couch, and she knew that he'd probably thought she would be in the bedroom, or in her office, as she had been last week and yesterday when he had finally come home.

"You startled me," Chris said with a half-smile. "I thought you'd be in bed by now."

"You thought or you hoped?" Arizona said as she pursed her lips. Chris walked toward the hallway and tried to ignore her. "If you stayed up just so you can argue with me, I'm not interested."

Arizona jumped up from the couch. "Tell me what you are interested in because I know you're definitely not interested in me."

As Chris entered the guest bedroom where he now slept, Arizona was hot on his heels, step-for-step. "Please, Arizona," Chris said with irritation, "I've had a long day and I really don't feel like getting into it with you." He loosened his tie and removed it from his neck. He walked over to the closet where he had begun storing his clothes, and hung it on the tie rack. "I'm glad Solomon's asleep because I'm too tired to even check in on him tonight, so I'll see him in the morning before I leave for work. But right now, all I want to do is take a shower, and go to bed."

"Solomon is at my parents' house. I asked them to keep him for a couple days."

Chris looked puzzled. "Why? And why did you ask them to keep him for a couple days without talking it over with me?"

Arizona shifted her weight to one leg and placed her hand on her hip. "I took him over to my parents' because I don't want him around while we clear the air about the problems we're having. Plus," she said with emphasis, "I don't have to ask your permission to do anything when it comes to my son."

Chris looked incredulous. "Solomon is just as much my son as he is yours."

"We both know that's not true."

"I don't even know what to say to that. What's really going on with you, Arizona? Ever since we got married you've changed into an entirely different person that I don't even recognize. You disrespected me on the plane when we got back from our honeymoon, and you kicked me to the floor the other night when I was trying to make love to you. I've been good to you, and to Solomon, and I bend over backwards to support both of you. I feel like you've been using me and now that we're married you think you can treat me any kind of way that you want."

Arizona was so livid that she felt as if her head was going to explode and pop right off her shoulders. She had been trying to practice tact, as Bernadette had often reminded her, especially when it came to Chris, but now she knew she'd reached her limit with him. "You must be crazy as hell if you think I'm gonna stand here and let you create your own reality. Have you supported Solomon and me? Yes. Did I ask you to? No. That's something that you did on your own, so don't you dare try and turn anything around on me."

"You didn't ask, but you sure didn't turn it down. Not when I paid your credit cards off, not when I paid your mortgage, and certainly not when I bought you clothes, groceries, or paid for Solomon's summer camp."

Arizona's eyes enlarged with shock. "Wow, I thought the things that you did were done out of love, I didn't know you were keeping a running tab."

"You should know that there's a price to pay for everything, Arizona."

Arizona looked into Chris's eyes, and it was becoming clear to her that he wasn't the man she thought he was. She remembered all the times that he had ducked and dodged from the truth, and had manipulated her without her even realizing it.

It had been Chris's idea to practice celibacy, and now she knew that it was because he had wanted to hide the fact that he had a micropenis. Remaining chaste had allowed him to date her long enough to make her fall in love with him before she learned the truth. It had also been his idea to take on the role of a father figure in Solomon's life because he knew that once he had endeared himself to the little boy, it would be hard for Arizona to let him walk out of their lives. And as things became even clearer, a bright light of reality illuminated something that nearly made Arizona gasp with shock.

It had been Chris's insistence and constant urging that had pushed her to quit her steady paying job at Bourbon General a year before she had planned to, in order to pursue her makeup artistry business, which had basically left her dependent on him for financial support. Chris had been able to turn the tables on Arizona without her even realizing it, and now she was beginning to see that he had zeroed in on everything that was important to her, and had played them to his advantage.

"That's the only thing that you've said tonight that I agree with," Arizona said. "There's a price to pay for everything and I've already paid it. I've been tip-toeing around the problems we have, but I'm not doin' it anymore, and I'm not gonna live a lie."

"What are you talking about?" Chris asked as he threw his hands up in the air. "I love you Arizona, and all I've ever tried to do was provide a good life for you. I work my fingers to the bone so that I can give you anything that you want."

"And that's the problem, Chris. You freely give me what I want, because you know that you can't give me what I need."

Chris drew in a deep breath. "I'm tired, you're obviously upset out of your mind, and I'm not going to have this conversation."

"Oh, yes you are!"

Chris unbuttoned his shirt and began to undress. "I'm going to take a shower and then go to bed because I have to get up early in the morning. Let's talk about this tomorrow, once you've had time to calm down."

"Solomon's biological father is in town."

Chris froze in place and stared at Arizona. Slowly, he lowered his body to the bed and sat as still as a statue. "You told me that you didn't know who Solomon's father was."

"I guess we both kept 'little' secrets from each other," Arizona said, making quotation marks with her fingers for emphasis.

"I didn't know you were so cruel."

"And I didn't know you were a manipulative asshole, but I'm beginning to see that you have some serious issues, and you need help."

"And you don't?"

"I admit that I have my share of problems. Hell, I allowed myself to go through with a marriage that I knew was built on straw and wishful thinking."

Arizona had to admit that Chris had been right about one other thing—they needed to end their conversation. It was late, she was tired, and their stressful exchange had veered so far over her limit for drama that she felt dizzy. She knew that she needed to wrap things up and clear her head. "I'll have the results of the paternity test in a couple days."

Chris shook his head. "Arizona, where does this leave us?"

She told him the one thing that she was absolutely sure of, "I don't know."

It was Wednesday morning. The middle of the week. Or as Arizona had always called it, hump day. Wednesdays were typically happy days for her, because it meant that she was closer to her favorite day of all, Friday. She lived for the weekend. But for the past two weeks, every day had seemed the same, dragging on from one to the next. She knew that this was no way to live, at least not the way she had envisioned. After her confrontation with Chris last night, Arizona had known that her marriage was over.

She usually rose as the sun was coming up so that she could get a jump on her day before Solomon's eyes opened. But because he was staying with her parents right now, she took advantage of a few extra moments in bed. She had heard Chris when he'd awoken this morning. She knew that he'd done all the usual things; wash his face, brush his teeth, brush his hair, and put on his suit and tie, but he'd done them down the hall, as if he were a houseguest staying for an indefinite amount of time. There had been a tiny part of Arizona that had hoped Chris would come into their bedroom and at least say good morning and apologize for last night, but he had toasted a bagel, made a cup of coffee, and walked out the door without a peep.

"I better get going and start my day," Arizona said with a yawn. She sat up in bed and stretched her arms high above her head. She looked around her empty room, which felt like a cave, and a thought came to her that she hadn't realized until now. Even though there was a window to the right of her, their bedroom was dark because it was situated on a side of the house that barely received light. "If that's not a sign, I don't know what is," Arizona said to herself. "Everything about this marriage is wrong."

Arizona willed herself to stand up and walk into the bathroom. She turned on the light and looked at herself in the mirror. Although she was stressed and hadn't been sleeping well, she looked like a well-rested beauty. Her eyes were bright, and her skin was smooth and clear. And when she stepped back to look at her body, she could tell that she'd lost another pound or two. "My marriage might be in the dumps, but I look damn good," she said with a smile.

Arizona reached into her cabinet, pulled out her half-empty tube of Crest and squeezed a straight line of minty freshness onto her Oral B. After brushing her teeth, she went about the business of getting herself ready for the day ahead, that included getting a swab sample from Jaquan later this morning, meeting with a bride-to-be for a makeup consultation this afternoon, and then sampling new products at ULTA Beauty for the store's makeup event later tonight. She hoped she would have enough time to write a quick article for her blog before she went to bed because she was serious about building her brand and her business.

"I think I'm gonna use peach and bronze to make the perfect cut crease," Arizona said to herself as she dabbed her brush in the highly pigmented eyeshadow palette. She was taking extra time to apply her makeup because she wanted to look especially good when she met with Jaquan. She knew she should feel this type of excitement about her husband the way she did about Jaquan, but the reality was that she had begun to lose her emotional attachment to Chris even before they had gotten married.

"I can't do a thing with this hair, so it's goin' up in a bun," Arizona said to herself as she pinned her hair into a low bun before fashioning a colorful, Kente-print headwrap on her crown. In addition to wanting to look good for Jaquan, Arizona also wanted to look good for herself, and she decided that even if she didn't feel emotionally well, she was going to make sure that her physical appearance didn't reflect it.

After she made a strong cup of hazelnut-flavored coffee, Arizona went into her office and logged onto her computer. Besides being a good mother to Solomon, the other thing that Arizona knew she did exceptionally well was makeup. She had perfected her skills over the years, and she was thankful that she was building a steady clientele of loyal customers through referrals and self-promotion techniques she was learning by reading articles and watching videos. She wrote her "To Do" list for the day, and then went to her YouTube account to see if anyone had watched the video she had uploaded yesterday.

"I don't believe it . . . this can't be right!" Arizona nearly screamed. She knew that her eyes were not playing tricks on her, yet it was still hard for her to believe that in less than twenty-four hours since she had posted her first makeup tutorial on YouTube, over two hundred fifty thousand people had viewed the video. "This is absolutely crazy," she whispered, still in disbelief.

Arizona scrolled through the comments that viewers had left:

You are an inspiration! Beautiful, genuine, and hella funny! Thank you for sharing your gift!

You are an authentic beauty. Your honesty, humor and genuine realness inspires me.

Beauty and inspiration in one. Thank you for the helpful makeup tips, and for being honest and real. You are awesome!

After watching your video, I learned so much more than how to apply makeup. Being true, authentic, and humble—that's what you taught me. Thank you, and please keep the videos coming.

I feel like I know you! Thanks for being honest, real, and beautifully you. You are an inspiration.

Arizona brought her hands to her mouth in awe. When she had filmed the video yesterday morning, she had been nervous about what to say. She'd worried if the thirty-dollar ring light that she had purchased on Amazon would give her the same type of professional quality she'd admired in the videos of some of her favorite beauty gurus. She worried if the background in the tiny, makeshift office she had put together in Chris's spare storage room would look chic and glam in the eyes of viewers. And she wondered if those same viewers would like her, and if her words would come out right because she knew that she was prone to making inappropriate gaffes at inopportune times. But as Arizona continued to read comment after comment, she could see that the precious moments she'd spent worrying had been wasted.

Once Arizona turned on the camera, she started her video by greeting her viewers, introducing herself, and then telling them, "As my grandmama used to say, 'I'm 'bout as nervous as a long-tail cat on a porch full of rocking chairs.' That's an old Southern saying, in case y'all didn't know." When she applied her eyeshadow with her angled brush, she advised viewers to, "blend real good or else you'll end up lookin' like you just stepped straight out a graphic arts class." Then she warned overzealous, would-be makeup novices to go light on the false lashes, telling them, "Y'all don't wanna look like you got two windshield wipers glued to your eyelids."

She told viewers that flawless makeup starts with good skin, and that she had learned that lesson the hard way because during her wild days she used to fall asleep with a full face of makeup on after partying at the club all night, and then wake up the next morning with a bumpy face. When she applied her lip color, she told them to be just as careful with lipstick as they were with their words, because both could paint you into a corner if you applied them wrong, and she followed up by saying, "I say the wrong stuff all the time, and I know I could've avoided so many fights in my younger days if I'da just listened and kept my mouth shut."

Arizona finished up her tutorial by spritzing setting spray on her freshly made-up face, telling her audience that she was a reformed bad girl who had a dream and a passion for what she did. She told them, "I know I'm not gonna be everybody's cup of tea, but I drink coffee, and if you drink coffee too, come on and roll with a sista and subscribe to my channel." After finishing her video and not doing much editing at all, she said a quick prayer, hit upload, and then grabbed her knock-off Louis Vuitton handbag before she walked out the door to meet with Jaquan.

"I thought I might get a handful of views, but not hundreds of thousands," Arizona said, still in shock. When she went to her Instagram, Facebook, and Twitter pages, her posts had gone viral across each social media platform and had so many likes, shares, and comments that it would take her an entire week to read and respond to them all.

Arizona pressed her back against the dining room chair that she was using in her office and burst into tears. "God, You gave me what I needed, exactly when I needed it," she whispered through tears. Just last night she had been feeling lower than she had six years ago when she'd had to tell her parents that she was pregnant and couldn't give them a straight answer about who the father was. Even though she'd known that her parents still supported and loved her, she'd also known that it didn't erase their disappointment in her. When lay in bed last night, half-asleep and half-awake, she had thought about what her parents would say when they found out that she was already sitting at the doorstep of divorce.

And aside from the emotional toll that ending her marriage would bring, Arizona had also worried about the very real financial impact that divorcing Chris would have on her bank account. She'd worried about how she was going to pay her mortgage once she moved out of Chris's house and back to her own. She'd worried about how she was going to afford food and clothes for a growing little boy, gas to fill up her SUV to chauffer Solomon back and forth to camp, school, doctor appointments, and activities, not to mention driving to her own business engagements and events.

But now, just as she knew that she shouldn't have worried about her video, she knew she shouldn't have worried about how she would make it without Chris. "I lived independently and supported Solomon and myself before I met Chris, and God will bless me to do the same after I'm divorced, and He might even bless me more," Arizona said with newfound confidence. Just then her phone buzzed, alerting her that she had a new text message coming in from Jaquan, and she also noticed that she had several texts and a few missed calls. She checked to make sure that she hadn't missed any messages from her mother, and she was thankful that she hadn't because that meant Solomon was fine.

Arizona read Jaquan's message and smiled.

Jaquan: Congratulations on your video!! Two thumbs UP You're a super star!

Arizona had told Jaquan yesterday afternoon that she had filmed her makeup tutorial, and she'd asked him to view it and give her a thumbs up if he liked it. She knew that he was going to be one of her biggest supporters. She reread his message, which she thought was goofy and cute, and had to once again marvel at the change in Jaquan. The man she'd known from back in the day would have never texted using exclamation marks, emojis, or anything other than bare-bones words. She thought about how Solomon would react to Jaquan and how she would introduce Jaquan to him. She didn't know whether to ease into it, or just tell him outright. She had so many thoughts running through her mind, but before she did anything, she knew that she needed to text Jaquan back, thank him, and ask him if she could drop by his Uncle Clem's so she could swab his cheek.

Chapter 19

BERNADETTE

Bernadette could barely keep her eyes open as William Snow, the director of purchasing at Bourbon General, presented her with the cost analysis information that she had requested last week. She could hear what he was saying, but she was so tired that each word he spoke ran into the next.

"Bernadette, are you okay?" William asked.

"Oh, um, yes, I'm fine," Bernadette said, blinking her eyes in rapid motion in an attempt to regain her focus.

William nodded. "I know I can be a little long winded, but I wanted to make sure I gave you the right information, especially since I'm late getting it to you."

"That's quite all right, William."

"Do you have any questions?"

Bernadette knew that even though she had only been half-listening to William, whatever he had said was going to be wrong, and she would have to spend the rest of the week correcting his mistakes. But she was too tired to go round and round with him as she usually did so she simply smiled and said, "Not at the moment, but I'll get back to you."

After William left her office, Bernadette kicked off her shoes, leaned back in her chair and closed her eyes because she needed a moment of meditation. It was only lunch time, but she felt as though it was midnight. She had stayed up late last night, unable to sleep because of all the worries that had bombarded her day.

She had been frustrated about the fact that Tess had asked for her advice about meeting with Antwan, but had done the complete opposite of what she'd told her cousin to do. If Tess had listened to her, Bernadette knew that she and Coop would have never run into Antwan at The Magnolia Room. But Bernadette also knew that regardless of their unfortunate meeting yesterday, Antwan would have eventually come knocking at Coop's door.

Bernadette had been glad that she'd finally told Coop about the evidence that she had found that linked him to Morris Fleming's murder. When Coop had asked her not to ask him any more questions about the Morris Fleming murder, she had known that he was trying to protect her because the less she knew, the better. But as his soon-to-be wife and mother of his children, she wanted to know all the details because every move he made going forward would affect them all, and vice versa. But Coop asked her not to worry, and she had put it out of her mind until Tess had called and then included Arizona on the line.

Bernadette had known that Arizona and Chris were on shaky ground, even before Jaquan entered in the picture. Their nightmare of a honeymoon, and then Chris's catastrophic attempt at pleasuring Arizona last weekend, only added to the unfortunate reality that her friend should have never gotten married in the first place.

Despite how uncomfortable it might be for Arizona to end a marriage and how challenging it might be to help Solomon adjust, there wasn't a doubt in Bernadette's mind that Arizona would land on her feet because she was a survivor. But when Bernadette thought about Tess, she wasn't so sure.

Tess was a spoiled drama queen who had lived a relatively comfortable life growing up. Her parents had had her later in life, and they had given her pretty much whatever she had wanted. Then, once she graduated from college, a year later she had landed her first book deal, and the very next year that same book had fallen into the hands of a well-known Hollywood actress and had landed on the *New York Times* Bestseller List, where all of her books had taken up residence ever since. She was adored by her readers and was the life of the party in the social circles where she hung. She loved being lauded, but Bernadette knew deep down that if Tess could have a loving and stable relationship along with children, she would gladly trade in every literary award and publishing accomplishment she had earned over the years.

Just as Bernadette knew that Arizona's marriage had reached its limit, she knew that after last night, Tess's and Maceo's engagement was coming to a quick end. Coop had called her last night while she had been talking with Tess and Arizona, and when she had seen his call she'd immediately clicked over.

"Hey Coop," Bernadette had said. "I'm so glad that you called me. I've been worried. How's Maceo doing?"

Coop let out a long and heavy sigh. "He's torn up. Tess had already called him earlier this afternoon and told him, and now he's back on the phone with her again."

"She must've just called him because I was just talking with her and Arizona when you called me."

"Yep, she called a minute or so ago . . . hold on, Bernie."

Bernadette could hear Maceo talking in the background and he sounded upset. She'd never heard him sound so hostile, and angry. Then she heard Coop's deep voice trying to calm him down. Knowing Tess the way she did, Bernadette had no doubt that her cousin had said something to set off the normally mild-mannered restauranteur. A minute or two later Coop came back on the line.

"Baby, I gotta go. Tess called Maceo and I need to calm him down."

"Okay, Coop. I'm so sorry about all of this, call me later if you can and if not let's talk in the morning."

From that moment on, Bernadette tossed and turned all night.

She was worried about Coop, concerned about Tess, sad for Maceo, and nervous about what choice Arizona might make. She knew that she needed to free her mind from too many burdens because the stress definitely wasn't good for her health.

When Bernadette had spoken with Coop this morning he had told her that he hadn't slept much either because he'd been up talking with Maceo all night. He had confirmed what Bernadette had seen coming—that Maceo had had enough of Tess, and he was breaking up with her. Coop told her that Maceo said that he wanted Tess out of his house within twenty-four hours and that he would hire people to move her if he had to. Bernadette wasn't sure if Tess would high-tail it back to Chicago, but she was prepared to once again open her home to her cousin if she needed a place to stay. But Bernadette also knew that this time she would need to set some boundaries and ground rules before Tess walked through her door.

"It's a mess," Coop had said. "You know I don't like bein' in folks' business, but this is family."

"I know," Bernadette acknowledged. "We're caught in the middle, but it'll all work out."

Bernadette could tell that Coop was tired from the fatigue that covered his voice, so she had told him to grab a few more hours of sleep and they would talk later this afternoon once she got home from work.

Now, it was late afternoon, and as Bernadette prepared to clear her desk of papers and wind down her day, she thought about how much life could change from one day to the next. Within two weeks' time, she had gotten engaged and found out that she was pregnant with twins. Tess had steered a relationship roller coaster straight off the rails, and in the process she crushed a man's spirit. And poor Arizona—she was the only person that Bernadette knew who had gotten married, honeymooned, and then was on the verge of filing for divorce, all within fourteen days. "I need to get out of here and clear my mind," Bernadette said.

It was nearly five-thirty when Bernadette steered her car out of the parking deck of Bourbon General and onto the busy intersection that lead into and out of the hospital. She was in the middle of what Bourbonites called rush hour traffic, which for her was a joke, compared to the hectic roads that she had grown up navigating in and around the Nation's Capital. She had just merged onto the highway when her phone rang. She glanced down and saw that Arizona was calling.

"Hey Arizona, how are you today?" Bernadette asked, hoping that her friend was still managing to keep her head up in spite of everything going on around her.

"Bernadette, I'm on top of the world," Arizona practically sang into the phone.

Bernadette couldn't believe the miraculous turnaround in Arizona's mood. Unfortunately, she knew in her gut that Chris didn't have a thing to do with her friend's happy disposition, and she was scared to ask what had gotten into her, lest her answer be Jaquan, so Bernadette simply said what was true. "It's good to hear you sounding happy again, and whatever has put a smile in your voice, I hope it stays."

"Girl, I can't wait to tell you, but hold on, I need to patch Tess in on the line."

"Okay," Bernadette said with reservation. After what Coop had told her this morning about Maceo calling off the engagement and putting Tess out of his house, Bernadette had fully expected to hear from her cousin by now, but it was the end of the day and she hadn't heard a peep from Tess. Bernadette knew that it could only mean one of two things, Tess was either in trouble or she was about to cause trouble, and either way, it wasn't good. Bernadette held her breath until her cousin came on the line.

"Hey Bernadette," Tess said, sounding as if she was actually in a good mood. "Arizona must've gotten her some good dick last night, and I know it wasn't from Chris 'cause she sounds happy as hell."

"Lucky for you, I'm a lady," Arizona said. "Otherwise I'd curse you the hell out right now. But even your sarcastic behind can't ruin my day."

Bernadette tried not to laugh at her cousin and her friend as she changed lanes in traffic. "Arizona, whatever you're happy about, please don't keep us in suspense."

"Okay ladies, remember when I told you that I was going to start promoting my business by filming videos, blogging, and posting on social media?"

"Yes," Bernadette and Tess answered in unison.

"Well, I filmed my first YouTube video yesterday morning and I posted a few photos on Instagram, Facebook, Pinterest, and Twitter."

"That's fantastic," Bernadette said. "You're so talented, Arizona, so you better get ready for the flood of clients that will be coming your way."

"I already am, 'cause as of a half-hour ago, your girl has over five hundred thousand views on YouTube."

"What?!" Tess screamed into the phone. "Are you shittin' us?"

"You know I don't play like that. My inbox and my phone have been blowin' up all day. And get this, I already have some companies that want to partner with me for product endorsements, sponsor my next video, and send me PR boxes."

Bernadette was smiling from ear to ear. "I'm so happy for you, and I don't know anyone more deserving than you, Arizona."

"I'm proud of you, Arizona," Tess said. "You're literally blazing your own trail, and like Bernadette said, I honestly don't know anyone who deserves this more than you."

"Aww, thanks ladies. I feel like it's a dream, but I know it's real."

"You're going to need to hire an assistant," Tess said, "I can put you in touch with some freelance admins who do work for me from time to time."

"I'm not at that point yet," Arizona said. "Plus, I know I can't afford the folks that work for you, Ms. New York Times Bestselling Author."

Bernadette stepped in. "Yes, you most certainly are at that point.

You're officially what they call an overnight sensation, which is rare, and in order to keep the momentum going you won't be able to do it all on your own. You're going to need some professional help if you want to keep climbing."

"Bernadette is right," Tess said. "She's the one who helped me get my ducks in a row when my first book took off like gangbusters."

"I'm so blessed that I have a corporate vice president and a world-famous author as my best friends."

"That's what good friends are for," Bernadette said. "And don't worry about the expense of hiring an assistant. I'll reach out to some of my contacts who can do the work at cost and I'll pay the fees to get you started."

"I can't let you do that."

"Why the hell not?" Tess asked. "It would be different if you were the type of person who was only looking to get over, but you're not. This is how sisters band together to help each other, and for the record, I'll split the cost with you, cuz."

Bernadette smiled into the phone. "It's a done deal. Arizona, get ready to be a household name."

Bernadette could hear tears through the phone.

"I really appreciate y'all," Arizona said through sniffles. "I have some homegirls who I've known all my life and instead of being happy for me, two of them sent me DMs sayin' my lighting wasn't bright enough in one of my photos, and another one texted me and said that I talked too much on my makeup tutorial."

"That's awful," Bernadette said. "I'm so sorry they said those hurtful things."

"Fuck them!" Tess said, "I'm on my laptop looking at your video right now and I have it on mute, so I can't hear what you're saying, but baaayyyybeeee, you look like a freakin' million bucks, so screw those jealous bitches."

Bernadette shook her head. "Although Tess's delivery is tainted, her truth is real. Any person who would contact you just to criticize the amazing job you did, especially if they know what this means to you, isn't a friend. And obviously, a half million people disagree with those bitter bitties. So tell them to go kick rocks."

"Amen to that," Tess yelled into the phone.

Bernadette sensed that something was wrong. She knew that this was Arizona's shining moment, and although she believed that Tess was genuinely happy for their friend, she felt that Tess sounded a little too happy, especially given that Maceo had broken up with her and had said that he wanted her out of his house. Then a thought occurred to Bernadette, *Maybe Maceo broke down and went running back to Tess.*

"You ladies are right," Arizona said. "I have to focus on the positive things and positive people in my life. And speaking of positive, I mailed off the samples I took from the paternity test and I should have the results emailed to me in two days."

"That's quick," Tess said.

Bernadette spoke up. "If you had gotten it done at the hospital you could get a rush on it and have the results by tomorrow."

Arizona sighed. "I know, but I also know the two techs that work in the lab, and I don't want anybody in my business."

Tess laughed. "So much for HIPAA and confidentiality."

Bernadette didn't breathe a word of contradiction. Prior to working at Bourbon General, she'd always thought that medical records were confidential, which for the most part they were, but there were also unscrupulous, unethical, and downright nosy people who mishandled information and didn't have any business with access to confidential files. "So, I take it that you talked to Chris about all this?" Bernadette asked.

Arizona told them about the conversation that she'd had with Chris last night after they had gotten off the phone, and Bernadette was more convinced than ever that after Arizona got the paternity results back this Friday—regardless of the outcome—she would be sitting in a lawyer's office come Monday morning.

"I have no one to blame but myself," Arizona said. "I walked into this marriage with my eyes wide open, and now it's up to me to

get myself out of this mess. I just hate that Solomon is gonna be af-
fected by my poor choices."

"Children are very resilient," Bernadette said as she veered her
car onto the exit that lead to her subdivision. "Solomon will be confused initially, and he may even feel hurt or angry, but he'll bounce
back from this. You're a great mother Arizona, and you'll make sure
that you give him the love and emotional support he needs, because
if Jaquan is his father, and Jaquan has made it clear that he wants to
meet Solomon and be a part of his life, Chris is going to have to accept that, regardless of what happens between you and him."

"You're right, Bernadette," Arizona acknowledged. "I'm divorcing Chris. I already know that."

"Even though I've never been in Chris's corner," Tess said and
then paused for a moment, "I just have to ask, are you sure that you
want to end it?"

"Yes, I'm sure."

"Okay, well, can I write about this in my next book? I'll change
your names, of course."

"Tess!" Bernadette said. "Don't even joke about that."

"Who's joking? I'm dead serious."

"If you do, I'll choke you with my bare hands," Arizona said.

"Damn, I guess that's a no," Tess said with a loud laugh. "Antwan's already investigating one murder here in Bourbon, and I sure
as hell don't want him to have to investigate mine."

"I knew there was something that I meant to ask my mom when
I called her and Solomon," Arizona said. "What's the name of the
guy who was murdered?"

"Morris Fleming," Tess answered and then hesitated for a
minute. "And um, I'm actually going to be talking with Antwan in a
few minutes."

Bernadette felt as if her throat was going to close up. "Excuse
me, but why're you talking to him? If anything, I would think you'd
be trying to talk to Maceo."

"Coop told you, didn't he?" Tess asked.

"Yes, he did. I was just waiting until later to talk to you about it."
Arizona spoke up. "I'm in the dark. What's going on?"

"Mace broke off our engagement," Tess said, sounding unaf-
fected, "and he wants me to move out of his condo."

"Oh, I'm sorry, Tess," Arizona said in a comforting voice.

"It's okay. At first he wanted me out by tonight, but I asked him
to at least give me until tomorrow, and he agreed. I should've seen
this coming."

Bernadette listened to how calm Tess sounded, and she immediately knew that something was wrong. The cousin she knew should
have been cursing Maceo's name in bitterness, but instead she
sounded perfectly fine, just as Arizona had sounded about Chris. But
the difference was that Bernadette thought that Tess had been genuinely in love with Maceo. *Maybe this is some kind of coping mechanism
she's using,* Bernadette said to herself as she pressed the remote to her
four-car garage. "Tess, what's really going on? Last night you were
drinking, and you were upset about the possibility of Maceo breaking
up with you, and now you sound fine. What happened?"

Tess didn't hesitate. "I fucked up, and I think I did it on purpose."

"You broke a good man's heart, and you 'think,'" Arizona said in
astonishment, "that you did it on purpose. What's wrong with you?"

"I have issues, Arizona," Tess shot back. "I'm trying to be real
with you and Bernadette, so please spare me your holier than thou
outbursts."

"Whatever," Arizona quipped. "When you know better you
should do better. And I know that's appropriate to say because I got
that quote straight from the late Maya Angelou."

Bernadette opened her car door and walked from her mudroom
into her kitchen as she listened to Tess and Arizona go back and forth
like grade school children. She knew that they loved each other like
family because only true friends could bicker the way they did and
still have each other's back no matter what. And although Bernadette

felt her cousin was finally beginning to take ownership of her behavior, she was sad that it had come at a steep price for Maceo, whose only fault had been trying to love Tess.

"Tess," Bernadette jumped in. "We all know you have issues, but if you did things to sabotage your relationship you owe it to Maceo to explain why you did it, and most importantly, apologize to the man."

The line was silent, and now Bernadette felt horrible. What had started off as a happy phone call to celebrate Arizona's accomplishment had turned into a contentious, prickly conversation. Bernadette wished that she had never asked Tess what was going on with her because once again, her cousin had managed to become the center of attention in the midst of Arizona's good news. It was as if she had been waiting for one of them to say something that would give her a sliver of an opening so that she could slide the direction of their conversation to what was going on in her world.

"You're right, Bernadette," Tess said in agreement. "Deep down, I knew the minute I texted Antwan and asked him to meet me for lunch that I was closing the door on any kind of forgiveness or trust that Mace was willing to extend to me."

"Then why'd you do it?" Arizona asked.

"It was easier this way," Tess replied in a genuinely sad tone. "If I hadn't given Mace a way out he would've kept hanging in there with me, trying to force something that's not right, only because he's a good and decent man. I'm not the woman for him and he's not the man for me. He needs to find someone who can give him kids and be satisfied living in Bourbon."

"You're not happy here?" Arizona asked.

"I would be, if the situation was right. But it's not."

There was another lull on the phone. Bernadette didn't want Tess to be unhappy, but she was determined not to let her cousin's continuous problems drag down Arizona or herself. So she attempted to put a positive spin on the mood Tess had created. "We've all had some pretty life-changing moments in a short amount of time, and I'm sure we'll continue to have our ups and downs," Bernadette said with conviction. "I'm just thankful that I have you two to share them with. God and good friends can get you through anything."

"Me too, and I second that," Arizona said.

"The three amigos," Tess belted out.

Bernadette set her handbag on her kitchen island and felt as though she was going to throw up from a wave of nausea that had been threatening her stomach on and off all day. She was hoping that her first trimester morning sickness would vanish soon, but for now she knew that she needed to get off the phone so she could get some relief. "Ladies, I just got home, and I need to change my clothes and relax because it's been a long day."

"I've gotta go, too," Arizona said. "I need to head out to an in-store event that ULTA is having for local makeup artists this evening."

"I gotta go as well," Tess said. "I'm meeting with Antwan in a few minutes."

"Oh Lord," Arizona said with worry. "I know it's gonna be some drama, so I'm gonna hold the fifty thousand questions that I have until our next conversation."

"Enjoy your evenings, Ladies," Bernadette said before she pressed the end button on her phone. She didn't want to venture into Tess's last comment about meeting up with Antwan, because as Coop had told her last night about the Morris Fleming case, the less she knew the better.

After Bernadette purged her stomach of the black bean salad she had eaten during her late lunch, she undressed and took a relaxing shower that loosened her muscles. When she came out of her bathroom she was startled to see Coop sitting on the edge of the bed holding a bouquet of roses. She instantly smiled. "You must've known that I needed a pick-me-up."

"I already told you, it's my job to know what you want and to give you what you need," Coop said as he stood and handed Bernadette the beautifully wrapped bouquet of flowers. He bent his head as she stood on her tiptoes so he could plant a soft and gentle kiss on her lips. "How're you feelin'?"

"Better, now that you're here. Thank you for these beautiful roses."

"You're welcome, baby."

After Bernadette changed into her silk loungewear set, she trimmed her flowers and put them in a crystal vase filled with water, then she and Coop sat at her kitchen island eating comfort food that he had gotten from Sue's. Crispy, golden fried chicken, seasoned cabbage, macaroni and cheese, and corn bread. Bernadette was hungry because she had emptied her stomach from what she had eaten earlier, and she hoped she would be able to hold down the delicious, home-cooked meal that Maceo had prepared.

"I pray this food won't make you sick to your stomach," Coop said as he bit into his chicken.

Bernadette put a fork full of cabbage in her mouth and felt as though she was in heaven. "Mmm, this is so good," she said through bites of food. "It's worth a little nausea."

Coop laughed. "Maceo sure can burn in the kitchen. That boy is just like his mama when it comes to cookin'. Sue used to have Maceo standing on a stool right beside her at the stove, so he grew up knowing his way around the kitchen." Coop smiled, and then his lips formed a flat line. "He's hurtin' right now."

"I can only imagine. I feel so bad about all of this. Tess has so many problems, Coop, that I'm beginning to think that it's actually a good thing for Maceo that he broke up with her."

"I told him the same thing last night."

"You did?"

Coop nodded. "As God is my witness, I told him that Tess had been givin' him signs all along, but he looked the other way. After they got engaged she didn't tell a soul, then she went about her life in secret, seein' doctors in Chicago, meetin' with her ex here in Bourbon. A woman who's committed to a man ain't gonna operate that way."

"That's true. I plan on talking to Tess tomorrow, just to see where her mind really is."

"When you talk to her, tell her to stay as far away from Maceo as she can." Coop put down his fork and let out a heavy sigh. "Losing his mother was devastating, and the way his divorce went down, with the paternity mess and all, it just about took him out. But even with all that hurt, he managed to stay open to love, and he thought he'd found it with Tess. That's why he's in a bad way right now."

Bernadette put her hand on top of Coop's. "I feel hurt for him, but like we've both said, this is for the best because what if they got married and then ended up like Arizona; ready to get a divorce."

"Divorce, already?"

"Yes, Arizona is so unhappy."

"They've only been married a couple weeks. I knew Jaquan's presence would cause a ripple, but not like this."

Bernadette bit into her cornbread and then dabbed the corners of her mouth. "Arizona and Chris's problems started way before Jaquan came back to town."

Bernadette told Coop about Chris's micropenis and his challenges in the bedroom. She shared that Arizona had wavered back and forth about marrying him, and now, their situation was worse than ever. She hadn't planned to tell him about the intimate details of Arizona's marriage, but Coop was going to be her husband, and she knew that she could talk to him about anything, plus, knowing the truth gave him insight into why Arizona felt as strongly as she did about getting a divorce so early in her marriage. Bernadette had never seen a look of shock on Coop's face until now, and she could tell by the tight lines across his forehead that he was stunned.

"I would've never thought they would have this kind of problem," Coop said. "I don't even know what to say."

"It's going to get even stickier. Arizona believes that Jaquan is Solomon's biological father. She mailed off the DNA samples today and she'll have the results back by Friday."

Coop nodded. "If she needs a place to stay, I'll make sure she's covered. I have a property that's vacant."

Bernadette smiled. "You have such a giving heart, and I love that about you. But I think she's going to move back into her house because she hasn't rented it out yet."

"Just tell her to let me know."

"I will, and I know she'll appreciate the offer."

"You never know what's around the corner. One minute life seems one way and then from outta nowhere, you can get blindsided before you have a chance to blink."

Coop's statement made Bernadette think about last month when she had been cleaning his office. One minute she'd been trying to decide how to reorganize his bookcase, and the next she'd been trying to rationalize the thought that she was in love with a man who was capable of cold-blooded murder. There had been a time when the thought of being with an ex-felon who had killed someone would have made her run as far as her legs would carry her. But now, as she looked at Coop, all she could think about was the fact that she was going to build a life with him, and she wasn't going to let anything stand in her way. She knew that Coop sensed that she was in deep thought about their situation.

"I don't want you to worry, baby," Coop said.

"Have you set up a time to meet with Antwan?"

"I called and left a voice message for him right before I got here. I hope I can meet with him tomorrow, so we can get things settled."

Bernadette put her hands in her lap and ran them up and down the smooth, silk fabric of her lounge pants. "I'm so nervous, Coop. I know that you said I shouldn't worry, and I try my best not to, but I can't help it."

"I don't plan on goin' anywhere. You hear me?"

Bernadette desperately wanted to believe him. Just as she was about to open her mouth, a feeling of nausea swept over her stomach. "Oh, no. I think I'm going to be sick."

An hour later, Bernadette lay in bed sipping a cup of warm Chamomile tea that Coop had made her, while he took his shower. Now that she was relaxed and feeling better, she once again thought about what had been on her mind right before she'd gotten sick. She had wanted to ask Coop what he intended to tell Antwan, but as she sipped her tea, she knew that the babies growing in her belly had sent her a clear message that she needed to focus only on what she could control. Coop had told her not to worry, and to trust that he would handle the situation. *I'm going to concentrate on the good,* Bernadette said to herself.

She was pulled from her thoughts when Coop emerged from the shower wearing a fluffy white towel wrapped at his waist and a smile on his face.

"You feelin' better?" he said as he walked to Bernadette's side of the bed and sat next to her.

"Yes, I am," Bernadette answered, and a thought came to her. She knew that she needed to ask him another question that had been on her mind. She cleared her throat and looked into Coop's eyes. "What do you think about getting married this Saturday?"

Chapter 20

TESS

Tess paced the floor and prayed that she was doing the right thing. She looked around the room at the elegantly appointed décor that harkened to a bygone era of the genteel South. The style wasn't her taste, but she appreciated the attention to detail and the craftsmanship of the aesthetic, from the plush, jacquard window coverings with braided tassel tiebacks, to the ornate scrollwork on the arms of the high-back chairs, to the elegant sconces that flanked the walls. Tess had only been inside the St. Hamilton Hotel on one other occasion, and that had been a little over two weeks ago when she had attended Arizona's wedding reception in the hotel's ballroom. But now she was standing inside a sleeping room, and the purpose of her visit wasn't for celebration, it was to get to the bottom of the truth with Antwan.

Tess had been doing a lot of thinking. Last night had been gut-wrenching for her because once she had begun to sober up in the wee hours of the morning, she'd been able to clearly see the error of her ways, and what a mess she had made of things between her and Maceo. She had cried until her eyes were puffy, and she'd thought about the cliché that had always annoyed her to no end, but she now knew to be true—hurt people, hurt people.

Tess was an emotionally hurt woman who went through life hurting others. She was hurtful with her words and her actions, and she knew that Maceo, Bernadette, Arizona, and anyone else in her life that she cared about didn't deserve the treatment that she dispensed.

She had gone into her temporary writing cave that had never really felt like her own, and opened a box of personalized stationary. She reached for her favorite Mont Blanc pen and began to write.

> *Dear Mace,*
>
> *I want to start by apologizing for the way that I've behaved. I messed up and there's no getting around it. You're a good man and you are deserving of someone who will love you the way you want, need, and deserve to be loved. I know that you desire a wife, biological children, and a legacy that will live on long after you're gone. And guess what? You will absolutely have all those things and I will be so happy for you when it happens, because that is your destiny. You are a wonderful man, Mace. You showed me love, patience and kindness, and for that, I will be forever grateful. Because of Bernadette and Coop, our paths will undoubtedly cross, and I sincerely hope that in time you will be able to forgive me, and that one day, you will actually thank me because I saved you, from me.*
>
> *Always,*
> *Tess*

After Tess finished the note for Maceo, she put it in an envelope and set it on the kitchen counter, then she returned to the tiny office and began to disassemble her computer equipment. She went into Maceo's small storage closet and pulled out the boxes that she had stored there shortly after she had moved her things into his house. She was thankful that she had put the bulk of her possessions into storage and the rest were still in her home back in Chicago.

It took Tess two and a half hours to remove all of her belongings from Maceo's condo. She put his key under his doormat and drove her car, loaded from front to back, straight to the St. Hamilton hotel. She had really wanted to stay with Bernadette, as she had done when she'd first come to Bourbon nearly six months ago. But given the circumstances, and the fact that if she stayed with her cousin, she ran the risk of being in close proximity with Coop, she knew that it was best for her to lay her head elsewhere until she could figure out her next move.

The sun had just begun to rise when Tess had pulled up to the grand portico of the St. Hamilton. She had shaken off the puzzled look of the valet when he had slid into her driver's seat and looked around the cabin of her late model luxury vehicle that was filled from top to bottom with her possessions. She had been thankful that there had been a skeleton crew working the front desk during that time of the morning, and she was especially thankful that Chris had been nowhere in sight. She had asked for a suite as far away from the elevator as she could get, and once she reached her room she immediately undressed, crawled under the sheets, and fell asleep.

Now, as Tess paced the floor, waiting for Antwan, she felt nervous. She had slept for eight hours and had awoken late in the afternoon. After ordering a pot of coffee, she had checked her phone for messages. She hadn't been surprised that Maceo had not contacted her, and she also wasn't surprised that Antwan had. He had texted her.

Antwan: Hi Tess, I'm not trying to cause trouble in your relationship, but you've been on my mind, so I'm reaching out. Are you okay?

Tess: No, I'm not.

Antwan: ??

Tess: My engagement has been called off.

Antwan: I'm here if you need an ear.

Tess had decided to pick up the phone and call Antwan. He had answered on the first ring and they fell into an easy conversation that had put Tess in a cheerful mood. Antwan had made her laugh, reminiscing about old times, and catching her up on some of their mutual friends whom she had fallen out of contact with. When he asked if she had eaten and she told him no, he invited her for an early dinner after he finished his last conference call of the day. Tess had told him that she didn't feel up to going out, so because they were staying in the same hotel, on the same floor, Antwan had told her that he would walk down the hall to her room, and they could order room service.

Tess had felt a jolt of renewed energy after talking with Antwan, and when Arizona called with her good news, she had been happier than she'd felt in a long time. But then the conversation turned toward her failed relationship with Maceo, and before she had known it she had done something that she now knew she needed to work on. She'd navigated Arizona's triumph to the sideline, relegating it to the back seat behind her own troubles. She had been thankful that Bernadette had salvaged the conversation by shifting the topic to friendship, which Tess was grateful for, and she made a mental note to apologize to both Bernadette and Arizona for her actions. She had been so engrossed in their conversation that she hadn't realized that Antwan would be at her door in a few minutes, and as soon as she hung up the call with her girlfriends, Antwan came knocking.

An hour later, Tess moved from the small in-room dining table for two where she and Antwan had eaten their dinner to the comfortable tapestry covered couch as they continued their conversation over dessert. After Antwan arrived, he had ordered an aged, angus ribeye for himself and baked, honey-glazed salmon for Tess. They each uncharacteristically forwent wine in favor of water, but they had allowed themselves the indulgence of chocolate lava cake for her and cheesecake for him.

Tess was comforted by how easy it was to talk to Antwan, and it led her to an eye-opening discovery. In all the time that they had dated—which had been two years—she had never felt the connection with him that she did now. It wasn't forced or propped up by image, looks, success, or hefty bank accounts—which both of them possessed. They were just a man and a woman who shared a mutual like and growing respect for each other.

"I'll say one thing about this town," Antwan said as he placed his clean plate on the table, "I haven't had a bad meal yet. Talk about some great food."

"The south is notorious for good food. Mace can cook his butt off and . . ." Tess caught herself and then stopped.

"Tess, I know that you may not want to talk about what happened between you two, but I think it might help if you let it out. We both know that breakups aren't easy."

Tess set her half-eaten dessert on the table. "It was my fault. I moved out early this morning, and right now my car is sitting in the valet garage, packed from top to bottom with all my things."

"I take it that the troubles in your relationship started long before you and I had lunch yesterday."

Tess let out a heavy sigh. "Yes, they did. I kept things from him. Important things, and while I didn't feed him lies, I wasn't upfront with him when it counted. Maceo Dennis has suffered a lot of loss and pain in his life. He never knew his father, which has had a huge impact on him, and the only people who have ever really stood by him were his mother, who passed away several years ago, and Coop, who you met yesterday, and who happens to be his uncle."

Antwan nodded his head. "Hmmm, interesting."

"I know, it's six degrees of separation. Anyway, Mace thought I could be 'his person,'" Tess said. "He wanted to build a family with me that he never had growing up, and he wants his family to be his legacy. I gave you that background to make a point about something very important that I kept from him, and you, too, for that matter."

Tess crossed her legs and adopted a serious tone. "I can't have children, and it's because of numerous gynecological problems that are too complex to explain in one sitting. But the short version is that my plumbing is so screwed up that I'm going to need a hysterectomy. At first, I resisted the thought of having the surgery because I held out hope that by some miracle I could conceive, but I had a doctor's appointment with another specialist the other day, and he confirmed what all the others have told me."

"I'm so sorry, Tess."

"Yeah, me too. But you know what? This just means that having kids wasn't in the cards for me. I guess God's got other plans."

"You never know."

Tess looked at Antwan with curiosity. "Do you want kids?"

Antwan nodded. "Yes, I do. But for so many years I was so involved in my career that having a family took the back burner, as you know. But after my relationship with Marie fell apart, it was like my eyes became open to so many things that I hadn't seen before . . . so many things that I've missed out on. I started thinking about things I'd never considered before, like growing old with someone, having kids, enjoying life, and actually feeling like I'm living and not just existing. As a matter of fact, the Morris Fleming story is going to be my last."

"What do you mean? You're not going to stop writing, are you?" Tess asked with surprise.

"I've been with The Post for twenty years, and I'm ready for a change. My work has been fulfilling and rewarding, and I've made a ton of money and had the opportunity to travel the world. But honestly, I'm tired of the rat race and I'm ready to jump off the hamster wheel. If there was one thing my bogus marriage taught me, it's that happiness is priceless. I want to be happy, Tess . . . you know what I mean?"

"Yes, Antwan. I know exactly what you mean." Tess smiled. "Why couldn't we have conversations like this when we used to date?"

"It wasn't our time back then. But maybe it is now."

Tess starred at Antwan, and the realization of what she had just discovered made the faint trace of hair on her arms stand at attention. When she had looked at Antwan in the past, she had always admired his outward attributes: the shape and color of his hypnotic hazel eyes, the plump fullness of his lips, the ruggedly masculine texture of his skin, and the soft-as-cotton, kinky coils on the top of his head. But just as she had done yesterday when they had lunch at The Magnolia Room, when Tess looked at him now, she searched for something deeper. She paid attention to the way he looked straight into her eyes and did not waver when he spoke, she watched the way his lips formed into a smile or the quizzical purse that matched his expression, letting her know that he was interested in what she was saying. She studied the fine laugh lines on his face that were beginning to tell his age and were a testament to the fact that he knew how to laugh and enjoy life. And she appreciated the unbothered freedom that he carried inside and expressed through the way he carried himself, with laid-back sophistication.

Tess realized that Antwan's pronouncement was right. It hadn't been their time back then because she hadn't taken the time to see who he really was, and for his part, he had never taken the time to do the same with her.

Tess had just collapsed one relationship, and although Antwan was familiar, and he was inviting, she knew that she needed to find herself before she could even begin to think about rekindling anything with him. "Antwan," she said. "You're just coming out of a bad marriage, and my engagement literally just fell apart. I don't think this is the right time for either of us."

"I hear you, and I understand why you would think that. But you know what I learned from my failed, crazy sham of a marriage?"

"I'm all ears."

"That love is worth the wait, and it can be better the second time around."

"How did getting an annulment from a psychotic serial cheater who drugged you help you reach that conclusion?"

"I'm going to ignore that."

"I'm being serious."

Antwan cleared his throat. "What I'm trying to say is that everything that I went through opened my eyes to how horrible I was to you. I lied, I manipulated, and I caused you emotional pain. It wasn't until those same things had been done to me that I fully understood how badly I had behaved. I can't tell you how many nights I wanted to pick up the phone and call you, just to say I was sorry."

"You were a real piece of shit," Tess said with a roll of her eyes, "and I'm glad that you realize it."

"Are you ever gonna cut me any slack?"

"Maybe. But you're gonna have to earn it."

"So does that mean you're willing to consider giving us another chance."

"It means that I'm willing to be your friend, and get to know you in the right way. Just like your relationship taught you things about yourself, mine did, too. And I know that I have issues that I need to work out before I can even think about getting back into a relationship with you or anyone else."

Antwan simply nodded his understanding. "I can respect that, and I'll honor your wishes about taking things slow. But I'm serious, Tess, I believe that it's our time."

"And what makes you so sure?"

"I don't think it's a coincidence that the last story that I'm working on in my career at The Post brought me here, to an obscure little southern town where you happen to be living. And I don't think it's a coincidence that as soon as I got here, your relationship ended. I think the universe set both of us free so we can be together."

"If you're tryin' to get some ass tonight you can hang it up," Tess said as she turned her eyes away from his.

Antwan didn't say a word. He simply continued to stare in Tess's direction, and that's when she knew that he could see through the brick wall that she had been hiding behind. She knew that what Antwan had just said was what he actually felt, and it scared her. She was scared of being hurt again, and of rekindling their relationship only to mess things up with him like she had done with Maceo.

"It's almost midnight, so I think I better let you get some rest," Antwan said as he stood to his feet.

"Yes, it's been a long day."

Tess walked Antwan to the door, but a part of her wanted him to stay a little longer because she had enjoyed their simple dinner inside her room more than she had enjoyed any of their lavish nights out on the town when they had dated. "I hope you have a good night's sleep," she said.

"You too."

Antwan turned, pulled Tess close to him and gave her a hug so tender that she felt she could melt in his arms.

"Will you join me for breakfast in the morning?" He whispered into her ear, still holding her close to his body.

"What time?" she answered.

"Whenever you get up, I'll be ready."

Antwan kissed her cheek with the reverence of a gentleman, and then walked out the door.

Five minutes after Antwan left, Tess was still standing at her door. She couldn't believe what had just happened, and she had so many emotions swimming through her head. She wanted to talk to Bernadette, but she knew it was late and that her cousin had to be at work early in the morning. Just as she was about to walk to the bathroom to take a shower, her phone rang, and it was Bernadette.

"Oh my goodness, I was just thinking about calling you, but I thought it would be too late," Tess said.

"I can't sleep, so I left Coop snoring in bed and I'm out here in the living room. You've been so heavy on my mind, Tess, so I thought I would take a chance and give you a call. Are you still at Maceo's?"

"No, I moved all my things this morning. I'm in a suite at the St. Hamilton."

"You're literally five minutes away from me. Why didn't you just come over here? You know that I have plenty of room."

"I knew you would say that, but Bernadette, you know Coop doesn't want to see my face right about now, and to tell the truth, I'm too embarrassed to see his."

"Oh, Tess, I'm so sorry about all of this. It seems like everything is a big mess."

Tess nodded on her end. She walked to the edge of the bed and sat down. "I've caused a lot of problems, cuz, and this time I'm going to own every one of them. I hurt Mace, and I've no doubt caused tension between you and Coop because of it."

Bernadette exhaled. "Coop isn't happy about how things went down, that's for sure, and honestly, neither am I. Tess, I'm glad that you're going to accept responsibility. I'm not trying to pile on to your problems, but cuz, you've got to stop walking around acting like you're mad at the world. I know that you've been through a lot, but we all have. Hard times isn't an excuse for treating people badly, especially people who love you."

"Twenty-four hours ago, I would've had a smartass comeback for you, but tonight I'm just gonna say you're right."

"So what are you going to do now, because you can't stay at the St. Hamilton forever."

Tess fell back onto the bed and looked up at the ceiling as she spoke. "I've been thinking about that. The buyers who had been interested in my house just put an offer on a different property, so maybe that's God's way of blessing me with a roof over my head since he knew I was gonna fuck up the one I was living in."

"Somehow using an expletive while talking about the Lord just doesn't sound right."

"You know what, you're right. Girl I've got to do better."

"So you're going back to the windy city?"

"Yeah, I had initially thought about going back to DC. Mom and Dad have been trying to get me to move back home for years. The winters are less harsh, so who knows."

"Actually, I think that would be a great idea, and I can speak from personal experience that changing your environment can change your life in wonderful and unexpected ways."

"Right now I feel like anything is possible," Tess closed her eyes

and shook her head. "I never thought my life would be li
now, cuz."

"I know what you mean," Bernadette said in a low voice.

"Yeah, but your situation is completely different because the
things that you didn't think were possible came true. You have a
good man who loves you and I can see you and Coop sitting in rocking chairs growing old together."

Bernadette cleared her throat. "With kids and grandkids by our
side."

Tess opened her eyes. "Are you and Coop thinking about adopt-
ing?" she asked with surprise.

"Tess, I'm pregnant."

Tess squinted her eyes as if that would help her understand what
she had just heard. "Bernadette, what did you just say?"

"I'm pregnant. I wasn't going to say anything until I made it out
of my first trimester, but yes, I'm pregnant."

Tess shot straight up from the bed as if an electric current had just
surged through her body. Her feet hit the floor and she began to
pace. "What?! How can you be pregnant?"

"Well, Coop and I had sex, and his sperm fertilized my egg, and
then . . ."

"I know how babies are made, Bernadette!" Tess said in a state of
disbelief. "I just don't understand how . . . why? . . . I just . . ."

Bernadette eased her voice into a calm and steady tone. "Other
than my mother, you're the person who I've been most worried to
tell about my pregnancy, Tess. I know that you want children, but
you can't get pregnant. And here I am, not trying to get pregnant,
yet, I'm going into my ninth week, and not only that," Bernadette
paused and then cleared her throat. "I'm having twins."

Tess felt the room begin to spin and she had to return to the bed
to regain her footing. "And you're serious?" she asked, still in disbelief. "You're not bullshitting me just to get a reaction, are you?"

"Are you insane?" Bernadette said, completely changing the tone in her voice. "Why in the world would I make up something like that? You know me well enough to know I wouldn't joke around about something so serious."

"Cuz, this is just so shocking. I didn't even know that you and Coop wanted kids."

"We didn't either, and trust me, we weren't trying. It just happened."

Tess listened as Bernadette told her that what she had thought was menopause had actually been the first symptoms of her pregnancy. She told her that she had been nervous about telling Coop, but after he had proposed to her the night of Arizona's wedding, she had no choice but to tell him right away. Bernadette also admitted that not a day went by that she didn't worry about miscarrying, and that she had agonized over how Tess might receive her news, in light of her own reproductive challenges. And finally, Bernadette told Tess that if she was blessed to carry to full term, she wanted her and Arizona to be godmothers to her children.

"Damn!" Tess said, and then shook her head. "You and Coop are gonna be old ass parents and I'm gonna be a fly ass auntie. Bernadette, we're gonna have a baby . . . I mean babies!" Tess said as she screamed with excitement.

"You're not upset?"

Tess was startled her cousin would even ask that question, but then it hit her, and she knew exactly why Bernadette felt the way she did, and it nearly brought tears to Tess's eyes. Tess knew that she had been so self-absorbed, rude, and downright difficult to deal with. This was why Bernadette thought that instead of being happy for her and Coop, Tess would lash out because of her own problems or feel jealous by making comparisons of their lives. And this time, Tess allowed her tears to fall.

"No, Bernadette," Tess said through small sniffles. "The only thing that I'm upset about is the fact that my behavior has been so shitty that it's caused you to have reservations about sharing something so joyous for fear I wouldn't be happy for you, and I apologize for that. I'm so, so very happy for you and Coop."

Bernadette let happy tears fall on her end of the phone as she spoke through sniffles of her own. "I'm so relieved, Tess. This has taken a big weight off my shoulders."

"Bernadette, I'm here for you every step of the way. You're going to carry your babies to full term, and they're going to be a beautiful blessing to you and Coop."

"Thank you, cuz. I receive your words, and I'm going to think positively about things each day."

"You better."

Bernadette told Tess that Arizona had already guessed that she was pregnant, and Tess felt a little sting of guilt because she knew that if she hadn't been so focused on her own problems instead of pointing out flaws in the cousin who loved her, she would have seen all the signs that Arizona had. Tess apologized again, and then they talked a few minutes longer about how quickly things in both their lives had changed. It was approaching one in the morning and they both knew they needed sleep.

"Oh, before I forget," Bernadette said. "Don't leave town until Sunday."

"Why Sunday?"

"Because Coop and I are going to the Justice of the Peace to get married this Saturday, and I want you there. But I have to warn you, Maceo is going to be there, too."

"It's not about me, or Mace. Saturday is going to be your and Coop's big day, and I can't wait to celebrate with you both."

"Prayers get answered every day," Bernadette said before they ended the call.

Twenty minutes later, Tess had showered and was in bed, relaxing from her roller coaster of a day. She had to admit that a small part of her wanted to cry out and say, "Why can't I get pregnant? Why can't I have a man who loves me the way Coop loves Bernadette?" But as she drifted off to sleep, a smile came to her face because her feelings of happiness for her cousin far outweighed her own longing, and in that moment, Tess knew that she had begun her journey, however long it might take, to becoming a better person.

Chapter 21

ARIZONA

Arizona felt tired, happy, and confused, but also empowered, all at the same time. The last two days had been hectic and filled with unimaginable highs and lows, and now, as she sat in front of her computer, ready to read the email that would let her know if Jaquan was Solomon's biological father, she reflected on the events that had brought her to this moment.

When she had walked through the door two nights ago at the ULTA Beauty makeup event, the room had fallen silent, and Arizona hadn't known what to think. But when the other makeup artists had started congratulating her and telling her that they loved her video, as well as her style, she had felt as though she could have floated home. By the time she left the store, she had made dozens of contacts and had gone home with so many promotional products that she'd had to enlist the help of two sales associates to assist her with transporting them to her SUV. Before she went home she had stopped by her parents' house, kissed Solomon good night, and shared her good news with her parents, who had been overjoyed and proud of her. But once she arrived home, Arizona's positive energy evaporated as soon as she walked through the door.

"Where have you been?" Chris asked in an irritated voice. He looked at the Seiko on his wrist, as if he were a coach who was clocking an athlete's time.

Arizona pursed her lips. "If you had checked your phone you'd know where I've been. I even sent you a follow up reminder from the original message that I texted you last week," she spat back. "Besides, you have some nerve asking me where I've been. It's barely nine o'clock, and you haven't gotten home before ten since we got back from the honeymoon."

"All of that talk still doesn't answer my question. Where have you been?"

"Didn't I just tell you to check your phone!" Arizona nearly shouted as she walked into their bedroom. She placed her handbag on the chair in the corner and tried to calm herself by taking deep breaths.

"Don't walk away from me," Chris called out as he followed her into the bedroom they'd never really shared.

She didn't want to deal with Chris, and she could already tell from the way that he'd spoken to her when she had walked through the door that their conversation wasn't going to end well. "Chris, I don't feel like arguing with you tonight. I've had a long day and all I want to do is take a shower and get some sleep."

"Your message said you were at some beauty event, but how do I know that's the truth?"

"Because I don't lie."

"How do I know you weren't out with that ex-con?"

"So that's what this is about? You think I was out with Jaquan tonight?"

"You've met with him before and you didn't bother to mention it to me, so why should tonight be any different?"

Arizona didn't know what to say because Chris was right. She had told him about running into Jaquan last Saturday night, but she hadn't mentioned that she'd had lunch with him just yesterday, and now she wondered how he could have known. *Maybe he's bluffing to see if he can catch me in something,* Arizona thought to herself. She didn't think that any of their very few mutual friends would have seen them at The Magnolia Room, but there was a possibility that someone may have spotted her SUV parked outside Jaquan's Uncle Clem's house this morning when she had stopped by to swab Jaquan's cheek before mailing the sample off along with Solomon's and one of her own. Arizona knew that Bourbon was too small to contain secrets for any length of time, and that eventually, all things would come to light. But even with that, she planned to remain silent until Chris presented her with definitive proof.

"Were you with him tonight?" Chris asked.

"No, I wasn't, and this is the last time I'm gonna tell you . . . I was at the ULTA event, then I stopped by Mom and Dad's to see Solomon before he went to sleep, and now I'm home, arguing with you for no good reason."

"Are you planning to leave me like Tess left Maceo?"

"What?"

"Don't act like you don't know that she checked into the hotel this morning. Her car is sitting in the valet garage packed full of all her things."

Arizona's entire body tensed because Chris was giving her information that she truly did not know. "Are you sure?"

"Of course I'm sure," Chris answered in a condescending voice that he had never used when talking with Arizona until this very moment. "I'm the general manager of the hotel, so I know everything that's going on there, especially when a guest checks into one of our presidential suites with an open-ended departure date."

"I honestly didn't know. I talked to Tess earlier this afternoon, and I knew that she and Maceo had ended their relationship, but she didn't mention anything about checking into the St. Hamilton. And honestly, even if I did know, Tess and Maceo have nothing to do with what's going on under this roof."

"Birds of a feather."

"What's that supposed to mean?"

"Don't play dumb, Arizona. You've been acting different ever since you started hanging out with Tess and Bernadette. Our relationship was fine for two years, and then bam!" he said, with a slap of his hand. "All of a sudden you started having second thoughts about us, complaining about me, and now you're coming home all times of the night."

Arizona was beginning to think that Chris had truly lost his mind. "I've had about enough of this foolishness. It's been a long day and you're making me extra tired." Arizona walked into the bathroom and began removing her clothes so she could take a shower, and Chris was once again right on her heels. "Do you mind? I'm trying to undress."

Chris gave her a judging look. "The last time I checked, I was your husband, and I've seen everything that you have."

Arizona blew out a deep breath of you're-about-to-get-cursed-out and looked directly into Chris's eyes. "I'm gonna hold back from saying some things that could cut you to your core and truly hurt your feelings, only because I'm a Christian. But if you don't get out of here right now, I promise you that all hell is fittin'ta break loose right here in this bathroom."

"I'll be waiting for you when you get out."

"Please don't. Just go back to the guest room and let's call it a night."

Chris shook his head. "I'll wait for you right here, in our bedroom."

"Why?" Arizona said in a raised voice. "I don't get you, Chris. You haven't shown me any attention since we got married, and other than to get a few clothes out of the closet to put into the guest room, you haven't been in this bedroom since you pulled that stunt with the vibrator. But now, all of a sudden you're in here, not to comfort me, or apologize for anything, but to start a fight."

"What do I need to apologize to you for? If anyone deserves an apology, it's me."

"You've lost your mind, and if I didn't know any better, I'd think you were tryin' to make me lose mine, too."

"I've been good to you, Arizona. And I've taken care of you."

Arizona shook her head and took a deep breath. "Did you click on the link to my video that I sent you?"

"Don't try to change the subject," Chris said in a heated tone. "You know that what I just said is true. I pay your bills, I'm raising Solomon like he's my own, and I work hard every day to provide for this family. But you don't seem to appreciate any of that because you're more interested in some low-life criminal straight out the pen, and now you're trying to move me out of my position so you can slide him in. I'm not letting that happen."

Arizona could feel her temperature boil, so she took a deep breath and tried to ignore ninety-five percent of what Chris had just said, and instead, she chose to respond to what she felt she could manage. "I wasn't trying to change the subject, I was trying to make a point."

Chris folded his arms across his chest. "What's your point?"

"If you had bothered to click the link in the message that I sent, you would've known that my video went viral, and as of tonight it has seven hundred thousand views and over two hundred and fifty thousand people have subscribed to my channel. All in one day."

Chris smirked. "So now this is all about you, huh?"

"Excuse me?"

"Forget it. You wouldn't understand."

Arizona threw her hands up in the air. "It took me a minute, but unfortunately, I do understand. You were good to Solomon and me because you wanted me to be dependent on you, that way it would be hard for me to leave you when you started trippin' like you're doing now."

"Don't try to make me out to be the bad guy. I've always been there for you, and it's not because I wanted to make you dependent on me. I do what I do out of love."

"That's a lie. If you loved me, you would've looked at that video and you would've been happy for me. Happy that my dreams are coming true. But you don't care about that because your real motives are clear to me, and it's all about control."

"Woman, you're crazy!" Chris said in a hateful, dismissive tone. "I can name at least twenty women who would trade places with you right now. Do you know how many women would love to have a good man who takes care of them, and their child?"

Arizona smirked. "And I guarantee you, all twenty of those women would be full of regret once they took a look at your invisible dick!" Arizona spat out. "Yeah, I said it, asshole. You got a little ass dick, and you don't know what the hell you're doin' in bed, so the only way you can feel like you have some type of control, as a man, is to keep me under lock and key. Well, I'm the wrong one."

Chris charged toward Arizona, but she put her hand up and stopped him in his tracks with her next words. "If you hit me, I won't have to call 911, because once my brothers and my cousins get through with you, your mama's gonna have to arrange a closed casket service to lay yo ass to rest. Now step." Arizona picked up her handbag and walked out the door, knowing that this time, Chris wasn't going to follow her.

Arizona had thought about driving back over to her parents' house to spend the night, but she didn't want to upset them, plus, she was too embarrassed to face them. Even though Arizona knew that Bernadette would gladly welcome her into her home, she didn't want to disturb her and Coop in the middle of the night. Then she thought about Jaquan. She knew that even though he was staying with his Uncle Clem, and he was limited on resources, he would either ask her to stay with him or do his best to put her up at a hotel for the night. But she decided against that option as well because she knew it would only lead to more complications.

She knew she had to reserve what little money she had in her bank account, so checking into a hotel was out of the question. Finally, she decided to go to her small, empty home that she had never fully appreciated until now.

"I'm so glad that I didn't rent out this place," Arizona said when she walked through the front door. "And thank goodness I didn't turn off the electricity or the water," she said aloud as she walked to the thermostat and blasted the cool air to relieve the stuffy heat that had settled inside. Her home looked much bigger inside now that all of her furniture was gone. She hated that she had sold most of her things on Craigslist and at the yard sale that she'd had last month, all at Chris's insistence. But she was thankful that she had what she needed, which was a roof over her head.

She sat in the middle of the floor and dialed Jaquan's number.

"Hey, A, are you okay?" Jaquan asked after picking up on the first ring.

"Actually, I'm not, but how did you know?"

"You're calling me late at night, which means that you're probably not at home, and if you're not home, that means that something went down with you and Chris."

Arizona let out a heavy sigh. "It did. He flipped out on me."

"Did he put his hands on you?" Jaquan asked with tightness in his voice.

Arizona could tell from Jaquan's reaction that although he was a changed person, he was still a man not to be played with, and his concern touched her because she knew it was sincere. "No," she answered. "But he did say a bunch of crazy stuff that made no kind of sense. I had to leave."

"Where are you now?"

"I'm at my old house. There's no furniture in here but at least I have a place to lay my head."

"Why didn't you call me, you know I got you, A. You can stay in the spare room at my Uncle's, and if you don't want to do that I'll get you a room at a hotel. But you don't need to be staying in an empty house, late at night. You know how it is around here in The Bottoms."

"I'll be fine, really. People know me in this neighborhood so nobody's gonna do anything foolish."

"What's your address, I'm coming over."

Arizona thought about Jaquan's offer and immediately became excited, but then she reminded herself that she shouldn't do anything that might escalate drama. "No, Jaquan, I'm tired and I'm just going to lay down and go to sleep. But how about breakfast in the morning?"

Arizona and Jaquan talked for a while longer until she finally convinced him that she would be safe in her house. They agreed to meet for breakfast in the morning at a small diner on the edge of town, and then said good night.

Arizona stretched out on the floor and used her handbag as a pillow beneath her head. She looked at the empty walls with the aid of the streetlight that shone into the room. "I feel more comfortable lying on this hard floor than I felt in the bed at Chris's house," Arizona whispered into the dark. But instead of feeling sad, she was filled with thanks. She was thankful about the doors of opportunity that she knew her video was about to open, and she had no doubt that those opportunities were going to help her provide for herself and her son. She didn't worry about Chris, her failed marriage, the bills that were due next month, or anything else as she drifted off to sleep, already aiming her focus on how she was going to conquer the day as soon as the sun came up.

★ ★ ★

Even though Arizona had gone to sleep late last night, she had risen early this morning to get a jump on her day. She waited until she knew that Chris was gone to work before she went by the house. After letting herself in, she took a quick shower, which felt like a therapeutic massage after having slept on the floor all night. She changed into a brightly colored sundress, applied her makeup, and then snapped a few pictures to post on social media.

Her YouTube views had surpassed one million, and again, she was still in disbelief. She looked at the comments which continued to pour in, so she took a moment to post a thank you to everyone who had viewed, left comments, shared her video, and given her support. She had thought about filming another quick video, but she decided against it, knowing that she had a lot to do before heading out to meet Jaquan for breakfast.

Arizona packed as many of her and Solomon's clothes as she could fit into two suitcases, and then filled a large storage container with her makeup and video equipment before loading them into her SUV. She knew that she would be coming back to get her things, but in case Chris went way off the rails and changed the locks, she wanted to make sure that she had the bare essentials of what she needed. "I need to get Solomon's camping gear," she said, as she remembered that he would be going on a trip through his summer camp this weekend.

She had stored Solomon's sleeping bag, canteen, and a few other items that he would need in the closet inside the guest room where Chris was now sleeping. "I hate to even go in here," she said aloud as she entered the room. She opened the closet and retrieved the items she needed. She was about to leave the room when she saw some papers peeking out from underneath the bed. As soon as she saw them, Arizona knew that the papers would reveal trouble, because as her mother had always said, "when you look for trouble, you find it."

"I'll pick it up and put it away because papers don't need to be on the floor," Arizona said as she rationalized her curiosity. She placed Solomon's camping gear atop the bed, bent down to retrieve the papers, and got the shock of her life.

Arizona had been in disbelief—in a good way—when she had seen the success of her video yesterday morning, and now, she was in disbelief—in a bad way—as she read the papers in her hand. She was holding the results of a physical that Chris had taken one month before their wedding, which until now she had known nothing about. Initially, she hadn't seen anything out of the ordinary until she flipped to the last few pages and read the doctor's notes.

Cluster B Personality Disorder: Borderline Personality Disorder

Arizona's mouth fell open and stayed that way for a full ten minutes. According to the information in Chris's records, his doctor had notated information about Chris's medication, which he had not been taking and his psychotherapy sessions, which he had not attended since January, right around the time of Arizona's birthday.

Arizona reached into her handbag, pulled out her phone and Googled Borderline Personality Disorder. As she read through the list of common symptoms, some didn't pertain to Chris, at least not that she knew of, but many of them did, and many things that she hadn't noticed before now stood out like big, bold danger signs.

Fragile self-image, chronic feelings of emptiness and fear of abandonment, pattern of unstable and intense interpersonal relationships, impulsivity, and identity disturbance were listed in Chris's chart. Arizona thought of instances where she could pinpoint examples of each of Chris's symptoms. His fragile self-image stemmed from his micropenis, which he had dealt with all his life. She remembered that he'd told her that he had even transferred schools during college to avoid ridicule after a girl that he'd been dating had discovered that his penis was smaller than her pinky. His feelings of emptiness and fear of abandonment had been front and center last night when he had thought she was going to leave him, and she also thought back to an incident several months ago when she had considered breaking up with him. He had been out of town, working at the St. Hamilton's sister hotel in Washington, DC, and had left the job and showed up at her door in the middle of the night, begging her not to leave him.

Arizona realized that many of Chris's actions, which she had seen as protective, caring, and endearing, were actually controlling, manipulative, and impulsive. And most of all, his symptom of identity disturbance stood out to her. She'd always found it strange that up until last night, Chris had disassociated himself with the reality of their marital problems, especially since he had been the primary cause of them. She discovered through a few articles that his identity disturbance and impulsive behavior were tied to his feelings of emptiness, which he exercised through manipulation.

"Why didn't I see this before now?" Arizona said to herself. She folded the papers, put them inside her handbag, and gathered Solomon's things before walking out of Chris's house.

Arizona called Jaquan once she was in her SUV and told him that she would no longer be able to meet him for breakfast. He was disappointed, but he understood once she explained to him what she'd found at Chris's house, and so that he fully understood the scope of her troubles, she shared the delicate information about her and Chris's pitiful, nonexistent sex life. She told him that she needed to act quickly so she could move the rest of her and Solomon's things, because she didn't know Chris's state of mind and she did not want to leave anything to chance. By the time she ended their conversation she was in front of her parents' house. Arizona felt her heart beat fast because this was a conversation that she didn't want to have.

Arizona sat in her driver's seat, looking at the modest, three-bedroom, two-bathroom, ranch style house she had grown up in, and thought about the two people inside who had raised her. She was the reason why her parents had to make numerous trips to the principal's office and attend regular parent/teacher conferences to correct bad behavior during her elementary school years. She'd caused her mother to experience premature graying during her middle school years. She'd kept both her parents up at night with worry during her high school years. And she'd raised so much hell during her early twenties that they'd told her that all they could do at that point was give her over to God. But even with all the worries and disappointments that Arizona had caused Myron and Carlotta Mays, they had always been there for her when she needed them.

"Now I'm married, I have my own business that's about to take off, and a son who's a straight-A student in the gifted and talented program," Arizona said as she looked at the welcome wreath on her parents' front door. "But I'm about to cause Mom and Dad more headache, just like I always do." As much as Arizona didn't want to upset her parents, she knew that she needed to tell them what was going on because once again, she needed their help.

A few minutes later, Arizona watched her mother and father's mouths drop as she told them the same information that she had told Jaquan, even the part about Chris's micropenis, which made her father look away and her mother put her hand to her mouth in what Arizona could see was pure shock.

"I can't believe it," her mother said. "I had no idea that you and Chris were having troubles, and the fact that you hid it says a lot, 'cause that's not like you, baby. But I don't blame you for leavin'."

Arizona's father was more strategic and to the point. "I'mma put a call in to Bud, Rabbit, and Squirrel"—the nicknames of her two brothers and her first cousin—"and we can have your things moved out before lunchtime."

Even before Arizona had read Chris's medical documents, she'd known that their ill-fated marriage was over. She had heard stories about people who'd dated someone for years, had gotten married, and then their spouse flipped the script into someone brand new, but she never thought she would be one of those people.

The more Arizona thought about how Bernadette had repeatedly told her that Chris's problems were just as much about his selfish manipulation and need for control as they were about his physical shortcomings, the more she realized her friend had been right. And even Tess, who in Arizona's opinion had no relationship skills whatsoever, had been right when she'd said that something about Chris's mental state wasn't quite right.

Arizona had been blinded by the façade that Chris had created through artful manipulation. But she also had to admit that the warning signs had been there all along, and instead of heeding them she had looked the other way, all so she could have a father for her son and a husband for herself.

Two hours later, Arizona's father had been true to his word. He, along with her brothers and her cousin, had moved every single item she owned—which had not been much—back into her house. They had even set up a twin bed in her bedroom that had been in her parents' storage shed. She had told her parents that the bed was the only furniture that she was willing to accept from them, and that she was going to start over from the ground up, on her own. After her relatives left, she dialed Bernadette and Tess on a group call and told them the crazy events that had happened to her since the three of them had spoken less than twenty-four hours ago. And like good girlfriends, they told her that they would be at her house later that night.

It was now eight o'clock, and Bernadette, Tess, and Arizona were at her house, sipping wine and unpacking Arizona's boxes.

"Girl, I told you that Negro was crazy as hell," Tess said. "But I didn't know that he had all these problems."

"He's not crazy," Arizona corrected as she shook her head. "He has a personality disorder."

Tess took a sip of wine. "Okay, well, the bottom line is that I'm glad you left him because who knows what could've happened."

"You're right," Arizona said as she poured more wine into her glass. "I wish I had listened to you and Bernadette, but you know how you have to experience something for yourself in order to believe it? But let me be clear, the main reason that I can't stay in this marriage isn't because of Chris's mental state, because that can be managed if he's willing to put in the work. But his micropenis and lack of sexual skills . . . that's too much for me. I tried to convince myself that I could live without good sex, but I can't."

Bernadette nodded her head. "You aren't the first woman who bought into a fantasy and you definitely won't be the last. But like Tess said, the good thing is that you got out while you still could. I can't believe that Chris actually acted like he was going to hit you last night."

Tess shook her head. "He wasn't going to do a damn thing."

"What makes you so sure?" Arizona asked. "What I know now is that one of the symptoms of people with BPD is intense anger and even violence, and Chris sure was mad enough to hit me."

Tess shook her head again. "If he had really wanted to lay hands on you, you would've never had a chance to talk all that shit that you did about having your family whoop his ass because he would've laid you out and worried about the consequences later. He just wanted to scare you."

"It was the control factor," Bernadette said as she took a large gulp of her bottled water. "He wanted to scare you into submission, and although anyone who knows you would laugh at the thought, Chris's mental state allowed him to think that he could, or at least try."

"Be prepared for him to call you, or come looking for you," Tess said. "I know he probably lost it when he came home and saw that you moved everything out."

Arizona sat beside Bernadette in one of the dining room chairs that her brothers had placed in the living room. "He probably won't be home from work for another hour."

"Do you think he'll try to come over here?" Bernadette said with worry.

Arizona sat back in her chair. "Absolutely not. I left a note for him along with the house key that let him know that I found his medical papers and if he comes anywhere near me he'll have to deal with Daddy, Bud, Rabbit, Squirrel, and every man that I know in the Bottoms."

"That's right," Tess said. "Some good ol' down home ass whoppin'. And I'm telling you now, if I see him at the hotel, I'm gonna give him a piece of my mind."

"I hope that's the wine talking," Bernadette jumped in, "because you definitely don't need to do that. You've caused enough scenes to write three novels."

Tess laughed. "I guess you have a point."

Bernadette shifted her weight in her seat. "I hope that Chris gets back on his medication and resumes his therapy, because despite how mad we all may feel about what he's done, especially you, Arizona, Chris needs professional help."

Arizona nodded in agreement. "You're right, Bernadette. But he's gonna be somebody else's problem now. I need to find a good divorce lawyer."

Tess piped up. "Girl, don't worry about a long, drawn out divorce. After all the shit that you've experienced with Chris in less than three weeks, you've got to have grounds for an annulment, just like Antwan did."

Arizona and Bernadette glanced at each other, and she knew that Bernadette had detected the same change in Tess's voice and tone at the mention of Antwan's name. She had never thought that Tess had fully gotten over Antwan, and now that she was back on the market, Arizona had a strong feeling that her friend would end up back in his arms.

"So, how long is Antwan gonna stay in town?" Arizona asked. "Is he just about finished with that murder story he's workin' on?"

Tess nodded. "Yes, he's wrapping it up. As a matter of fact, he texted me right before I came here and told me that he and Coop were about to meet for dinner."

Bernadette looked at Tess. "Coop told me they were supposed to meet tomorrow afternoon."

"Yes, that was the original plan, but Antwan's text said that Coop had a change of plans and wanted to meet earlier," she said and then paused. "And guess where they're meeting?"

Bernadette reached into her handbag and pulled out her phone. "I'm going to see if Coop texted me."

"Where are they meeting?" Arizona asked with curiosity.

Bernadette spoke up as she looked away from her phone. "According to Coop's text they're at Fried Green Tomatoes."

Arizona rose from her chair. "You've got to be kidding me."

"Somehow I missed Coop's call and his text," Bernadette said. "But that's where they are."

Arizona shook her head. "I guess it makes sense because it's closer to the St. Hamilton, where Antwan's staying, and the food is good." Arizona reached for her glass and took a sip of her wine. "Are y'all thinkin' what I'm thinkin'?"

"What's that?" Bernadette asked with a touch of worry in her voice.

"Cuz, are you okay?" Tess asked as she looked at Bernadette. "We need to make sure you and the babies are all right."

Bernadette nodded. "I'm okay, just a little tired. I think I need to head home," she said as she looked at Arizona and then at Tess. "Are you ready?"

"Yea, I'm ready, but I wish I'd driven my car instead of riding here with you, that way you wouldn't have to take me back to the hotel, and you could just go straight home."

"Tess, you know I don't mind. Besides, it'll give me a chance to walk you to your room and make sure you don't curse anyone out on your way up."

Before Tess and Bernadette left, Bernadette handed Arizona a greeting card. "This is to cheer you up," she said with a smile. "Oh, you forgot to tell us, what were you thinking?"

Arizona chuckled. "That all our men are at the same place to-night."

"Girl, Antwan's not my man," Tess said with a wave of her hand.

For the second time tonight, Arizona and Bernadette exchanged a knowing glance before they said good night.

Now, it was Friday afternoon, and Arizona was nervous as she sat in the passenger's seat of Jaquan's jeep, staring at the email from the testing lab that contained the confidential DNA paternity results.

Jaquan had called her last night right after Bernadette and Tess had left, and told her that he was worried about her safety and that she shouldn't be in her house alone a second night in a row. He told her that he was going to come over after his shift ended, and if she didn't feel comfortable with him spending the night inside, he would sleep in his jeep, parked in front of her house.

Arizona had been glad that she agreed to let Jaquan come over, and she'd been especially glad that she had welcomed him inside. They shared a delicious meal of tender rosemary chicken, mashed potatoes, and asparagus that he had brought from work. After they finished their meal, Arizona lit one of her scented candles and they talked into the wee hours of the morning before falling asleep—she on her twin bed, and Jaquan on the floor beside her.

When Arizona had awoken, she had looked down and saw Jaquan sleeping peacefully, and at that moment she felt in her gut that regardless of what the DNA results were, Jaquan was going to be a part of her and Solomon's life.

"It just came to my inbox," Arizona said in the present, bringing her mind back to the moment at hand as she and Jaquan sat inside his Jeep.

He nodded. "Please don't keep me in suspense."

Arizona clicked on the message and began reading. At first she did not understand all the columns and numbers until her eyes landed on the portion that listed the paternity probability percentage. She closed her eyes and laid her head back against the headrest.

"What does it say?" Jaquan asked, trying keep his voice steady.

Arizona opened her eyes and handed him her phone without saying a word.

She exhaled a deep breath and watched the expression on Jaquan's face as he read the results. He nodded his head and handed her phone back to her.

"Let's go to your parents' house so I can finally meet my son," Jaquan said as he smiled wider than Arizona had ever seen.

Chapter 22

BERNADETTE

Bernadette was a nervous wreck after she and Tess left Arizona's house. Coop had called her on her drive and told her that he would tell her all about his meeting with Antwan once she got home. After dropping Tess off at the St. Hamilton, she'd felt as though it had taken her an hour to reach her house, instead of the actual five-minute route because the closer she got to her home, the more pressure she felt.

Bernadette walked into the house and found Coop waiting for her with a bowl of Rocky Road ice cream on the island countertop.

"This must be bad," she said with nervousness.

Coop kissed Bernadette on her cheek and helped her to the barstool. "I hope that once we're married you start listenin' to me. Didn't I tell you that everything was gonna be fine?"

Bernadette blinked her eyes with questions. "What happened?"

Coop took a seat beside Bernadette. "Antwan asked me a lot of questions. He's thorough, and he's a good reporter. But the truth about what I've been keepin' to myself for all these years is finally out."

Bernadette was so nervous that she bit her bottom lip as she watched her ice cream melt into a brown puddle.

Coop reached for Bernadette's hand. "I'm not goin' to jail. I didn't kill Morris Fleming."

Bernadette's eyes grew wide. "If you didn't, who did?"

Bernadette listened as Coop told her the details of the night that Morris had been killed. It was true that Morris had beaten Sue after he'd found out that she was pregnant, in hopes that each blow he dealt her would cause her to miscarry, freeing him of responsibility for a child and a life that he didn't want. And it was also true that Coop had been crazy with rage when he had come home to his sister's house where he'd been staying and he'd seen her badly battered face and body, bloodied and swollen. But by the time he had helped clean and bandage Sue's wounds, Morris had already been dead for more than two hours, lying in an alley with a bullet through his heart that Sue had put there.

When the police had found Morris's body the next morning, they couldn't find a single person in The Bottoms who had heard a gunshot or seen a thing. Everyone's lips were tight. Everyone had speculated about what had happened to the stranger who'd been found dead in an alley, but no one had known for sure, and no one was going to talk. Coop's reputation had ensured silence, and that was the way it was to this day.

Coop had never wanted the truth to come out, especially after Sue passed away, because he didn't want to taint her legacy, or bring more trauma to Maceo by revealing that his dear, sweet mother had killed his father. And even now, Coop was still protecting Sue's good name.

Bernadette looked down at her melted ice cream. "Coop, why didn't you just tell me from the beginning. I thought there was a real possibility you had killed that man."

"I'm sorry, Bernie. I know it was eatin' you up inside, and after talkin' with Antwan, I realized that I should've told you. But I didn't want to get you involved because if it came down to you havin' to tell what you knew, I didn't want to put you in that position."

"What made you tell Antwan?" Bernadette asked.

Coop let out a tired sigh. "Actually, I didn't tell him a thing. He'd already figured it out, and when he asked me questions, I didn't confirm or deny. Then he told me somethin' that made me change my entire opinion about him, and Tess, too.

"After Antwan laid out every detail that he'd investigated, he said that Tess had told him a little about Maceo's background, and that she had felt bad about hurting him because of all the pain and loss that he's already endured. Then Antwan said it was a shame that after all these years the details of the case may never see the light of day because he was gonna have to walk away from the story."

"What?" Bernadette said with confusion. "I don't understand. I get that he probably wants to do the compassionate thing and spare Maceo, and you, too. But Antwan's a hard, stone cold journalist, and I can't believe that he's going to just let this go."

"Like Antwan told me, sometimes whether it's right or wrong, you gotta listen to your gut, and he said that he doesn't have the heart to finish the story, and because this is his last project before he retires and he's sacrificed so much in his career, he's gonna tell his editor that he's bowing out."

Bernadette shook her head. "That's so unlike him. I just can't believe it."

"I can," Coop said with a serious look. "The thing that killed that maggot, Morris Fleming, is the same thing that made Antwan drop the case, and that's love. Even though Sue loved Morris with all her heart, he took advantage of her and abused it, so she shot him clean through his. And even though Antwan loves what he does, I believe that he loves Tess more, and hurting Maceo would hurt her, so he let his heart make the decision for him."

Bernadette leaned into Coop's arms and he rocked her back and forth as she shed a few tears.

"Bernie, didn't I tell you that everything was gonna work out?"

★ ★ ★

Bernadette was thankful she had made it through the week. The past five days had been filled with shocking discoveries, hard conversations, tragic endings, and new beginnings.

Now, it was a bright and beautiful Saturday afternoon, and the temperature in Bourbon was close to one hundred degrees. But despite the stifling heat, Bernadette felt as cool and fresh as a spring morning because she was about to marry Coop.

The day after Coop had revealed the truth behind his decades-long secret, Bernadette had gone to a specialty boutique not far from where she lived, and found an elegant cream-colored off-the-shoulder sheath dress with a delicately designed matching shawl. She completed her look with a pair of champagne-colored flats that comforted her swollen feet and ankles, and accessorized the ensemble with a beautiful pair of pearl and rhinestone earrings. She wore her hair in her signature chignon, and because it had been growing like weeds since she'd become pregnant, she let the front fall to one side, resting against her chin in neat spiral curls. Her finishing touch was the flawless makeup that Arizona had expertly applied. It had been especially meaningful to Bernadette because Arizona had filmed her makeup application from start to finish, and was going to upload the video as her first bridal makeup tutorial.

When Bernadette arrived at the magistrate's office with Tess and Arizona, she was so excited that not even the heat and humidity bothered her. And although her mother wasn't there to celebrate her big day, she had called Bernadette earlier that morning to wish her and Coop a lifetime of happiness. Rosa had told Bernadette that Tess had called her last night, and that they'd had a long, heart-to-heart talk that had been difficult at times, but also eye-opening, and while Rosa hadn't gone into all the details, she told Bernadette that Tess had made her realize that old dogs could learn new tricks.

As Bernadette stood in front of Coop, waiting to say their vows, she admired her handsome groom in his charcoal gray suit, cream-colored tie and matching pocket square. Bernadette handed her simple bouquet of hydrangeas, eucalyptus, and cream-colored roses to Tess, as Coop slipped a dazzling band of diamonds onto her finger that perfectly complemented her custom-made engagement ring. Then she slipped a polished, platinum band with gold trim onto Coop's ring finger.

Bernadette glanced at Maceo, who was standing by Coop's side. She could tell that he was still hurt from all that had happened between him and Tess, but she could also see that he was happy that his uncle had finally found true love.

After the officiant pronounced them husband and wife, Coop kissed Bernadette more gently than she had ever remembered him doing, and they were officially Mr. and Mrs. Dennis.

A few hours later, Bernadette and Coop stood in front of a select group of friends, family and loyal Southern Comfort regulars and thanked them for coming out to help them celebrate their special day. Bernadette was overjoyed. Tess and Antwan raised their glasses, and so did Arizona and Jaquan, as they toasted to love.

Bernadette knew that just as the past six months had been turbulent, the days and months ahead would most likely present even more unforeseen challenges. She didn't know what the future held, but she knew that as long as she had her loving husband and her good girlfriends in her corner, she would surely make it to the other side.

A Message About Mental Illness/ Mental Health

If you or someone you know has a mental illness, is struggling emotionally, or has concerns about their mental health, there are ways to get help. Please use these resources to find help for you, a friend, or a family member.

National Institute of Mental Health
866-615-6464
https://www.nimh.nih.gov/health

NEABPD (National Education Alliance for Borderline Personality Disorder)
914.682.5496
https://www.borderlinepersonalitydisorder.org/resources/treatment-resources

National Suicide Prevention Lifeline
1-800-273-TALK (8255)
https://suicidepreventionlifeline.org

Veterans Crisis Line
1-800-273-TALK (8255) and press 1 or text to 838255
https://www.veteranscrisisline.net

Stay Safe and Stay Healthy

BLINDSIDED

Trice Hickman

ABOUT THIS GUIDE

The suggested questions are included to enhance your group's
reading of Trice Hickman's *Blindsided*!

If you're a member of a book club I'd love to join you at your next monthly meeting, in-person or via your preferred video conference platform. To schedule a meeting please visit my website at www.tricehickman.com, and we'll make it happen.

1. Bernadette, Tess, and Arizona share the same birthday, ten years apart. Other than being Aquarians, what other characteristics do you think they shared? In what ways were they opposite?

2. Each character had their own set of delicate situations to navigate. In your opinion, which character do you think faced the biggest challenge and why?

3. Which character do you think grew/changed the most, from the beginning to their journey to end of the book?

4. Bernadette faced a moral dilemma as it related to Coop's involvement in an unsolved murder case. If you had solid and indisputable evidence of a crime that had been committed by someone you loved, would you turn them in to the authorities, or would you remain silent?

5. Tess kept her fertility issues from Maceo for fear that he would break up with her. Conversely, when Antwan reentered her life, she told him almost immediately. Do you think that Tess and Antwan will have a better relationship the second time around? If so, why? If no, why not?

6. Arizona and Chris struggled with sexual dysfunction in their marriage. How important do you think sex is in a relationship/marriage?

7. Chris struggled with mental illness and hid it from Arizona. What were some of the signs/symptoms he displayed that Arizona missed?

8. Bernadette and her mother, Rosa, had a complicated and strained relationship that stemmed from the hurt that Rosa carried from her failed marriage. What effects do you think parents' relationships have on their children?

9. By the end of the book, Bernadette, Tess, and Arizona had all successfully dealt with challenges; however, new ones arose. What do you think is each character's biggest challenge moving ahead?

10. If you could look into the future of Bernadette, Tess, and Arizona, what would you like to know?

Loved *Blindsided*? Don't miss Trice Hickman's first Complicated Love novel . . .

THE OTHER SIDE

After one too many failed relationships, businesswoman Bernadette Gibson is resigned to singlehood. Yet on the heels of her fiftieth birthday she meets Cooper "Coop" Dennis, a charismatic nightclub owner who literally sweeps her off her feet. But just as they're ready to make the ultimate commitment, a secret from Coop's past threatens to end their relationship . . .

As her fortieth birthday approaches, bestselling novelist Testimony "Tess" Sinclair is hurting—especially since her ex-boyfriend got married. For a change of scenery, she travels to the sleepy southern town of Bourbon, NC, to visit her cousin, Bernadette—and finds unexpected love. Yet as wedding bells promise to ring, Tess wrestles with a secret that could end their happily ever after before it begins . . .

Up-and-coming makeup artist and single mom Arizona May is thrilled to be just a few months away from marrying the love of her life. Until then, she and her fiancé are committed to celibacy. But on the eve of Arizona's thirtieth birthday, they surrender to passion—and she discovers something about her Prince Charming that leads her to rethink their plans . . .

As Bernadette, Tess, and Arizona strive to find happiness, they develop a bond that strengthens and surprises them—and carries them through their struggles, to the other side.

Chapter 1

BERNADETTE

Five Years Ago

Bernadette Gibson had suffered many disappointments in her forty-five years of living, but in all her experiences, she knew without a sliver of a doubt that Walter Pearson was her worst and most costly mistake to date. Their relationship was the reason why Bernadette completely understood how someone could be pushed to the brink of committing premeditated, cold-blooded murder . . . with one's bare hands.

Bernadette had met Walter at the Prince George's County Urban League's Annual Black Tie Gala. She had immediately been attracted to his engaging smile, witty conversation, and charismatic style, not to mention the fact that he was easy on the eyes, with the type of looks that could have easily earned him a spread in the pages of *Esquire* magazine. She'd thought his perfect diction, refined mannerisms, and air of entitlement were the telltale signs of a man who most likely hailed from a pedigreed family with good genes and deep pockets.

Bernadette had worked hard clawing her way out of the projects of southeast Washington, DC, for the opportunity to be in the company of men like Walter. She'd earned excellent grades in high school, which had given her a full ride scholarship at Georgetown University. Getting into such a prestigious college had allowed her to join the right social and professional organizations, and those accomplishments had provided her access to attend the right churches, socialize with the right people, and land the right, well-paying corporate jobs. This was all in an effort to meet the right kind of man with whom she could build a happily-ever-after life. Walter Pearson had checked off the boxes for what Bernadette had deemed a good catch, and from their first hello, she'd been determined to have him.

"He's perfect," she'd told her mother.

"Ain't no such thing as a perfect anything, let alone a perfect man," her mother had quickly rebuffed.

"Well, he's perfect for me!" Bernadette had shot back.

Bernadette loved her mother dearly, but she also felt that her mother's bitterness toward men often clouded her judgment. Bernadette's parents had divorced when she was five years old. Her father had cheated on her mother for years before finally leaving her for a much younger woman, the pain of which her mother had never overcome. Growing up, Bernadette couldn't recall ever seeing her mother date or show affection toward a man, and she'd never supported Bernadette in any of her relationships, always giving her boyfriends a serious side-eye. So when her mother objected to Walter and told Bernadette that he was a snake who couldn't be trusted, that warning went unheeded.

Bernadette loved that Walter was equally determined to have her—but what she hadn't realized was that his dogged pursuit was for vastly different reasons than her desire to be with him—and he'd played his hand like a professional croupier, dealing out deceit coated-lies. He'd wooed her with candlelit dinners at upscale restaurants, taken her for long, romantic walks in the park, and surprised her at home and at her job with weekly bouquets of softly hued flowers accompanied by sweet notes that read "Just Because" and "You

Mean So Much to Me." Walter had even cooked gourmet meals for her in his marble-tiled, stainless steel cook's kitchen, replete with signature cocktails on his sprawling lanai and ending with hours of beautiful lovemaking.

Walter was always on time, always answered his cell phone when Bernadette called, always treated her with respect, and always did exactly what he said he was going to do. Bernadette had known that men like Walter were like unicorns, especially in the dog-eat-dog dating pool of eligible men in Washington, DC. Looking for a good man who was straight, employed, and single with no attachments or serious baggage was the equivalent to mining for gold; the prospect of striking the mark was extremely slim.

"I feel like I need to pinch you, and myself," Bernadette had said to Walter, "to make sure you, and this, is real. This seems too good to be true, which my mother says it is. And I guess a part of me believes her because no one has ever treated me like this."

Walter paused for a quiet moment, then looked directly into Bernadette's eyes. "Bernie, I understand where your mother is coming from because she loves you and she's just being protective like any parent would. I can't speak for the men who came before me, but I can assure you that I don't want any to come after me. I want to be your one and only, because you're my one and only. I love you, Bernadette."

Tears formed in Bernadette's eyes. "I love you too, Walter."

Statistics had told Bernadette that as a single, middle-aged African American woman with a college degree, making a mid-six-figure salary, living in an upper-middle-class neighborhood in the heart of the nation's capital, her meeting and marrying an African American man of equal standing was a long shot. She counted herself lucky to have a man like Walter in hot pursuit of her affections, professing his love for her. She thought he was a dream come true, and after a three-month-long whirlwind romance, Walter proposed with a flawless, brilliant cut, four-carat Tiffany ring. Bernadette enthusiastically said yes and within days she picked out a date and began interviewing caterers and florists for what she envisioned was going to be a wedding to rival all weddings.

"Bernie, I don't trust him," Bernadette's mother had said, when against Bernadette's better judgment, she'd asked her mother to accompany her as she tried on wedding dresses.

"Mom, please. For once can't you just be happy for me, or at least don't discourage me? I've finally found someone who loves me, and I love him."

Her mother shook her head. "I love you too much to lie to you, baby. You're my only child, and I wouldn't tell you anything untrue or that I thought would hurt you. I'm trying to help you," she'd said as she'd assisted Bernadette out of the ivory-colored sheath wedding dress she'd just tried on.

"I thought this was going to be a great mother/daughter moment for us, and that it would help you get over your bitterness so you'd find a way to be happy for me. If I'd known you were going to act this way I would have never asked you to come."

Her mother snickered. "Is that what you think? You think I'm not happy for you because I'm bitter?"

"You've never gotten over what my father did to you, and you've let your anger and resentment rule your life. But, Mom, as much as I love you, I can't allow you to poison my relationship with Walter or cast a shadow over the happiness I feel when I'm with him."

Bernadette's mother reached out, took her hand, and gave it a gentle squeeze. "Oh, honey, you don't have a clue. Yes, I might be bitter, but don't mistake my shortcomings as a reason for why I think your relationship with Walter isn't going to last. Trust me, time will prove me right."

Bernadette's mother/daughter dress-shopping excursion came to an abrupt halt, as did their daily phone calls. Bernadette vowed to surround herself only with people who were supportive of her relationship with, and impending marriage to, Walter.

With more determination than ever, Bernadette continued her

wedding plans. She knew that Walter's custom-built, seven-thousand-square-foot home would be the perfect setting to celebrate what would be the beginning of their fairy-tale life together. His home sat on several acres of land in Prince George's County, close to a beautiful man-made lake, and Bernadette couldn't wait to host a lavish outdoor wedding befitting the power couple that she and Walter had become. She couldn't imagine being any happier than she was today because although at her age she had ruled out the possibility of having children, her dream of growing old with someone was finally within reach. But one month after Walter had proposed, Bernadette's happily-ever-after came to an end with breakneck speed.

Walter's work schedule had been hectic ever since they'd met, which made the fact that he always found a way to make himself available to her even more special in Bernadette's eyes. But after he'd proposed, his long hours kicked into overdrive.

"I'm working hard so you won't have to," he told Bernadette one evening over steak, lobster tails, and vintage wine.

She'd been so touched by his dedication to their relationship and the loving care he consistently showed for her that she wanted to do something special to show her appreciation for his thoughtfulness.

Wednesdays were Walter's work from home days, so Bernadette decided to surprise him with lunch from Panera Bread, which was the spot of their first lunch date. She slipped inside Walter's house unnoticed through a side entrance near his garage. She planned to set up their romantic feast of delicious sandwiches, savory soup, and tasty pastries in his bedroom and then cap off the meal with an afternoon tryst. She smiled with anticipation because she knew Walter would be pleasantly caught off guard and thrilled about spending time with her.

Bernadette didn't think Walter was home because she hadn't seen his luxury sedan when she'd peeped into his garage, so she was startled when she heard his voice booming from the direction of his home office. But instead of sounding his usual calm, confident, and polished self, his voice had taken on a hard edge, filled with the frustration and desperation of someone about to lose control. Bernadette was shocked and momentarily couldn't believe what she was hearing.

"Uh-huh, yeah . . . I understand," Walter said to the person on the other end. "I'm tellin' you, just give me a little time and I'll get you your hundred grand in another month or two after I lock up this trick I'm about to marry."

Bernadette covered her mouth in disbelief as she continued to listen to her real-life nightmare unfold.

Walter smirked on his end. "Yeah, man, the one you saw me with last month . . . yeah, she's gonna be my ticket to easy street, and once we make things legal I'll have access to everything she's got. And I'll need it, too, 'cause trying to pay for all these fancy restaurants and flowers is adding up."

Bernadette continued to listen to a story that sounded as if it was ripped from a novel. Walter went on to say that he didn't have the money to pay off his $100,000 gambling debt because every penny he made went to spousal support for three ex-wives and child support for seven children, not to mention the fact that his girlfriend on the side had just announced she was pregnant with his child.

Bernadette was rendered motionless and speechless in the middle of Walter's hallway, tightly gripping her Panera Bread to-go bag. But slowly, she summoned the strength to put one foot in front of the other and make her way into Walter's office.

Walter kept talking on the phone, oblivious to the fact that Bernadette was standing in his doorway. "You son of a bitch!" Bernadette yelled.

Walter's eyes enlarged to the size of baseballs and his face looked as if he was staring at a ghost. "Baby, I can explain."

"My mother was right about you!" Bernadette threw the cup of fresh-squeezed lemonade she was holding and hit Walter square in his face, then she reached into the bag, pulled out a steaming hot container of broccoli-cheddar soup and drenched him in the creamy greenish-yellow liquid.

But in that instant, Bernadette realized she'd gone too far because Walter flew into a rage.

"Uuggghhh," Walter cried out. "You just burned me, you crazy bitch, and you ruined my brand-new shirt. I oughta kick your high siddity ass!"

But instead of feeling fearful of the man standing in front of her, whom she now viewed as a stranger, Bernadette gathered all the years of hurt and bad relationships she'd experienced into the moment. "You ought to kick my ass?!" Bernadette screamed back. Her voice was a mixture of controlled anger mixed with a touch of set-it-off. "I'm the one who should be kicking your ass!" Bernadette said, gritting her teeth. She lunged at Walter, and in one quick motion she picked up the stapler off his desk and launched it like a missile at his face, hitting him in his nose, causing blood to gush.

Walter grabbed his nose in pain, but Bernadette showed no mercy. She reached for the sharp metal letter opener and stabbed it into Walter's forearm. He cried out again and staggered backward as he pulled the office tool turned deadly weapon out of his bleeding flesh. "Bitch, I'm gonna kill your crazy ass!" Walter yelled.

"Dead men can't fight," Bernadette said as she lunged at him with full force. She didn't know where her strength came from—it could have been from pent-up hurt, feelings of abandonment from her father, bitterness from her mother, unrequited love from her past relationships, or a combination of them all. But one thing Bernadette did know was that her raw emotions led her to fight Walter like a man and beat him to a pulp. But she didn't come out unscathed. She suffered a fractured right hand and a nasty black eye.

"Press charges and put his butt behind bars," her mother told her later that evening. "If he tried to swindle you, I'm sure he's involved in all kinds of shadiness."

After what Bernadette had just lived through, all she wanted to do was put Walter and his deception behind her. In the days that followed her shocking discovery and violent breakup, Bernadette learned that Walter's luxury car had really been a rental from Prestige Foreign

Cars, and the beautiful home he lived in was the property of one of his real estate clients who'd been living abroad for the last six months while Walter house-sat for him.

Bernadette shared a few details with her mother and poured her heart out only to her close cousin, whom she considered a sister. But she was much too devastated and embarrassed to reveal the full truth to the rest of her family and friends.

Over the next few weeks she retreated into the four walls of her luxurious Dupont Circle townhome and eventually told everyone that she'd realized that she and Walter had been incompatible. She knew that no one really believed her story, and she was grateful that not a soul had pushed her for the ugly details of their breakup, especially after Walter was arrested two months later for wire fraud.

Walter Pearson's deception had done more than embarrass Bernadette; he'd hurt her to her core, and she vowed to never allow herself to be deceived by another man, ever.

Connect with Us

Visit us online at
KensingtonBooks.com
to read more from your favorite authors, see books
by series, view reading group guides, and more.

for sneak peeks, chances to win books and prize packs,
and to share your thoughts with other readers.

facebook.com/kensingtonpublishing
twitter.com/kensingtonbooks

Tell us what you think!

To share your thoughts, submit a review,
or sign up for our eNewsletters, please visit:
KensingtonBooks.com/TellUs.